An
Unorthodox
Match

Also by Naomi Ragen

An Unorthodox Match

Naomi Ragen

ST. MARTIN'S PRESS ⚏ NEW YORK

First published in the United States by St. Martin's Press, an imprint of St. Martin's Publishing Group

AN UNORTHODOX MATCH. Copyright © 2019 by Naomi Ragen. All rights reserved. Printed in Canada. For information, address St. Martin's Publishing Group, 120 Broadway, New York, NY 10271.

www.stmartins.com

Designed by Steven Seighman

The Library of Congress Cataloging-in-Publication Data is available upon request.

ISBN 978-1-250-16122-2 (hardcover)
ISBN 978-1-250-16124-6 (ebook)

Our books may be purchased in bulk for promotional, educational, or business use. Please contact your local bookseller or the Macmillan Corporate and Premium Sales Department at 1-800-221-7945, extension 5442, or by email at MacmillanSpecialMarkets@macmillan.com.

First Edition: September 2019

10 9 8 7 6 5 4 3 2 1

Printed in Canada

For Alex
Half a century of friendship, love, support, joy, partnership
Thank you, my dear husband

I will lead the blind by a road they did not know, and I will make them walk by paths they never knew. I will turn darkness before them to light, and rough places into level ground; these are the promises, I will keep them without fail.

—Isaiah 42:16

1

Leah Howard sat there facing Rabbi Weintraub's empty chair, rehearsing what she was going to say to him. She was surprised by her nervousness. After all, she'd been a top marketing executive in a spectacularly successful start-up. Sales pitches were her lifeblood. And this was, after all, in the final analysis, just another product she was trying to sell, even if that product was herself.

How truthful should I be? she wondered. Should she talk about her parents? Her childhood? The FBI investigation and avalanche of lawsuits that had bankrupted her company and put her on the unemployment lines? Or should she start at the beginning, with the sleazy, deserted park where she had encountered God for the first time as He reached down and plucked her—a terrified eight-year-old—from the horror of the fate unfolding before her eyes? Or perhaps it was best to dive into the immediate present, and the two-year spiritual journey that had led her to apply now to a women's study program for newly observant Orthodox Jews in the haredi enclave of Boro Park, Brooklyn?

She opened up her purse—a ridiculously expensive mini Kelly bag from Hermès she'd purchased from her first bonus check in the mistaken belief that she could afford it—pulling out a tissue and dabbing her eyes. Why go into any of that? It would just make her sound pathetic. Worse, she'd come across like one of those typical druggie-misfit-instant-converts that usually came knocking on the doors of Chassidic outreach programs when they needed to be rescued from their lives.

The door opened and closed as a secretary in a brown wig covered by a fuzzy white mohair beret went in and out shuffling papers. "He'll just be another minute." She smiled, probably forgetting she'd said the same thing fifteen minutes ago.

Leah nodded, smiling back. She was in no rush. She peered out of the window into the freezing, rain-swept Brooklyn streets, catching glimpses of men in black overcoats, plastic bags protecting their large-brimmed black hats from ruin; women in staid, calf-length blue raincoats with sensible low-heeled boots hurrying past. She thought of the last conversation she'd had with her mother.

"It's not a cult, Mom. It's exactly the way your parents brought you up. Exactly the way my grandparents and great-grandparents lived their whole lives! The way our people have lived for thousands of years."

"Which is exactly why I jumped into a hippie van in the eighties and disappeared! Why are you doing this, Lola? Is it because of what happened with your company? Or with Andrew? Or is it . . . still . . . Josh?"

"Leah. I'm called Leah now," she'd corrected her, cringing. Lola feathers in her hair. How she'd always hated that name! She refused to answer, her stomach somersaulting at the questions.

"I can't believe you are moving back to Brooklyn, sinking into everything I ran away from! I brought you up with freedom!"

"Freedom. Yeah, your generation was so big on that. And where has it gotten us? There's a rape every six minutes in this country. And forty-three thousand people dying of drug overdoses every year. And half of all kids under eighteen have watched their parents get divorced. Some of them more than once. Forty percent are growing up with no fathers. Great job!"

There was a pause. Shocked silence? Probably not. Just a recalibration if she knew her mother.

"Do you know how these people treat women, Lola? Why would you, with your education, want to become some man's kitchen slave and baby-

maker? Why would you want to be a second-class citizen? And don't think
he won't send you out to support him while he's drinking coffee and turning the pages of his holy books. How can a feminist buy into all that?"

"Oh, feminism, the Holy Grail! They are so bankrupt. They have no
answers for women who want to be women, to be wives and mothers, to
have a real life! They've pretty much destroyed marriage and courtship. If
she's equal, why shouldn't she pay for dinner, hold open her own door? If
she's equal, why shouldn't she go back to work two days after giving birth?
After all, that's what fathers do! You know what Joan Didion said about
feminism? She said it was 'no longer a cause but a symptom.' I did the
successful-career-woman bit, remember? And where did *that* leave me?
I'm thirty-four years old, Mom. Do you even see a man around me who
wants to get married and settle down and help me raise a family? Men
don't want that anymore, not modern men. They want to play with you
until they get tired of you. They have no morals, no commitment, no self-
discipline.

"The world I'm going into is the opposite. They respect women as
wives and mothers. They don't toy with a woman's feelings. You go out
a few times, and then they ask you to marry them—or not. But they
don't—they're *not allowed*—to leave a woman dangling *for years and years
and years*." She felt her throat clench as she fought back tears. "They're
not running away from marriage and fatherhood. They're running
toward it. They have to have a woman in their lives. They *need* her. They're
committed to her. And they *have* to treat her well. That's the law. Jewish
law."

"Yeah, and I just bet everybody there is a law-abiding citizen." Her
mother snickered.

Leah made a supreme effort at self-control. *Honor thy father and
mother.* "Look, Mom, I respect your opinion, and I know you are trying
to help me. You're right. You raised me with freedom to be just like you.
But didn't you run off and do stuff that horrified your parents? Well, this
is *my* choice. This is the life *I* want."

"That's what you say now. But it's one thing to admire someone's life
from the outside. Another thing to live it. And when you're inside and
your eyes are opened, you'll see the ugly truth. And you won't be able to
just swallow it, like some Stepford wife, or some pious little sheep. Not

you. You'll leave, all right, and then, when you go looking for another job, how are you going to explain that big blank spot on your résumé? You're throwing everything away, Lola—your education, your career. You'll regret it. You'll change your mind. You're just depressed, honey. I understand that. Ravi and I want you to know—"

"Ravi! Why should I care what Ravi thinks? You're not even married."

"Okay, not technically, but he cares."

"Which is why he asked me the day after I arrived 'what my plans' were."

"He didn't mean anything by it! He was just concerned."

"Yeah, concerned all right, that since I'd lost my job I'd be sponging off him, living in the basement. Admit it. You both were."

There was a short silence.

"They prey on depressed people, you know. It's so easy to mess with their heads. Honey, you're all hepped up with all the brainwashing, and God knows what you went through in that year you spent in the Middle East—"

"Israel, Mom! Jerusalem! It's not a backwater! It's the high-tech leader of the world!"

"Whatever. But at the bottom of all those fine words, there's a really ugly reality."

For some reason, of everything her mother said, this rattled her. *What if she's right?* she thought. *She's not,* she answered herself emphatically. *She's never been right about a single thing her entire life.*

"I love you, Mom. Just accept that we are very different people. Always have been."

"You know, if you ran off with Hare Krishna, I could accept it. Just not this. It's a tragedy."

"No, it isn't. I lived through a tragedy. Remember?"

That ended the conversation. They had not spoken since. That was three months ago.

She couldn't say she was surprised. After all, her mother was the mirror image of the child her strict, middle-class Jewish parents from Flatbush had struggled to make her. According to her mother, her grandparents were square, un-American, completely unreasonable fanatics. Her litany of proofs included the fact that they wanted her to wear skirts that touched her knees and elbow-length blouses, even in the summer; that they wouldn't let her go to rock concerts by herself in the city at night when she was fifteen, even when the Rolling Stones came to town. According to her, all the vicious fights they'd had were entirely their fault, and it was therefore perfectly reasonable for her to have jumped out of her first-floor bedroom window one night to take off with some people she'd met at a punk rock concert who were heading to California. She was seventeen. By the time they'd tracked her down, she was already of age and beyond their juris-diction.

Her mother had never looked back.

When Leah finally got to meet her grandparents just after she turned eight, she was shocked to find two frail, elderly people with warm smiles who hugged and kissed her like they never wanted to let go. They were nothing like the powerful ogres who starred in her mother's tales. They gave her a gold Jewish star necklace, which she never took off. And when they passed away, one right after the other when she was eleven, they left her a pair of silver candlesticks that had belonged to her great-grandparents in Poland. She treasured them.

She'd always envied her mother's childhood. And her parents.

Like most people, Leah thought, her mother had tried to raise her the way she herself would have wanted to be raised. And like most people, she had gone overboard, her good intentions having terrible consequences. The lack of rules and limitations, even good advice, didn't feel like freedom; it felt like abandonment. She was a baby gazelle wandering the savannah, open to all predators, the only safeguards those she could figure out herself from what her friends' parents wouldn't let *them* do.

"Grow up to be happy," was her mother's mantra.

That was easier said than done in San Jose, California, a place that at-tracted rootless drifters who tooled up the highway from the East and Midwest, escaping bad marriages, child-support payments, or hot pursuit by law enforcement. Throughout her childhood, she experienced a con-stant current of low-level fear.

While they lived on a good street, right around the corner were rows of rentals where people drove filthy pickups and had soggy cardboard pizza boxes decorating their front lawns. There were a lot of new immigrants and vagrants, people who slept on mattresses on the floor in rooms that smelled of unwashed dishes and kitty litter. There was a lot of noise, a lot of kids screaming and being yelled at, a lot of domestic abuse. The sounds of police sirens, barking stray dogs, and beer bottles smashing against their fence provided the soundtrack to a childhood filled with the repulsive backdrop of used car dealerships and strip malls that went on for miles and miles on El Camino Real.

Once she'd read a newspaper story about a woman whose car had broken down on the highway. She hadn't been waiting more than five minutes when a supposed Good Samaritan picked her up. Of course, he turned out to be a rapist-murderer who just happened to be passing by. The police found the poor woman's body a few hours later. As young as she was, Leah had been shocked by the possibility that the people tooling up and down the highway right near her, who knew how to drive and who looked perfectly normal behind the wheels of their cars, were actually monsters.

She longed for safety and stability, a conservative, conventional life, like *The Cosby Show* or those old fifties sitcoms that she'd found on video—*Father Knows Best* or *The Donna Reed Show*—half-hour morality lessons with canned laughter and commercial breaks where mothers wore aprons and fathers came home to the suburbs wearing a hat with their suit jackets flung over the shoulder of their white, starched-collar shirts. She would watch episode after episode after school in the empty house as she waited for her mother to come home from her job in the hair salon, the doors double-bolted and the windows locked.

Most of all, she longed for a father, someone wise, strong, and lovingly protective.

Her stepfather, Don Howard—the only father she remembered—had died suddenly when she turned four. He'd been a ball-tosser, a let's-all-go-out-for-pizza-and-bowling type. She hardly remembered him. The rest, all the boyfriends, were strangers.

And then one day it had finally happened, the thing that happened—more or less—to the child of every negligent parent. While she had gotten off incredibly easy, the experience was indelible, a point from which there could never be a return to an innocent trust in her mother's ability and wisdom to keep her safe.

———

The door opened. "Sorry to keep you waiting." Rabbi Weintraub smiled.

She stood up, alert, her hands reaching back to make sure her hair was still held in severe check by clips and bands. Making her natural strawberry-blond mass of outlandish and uncontrollable curls look respectable was such a hopeless task that she'd once seriously considered cutting it all off or dyeing it brown and having it straightened. She'd resisted the impulse, refusing to succumb to the self-hatred she'd encountered all too frequently among other newly observant women. There was a limit to what she could do and still remain herself.

She tugged at her already mid-calf skirt. Although it was new, it was already straining at the seams. Ever since stopping her daily run, the weight had larded her body like a fat suit. It disgusted her, but at the moment, she felt helpless to do anything about it. Putting on trainers and jogging up the street would be looked down upon as immodest and attention-seeking, for a man or a woman, among the people whose respect and acceptance she craved. And even if she was doing it among strangers in Manhattan who wouldn't give her a second glance, it didn't seem honest. If she sincerely wanted to be part of this community, she needed to make an honest effort to conform to its rules.

He wore a long black coat, glasses, a black hat with an impressive brim, and a beard that, if it had been white instead of coal black, would have made him a dead ringer for Santa Claus. His eyes were an intelligent, sharp blue.

She had been living long enough among religious people not to be offended when he didn't offer her his hand. Religious men didn't touch women other than their wives, daughters, or granddaughters. She had always found that stringent regard for strict boundaries admirable, a surprising oasis in a world rife with sexual harassment and abuse.

"Please, sit." He gestured affably, lifting the sides of his long black coat and sitting down behind his desk. "And so, Miss . . . ?"

"Leah," she helped him. "Leah Howard."

"Of course. Leah. What brings you to us today?" He looked at her expectantly.

"I want to enroll in your women's program."

He nodded. "Very nice! Can you tell me a little about yourself?"

"I've been in other study programs. I started out with Chabad—Bais

Chana—and I spent some time in Ohel Sara in Israel. When I got back, I started going to the Beginner's Minyan at Washington Avenue Synagogue in Manhattan."

He sat back. "You went from chassidish to yeshivish to modern Orthodox, and now you are back here with us black hats?"

She was confused. Was that what she'd done? "Listen, Rabbi," she told him honestly, "the truth is I went from knowing nothing to knowing something—about HaShem, about Judaism, and mostly about myself. Along the way, I found out what I wanted and what I didn't want." She paused. "That's why I'm here, at your school, in your community. *This* is what I want."

He rested his elbows on his desk, pressing his palms together. His eyes were searching, she saw. But also amused.

"Tell me why."

"Well, as I mentioned, I started out with Chabad. It was something I came across online. A 'summer camp for adults,' they called it. The ad said no matter what your age or background, if you were a Jewish woman, '*this is the right place for you.*' I'd just lost my job and my boyfriend. I couldn't afford my Manhattan apartment anymore. And my family made it really clear that they didn't want me moving in with them. The camp was in Minnesota, and they offered me a scholarship. And I thought, *Let me take some time to think about my life.*"

"So Chabad was not for you?"

She hesitated. "I really enjoyed it at first. They were all so friendly. I loved the singing, the beautiful Shabbos rituals, the feeling of sanctity and closeness with others and with God. I learned so much . . . everything, really. But then I hit a wall." She hesitated.

"Please, be honest."

"Okay, I got tired of all those stories about how the simple man or woman with terrible problems goes to the rebbe, and how the rebbe tells them exactly what to do, and how his advice is always perfect and solves everything. I couldn't see where that left me. After all, the rebbe died more than twenty years ago. And even if he were still around, what kind of way is that to live, to ask someone else to make all your decisions for you? To be afraid to have a single thought, or idea, of your own? I shared this with one of my teachers. He was actually very nice about it and steered me to another program in Jerusalem."

"How did that work out?"

"I'd never been to Israel before. It was overwhelming. I saw people, whole communities, actually *living* their daily lives according to the rules I'd only read about. Many of my teachers invited me to their homes. They had these big, noisy, happy Jewish families with everyone from the tiniest toddler to the great-grandparents living totally committed Jewish lives rooted in traditions that went back centuries. That somehow made it real for me. It showed me how such a thing was possible. It didn't feel primitive or reactionary. It felt homey and right. It felt holy."

"So why didn't you stay? I'm sure Ohel Sara had plenty of matchmakers looking out for you." He smiled.

She smiled back, a bit uncertainly. "Ohel Sara was good. I enjoyed some of it." Again, she hesitated. "But it was so big! I was one of something like seven hundred women. I got a bit lost there, I think. And also, by this time, I felt I wanted to deepen my intellectual understanding of the laws, the lifestyle, not just to be told: do this, don't do that. Many of the classes weren't geared for that. Many of the women had just taken out their tongue rings—" She blushed fiercely, looking up. "I'm . . . I . . ."

He waved dismissively, his blue eyes mischievous. "Believe me, we've seen everything here, too."

"Well, anyway. They went straight from that into trying to imitate everything their teachers said and did, even if they didn't understand a thing. And they were very judgmental toward one another. It was sometimes like high school and the mean girls. Still, I had some very inspiring teachers, and I went up a few more spiritual rungs there. But I was running out of money, and honestly, I wasn't ready to leave America. So I came back and looked for work. A high-tech company in Manhattan hired me. I rented an apartment not far from where I used to live. I was terrified of falling back into my old lifestyle; I didn't want to forget everything I'd learned. So when I got involved in the Washington Avenue synagogue, I was relieved. Here was a modern Orthodox congregation where people had a similar education to mine and were working in top-notch professions. Many were *baale teshuva,* and quite a few were single. They were so much less restrictive than either Chabad or Ohel Sara. They had television sets, went to movies and the theater, and read the latest *New York Times* bestsellers. They were exactly like I used to be, except that they were Sabbath-observant and ate kosher. With them, I didn't get the highs I got in Jerusalem or even Chabad, the spiritual uplift from prayer, the sense of being in conversation with God. It reminded me a little too much of the Reform and Conservative style of abridging God's demands to make them easier and more popular. But I wasn't looking for easier. I wanted something true and tested. Something eternal. But I was also tired of searching. I was hoping it would be enough even if the fit wasn't perfect. Part of that, I'll admit, was the fact that there were quite a few eligible men in the congregation. I wanted so much to settle down and have children."

She paused, self-conscious, suppressing an audible sigh. "I met someone there. He was my age. A systems analyst. He was also a *baal teshuva.* We went out for six months, seeing each other two, three times a week. I expected, I hoped . . . But then, someone else from the congregation took me aside and told me that I wasn't the only member of the synagogue he was going out with. There were at least two other women."

She looked up, staring across the impersonal desk in this nondescript Brooklyn office at the bearded stranger facing her, his brows creased with sudden pain. *He understands,* she saw gratefully.

"So, there was a little too much 'modern' in the Orthodox."

She nodded wordlessly. Like Venetians who had fled an enemy right into the ocean, building houses on stilts, she had run from modern morality and modern business practices, finally reaching the edge of America, a world as alien and opposed to everything "modern" as one could possibly imagine.

"Rabbi, I am thirty-four years old. I want to stop running. I want to live here, build a Jewish home, find a good husband, have children. I know that the women who finish your program find shidduchim in this community. I am hoping . . ."

"Leah, what is your current level of observance?"

She knew what he meant. He wasn't talking only about her faithfulness to the laws of the Torah but also to the stringencies imposed upon those laws by thousands of years of rabbinical decrees and custom. Truthfully, she'd never met two Jews who were on the same level as far as observance. It was endless, depending on what you had observed at home and been taught in school. She had been privy to neither, randomly picking up customs and stringencies here and there and doing her best.

Just be honest, she told herself, trusting those kind, intelligent eyes that looked at her so intently. "I pray every morning, but in English. I don't know enough Hebrew yet. I'm strictly observant of Shabbos and holidays: I don't use electricity, and shut off my phone and computer. I don't use money, or carry or drive. I light candles and go to the synagogue even though sometimes I'm the only woman there." (The more Orthodox the shul, she'd found to her surprise, the fewer women attended. Why was that?) "I prepare or get invited to festive meals. I'm very careful to buy only foods that have proper rabbinical certification. But most of all, I try to be careful about what I say to and about other people. I try never to hurt anyone's feelings or be dishonest with my words or with my actions. When I can, I try to do good deeds."

He straightened in his chair, noting her long skirt and modest blouse. "I don't know if you need any more lessons, Leah. You seem to have learned all the most important things already!"

She relaxed. "I still feel very ignorant."

There was a short silence. "There are many places you can take *shiurim.* But, to be honest, I don't think this program is right for you. You see," he said very gently, "most of our students are under twenty-five."

His words pierced her heart like pincers, plucking out what was left of her hopes. *Too old! She was too old.* She nodded wordlessly, gathering her things together. "Thank you for listening to me, Rabbi. I'm sorry I wasted your time."

He didn't respond, staring at her.

Abruptly, she stood up.

He gestured impatiently. "You're in a rush? Sit, sit."

She fell back into her seat, confused, her face flushed with humiliation and disappointment.

"Tell me, Leah-le, what really happened to you before you went to Chabad?"

She sank back into her seat, clearing her throat with difficulty, aware of the rabbi's intense, discerning vision resting on her without judgment but also without pity. "The company I worked for, PureBirth, was a start-up that produced a revolutionary genetic screening test that promised to detect cystic fibrosis, Huntington's disease, sickle-cell anemia, Tay-Sachs, and all kinds of other genetic diseases through a simple blood test. I worked in the marketing department, helping to sell millions of these test kits all over the world. We were making huge profits. Everyone got bonuses and stock options.

"And then one day, I went into the office and there were police everywhere. People were standing by their desks filling cardboard boxes, crying. My boss, Juliana Hager, a woman I admired and looked up to more than almost anyone I'd ever met, was taken into custody. They actually handcuffed her right there in front of everyone! Our 'revolutionary, cutting-edge' product was a fraud! Dozens of couples all over the world had started having children with genetic diseases we'd guaranteed they were free of. The lawsuits began, and then a criminal investigation."

She twisted the tissue in her hands. "I know it wasn't my fault. I was just a small cog in a huge machine. But if I hadn't convinced the buyers in drugstore chains to stock our product, maybe those couples would have gone to doctors and had reliable tests done. Because of me, they'd had access to this fake test. They'd trusted it. And now, they and their children are going to suffer for the rest of their lives." She dabbed her eyes, the tears that had slowly built up beginning to fall. "And the worst part, the *very* worst was *this*." She held up her purse. "I got rewarded for it! But God was watching, Rabbi. He punished me. Not only did I lose my job, but a long-term relationship I was sure would lead to marriage and children suddenly ended. I'd invested five years of my life—my youth—in it. I was left with nothing."

He nodded. "God is certainly trying to get your attention, Leah Howard. Sometimes this kind of personal crisis is His way of pushing us to look inside our hearts and then outside to Him." He tapped the desk thoughtfully with a pencil, leaning back into his chair, sighing. "Leah-le, Leah-le," he said, shaking his head and looking her over. "What are we going to do with you?"

2

Yaakov Lehman opened his eyes as the sun streamed into his bedroom. *"Blessed be you, living, everlasting King, for giving me back my soul in Your great mercy,"* he whispered in Hebrew, the first thing he did every morning. He propped himself up on one elbow, peering in the direction of his wife Zissel's bed. This morning, like every morning for the last year, he was shocked to find it empty.

His heart ached.

He reached over to grab his undershirt, bringing it under the blanket as he took off his pajama top, quickly covering himself. Next, he reached out for the mug filled with water he'd prepared the night before, stored inside a small basin. Taking the mug deliberately into his right hand, he transferred it to his left, pouring water over his right hand into a small basin, then passing it back and pouring water over his left, repeating three times. He dried his hands, then reached for his large black velvet skullcap, covering his head.

He stood up, picking up his tzitzis and carefully fingering each set of strings to ensure they had eight long threads, then he pulled it over his head as he recited the proper blessing for this mitzvah. In his closet, he found a single clean, white shirt—his last—and black cloth pants.

He thought back to the official thirty days of mourning immediately following the funeral, the *shloshim,* when his neighbors, friends, mother-in-law, brother, and sister-in-law had all crowded around them, ready to take up the slack. Long since, everyone had gone back to their own lives, which was as it should be, he told himself, as a frisson of fear and doubt passed through him, making him shudder.

He had not known exactly what to expect, imagining vaguely that eventually things must fall back into place, into some kind of normalcy. He had no idea how that would happen but thought it would be taken care of by someone, the way things in a yeshiva boy's life were always taken care of. It was not that he objected to taking over household duties himself; he just did not have the slightest clue how to begin. A yeshiva boy never had to operate a washing machine or use an iron. His clothing had always magically appeared on hangers and in drawers, crisp and immaculate. Shabbos and daily meals were prepared for him and served to him. The refrigerator was stocked. From childhood, it had been taken care of by his mother and sisters, and then his young wife, whom he had married when she turned eighteen and he barely twenty. After his children were born, they too had always been well dressed and well fed. He had never even given a thought to how that happened.

Now his sock drawer was completely empty, he saw as he searched futilely for a clean pair. Sinking into a chair, he pulled on the pair from the day before that were still lying on the floor where he had left them. *Don't think about it,* he told himself, continuing the rituals of dressing with pious care, the mindless routine imposing order on the chaos of his existence. *Place your right foot in your right shoe, but don't tie it. Place your left foot in your left shoe and tie it, and only then tie the other.*

Picking up his washbasin, he carefully emptied it into the toilet so that the water, defiled by the unclean spirits of night on his hands, should not contaminate anything else. Sitting on the toilet, he uncovered himself to the minimal degree possible, careful not to touch his private parts and to wipe himself with only his left hand. Once again, he washed his hands, then poured water over his clean hands in the same order he had done before.

Only when he brushed his teeth and combed his hair and thick, gold beard in front of the mirror did he allow himself to focus and think. *Who is that?* he wondered, shocked. An older man, much older than himself, who had only just turned forty. A man with silver strands in his gold hair and beard, little snowy tufts like weeds. Instead of gentle laugh lines around the mouth, there were the inverted creases of a deepening frown.

Who was this person who frowned, this miserable man? He himself never frowned! He was a happy, fortunate man, blessed by God in all ways! And the eyes, those clear blue eyes as calm as a summer sea, what unfamiliar depths they had now! He peered into them deeply seeing shock, shock, and more shock. The suffering there was so dense, the sorrows so deeply intertwined that they could never be untangled, smoothed over, and left to heal in the simple light of day. It was almost like looking at something not quite human, he thought, an angel or a devil, some otherworldly creature that was never meant to be confronted by any mortal on this earth.

Frightened, he turned away, combing out the long strands of his side curls with his long fingers, then twisting them into neat bundles, which he tucked neatly behind his ears.

Unlike his fellow Talmud scholars in the kollel, who, after following the same morning rituals, would now be hurrying directly to the synagogue, velvet bags holding their phylacteries and prayer shawls tucked beneath their arms, Yaakov instead went to wake his children.

He remembered the good days he had always taken for granted, when the little apartment had hummed with activity: the clink of plates and mugs and spoons being laid on the kitchen table; the smell of toast and scrambled eggs perfuming the air; the two older boys on their way to yeshiva; his daughters' giggles coming from the bathroom. And Zissele—his lovely, pretty Zissele!—at the center of it all, cooking and talking and laughing, a gentle smile on her lips as she nursed the youngest. Now there was only an eerie silence except for the rain slamming wildly against the windows, their thin panes the only barrier between himself and the unpredictable world.

He knocked on the door of the bedroom his two daughters shared. "Shaindele, are you up?"

"Yes, Tateh," the voice came back.

She opened the door. She was small for her age, still a little girl at fifteen, but smart and competent beyond her years, he thought, like all girls in large, devout Jewish families, accustomed to taking care of her siblings. She was already dressed in her school uniform—a calf-length plaid skirt and a sky-blue blouse that buttoned up to her neck with wrist-length sleeves. With surprise, he noticed that her thick, dark hair hung unfettered down her back and across her shoulders.

"Your hair?"

She patted it down. "It's gotten so long it's hard for me to braid by myself. Ima always used to help me. But I'll do it, Tateh. After I dress Chasya."

Who, he mourned, would help braid his Shaindele's hair? He turned aside, fighting the tears that sprang into his eyes. *Why am I so useless?* he thought. *Why is it that I do not know how to do anything?*

"Tateh, I will take care of Chasya and make her and the baby breakfast and pack their lunches. You'll be late for davening."

How can I leave? he thought. *The house, my children, everything is in such disarray? But how can I come late to kollel?* Despite everyone's sympathy for his plight, by now, he was sure, he must be losing the respect of the rebbe along with his chances of gaining a permanent position as a *maggid shiur,* something he had spent his entire life working toward. This was not only his heart's desire but the only path toward financial stability. Now, more than ever, with Zissele's salary as a teacher gone, it was vital.

Before this, he'd always believed he had a chance; the rebbe liked him, and while others could occasionally outshine him with brilliant insights into the Talmud, no one surpassed him in piety and diligence. But now, as he regularly took days off to deal with household emergencies, often showing up long after everyone else was already deeply immersed in learning, he imagined he was losing his edge. The idea terrified him.

"May HaShem bless you, Shaindele. Can you manage?"

"Don't worry, Tateh. Chasya is already up and getting dressed." She hesitated. "But Tateh, what about the baby? Who will drop him off at day care?"

He was confused. So many friends, neighbors, and even strangers regularly came by to help them in their bereavement he couldn't keep track of who did what. "Who usually takes him?"

"Mrs. Glick. But her baby is sick; she can't come. She called yesterday. I left you a note."

That piece of paper on his night table, the one he'd meant to read. He looked at his daughter and just beyond to where five-year-old Chasya was making her way sleepily into the kitchen. Her legs, he saw, were bare. "Chasya has no tights."

"I'll take care of it," Shaindele promised, her voice going shrill.

His children. His firstborn, Elchanon Yehoshua, and a year later Dovid Yitzchak, now bright, handsome yeshiva boys in their late teens, both boarding at a top yeshiva in Baltimore, where his brother, Chaim, could keep an eye on them. He missed them so much but was proud they'd gotten accepted and agreed it was better for them not to see what was going on at home and to concentrate on their studies. And then there were the girls, first Shaindele and then—after ten hard years filled with mourning over miscarriages and disappointed prayers—Chasya. Their last, Mordechai Shalom, had been orphaned so young he would never even remember what a lovely mother he'd had. During the barren years, it had often felt as if God were punishing him. But now he knew better. God in His infinite wisdom had simply shown mercy. The very thought of having more young children to care for made him shiver.

"Can't *you* drop the baby off, Shaindele?"

"They only open at eight, and it's a different way from Chasya's. I'll be late."

Of course. How was it he didn't remember that? It was all out of control, he thought, panicking. His learning, his family. He needed to take charge, to be more diligent, to organize more. But how? He had no experience.

His whole life, it had been impressed upon him that he had but one task, one thing worth living for, the only true contribution he could make to the betterment of his family, his people, and the whole world: to learn God's laws and to teach them, so that the world became a better and holier place, deserving of Divine mercy.

For the first time in Yaakov Lehman's life, a small, niggling doubt crept into his heart over what he had learned and what he had been taught that had left him so helpless in the face of tragedy, a burden to his family instead of its savior. He felt a frightening burst of anger at his ignorance, at the knowledge that all these practical skills had been denied him. He clenched his fists. Now he must learn, he must teach himself, or he and his family would not survive.

The baby's soft gurgling sounds interrupted his thoughts. When he entered the nursery, the baby had climbed out of his crib and was standing by the door. When had he learned to do that? he thought, astonished. Smiling, he lifted the child into his arms. His diaper was full.

"Oh, Tateh, you'll get your clothes all dirty! Here, give him to me," Shaindele insisted.

Yaakov looked at the cooing baby, then down at himself. He had nothing to change into if these clothes got soiled. Helplessly, he kissed his son, placing him gently in his daughter's outstretched arms. The child burst into furious wails of betrayal and loss.

"Go, Tateh! You'll be late."

"But the baby—"

Her jaw was set firmly. "He'll stop crying in a minute."

"But how will he get to day care?"

"I'll take him."

"But you said you'll be late!"

She sighed. It wouldn't be the first time. "My teachers will understand. Just go."

Even as he closed the door behind him with guilty relief, he was immediately battered by a wave of misery so strong it paralyzed him. *How can I allow this?* he thought wretchedly, his hand still on the doorknob. *I am the father, the adult, the caregiver, the protector. Shaindele is just a child, my child.* It wasn't right. It wasn't fair. But then, what was fair about his life? He thought of the rebbe walking through the kollel and turning to stare at his empty seat, and the vision propelled him down the stairs and out into the street.

It was still pouring. A sudden realization sent him flying back up the stairs.

"Shaindele, here!" He opened his thin wallet, taking out a ten-dollar bill, his last for the month. "Call a taxi. Wrap yourself and the children up warmly. Take an umbrella."

"But, Tateh, Mr. Belkin at the grocery—this month's bill, it's still not—"

"Reb Belkin is a merciful Jew. He will understand. Tell the taxi driver to wait. I want he should take you also to school. I don't want you should get a cold."

"I'll be all right, really!"

"Please," he begged.

"All right, Tateh," she finally agreed, taking the money. "And don't forget to cover your hat," she reminded him, running to get him a big plastic bag.

His hat! He wiped off the beads of moisture that had already accumulated in the folds, drying it as best he could. He could not afford another. Gratefully, he took the bag from his daughter, covering his big, black hat and placing it carefully back on his head.

How would it all end? he wondered as he hurried through the streets as fast as a respectable Talmud scholar dared without being undignified or calling attention to himself, praying hard all the way that his tardiness would not be noticed. His heart pumped so hard it hurt. Who, he thought with despair, would take care of them all now?

3

"Those steaks ready anytime soon?" Cheryl Howard called out, her nostrils flaring as she breathed in the perfume of roasting meat on the outdoor grill. It was the thing she loved most about lazy Saturdays, when her shift at work ended at noon and she had the whole afternoon to do whatever she pleased.

"Two secs, hon," Ravi answered her calmly, his deep baritone surprisingly accommodating.

He had a trigger temper and didn't like being nagged. Usually, Cheryl was cautious about it. But now her focus was on her cell phone as she tried once again dialing Lola. The phone rang and rang with no answer. *She's probably mad. But not to answer at all?* She bristled, telling herself she had nothing to feel sorry about. A mother was allowed to speak her mind. She just wondered when Lola would get over it, hoping it wouldn't take another three months. They'd disagreed plenty over the years, but these long silences were something new. It was freaking her out.

Annoyed, and a bit frightened, she put the phone facedown on her bare stomach. The cool glass felt good against her warm skin. Leaning back, she stretched out her tan, shapely legs to the full length of the chaise longue.

Soon she was slowly sautéing, the waves of heat positively spiteful, she thought, shielding her eyes with the back of her hand and directing her irritation at the relentless Florida sun. A sudden ache for San Francisco's chilly gray summer skies swept over her. She turned over.

"What did you do with the beach umbrella? I'm frying back here!" she accused as the backs of her knees began to itch from sunburn.

There was no reply.

Uh-oh, she thought uneasily, sitting up and swinging her legs over the side. She gave him a cautious sidelong glance, gauging his emotional temperature.

His hands were crossed over his chest, and he was glaring.

"Okay, okay, sorry, sorry," she said contritely. "It's my daughter."

She watched in relief as he slowly unfolded his arms and picked up the grill fork, turning his attention back to the meat. "You were the one who put the umbrella in the shed. You said the rain would ruin it."

"Right, right. Sorry, honey," she cajoled. She loved him, but he was a handful.

"You heard from her?"

"She called me last week. After three months."

"So, what's up?"

"Well, she went for this interview, see, to get accepted to some brainwash program in this fanatically religious neighborhood in Brooklyn. Guess what? They turned her down! Said she was too old."

He nudged the sizzling steak onto its still bloody raw side. Without looking up, he said, "So you're happy, right? That's what you wanted."

His tone was unfriendly, she thought. Judgmental. "No. I didn't want her to get turned down," she fumed. "What I wanted was for her to wise up and go back to Manhattan to get a job. But getting turned down only made things worse."

Now he suddenly gave her his full attention. "How's that?"

"Well, see, the rabbi who told her she was too old and too smart to be a student in his program offered her some job doing something online for the yeshiva. Imagine, with her degrees and experience to be stuck working for some rinky-dink little Jewish outfit in Brooklyn for peanuts! Makes me sick to think about it."

"Is she complaining? Asking you for money?"

She felt her temper rising. "You're not getting this, Ravi! Those fanatics are clever. They didn't ask for money, just slave labor! And of course they were clever enough to throw in a place to live with free meals and as many free brainwashing courses as she needs to permanently screw up her life for good! She says the rabbi wants her to see if this life is really for her by trying it out for a few months. Oh, they are diabolical, that bunch. Once they get their claws into you, you can never escape. And they make you think it's *your* choice! That it's what *you* want! I tried to tell her, but she can't see any of it. She says she's happy! It's insane."

"And this is what you told her?"

"What, you think I should have lied?"

"And how did she take it?"

"She hung up on me. And now she won't answer the phone at all."

"What did you expect? And what do you care? She's an adult. She's not asking us to bail her out of jail. Leave her be."

"Yeah, you're the expert at that. When was the last time you spoke to *your* daughter?" she asked him spitefully before she could stop herself.

He slammed down the fork and threw the apron at her.

"Cook your own damn dinner!" he said, storming off to sit by the pool. On the way, he grabbed a beer.

Her eyes followed him, the idea of going after him, pleading for forgiveness, flashing through her head. But it was just too damn hot. *What the hell. I don't need this crap.* Besides, if it wasn't for him making Lola feel so unwelcome that time she came home after losing her job, maybe none of this would have happened. She was sick of it. Sick of him.

Reluctantly, she picked up the apron, walking over to the grill. *It looks done to me,* she thought, poking at the steak, then lifting the still-bleeding meat to her plate. The rarer the better as far as she was concerned. She thought about those soccer players stranded in the Andes after a plane crash who wound up eating each other. There was an inner cannibal in all of us.

She sat down at the table and poured herself a cold beer, chugging it down until the alcohol spread a pleasant, drugged calm inside her chest. She took two or three bites of the meat but spit it out, her appetite disappearing. Yeah, too raw. Even for her. She got up and put it back on the grill, poking at it absently, glancing over to where Ravi sat with his back to her, dangling his bare feet into the pool.

Most of the time, they got along just fine. But when it came to family, he was one big wound. She'd never met his parents or siblings, who were all back in India. Only once had he even shown her a photo: very gray and grainy. She imagined them scurrying around without shoes in the squalor of some third-world backwater. The only other photo she'd seen was of his daughter. In it, she was about two years old. Last she'd heard, the child was already in second grade. She had no idea if he kept in touch with any of them. He, unlike her, never talked about his family.

She remembered the first time he'd walked into her hair salon in San Jose looking like an extra for Aladdin, an enormous turban wrapped tightly around his head. When he sat down in front of her and removed it, mountains of thick black hair cascaded down his shoulders like an avalanche.

It took her a while to exhale.

"You sure about this?"

He closed his eyes and gnawed his lips, giving a sharp nod and a guttural sound almost like a bark.

When she was done, hair carpeted the floor.

"Well, don't you look handsome?" She smiled proudly, holding up a mirror behind his head so he could admire her work.

Instead, he stared, devastated, his large, dark eyes welling.

"I am a hopeless sinner," he whispered, trembling as he took out his wallet.

"Aren't we all, honey," she answered, touching his shoulder sympathetically.

A moment passed between them as his dark eyes searched hers, a question asked and answered.

She wasn't surprised to find him waiting for her outside the next day when she closed up shop, looking sweet but forlorn. Without the distraction of the odd headgear, he was actually quite attractive, she noticed, tall and graceful. She was touched to see that he had trimmed his beard and mustache meticulously.

"I didn't thank you properly yesterday. I was in shock. Can I take you out for coffee?"

"Sure, why not? I like sinners."

She found him really easy to talk to. She told him all about her fanatic parents and how she'd run away from home with some musicians, and how happy she was.

He seemed to admire that. "Like all good Sikhs, I started wearing a turban at the age of fourteen," he told her. "I was an expert in tying it beautifully tight. I married a Punjabi girl, and we came to America. We were happy at first, but she started feeling very homesick. All she talked about was going back to Punjab. She missed her family, her sisters, the food, the rituals, the climate. I don't buy it. There is a big Sikh community in San Jose, and a big gurdwara—that's our temple. We already had a kid by then, a daughter we named Balvindra—which means *strength*. But then one day, I look on my wife's computer and I see she's writing to this old boyfriend, some guy who her parents didn't like. A Hindu. It was bad . . . I got a little carried away."

She stopped, searching his face, cautious. "What do you mean?"

"I threatened to take the kid away and leave her. I didn't mean it. But soon after, I come home after work and she's gone. Just took the kid and got on a plane. I called, I wrote. Divorce is very taboo among Sikhs. But she wasn't coming back. She wanted me to come and live in Punjab." He shook his head in bewilderment. "Her family missed her and took her and the child in and helped her file for divorce. I signed everything she sent me. What can you do? I went to see the kid once. My ex was remarried by then—not to the Hindu, to some Sikh engineer. Very rich. And Bal didn't even know who I was."

"Ouch."

He nodded slowly. "Right after that, I started getting headaches." He pressed his fingers into the center of his skull. "There was this pain in the middle of my head, right above my turban on my forehead, and my ears would ache like hell. I used to bow down my head every two, three minutes, press my turban near my ears and push it forward to get some relief. This went on for about a year. Finally, I got these bumps by my ears and in the back under the turban. I couldn't concentrate. I was sure they were going to fire me. And also, I met this girl at work, a Californian, but she wouldn't go out with me because she thought the turban was too weird. I also began to feel it was too weird. I started feeling like the only Sikh in

San Jose. After my divorce, I stopped going to the gurdwara. I just didn't fit in there anymore."

"Oh, so the haircut was not the beginning of your war, it was the end?"

"Exactly."

She shrugged. "Religion is a pain. Run away as fast as you can, is what I say, and never look back. That's what I did. I haven't been struck by lightning, tornadoes, or plague even once," she said, grinning.

But his face was serious. "It's not a joke to be cut off from your past, your beliefs, your heritage. It's a tragedy."

She didn't pursue the subject. Soon after, they moved in together. He and Lola had never gotten along, which didn't matter since Lola had long since moved out. But after she lost her job and moved back in, there had been daily flare-ups.

"She's becoming a born-again," she told him accusingly when Lola left for the Chabad camp. "I mean, a Jewish born-again, if that's the expression to use. She's getting herself involved in this cult! All because you weren't nice to her!"

"Are you Jewish?" he asked levelly.

"Like we never discussed this." She rolled her eyes.

"And your husband, her father, your parents?"

"As I told you, he was her father, but not my husband. And yeah, he was a Jew—which I didn't know until much later, by the way—and so were my parents, as you know. What's your point?"

He looked puzzled. "But you are not happy? Because your daughter wants to follow her religion, your family's religion?"

"I didn't bring her up that way."

"Why not?"

"I wanted her to be free. Make her own choices. Not like how I was brought up."

"I see. And you, Cheryl, are so, so happy."

From then on, she had made every effort to avoid the subject. They'd been living together for four years when he got a lucrative job offer in Boca Raton. She'd followed him, using all her savings to open her own hair salon. Some, maybe even most, of the time they were good together. He didn't drink or smoke or find ways to make her jealous. Like her, his tastes were simple: movies, barbecues, speedboating, nights on the couch in front of the television. Sex was sporadic, but friendly. Most of all, their combined incomes left her more financially secure than she had ever been in her life. They never spoke about marriage, which was fine with her. She had never needed a man to make her feel secure. For the life of her, she couldn't understand her daughter. Not that she was unsympathetic. To lose the man you love in the heat of that passion . . . it was a tragedy. Then for it to happen again! But Lola was so young still, so smart! Why was she so desperate to tie herself down, to be subservient to some set of rules made up by a bunch of self-serving men with long beards?

She looked at Ravi, startled by the beard. She was so used to it, she almost didn't see it anymore. Besides, there was no comparison. Ravi wasn't religious, not anymore, she told herself uneasily. She should never have shared the Lola stuff. Of course he would side with her! He'd never forgiven himself for taking off his turban. Any day now, she expected him to start growing his hair again. It would have happened already if he hadn't been living with a hairdresser who watched him like a hawk and brought out the scissors the minute his hair grazed the tops of his ears. The God she didn't believe in had a wicked sense of humor saddling her with the two of them!

She took the steak off the grill and put it back on her plate. Truth was, she wasn't all that hungry anymore, all this tension upsetting her stomach. Even though she'd hardly eaten more than a few bites, she was sure to get heartburn now. It was so bad these days. Like angry villagers marching with torches through her stomach and chest, threatening to burn down the whole building. None of the pills were working anymore. She looked at the picnic table with its cans of diet cola and Heineken, bowls of potato chips, and soft white hamburger rolls. It was like committing hara-kiri, she thought, imagining the dragon fire that would leap up and torch the back of her throat at midnight.

"Lola had a hard childhood," he said suddenly, sitting down in the chair next to her.

She tensed. "What makes you say that?"

"Single mom, bad neighborhood . . ."

She bristled. "San Jose was a very expensive area."

"So what? It's still full of bums and drifters."

"Our street was just fine! It was a nice house, and I owned it!"

"She was probably scared to walk to the playground by herself."

"Actually, I didn't usually allow her to walk around the neighborhood by herself. That's normal in most American cities."

"You are proving my point! Tabloid horror stories, Parents of Murdered Children support groups, American junk food and junk television and junk culture. That's your normal life here." He shook his head. "But it's not normal, hon. It's not right."

"She graduated with honors from one of the best schools in California, Santa Clara University!"

"So? I also graduated with honors from San Jose State, but I'm totally screwed up," he said placidly, getting up and heading back to the grill. He put on another steak, sprinkling it with generous amounts of some pungent spice that rose like a cloud of incense. Just the smell made her stomach ache.

"What makes you think it has anything to do with her childhood?"

"When people are looking to make big changes in their lives, it doesn't happen overnight. It starts slowly and builds bit by bit. Believe me, I know. When was the first time you noticed a change in her? I bet she was eight or nine, right? Maybe even earlier."

What the hell? she thought. How could he know *that?* The "incident," as she had labeled it in her mind, was never brought up. Something awful had happened, but it had not been the tabloid horror story it might have been. In the end, it was all right, she told herself. Lola never talked about it. But afterward, she'd never really gone back to being the same kid. She'd begun asking strange questions: Who made the world? Were there angels? Where did bad people go when they died? All kinds of questions about subjects that no normal kid ever talked about, questions for which she had no answers. It got so bad, she'd even called Lola's biological father, who, in typical self-help guru fashion, told her not to worry about it. "Everyone has a religion, a way of living in the world, of making sense of it. As long as you aren't pushing anything down her throat and she's free to find her own way, she'll be fine."

Dr. David Kannerman.

It had all started with a new car. She was desperate. In San Jose, only people with canceled driver's licenses and outpatient mental cases used public transportation. There weren't even any sidewalks! You'd have to walk in the middle of the road. And unlike Brooklyn, everything was so spread out. If you asked directions, people would say, "Oh, it's five minutes away." And then you'd start to walk and walk and walk until you finally realized they'd meant five minutes *by car.* Nobody walked anywhere.

She'd had no choice but to take out an enormous car loan. To pay it off, she took on a second job, a part-time gig at the Fairmont Hotel hair salon. One night, the concierge called and told her to throw on some clothes because a big shot needed an emergency haircut. It was already after 9:00 p.m. She'd almost told him to go to hell. But then she thought about her adorable new red Honda Civic and the repo men. She got dressed and headed downtown.

It was the year she'd turned nineteen. She'd been on the road for two years, living in communes and couch surfing with members of a thrash metal band she'd met in San Francisco. But then her boyfriend, the lead singer, suddenly and shockingly got tired of the rocker lifestyle and wanted to settle down—with somebody else. She enrolled in hairdressing school and got her diploma. It was either that or back to Flatbush prison. That year, she was the thinnest she would ever be, her long, curly, reddish-blond hair drifting wildly down her back, her eyes big and green and expressive.

He was sitting in the Fairmont lobby, imposingly tall, his back straight, his long arms folded serenely in his lap. His beautiful blond hair was tied back in a ponytail.

She'd always had a thing for men with ponytails.

He looked familiar. It took her a few moments to realize that was because his face had been plastered all over town on posters and billboards advertising a self-help book. He was also the principal speaker at the psychoanalysts' convention being held in the hotel's conference room.

"Sorry for dragging you away from your family so late. My agent called and demanded I get shaved and shorn. He said it would give me more credibility and I'd sell more books." He smiled, a wondrous flash of beautiful white teeth.

"I was just watching television. *The A-Team.*" She shrugged. "No biggie."

And when she leaned over him in the chair, clipping the apron around his throat and shoulders, she inhaled a scent of cleanliness mixed with a subtle and expensive cologne that made her ache with desire.

She hadn't been a hairdresser very long, and touching someone's hair still felt intimate. "Listen," she said, because she couldn't help herself, "I think your agent is nuts. Don't touch it. It's perfect."

He leaned back and laughed, a good strong sound that was free and somehow innocent. "Ah, you think so?" His smile was broad and familiar, as if they'd shared a secret joke. "Well." He sighed. "That may very well be, but I promised him I'd do it." He closed his eyes, leaning back. "I'm in your hands."

She wielded the scissors gently, watching with dismay as the silky golden strands fell to the floor. Perhaps he could see how it pained her, which made him smile. To distract her, he started asking her questions about herself, her family, her job, San Jose. He made a real effort to sound interested.

When she finally finished, brushing the stray hairs from his shoulders and undoing the apron, it almost felt as if they knew each other. She contemplated her work. Considering he was perfect to begin with, she thought she'd done a decent job. She always did, especially on men. It was as if she were molding them into someone she could admire, even love. That was even true of the old ones, the fat ones, the sorry ones.

Catching her admiring glance in the mirror, he nodded his approval, opening his wallet and handing her a generous tip.

She accepted it shyly. "I don't read much," she told him. "But I'm planning to go out and buy your book."

He frowned. "Don't do that. I've got boxes and boxes of them upstairs. I'd be happy to give you one. Come up with me?"

Of course, she should have said no, thank you very much. She should have been stronger, wiser, and more perceptive not only about what he was capable of but what *she* would allow to happen of own free will.

She remembered that innocent ride up in the deserted elevator, the silent walk down the elegant corridor toward the brightly polished door of his expensive suite. At first, they just talked, he on the couch, she in a chair. He told her about his wife of many years—his college sweetheart—and about their two children with whom he did not spend enough time. The soft yearning of his voice and its buried sadness reached out to her own loneliness like embracing arms, so that when he finally got up and took that one step toward her, one was all that was needed.

She didn't judge herself. Not anymore. She'd thought about an abortion—for about two seconds. No way she was killing any part of herself willingly, no matter how convenient it might be, especially for her scandalized parents. She never involved Kannerman. Why would she? It was her body, her choice.

The sad truth she had learned about life was that it picks you up like a tornado and sets you down full of bruises and astonishment wherever it wants. Nine months later, when Lola was born, and her sad financial situation became desperate, she'd contacted him. He was surprisingly nice about it, although he did politely ask her to provide some saliva samples for a paternity test. She wasn't offended, even though she knew what the results would be. After that, he even came to visit a few times, bearing baby presents. Then she got a letter from a lawyer asking her to sign some papers in exchange for a lump sum. It had been more than generous, she thought. She'd used it to put a down payment on a house. Soon after, she'd met Dick Howard, a food-and-drink manager at the hotel, who had two teenagers from his first wife.

It was a decent, if not passionate, marriage. They were both tired, looking for a safe harbor away from storms. He died swiftly and unexpectedly from a heart attack at work four years later. He was only forty-four.

She had done her best as a single mom, but Lola was always a strange kid. Instead of bugging her for the latest styles and brand names, she was happy to wear stuff they got on sale or even in Goodwill. After what happened, she never liked playing outside the house or going to the playground, preferring to read or draw inside her room. She did her homework without being asked, studied for tests, and got excellent grades. In fact, at parent-teacher conferences, the teachers seemed shocked when Cheryl showed up with her jeans and biker jacket, like they were expecting someone in a skirt and twin-set.

It was a typical California school, filled with new immigrants who spoke Spanish or Vietnamese and needed to take English as a Second Language. Lola always envied that. She'd go to the library and look up their home countries, thumbing through touristy photographs of teeming rain forests full of brightly colored birds; watery, colorful souks on canoes. "If we lived there, I wouldn't have to be afraid to walk outside by myself," she'd say, without elaborating where she'd gotten that crazy idea from. "People there are kind and smart. Not like here in San Jose."

"People are the same all over, honey," she'd tried to tell her daughter, then wondered if she were doing the right thing. Maybe it was good for a kid to dream, to think there were places in the world that were beautiful and safe. But on the other hand, to encourage such a dangerous fantasy might have terrible consequences for the future. In the end, instead of deciding, she'd say nothing, lighting up another cigarette and blowing perfect smoke rings toward the ceiling while Lola rushed around opening the windows.

All she ever wanted was for her child to grow up free and happy. Was that too much to ask?

Lola hadn't seen it that way.

Once, when they were sitting side by side on the couch in front of the television set watching young Olympic gymnasts fly through the air, Lola stood up and cried out, "I wish I could do that!"

"No, you don't, Lola," she'd told her. "You don't have any idea what that poor girl has been through! The pushy parents waking her up at five, driving her to some freezing gym, counting her calories, not giving her time to be a kid, to have friends. That there is *child abuse*."

Lola had stared at her stonily. "Anything worth having you have to work for, Mom."

Talk about role reversal! The kid was barely ten years old.

"Well, I don't believe that. Life is hard enough without making it worse with all kinds of rules and restrictions. My parents did that to me: 'Don't stay out late, don't wear shorts, don't ride in cars with boys.' Listen to what I'm telling you, girl. Do what makes you happy."

She never sent her to Hebrew school, and there had been no bat mitzvah. She would have been perfectly content if her daughter never knew a single thing about any religion. As it happened, that was not to be. A friend from school, daughter of a high-tech Israeli genius working in Silicon Valley, had invited both of them to join the seder at the local conservative temple. Lola wanted to go, so they went. It wasn't the traditional seder Cheryl remembered, but long and boring nonetheless. But Lola's eyes had lit up as she'd followed every word, dipping her pinkie into the wine ten times to count the plagues, standing by the door to welcome in Elijah the Prophet—who, as usual, didn't show up. The following year, she begged her mother to make their own seder. Cheryl agreed, but on condition she could make up all the rules. She invited the neighbors from Guatemala and Cambodia, all of whom could relate to long journeys fraught with peril; and alongside the horrible flat, inedible cardboard matzo, she made sure to place an organic loaf of sourdough nut bread.

Still, Lola enjoyed it. After that, once in a while, just for the heck of it, she told herself, she'd brought out the silver candlesticks on Friday night, Lola's inheritance, allowing her daughter to light them while immediately afterward making sure to put on a video she'd gotten from Blockbuster, something silly and full of laughs.

Lola would watch for a while, then go into her room and stick her head inside a book. Lord only knew where the kid had picked up the book-worm bug. Certainly not from her. The only books they had in the house were Danielle Steel and an autographed copy of *The Life Choice* by Dr. David Kannerman, which she herself had never read.

And now—despite Cheryl doing everything she could to raise her completely differently from how she herself had been raised—Lola was morphing into her grandmother.

Go figure!

She was hurt and insulted and personally offended by the road her daughter had chosen to take. She would *never* accept it and do everything she could to bring her back to her senses. This wasn't over yet, not by a long shot.

"Want me to put your steak back on for a few minutes?" Ravi asked.

"Nah. Don't bother. Just open up another beer for me, will you?" she asked him morosely, tapping out Lola's number on her iPhone once again.

4

Fruma Esther Sonnenbaum pinned her chin-length dark wig firmly to her head, covering it with an elaborate hat held in place with at least three lethal-looking hatpins. Only after shaking her head vigorously to make sure her head covering would stand up to hurricane winds before flying off to reveal the forbidden sight of her fuzzy gray hair did she put on her coat. Carefully examining the dark material for lint or stray hairs, she buttoned it up to her chin. When she was done, she stared into a full-length mirror. She lifted her chin, satisfied. A queen! An absolute queen, as befitted the widow of the late Admor Yitzchak Chaim Sonnenbaum—of blessed memory—as well as the sister of the deeply revered late Rabbi Eliezer Ungvar.

She glanced at her watch. Oy! It took her so long to get dressed every day. But what could she do? To walk out into the streets of Boro Park without being impeccable to the last detail would besmirch the family name. It was a heavy responsibility.

She reached for the carefully wrapped packages on the kitchen table: two pounds of freshly baked rugelach in an aluminum pan, a jar of homemade prune compote, and a plastic container of cold cuts. They would be waiting, her poor, orphaned grandchildren. Her son-in-law depended on her now. Once again, her heart filled with guilt that she had moved out of her late daughter's home and back into her own. But what could she do? She'd stayed as long as she could. At seventy-four, she just didn't have the strength to take her daughter's place indefinitely. You did what you could, she kept telling herself unconvincingly, pressing the elevator button a little harder than was necessary.

To assuage her guilt, she visited several times a week, bringing over home-cooked food and supervising the children for as long as she felt able. And when people asked her with concern how she was managing, she answered as was expected of her: "God be blessed! I'll have plenty of time to rest in the grave!" Only in the privacy of her mind did she allow herself to admit the inexcusable truth: she was exhausted.

"Good morning, Rebbitzen!" the people of Boro Park greeted her as she walked through their busy streets, sometimes waylaying her, clutching her hands and pouring blessings on her head as they implored her to send their good wishes to her poor, dear family. "How is your son, the children?" they asked, their faces filled with compassion and concern.

While she had no reason to doubt their sincerity, she couldn't help but feel resentful. Deep in their hearts, she knew, they asked themselves why the Sonnenbaums had been visited with this catastrophe. After all, HaShem, may His name be blessed forever and ever, was just and full of mercy. So, when such a tragedy struck, as much as one tried not to fall prey to the Evil Inclination of slander and libel, ordinary pious Jews could not but ask themselves—as she herself had numerous times concerning herself and others—what fault, what transgression, had merited such retribution?

Her rancor was soothed by the knowledge that if asked, not one of them would refuse to help if they could. Compassion for the suffering was not only a religious obligation but the norm in their little town. Wherever Torah-observant Jews gathered into a community, they became one big family. People prayed for you when you or yours were ill; they brought you meals when you were mourning or convalescing; they had numerous organizations eager to provide you free of charge with everything from children's medicine when the pharmacies were closed, to tables and chairs for a family event, to fans to cool you in the summer, to heaters to warm you in the winter, to interest-free loans. You could get everything free of charge—from a wedding dress to pacifiers, from wigs to the special pillow meant to cradle a baby during circumcision to soften the blow. There was no end.

But like any family, there was a pecking order, people who were in charge, who had to be obeyed and respected, whose word was law. If you fell afoul of them, the family that could be so giving and compassionate could turn on a dime, their backs a solid wall blocking you from escaping from the cold into the warm, lit rooms of their loving acceptance.

Fruma Esther Sonnenbaum was one of the people in charge. That knowledge glued together her broken heart as she made her determined way to her late daughter's family.

Her lovely, lovely Zissele! Child of her old age, born after all her other children were teenagers. Her other children—two girls and a boy—had moved far away. The girls were both in Israel, married to respectable scholars in Jerusalem and B'nai Brak, and her son was busy teaching in the renown Telshe Yeshiva in Chicago. He had ten children of his own to care for. While all of them—God be praised!—were diligent in showing her concern and respect, they had left her behind. Only Zissele had been there. They had been very close, especially at the end.

She knew that one should never question God—blessed be He—but often her thoughts betrayed her, wandering dangerously close to the edge of blasphemy. Why had this happened to her lovely, pious daughter, her strictly God-fearing observant family? Why had there not been *hasgacha pratis,* Providence, divine intervention? Why?

As much as she tried to comfort herself by counting her many blessings, she found the loss unbearable. Sooner or later, she knew, it would bring her down to the grave. She did not wish for such a thing. God forbid! To do so would have been a direct affront to He Who gives us life and sustains us day after day. But the relentless flow of sorrow that dampened her pillow and the pages of her prayer book could not go on forever.

Often these days, she found herself sitting alone in the evenings staring out the window with her increasingly fuzzy eyesight at the halo of light from Boro Park's streetlamps, imagining the pain that would strike her down, the visit to the doctors, the test results that would finally, finally give her ordeal an expiration date. Still, she prayed that would not happen until her daughter's family were settled and taken care of; until the right wife could be found for her saintly son-in-law, the right step-mother to care for her suffering grandchildren.

There was no other choice. Life only went in one direction: forward.

Yaakov's own family was not in a position to help. He had lost his saintly father at such a young age, and his mother had never remarried. And now—God save us!—his mother was in a nursing home with that unspeakable disease that robbed old people of everything they had struggled so hard to learn from infancy, stealing away a lifetime of education, accomplishments, connections, and precious memories. That alone terrified her, more than any debilitating physical pain. People could live for years like vegetables, a burden to everyone they loved, dependent on the mercies of indifferent strangers.

Only not that, dear God, she prayed. Only not that. Death would be a blessing compared to dependency.

Yaakov's siblings could also not help. His brother, Chaim, was in Baltimore, married with a large family, and his three sisters were spread out around the country and in Israel with their devout, scholarly husbands, each one working hard to support Torah learning as well as to care for their large families.

She blamed the breakup of close-knit families on the high price of apartments in Boro Park and Flatbush. You had to be King Solomon to buy a normal house these days, the little redbrick town houses selling for over a million dollars. Besides, the neighborhood was being taken over by chassidim moving in from Williamsburg, many Litvish families like her own moving to Lakewood, or Israel, or wherever jobs in far-flung religious institutions seeking Torah-true leadership were plentiful. As a result, large families had been dispersed, making it impossible for them to help each other through a tragedy such as that which had befallen her poor son-in-law.

Of course, friends, neighbors, and merciful strangers were temporarily taking up the slack of Zissele's loss, as was the rule in their holy community. Women sent meals to stock their refrigerator, others their teenage daughters to babysit in the afternoons. A day care center had been found for the baby, and one of the mothers had been dropping off Mordechai Shalom every morning along with her own. But if somebody got sick and needed to stay home during the mornings, who but she would be available? Yaakov, of course, could not be disturbed from his Torah learning.

It was all piling up: the laundry, cooking, shopping. Her little granddaughter was trying, but she couldn't cope. She was a child herself. Fruma Esther shook her head. You needed a full-time mother for five children. Not to mention a second income.

People did not like to discuss that—money. After all, according to halacha, a man was obligated to support his wife and children financially. That was the law, written specifically into every Jewish marriage contract. But custom was stronger than law, and the rabbis had long circumvented this absolute religious requirement by allowing women to "voluntarily" give up their due. Bais Yaakov girls were instructed that the highest rung of womanhood was not only to renounce their husband's financial support but also to put the yoke of making a living around their own slender necks, sparing their husbands all monetary worries that might interfere with their single-minded pursuit of greatness in the halls of Talmud study. Girls competed with each other for the honor. A prospective groom who admitted he planned to earn a salary at some profession was denigrated as balabatim and had a hard time finding a willing bride.

Her Zissele, of course, had been the same. Not that she hadn't struggled. Especially after every birth. She often had what people called "sad" days, days when she had been too exhausted to get out of bed and needed pills to fall asleep. But she was such a saint, never complaining and always managing to pull herself together and continue until . . .

She stopped walking, taking a deep breath and letting it out with an audible sigh. She must sweep that thought out of her head forever, the memory of the day when her Zissele had been unable to continue.

With great effort, she readjusted her thoughts, focusing on that which she could comprehend. The income! What would the family do without Zissele's income? A teacher in a religious school didn't make much, but added to Yaakov's kollel stipend, it had made the difference between being able to pay the rent, the grocery store, the butcher, and their medical insurance. How would they manage now? If only she had been able to help them. But between her social security and the small pension from her husband, she herself barely scraped by. Yaakov was borrowing money, she knew. But how many more loans could he take from the free loan societies? Even if no interest was charged, this money still needed to be repaid! Otherwise, the family's reputation would suffer. It was a stopgap, not an answer.

The only solution, she thought, was to find Yaakov a wife—an efficient, clever housekeeper who knew how to manage money and who would work as well, bringing in a monthly salary; a kind, pious woman who would care for her precious grandchildren as if they were her own.

This was urgent.

Waiting what non-Jews called a "decent interval" before beginning arrangements for such a new shidduch was not part of Jewish tradition. Such niceties had been erased from Jewish life by the unceasing struggle to survive each generation's pogroms and persecutions. If Jews had learned anything of value at all from their sufferings, it was this: the dead were to be honored and deeply mourned, but they were not irreplaceable, especially if there were children involved who needed a kind hand to wipe away their tears; especially if there was a Torah scholar whose learning was interrupted by material cares and whose natural, physical needs were not being met.

Practically from the moment the thirty days of mourning had ended, the matchmakers had been bombarding Yaakov with prospective brides. She not only knew of this but forced herself to approve. It was Yaakov himself who had refused to cooperate. Even now, after a year, he insisted he had no intention of returning their calls.

She was sympathetic. In fact, his reluctance served only to raise him higher in her esteem. Of course he missed her Zissele! What kind of monster would he be if he could so easily forget the lovely bride of his youth, the mother of his children, and just move on? But that was neither here nor there. The fact was, he and his children needed a woman in their lives, a mother and a wife. The family—her family—wouldn't survive without one.

She straightened her shoulders, clutching her aluminum and plastic containers closer to her ample bosom. It was a problem urgently requiring an immediate solution. With God's help, solve it she would.

5

The moment Yaakov Lehman entered the study hall and heard the noisy, passionate chant of learning, his soul expanded, shedding all the constraints that sorrow had placed around it. He searched for his *chavrusa,* Meir Halpern, happy to see him in his familiar spot.

They had been learning together for ten years. Aside from his wife and children, it was the closest relationship he had ever had with another human being, closer even than his parents. A good *chavrusa,* a study partner you chose to learn with, was a gift from God. Sometimes it was random—someone who just happened to be sitting near you and needed a partner. Sometimes the rosh yeshiva played matchmaker between two students. And sometimes, over the voices of the other students, you heard the comments of someone who intrigued and motivated you. It could be because you complemented each other: one was precise and practical, pointing out all the tiny details—the how—while the other was deeply spiritual, delving into the mystical meanings, the significance—the why. And sometimes, you were exactly on the same wavelength, able to finish each other's sentences.

Study pairs often lasted a lifetime, and students would change yeshiva to follow a partner, even moving to another city. Often it was also a relationship that dissolved the moment you stepped outside the study hall. But inside, you were soul mates and partners in the most intense, meaningful endeavor imaginable.

Each day as he sat down behind his *shtender* and opened his Talmud, it was as if he were embarking on an incredible treasure hunt, sifting through the often opaque text until the light of insight illuminated all its startling hidden inner meanings, the very secrets of life. Like all great explorers, each man had his own style.

Sometimes, ignorant people compared learning Talmud to studying in a university classroom. Nothing could be further from the truth! Professors had high intellect, perhaps, but no passion. There was no hidden, Divine truth to be uncovered. Quite the opposite. Their need was to pin down the ordinary, to expose the commonplace nuts and bolts. All they saw was the dark and light of bones and sinews. They missed the soft skin, the beautiful eyes, the sweep of eyelashes on a delicate cheek.

What lover would keep an x-ray of his beloved in his wallet?

A Talmud scholar did the best he could to connect to something much deeper. It was not like praying to God; it was like working for Him, joining *with* Him to shape the world.

As Yaakov neared Meir, a smile lifted the corners of his mouth. He sat down in his chair, a sense of peace flowing through him that eluded him everywhere else in his life, which was chaos, as was the world. Only here could he search for and find the Divine order, the secrets of reality. This was the true work of men, he believed, to discover how to live the right way, by learning God's laws. And once he uncovered these secrets, it would be his task to enlighten others, to fill their lives with good, to save them from the misery of ignorance, from a life of walking blindly through darkness where jagged, sharp stumbling blocks pierced, blocked, and injured one at every turn. It was the noblest of occupations and the most selfless.

He was not here because he had to be, or to fulfill the expectations of others. He was here to fulfill his heart's desire.

"Reb Alter is looking for you," Meir whispered.

Reb Alter's authority permeated every corner of the yeshiva. As rosh yeshiva, he decided who was admitted and who rejected, who earned a stipend, and how much, who was in line to be promoted to a *maggid shiur*, and who was to remain in limbo. He was not a person with time to waste—his or his passionate students'. If he wanted to speak to you, there had to be an important reason.

A shadow, like a cloud passing over the sun, darkened Yaakov's spirit. Could he know? Could someone have told him just how bad things really were at home?

"Did he say what it was about?"

Meir shrugged. "He told me to tell you to go to the office."

Yaakov settled himself more firmly into his chair.

Meir raised an eyebrow, surprised.

"I will go, but not now," Yaakov said obstinately. "We will learn for a few hours, and then . . ." He turned the pages eagerly. "You begin."

Meir shrugged. He began, and Yaakov allowed himself to breathe.

Rav Alter viewed time like precious drops of water in the desert. From the moment he got up and made his way to the earliest minyan at the yeshiva to greet the sunrise, to the moment he uttered his bedtime prayer before closing his eyes at midnight to sleep, he was besieged by students and ordinary neighborhood people seeking his advice, help, understanding, and religious rulings. Often, he found himself skipping lunch as the parade of visitors clogged his waiting room, people standing crowded together against the walls when all the chairs were fully occupied. How many times had he found his whole being yearning to once again be a simple yeshiva student sitting behind a *shtender* in the study hall with nothing to do but delve into the holy words of the sages! But as it is written: *Not the expounding of the Law is the important matter, but the doing of it.* He sighed, beckoning his beadle to usher in the next supplicant.

When he saw it was Yaakov Lehman, he rose with a warm smile. "My dear Yaakov, may the Holy One Blessed Be He give you long life and strength. How goes it?"

Yaakov shrugged, taking a seat. "Not good, Rebbe. Not good."

The rav sighed. "How can I help you, my son?"

Yaakov looked up, surprised. "It was the rebbe who summoned *me* here!"

Rav Alter pulled at his beard. "As it is written: *You cannot be saved from forgetfulness.*" The repetition of this gave him just enough time to search his brain. An image was forming: an elderly woman with a blue hat covering a brown wig. Fruma Esther Sonnenbaum. Of course. She had practically taken up residence in his outer office, demanding that he convince her widowed son-in-law to return the calls of the matchmakers.

"Your mother-in-law, God give her health and strength, is very worried about you."

Yaakov felt his heart sink. Was there to be no end to the demands and pressures from every quarter to find a new wife?

"Rebbe, I'm just not ready," he said honestly. "Besides, what would it look like if I were to put Zissel Sarah behind me so quickly?"

"Is it your heart that isn't ready, Yaakov? Or is it your mind?"

"I don't know!" he cried, a bit desperately. "I just wish everyone would leave me alone!"

Rav Alter sat back in his chair, shocked. He had known Yaakov Lehman from the time he had entered yeshiva as a serious little boy with big, dark eyes that always seemed touched by sadness. It had been a great tragedy to be orphaned of his sainted father at such a young age. But to his great joy and admiration, he had been able to watch the sad child follow in his saintly father's footsteps to become a respected and diligent scholar with a bright future ahead of him. Clearly, Yaakov's mother-in-law had been right. Circumstances were indeed becoming desperate if Yaakov Lehman could express himself with this kind of chutzpah.

Rav Alter got up and walked around the desk, putting a fatherly hand on Yaakov's shoulder. From there, he made his way to the enormous bookcase, pulling a large volume off the shelves. He pulled a chair up next to Yaakov's.

"Are you lonely?"

"More than you could ever imagine," Yaakov whispered. "More than I ever thought possible."

Rav Alter nodded. "But you think to consider a new shidduch would be disloyal to the memory of Zissel Sarah. Is that right?"

"It hasn't been long enough!"

"It's been a year, my son," Rav Alter said quietly.

Yaakov looked down at his hands, troubled.

"Yaakov, do you believe in the Torah and that it was written by God, Blessed Be He, who is all-knowing?"

"Of course, Rebbe!" his eyes darted miserably, wondering what he had said to warrant such a question.

"Is it not clearly written in the Torah: *It is not good for man to be alone*? How can fulfilling the commandment of the Holy One Blessed Be He be wrong? Would Zissel Sarah have wanted you to go against God's laws? Yes, you were married once. But that marriage has ended. It is your religious obligation to find a partner, a helpmate. Now, look at this." He opened the book and began to turn the pages. "You can clearly see that there is an obligation to procreate, even in later years. Rabbi Zerahyah HaLevi, the Great Light, commented that to procreate is a rabbinic obligation."

"With all due respect, *kvod harav,* the Rambam doesn't agree," Yaakov answered softly, trying to make up for his former outburst with extreme deference. "He writes it is a *recommended* way of living but not a rabbinic *obligation*. Surely, with five children, two boys and three girls, I have fulfilled my religious obligation to procreate."

Rav Alter gazed at him fondly but unwaveringly. "It is not a question of obligation but of wisdom. King Solomon writes: *Two are better than one.* Your own soul is telling you this, Yaakov, is it not? Besides, your children need a mother. And you need a helpmate."

Yaakov raised his head and looked into Rav Alter's eyes. "The rebbe doesn't understand."

"So help me, Yaakov."

"I don't *deserve* another wife. Not after what happened to Zissele. If I had been a better husband, perhaps I could have—"

"Could have what? Are you God who measures out the days of all His creatures, who shall live and who shall die?"

Yaakov sobbed, big racking cries that rattled his broad, manly shoulders. Rav Alter, shocked, patted him gently on the back, his own eyes filling with tears.

Finally, Rav Alter handed him a tissue and took one for himself.

"I understand how you feel, my son, but there are other reasons, practical reasons, are there not? Zissele was a teacher, no?"

Yaakov wiped his eyes and nodded. "She taught third grade in Bais Yaakov."

"And now her salary is no longer coming in, is that correct?"

Yaakov nodded wordlessly. For the first few months, he had been entitled to certain insurance benefits and payments, but now they, too, were coming to an end.

"I understand that you have taken out heavy loans from all the free loan societies?"

Yaakov swallowed hard. "Yes, Rebbe."

"And that every day you struggle to find someone to care for your children?"

"My mother-in-law has been an angel."

"She is, unfortunately, very human and close to seventy-five, no?" He paused. "She can't go on much longer," he argued reasonably.

"She has been here? She has spoken to you?"

The rav nodded. "But only because I sent for her," he lied to keep the peace, as God Himself had done when He repeated Sarah's words to Abraham, changing her wording from "How shall I conceive, *my husband being old?*" to "How shall *I* conceive, being that *I* am old?" Forging peace between people always outweighed truth.

"Rebbe, the truth is, I don't know what I'm going to do. I can't manage anymore on my stipend. I was going to ask you if you knew of a part-time job I could do a few evenings or afternoons a week."

"If that is what you want, I will, of course, look. But will you think about what we've discussed? Please?" Rav Alter continued gently.

"Yes, Rebbe," he answered, miserable beyond words.

He finished his day early, weighed down by uncertainty and dread. In order to learn, a person needed peace of mind. And his mind, like his life and his family's, was in turmoil. *Seek peace in your own place and pursue it in others,* taught the Talmud, but it also taught that *a wifeless man has no peace.*

His heart heaved in unhappiness and despair.

He could not support his family without his wife's income. But was the only solution to marry? Could he not go out and earn this money himself? Was that not, after all, the duty and responsibility of a man in the world?

He discussed this with Meir.

"It would be a drastic step," his *chavrusa* answered. "Perhaps in such a case, it is better to ask for support. You could apply for welfare from the government. Almost everyone in Boro Park who is learning is at least getting a housing subsidy."

"Why are they entitled to help from the government?"

"A widower with five children and no income is entitled."

"But you say everyone in Boro Park—"

"Not only. In Monsey and Lakewood and Square Town." He sighed. "They lie on their applications. Or the couples don't register their Jewish marriages with the government. So that way, the wife is considered a single mother, and she is entitled to benefits, housing subsidies that pay off their mortgages."

Yaakov was shocked. "It's disgusting. Is it not written: *Be holy, because I am holy*? This is cheating, stealing from the government."

Meir shrugged. "They all feel the end justifies the means. This is how they support their learning. Besides, you *really are* a widower, and you have no money. You would not be cheating."

He thought about it. Charity, nonetheless. He found the idea sickening. But if he could get some help with the rent, maybe some food stamps, for a little while at least until he figured something out.

"And then, you could ask for help from kind Jews."

At first, Yaakov didn't comprehend. "You mean schnorr?" He was stunned at the idea.

Meir nodded. "You are an important scholar, Yaakov! If you abandon your learning, the secrets that will lead to the well-being of the whole world might well be lost, the time for the coming of the Messiah postponed! Think of the misery! Why not ask other Jews to help you? Isn't your learning for their benefit as well?"

Yaakov pondered this, tossing in his bed. He didn't mind the government subsidies if he was honestly entitled to them. But future subsidies would not help him to clear up the debts of the past.

As usual, when faced with any dilemma, he turned to his holy books, the only true source of knowledge. According to the Rambam, anyone who decides to study Torah and not work, making his living from charity, desecrates HaShem's name and disgraces the Torah. Moreover: *Any Torah that is not accompanied by work will lead to its own undoing and cause sin.*

But in another passage, the Rambam also wrote:

> *Any person whose spirit moves him to separate himself and stand before HaShem, to serve Him in order to know Him . . . behold he has become sanctified as the Holy of Holies, and HaShem becomes his portion, his inheritance forever. And He will provide his basic necessities for him in this world, as with the priests and the Levites.*

Elsewhere, he found written that the tribe of Zebulun occupied itself with commerce in order to support the tribe of Issachar, who were Torah scholars. For this reason, according to the midrash, when Moses came to bless the tribes of Israel, he blessed Zebulun before Issachar, in accordance with the verse: *It is a Tree of Life for those who cling to it, and those who support it are content.*

Something inside him cringed at this. After all, was not the great sage Hillel a woodchopper before he became the president of the Sanhedrin? And was not Shammai the Elder a builder? Rabbi Yochanan Ben Zakkai was a businessman for forty years, and Abba Shaul was a gravedigger! He knew many other examples.

He talked it over with Meir, who shook his head sadly. "Perhaps this was possible thousands of years ago when there were only a few tractates, but today, Torah learning is vast, a thousand years of opinions and interpretations. There is no way true Torah scholars can learn part-time. It's futile. Their lives would be wasted. In our times, without support, no real Torah scholars would exist at all for the Jewish people. And if the community did not finance the study of yeshiva students, who would there be to teach and guide the next generation? And what then would happen to the Divine plan? To the universe? Was it better to neglect the most important work that he was put on earth to accomplish, and gifted by God with the abilities to excel in, work that would advance good in the world for all mankind, in order to work in a store selling cameras?

Was it better? He pondered this idea. To earn a respectable living was better for him, for his family, yes. But for the world, no. *And for the good of the world,* he thought, *I must be ready to humble myself. I must be ready to beg.* But that, too, required training. That, too, was a kind of job, he thought. A job for which he had never developed any skills.

There were always beggars at the synagogue and yeshiva asking for charity. He gave them what he could but had never paid much attention to the beggars themselves. Now he studied each one. How did they look? What did they wear? What words did they use in making their approach? Did they tell a story that evoked sympathy, or did they simply put out their hands?

The put-out-your-hand approach, he saw, was the least remunerative. If you put out your hand or jingled the coins in a charity box, people automatically responded by digging into their pockets for a few coins. But if you dressed like a yeshiva scholar and had a letter of introduction from a well-known and respected rebbe vouching for you, they opened their billfolds or took out their checkbooks.

If Rav Alter was surprised to see Yaakov Lehman the very next day, he did not show it. "How can I help you, Yaakov?"

Stammering and turning red with shame, he asked Rav Alter to compose and sign a letter of introduction for him to show to potential donors.

Rav Alter listened patiently, nodding in wordless agreement.

"Come back this afternoon, Yaakov. My secretary will have it ready for you."

Only after Yaakov Lehman closed the door behind him did Rav Alter allow himself a deep and painful sigh.

He did not reveal his plans to anyone, merely arranging with his mother-in-law to watch the children. "I'm going to Lakewood," he told her.

Hearing the name of the great center of Torah scholarship, she asked no questions. Talmud scholars often visited there to discuss weighty points of law with distinguished scholars.

For Yaakov, Lakewood's proximity yet its distance made it the perfect place to begin his new venture in obtaining relief from his financial nightmare. Only eighty miles from Manhattan, Lakewood had grown into a small city from a summer village near the Jersey Shore for well-heeled gentiles. Now it mirrored the great centers of Torah learning destroyed by the Nazis in Europe, its flourishing yeshiva complex encompassing over six thousand Talmud scholars, roughly the same size as Harvard. This devout community was the perfect place to try his luck, he thought. It was close enough so that he could catch the Lakewood Express bus on Forty-ninth Street and Eighteenth Avenue and be there in an hour and a half.

It was the first stop for any serious Jewish beggar.

Before leaving, he examined himself in his bedroom mirror, brushing lint off his handsome black suit, his Sabbath best, and rubbing his sleeve over the brim of his expensive black felt Borsalino hat before placing it on his head. He was startled. He looked tall and handsome and prosperous, he thought in sudden dismay. Why would anyone, especially a struggling yeshiva student, hand over his precious tithe money to someone who looked as if he had no cares in the world, letter of introduction or no?

He rehung the suit inside its plastic bag and took off the hat, redressing in everyday black pants and a clean white shirt. In the back of the closet, he found an old suit jacket that was a different shade of black from the pants. It was worn at the elbows and frayed at the cuffs. Satisfied, he turned his attention to the hat. It was an expensive item, usually gifted to young men by their brides' parents or to lucky bar mitzvah boys whose parents could afford to show off. It was destined to be worn for years on every Sabbath and festive occasion over a black velvet skullcap, especially when davening before the King of Kings. Surely those he asked for charity would not hold that against him? But then again . . .

He put it back into its box, replacing it on the high shelf in his bedroom closet. There, on the shelf just above, was Zissele's wig hugging the Styrofoam head form. It was still shiny and clean, the dark brown curls dripping down the sides as they'd done on his dear Zissele's pretty face. Her sisters and mother had disposed of the hats and clothes, but he would not let them take the wig. He couldn't even explain to himself why. And each time he saw it, the vision kicked him in the gut like an enemy. He embraced the familiar violence. Surely, he had it coming. He left with only the velvet skullcap. Finally, he put on his long black everyday raincoat.

When he neared the stop, he quickened his steps. The bus was already there. Men who looked like him, and women who looked like the wives of his friends and neighbors, had already begun to board. There was separate seating, the women moving to the back, the men sitting in the front for the sake of modesty. This made him comfortable and uncomfortable in equal measure. On the one hand, it was familiar and pleasing to his sense of propriety. But on the other, it was as if the whole neighborhood were accompanying him on this shameful journey.

As soon as the doors closed, his jittery hands reached for his book of psalms. There among the sacred verses written by a King David lost, hounded, and afraid for his life, Yaakov found himself, reciting the moving words with a devotion and desperation that their author would have found familiar.

"Are you on your way to the yeshiva?" the young man sitting next to him asked in a friendly way.

Yaakov looked up, his heart sinking. *He means well,* he tried to convince himself without success, hoping he wouldn't ask anything else. Although he didn't doubt the utter rightness and necessity of the path on which he had now embarked, a massive residue of shame clogged his heart and made his face flush.

"Thinking about transferring?" his seatmate continued.

Yaakov leaned back, resigning himself to the interrogation. "Actually, I'm a *shaliach,*" he improvised, using the professional term for those sent to collect charity on behalf of others.

"Ah, may God bless you with success." The young man nodded, his face open and friendly with no trace of pity. *That's because he thinks I'm collecting for some institution. Or for some cause in Israel. If he knew it was for myself . . .* Yaakov's heart raced.

"Where will you go?"

His mind was blank. "I didn't think about this," he admitted.

"Ah, so it's a new thing by you?"

"First time, yes."

"God be blessed. Well, definitely a person should go to the yeshiva, and then to the Brookhill area, where many frum people live who are also blessed with a fine income. Will you go door to door?"

Yaakov swallowed hard. "I don't know," he admitted. "Is that your advice?"

The young man smiled. "Don't look so worried! People there are so generous. This is known. So the town has to be careful. Everyone who wants to collect tzdaka first has to get a certificate from Tomchei Tzdaka. Without that, no one will give you a penny."

"Tomchei Tzdaka?"

"Yes, the town's charity committee. They investigate. If someone says they are collecting for a yeshiva, they call the yeshiva. Or if they say they are a yeshiva student collecting for themselves . . ."

Yaakov turned a deep red, but his companion didn't seem to notice, chattering on, "They will ask you how many students are in your yeshiva, and who is the rosh yeshiva . . . you know, questions to check. And when they see a person is telling the truth, they give him his certificate."

"But I already have a letter from my rosh yeshiva."

"I am sure you are a righteous man. But others . . ." He scowled. "In Lakewood, they have experiences you shouldn't know from, people who make up letters, forge signatures . . ."

His heart sank. He had no choice then. "Where is this office?"

"Not too far. You can walk to it from the bus stop. I'll show you."

When he finally got off the bus, he thanked his companion profusely and followed his directions. He walked and walked and walked, his heart beating at an exhausting pace as his mind filled with frightening images of angry confrontations with balabatim demanding his certificate, people who would have shouted at him insolently when he was unable to produce one, chasing him away like a charlatan. Sweat broke out all over his body as he imagined it. Silently, he blessed God and his traveling companion for having saved him.

More than once, he lost his way and was forced to ask directions once again. When people heard *Tomchei Tzdaka,* they examined him curiously, their eyes widening in what he hoped, but could not be certain, was compassion. By the time he arrived at the nondescript office building, his white shirt was drenched in sweat. He took off his coat, hoping the shirt would dry and that at least there was no odor. He felt tired and near despair.

There was a small waiting room with a bench and a few chairs, almost all occupied. The faces that turned to stare at him when he entered had unkempt, scraggly beards, and eyeglass frames held together with Scotch tape. He noted that most wore clothes that had not been washed recently and which perhaps had never been ironed. They examined him at their leisure, leaning back in their seats with the air of retirees who had no place to go and nothing to do. Yaakov nodded, trying out a tentative smile. They smiled back, their sad, neglected teeth crooked and discolored.

Despite his tired feet, he could not bring himself to join them.

"First time?" one of the men asked him in Hebrew.

Yaakov nodded.

He patted the seat next to him. Yaakov hesitated, then sat down gratefully. "Exactly! Take a load off your feet and don't look so sad! God made us beggars so that rich Jews won't go to hell. What would Jews do if no one needed their charity? Besides, this is God's choice, not mine. He could have made me rich, but He didn't. He made me what I am, so I do the best with it. I try to make them laugh. They like that, a joke. Makes their wallets open easier. If you are taking their money, at least leave them with a smile!" His eyes narrowed. "If that doesn't work, then I take out this picture" He unfolded a photograph of ten bedraggled children which he displayed without explanation. "Until I get something out of them, I don't move. I'm like a piece of furniture."

Yaakov didn't know how to react to such talk, which he found undignified, bordering on trickery. He was happy when he heard the door open and saw a young yeshiva student sitting behind a desk, talking to a potential beggar. When his turn came, he was asked to fill out a questionnaire: name, address, synagogue, marital status, number of children. There were little boxes to check next to a variety of needs that included wedding expenses, health, or emergency. He filled it out and checked *emergency*. When it was his turn, he handed the paper to the young man behind the desk who studied it with a frown.

"I have a letter of introduction from Rav Alter," Yaakov said hurriedly, wanting to reverse the downward turn of the man's mouth.

It worked. He looked up and smiled broadly. "Rav Alter!" He motioned to Yaakov to hand it over. He read it quickly, shaking his head in commiseration. A few times under his breath, he whispered, "*Nebbech, nebbech,* may God watch over us." When he finally looked up, his eyes were filled with sympathy. He handed Yaakov the certificate and shook his hand warmly, wishing him well. "May you know no more sorrow."

Yaakov thanked him, the kindness a balm to his wounded pride. When he turned to leave, he saw that his empty seat had already been filled by another hopeful beggar. Lakewood, it seemed, had no shortage of those down on their luck.

Out in the street, his tired legs moved slowly, without enthusiasm, his heart slowing down to the pace of his tired brain. While in the study hall, his mind was quick and supple, filled with a wealth of ideas and facts and intellectual vigor; now he felt dull, even stupid. He could hardly remember what he was doing in this place. His needs had become primal. *Where can I get a drink?* he thought. *Something to eat?* Then he remembered the brown bag his mother-in-law had shoved into his hands as he went out the door. He searched for it in his black leather briefcase. Gratefully, he opened it, reaching in and unwrapping the cold chicken smothered between two thick slices of challah. There was also an orange and a small cardboard box of juice. Making the proper blessing, he stuck a straw into the juice and drank gratefully, draining it to the last drop. Then he looked around for water in order to ritually wash his hands before reciting the blessings over his sandwich, but there wasn't any. The sandwich crumbled in his hands, little pieces falling to the ground. He bent down, about to clean them up, when he noticed a train of ants that had quickly formed a line and were industriously handing the tiny crumbs to one another with admirable fortitude and industry. He moved his leg carefully to keep from harming them. The wonder of all God's creatures! "*He gives sustenance to all that live*," he recited with piety, thinking of the compassionate Father of all creation who had placed him and his sandwich in this exact spot to help these tiny creatures. He was glad for them.

Sadly, he put the sandwich away, putting one foot in front of the other for what seemed like hours until he finally found himself at the Beit Medrash Govoha campus. It was an impressive modern building of light tan brick, cared for and prosperous, the very opposite of his own miserable state, he thought sorrowfully. He made his way through the complex to the massive doors of an impressive synagogue, where students were streaming in for afternoon prayers. He joined them. Surely there he would find water.

The main hall of white marble columns and gold decoration took his breath away. Students crowded in, nudging him forward. There was no way to turn around and walk out without calling attention to himself. And that, almost desperately, he did not wish to do.

As he studied the faces of the healthy young men around him, he decided that they must be filled with happiness and animation, projecting on them the joy he himself had always felt in having spent an entire day delving into the mysteries of the Divine word. That any one of them might be bored or miserable seemed unfathomable. How could a yeshiva student in Lakewood, unburdened by care, be anything less than overjoyed at his station in life? Once, he, too, had been like them. His Zissele had made that possible. And he had never known, never realized, that it was all her doing, her hard work, her selflessness. He had taken it all for granted that there was a second income, someone to care for his children, to clean his house, cook his meals, and iron his white shirts. He had thought his life would continue that way until the children were grown, and both he and his wife grew old.

But without his wife, without Zissele, nothing was possible anymore. It was his own fault, he knew, despite what Rav Alter had said. He had been totally responsible for everything that had happened.

He felt something suddenly break inside him. The dam that had for so long held back from him the full knowledge of the immense change Zissele's death had brought suddenly collapsed, flooding him with sorrow so heavy and overwhelming he had to sit down. He touched his cheek, his fingertips tracing the curve of his cheekbone and the soft hairs of his beard, the arch of his nose and the hard curves and soft flesh inside his ear. Who was this? he thought, frightened. Who did this face belong to now? What kind of person? What would be his place in the world? He felt confused and lost. His entire body ached as if overcome by sickness.

When he heard the cantor begin the Eighteen Benedictions prayer, the center of Jewish liturgy, which required one to stand facing east toward Jerusalem and recite in total silence, he pulled himself up. Weak, his stomach growling with hunger, he joined the others in a collective and personal plea to his creator:

Blessed be You, Lord our God and God of our fathers, God of Abraham, God of Isaac, and God of Jacob; the great, mighty and

awesome God, God Most High, who bestows acts of loving-kindness,
who creates all, who remembers the loving-kindness of the fathers
and will bring a Redeemer to their children's children for the sake
of His name, in love. King, Helper, Savior, Shield.

When he completed the sacred prayer, he took three steps backward from the Divine Presence, clicking his heels as if leaving the court of a king. He felt exhausted, ennobled, scourged. He gathered his things together, avoiding the curious and friendly glances of those around him. To his surprise, he was no longer hungry or thirsty. He did not feel like himself. He did not feel human. He was a walking ache, a disgrace, consumed in his entirety by the sickening, humiliating task still before him.

He asked directions and found his way to the door of the rosh yeshiva. This would be his first stop, he told himself, the beginning of his new life of shame. He clutched the door handle, imagining the face of the beadle as he asked for permission to enter and then being led into the great man's august chamber. What would he do? he thought in panic. Hand over the shameful certificate and then his letter of introduction from Rav Alter with its sad, undignified personal revelation of failure, personal loss, and need? He, who wanted to be recognized by the great man as a talented scholar, would now meet him as just another beggar. There would be endless compassion and kindness from the great man. And pity. Because he was now pitiable, was this not so? Did he not now have official certification of his pitifulness?

The thought blinded him with hot tears. He felt his hand drop down off the doorknob. He turned, fleeing down the steps and out of the building, making his way back to the bus stop, where the Lakewood Express was waiting to take him, empty-handed, back to Brooklyn.

When he got home, his mother-in-law opened the door. The expectation in her face soon turned questioning and then to alarm. "What happened to you, Yaakov?"

He took off his old jacket, letting his bag fall to the floor. "You can call the matchmakers, Bubbee Fruma. Tell them Yaakov is ready."

6

Dear Mom,

So you're mad I haven't been in touch, and I'm sorry. I could give you a good excuse—like my phone died and I got a new one—true, by the way—but that doesn't explain why I didn't send you the new number.

I'm so sick of all your criticism. I'm sick of thinking twice about every word I say to you so you won't use it against me. I'm tired of trying not to feel angry and resentful and holding myself back from telling you off, which I can't do because my rabbi tells me not honoring parents is right up there with murder and adultery.

You think you're telling me things I don't know, that I don't have doubts? Of course I do! Every single day. But I can't go back to my old life. I was miserable there. And after all my horrible sins, I have to do some good in the world.

Yeah, I know what you're going to say: PureBirth wasn't my fault. We're both so committed to that big lie, aren't we? But the truth is, I should have investigated all those rumors. I should have quit. But I didn't. I kept selling that crap because I wanted my salary *and all those juicy bonuses. Only after I got laid off and found Andrew in bed with the CEO did I suddenly go hunting for answers. That's the disgusting truth we both have to live with. I'm guilty, all right. But I'm also horribly sorry, and in my own way, and for the rest of my life, I am going to try to make amends.*

I can't understand why so many people are worried about polluting the environment but don't give a second thought to polluting their own hearts and minds with what they see and read. Remember that movie we both loved, It's a Wonderful Life? *There was this guy, Potter, who wanted to cheapen and destroy the wholesome little town of Bedford Falls, turning it into Pottersville. In the movie, the little town stood united and stopped him. Well, now, people have been brainwashed into thinking this would be wrong, an infringement on "freedom" and "self-expression." And so the whole world has turned into one big, ugly Pottersville. Everywhere I look, I just see so much violence, sleaziness, and stupidity. I just needed to escape. Can you understand that, Mom?*

So this is my life now: I'm living with a lovely family in their spare room in Boro Park, Brooklyn. They're an older couple with nine children (close your mouth—there are people here with twelve and even fourteen!). Most of their kids are married, and there are dozens of grandchildren. Their two unmarried sons spend the week in a yeshiva in New Jersey, so it's only their youngest girl, Gittel Ruchel—a cute but standoffish fourteen-year-old—who still lives at home. She and I both have our own bedrooms.

It's a serene home. No television, no internet, and only a little radio mostly tuned to a religious music and sermon channel, and even that gets turned off on Shabbos (Saturday), when everything changes. The house fills up with people, noise, and laughter, and the kitchen counters and refrigerators (there are two!) fill up with a catering hall's stash of food and drink to feed their own huge clan and so many guests.

I help with the cooking. You'd roll your eyes if you could see me up to my elbows in ground carp, onions, eggs, and matzo meal for something called gefilte fish. Big difference from the gravlax with mustard sauce or beef fillet with truffle mayonnaise I made in college, I admit.

Friday night, everyone—even the babies—stays seated around the table listening to stories and parables. Every once in a while, someone—usually Rav Aryeh—pounds on the table and begins to sing yet another lively, out-of-tune Shabbos song. We make up with enthusiasm for what we lack in vocal chords. This goes on for hours. I can just see you rolling your eyes. But I'm not you. Try to remember how much I always wanted brothers, sisters, cousins, aunts, and uncles—big, noisy, happy family celebrations. But it was always just the two of us.

Rav Aryeh treats me like one of his daughters, and Rebbitzen Basha fusses over me, ironing my clothes and making me extremely delicious and fattening bag lunches to take to work at the yeshiva office where I spend my days setting up web pages and building a mailing list for fund-raising and publicity. So you see, you don't have to worry. I'm actually using many of the skills I learned in college.

When I finish work—usually around five in the afternoon— Rebbitzen Basha always has dinner waiting for me, something warm and nourishing. And then I go back to Rabbi Weintraub's program and join the other young women in learning about Jewish history, the Prophets, Jewish laws for women, and something called mussar, which is basically how to build character and become a good person. I suppose that's what I need most. That, and praying, which, by the way, I finally get. It's not only about what you say but about what you hear back. Sometimes what I hear comes through like a local AM radio station, and sometimes like a shortwave channel in another language. I'm always struggling to understand. They say that takes patience.

The other thing I like best is volunteering. Today, I'm helping out this young family whose mother passed away not long ago so that the father doesn't have to take out time from studying. He's a Talmud scholar but just enrolled in an evening program to get his CPA. Apparently, they're broke. So sad. I'm glad to help. Lives here center around performing good deeds like this. That's the kind of world I'm in now.

Mom, let's not fight anymore. My life doesn't need that. Try not to worry about me, and please write me back. I promise to answer you. I love you.

Say hi to Ravi.
Leah

She folded the letter, sliding it neatly into a stamped envelope, feeling a wave of regret on how much she'd left out.

If only she knew how to distill everything she felt as she looked around her: She loved the homey takeout food stores, the candy stores with their chocolate menorahs, the neat little neighborhood grids made up of family homes, synagogue buildings, and educational institutions. And most of all, she loved the children, the little girls in their long dresses and tight braids, the little boys in their velvet skullcaps and long sidecurls, crowding the playgrounds and the fenced backyards of synagogues filled with push toys and bicycles to keep them occupied while their parents entreated God for love and mercy in long, unhurried prayer sessions.

She loved the fact that here, men not only didn't stare at women and girls, they deliberately averted their eyes. Of course, no one would—Heaven forbid!—catcall or worse, the way men did in the city, even though there was no shortage of very pretty young girls who walked alone here, even in the dark.

The women, intent on their children, their slim arms straining under the exertion of pushing strollers that often held both a baby and a toddler, were so brave, so resourceful, she thought. Often, they cut up a chicken into twice as many pieces as had ever been imagined and made up for the lack with plentiful potatoes cooked a hundred original ways. And as busy as they were, they embraced the time-consuming weekly task of creating handmade challah bread so delicate, fragrant, and delicious that no one partaking of a slice or two could feel deprived or hungry. They added water to the wine after their husband's mandatory sip, so that each child and guest might taste a little bit of Eden and the bottle remain almost full until the next Shabbos meal. It was not an easy life.

During the weekdays, the men studied their holy books, trying to untangle the knotty, ancient word of God, to strain out the confusion and uncertainties so that it might flow smoothly and relevantly into their lives and the lives of their families. And the wives, whether the pampered daughters of wealthy merchants or the youngest in a family of ten on the edge of poverty, took up a reciprocal burden to ease the men's labors, to keep them glued to the task that they sincerely believed would bring them all blessing.

She remembered the fading sepia photographs of her great-grandparents who had fled Poland at the turn of the century. Her great-grandmother Chana had been a young unmarried woman courageous enough to accept an arranged match with a young widower with two small children. She had braved the many perils of the sea voyage to the new world, resolutely leaving behind her familiar life in a homeland filled with ugly hatreds, poverty, misery, and the constant threat of brutal, senseless violence, entrusting her future to her new husband and to America.

When she saw their photographs for the first time at the home of grandparents she hardly knew, she was shocked. The family resemblance was unmistakable. She stared up at the photos, mesmerized by the woman whose eyes and thick brows looked so much like her own, elegant in a dress of somber, black brocade with a lace collar so high it almost touched her small, determined chin. Her only ornaments were an elaborate gold watch held by a long, glittering chain, and tiny gold earrings. Her thick gray hair—so incongruous atop her unlined, youthful face—was parted in the middle and gently pulled back into a heavy bun on her long neck, emphasizing her beautiful high cheekbones and large, light eyes. Her full, well-shaped lips were closed and unsmiling before the intrusion of the camera.

Her great-grandmother Chana, she was told, had taken care of her husband's orphans, then given birth to her own two daughters. But the effort proved fatal. Her youngest died in infancy, and Chana soon followed, whether from the foulness in the air of the teeming Lower East Side or grief, no one alive remembered. She and her infant were buried side by side in a Queens cemetery, leaving her husband to care for yet another motherless child, her grandmother Shirley, who was barely five.

Her great-grandfather—distinguished in his short beard and American suit and tie, his head bald under a large, square skullcap, already seemed to be looking into tragedies as yet to unfold. According to her grandmother, he was a pious man who never for a moment abandoned his religious beliefs and practices. "He wouldn't drink a glass of water in anyone's house because it might not be kosher," her grandmother told her proudly. Although he'd been a prosperous landlord in Poland, in America he'd worked as a house painter to be master of his time. Unlike so many other immigrant Jews in New York, who felt it was work or starve, he'd adamantly refused to work on the Sabbath.

He wasn't alone. But for so many of the Jews who forwent the American dream to hold fast to their God and their religious beliefs, they'd been unable to pass on an iota of their piety to their progeny. She thought of her mother running off to California. She might as well have been a child of Cossack peasants or Irish coal miners, so antiseptically had she wiped away her heritage, leaving nothing behind.

But these people, she thought, wide-eyed, filled with the wonder of the newly initiated determined to see only good to justify their great leap of faith, they were the living repository of thousands of years of tribal belief and faith and ritual, transferred to them intact with rare success by their great-grandparents, grandparents, and parents. And now they were in the process of doing the same for their own children.

Considering the odds, it was a miraculous accomplishment. So many powerful forces had been aligned against them, determined to squeeze them dry of their old ways in the hope of producing an empty receptacle into which could be poured the watery thin, "progressive" life of a made-up new country with no past, desiccating them of all that had made the lives of their ancestors plump and joyful, rich with meaning. For those who cooperated, their reward was gadgets and appliances, the false hilarity of commercial amusement parks and crowded, noisy beaches; but most of all, the anonymity of assimilation that opened so many desirable doors.

This place was hardly America at all, she thought as she studied the modest brownstones, crushed together with no room for driveways or garages. The people too crowded together, leaning upon one another, part of each other's lives, with all the good and bad that entailed; a tightly woven community where people lived, worked, prayed, schooled their children in the same ancient values, and married into each other's families. It was not easy for an outsider to squeeze inside.

While the Blausteins and Rabbi Weintraub could not have been nicer, treating her like one of the family, she was keenly aware she wasn't.

She sometimes saw and felt this acutely through children who pointed at her, whispering in derision behind cupped hands as they stared in contempt. Like little Geiger counters, they detected outsiders immediately, set off by the length of a sleeve, the shade of tights, the inflection of a word. Through them, she experienced the invisible social barrier that was as high and as firmly impenetrable as that seven-hundred-foot ice wall in the *Game of Thrones,* erected in the far north to keep out the wildlings. On one side of that wall were the FFBs—or frum from birth—people born and raised in Orthodox tradition, and on the other, everyone else. And straddling the precipice were people like herself, BTs—or *baale tshuva*—the newly observant, trying desperately to make the leap over without smashing to the ground or being hounded back out.

She smiled a bit mournfully. It would take time. They'd have to be sure she was sincere. She didn't resent that. No, this place, and places like it, *needed* to be sealed off, she told herself. There was a tsunami of immorality and ugliness sweeping over the world, its greatest victims women and children who no longer had any protection from abandonment and exploitation. All shame and decency had disappeared. She was living proof of that, starting with her philandering father and ending with her unfaithful partners who had destroyed her hopes for love, marriage, and family without so much as a backward glance.

Here was an alternative universe, one so far unsullied by this modern plague, its people still living according to a moral code that made such things impossible. While no doubt there were sinners here, too, she so much wanted to believe it wasn't the norm, nor were one-night stands, illegitimate babies, and live-in unmarried couples. It was a different world, she told herself, where people had internalized those ancient Jewish laws she'd encountered for the first time, ironically, only as a college freshman in a comparative religion class taught by a Jesuit Catholic priest. Father Joe.

7

Father Joe.

Her mind went back to the day she started college.

Even though Santa Clara University was only a short drive from where she'd grown up, it was light-years away from her childhood. It was old California, site of one of the original twenty-one missions founded by the Franciscans and Spanish soldiers almost two centuries before. As she strolled through the wisteria-covered walkways in the mission gardens near the old bell tower, she felt joy bubbling inside her. All those lush, lovingly tended lawns and towering palms! All that jasmine-scented air tinged with the fresh, spicy odor of newly mown grass! All those carefree, healthy, uncomplicated young people in tank tops and shorts who were going to inherit the earth, and in the meantime were entitled to enjoy the fun of being in this lovely place! Now, finally, after a dreary and often complicated childhood, she'd earned the right to be one of them.

A black-garbed priest walking past noticed her smile. "Lovely day!" he called out, nodding and smiling back. He was young and startlingly handsome, with thick dark hair and large, heavy-lashed blue eyes. She blushed, smiling back, turning her head to follow his progress as he threaded his way through the bikini-clad coeds sunbathing all over the campus lawn. Did it bother him, she wondered, all that naked female flesh? And why would a man like that choose to be celibate?

She had a fascination with people who'd chosen to live religious lives: Buddhist priests in saffron robes, nuns, Chassidic Jews, people who had allowed their beliefs to shape their lives. What did they do every day? How were their lives different from her own? Were they happier? Kinder? More fulfilled?

While she hadn't mentioned it to her mom, one of the reasons she'd chosen Santa Clara—a Jesuit Catholic institution—over San Jose State despite the extra cost was because it had a religion requirement. Whatever your major, every graduate had to take at least three courses in religion.

She hadn't known what to expect that first day when she took her seat in the Introduction to Religious Studies course. To her surprise—and delight—the lecturer turned out to be the priest she'd passed on the lawn. His name was Father Joseph, "but you can call me Joe," he said right off, putting the class at ease. "I guess you're all wondering what you're in for," he said. "How many of you have heard stories about the Jesuits?" He looked around the room. "Come on now, be honest."

A few people giggled. A few hands went up.

"Okay, a few truth-tellers among the liars." He smiled. "No, I'm not going to ask you what you've heard. I can guess. But here is the truth. A Franciscan, a Dominican, and a Jesuit are arrested during the Russian Revolution for spreading the Christian, capitalist gospel. The Bolsheviks throw them into a dark prison cell. 'Oh, if we only had light!' the Franciscan mourns. 'I know. I'll put on sackcloth and ashes and pray for light.' Nothing happens. The Dominican then begins to preach, delivering an hour-long lecture on the virtue of light. Still, nothing happens. Then the Jesuit gets up and mends the fuse. The light comes on."

He paused, allowing the appreciative laughter to swell and subside.

"We are known for many things, but like all religious, God-fearing people, we have much in common with all people who seek to love and obey God. In this class, we will dwell on what we share. So no matter your own heritage, you have a little Jesuit in you, as I have a little Jew and a little Buddhist in me. What I'm hoping is that this class will help you to start on a journey of self-reflection. 'Who am I?' is your first stop. What is your self-identity in the midst of community? It is also the title of the essay I want you to hand in next time we meet."

She sat in her dorm room, staring at her computer. Where to begin?

Hall noises, and the phone chatter of her roommate, a devout Baptist from Wisconsin, seemed to grow louder and louder. It was driving her crazy. So she unplugged her computer and carried it across the lawn, finding a quiet spot beneath the trees.

Who Am I?

My father was a famous psychiatrist who wrote a book that was a bestseller all over the world. People often said it started the whole genre of "self-help." I thought, when I finally read it a week after my fourteenth birthday when my mom dropped the bombshell of my paternity, that it must have been written by a god: it was filled with compassion, goodwill, understanding, and love. He wrote such profound thoughts in such a deceptively simple way. Right off the bat, first paragraph, he tells you life is hard, that there are no simple answers, and that we should all stop moaning about it and get on with it. Love, he wrote, was action, not emotion. In his book, he tries to create in the reader the desire to become a genuinely loving person who can reach out in loving action even to enemies. It's beautiful.

You'd never believe the author was a bitter alcoholic who beat his legal wife and left illegitimate children all over the country and beyond, myself included. I guess I'll never know the extent of it, and frankly, even if I could, I'm pretty sure I'm not motivated. What would we do, these sperm-sharing strangers and I? Talk about what a contradiction our dad was?

His first wife—I think there were two, but that one lasted forty years, the second only a few months, just long enough to nurse him through a horrible double cancer that ate away at his liver and pancreas and left him totally, horribly destroyed by unbearable pain—was an eminent psychiatrist herself who had also authored a number of books that were equally good but not nearly as successful as his. I've read them all—his and hers—and I guess I can understand why: she, alas, had nowhere near his facility with language.

*He was a brilliant man. And yet, despite the fact that he makes
a cogent case for a truly moral secular life, his own life was the
opposite. This always made me wonder if even the most saintly
secular person is incapable of true morality without the trappings
and discipline of religion.*

*My mother equated living a good life with being happy. With
a strange look in her eyes—part ironic and part Mick Jagger
groupie—she'll happily tell anyone who asks how happy her one-
night stand with my father made her. He was the handsomest man
she had ever seen, she says. And so clean! Cleanest, best-smelling man
she had ever come across in her life. She will never admit having any
regrets, despite the consequences—which, in my opinion, were dire.
Notwithstanding our society's current campaign to champion every
variation of the fatherless and motherless family unit, I still believe
that to grow up without a father or mother is a tragedy for any child.
At least that was my own experience, even though my mother tried
her best to raise me alone and to instill in me her own very modern
attitude toward life. Mostly, I think she failed.*

*The neighborhood didn't help. We lived in a modest little house
on the outskirts of San Jose. Even though Silicon Valley has pushed
housing prices there up into the stratosphere, it never felt like a safe
neighborhood. There was never any sense of community. Neighbors
would appear and then disappear just as you got to know them.
I always felt surrounded by dangers. I wasn't being paranoid; San
Jose had the same murder rate as Albania.*

*Only school gave me some sense of stability. It was a bright, clean
building surrounded by grass. Almost all my school friends were
immigrants. Why on earth their parents had chosen to bring them
to San Jose from such interesting, exotic places I could never fathom.*

*"People do what they do," my mom would answer unhelpfully
when I asked her.*

*She was happy in San Jose. The rootless, mind-your-own-business
ethos appealed to her. The closest person she had to a spiritual guru
was John Lennon. She, too, believed there was nothing worth
fighting or dying for and that people should just live in peace.*

But then came the day when I discovered that my mother

*didn't know everything. A life-changing childhood experience
convinced me that something—someone?—was watching over me
and protecting me. Despite my secular upbringing, I still believe that.
There are forces that guide the universe, that intervene in human
affairs and human history, and for the most part, these forces favor
good over evil, kindness over cruelty. I don't know how this connects
to formal religious beliefs, but I feel I am on a journey toward
greater understanding of these forces and my place in the world.*

She read it over, frustrated. It lacked coherence, precision, philosophical depth. *I don't really know anything except what I feel,* she thought. And that was childish. It was also the truth. Reluctantly, she clicked Save.

She felt impatient for her next religion class, dragging herself through her business courses: Multichannel Retail Marketing and Introduction to Economics. After Father Joe collected the papers, he drew a huge circle on the blackboard.

"The world and everything in it. How do we explore this place into which we were born?"

Hands were raised.

"By using our senses," a girl in a green sweater proclaimed.

He nodded. "Yes. What else?"

"By using our intellect," someone else said.

"By reading what others have written of their experiences," a third person said.

He nodded and nodded. "Yes, all true. But let me ask you this. Have any of you ever experienced something that couldn't be explained by your reason or intellect, or defined by your senses? Something you never read about in someone's book?"

Timidly, Leah raised her hand.

"Can you describe what happened?"

"I'd rather not," she said. "It was pretty traumatic, and I was a child. But in the end, I perceived that according to the natural course of events, my life would have been ruined. I could even have been killed. But something outside myself, outside reason, outside the world, intervened. It was something I knew was true but could not reasonably explain."

He massaged his chin, studying her for a moment, his eyes serious and full of compassion. "Thank you. That was exactly what I was looking for." He turned to the class. "How many of you have had similar experiences, or at least moments when this kind of feeling came over you?"

Almost everyone raised their hand.

"From the beginning of mankind, all human beings have expressed a belief in powers outside reason, outside our logic. In fact, it is only in the last two hundred years that the disbelief in higher powers has become acceptable to express publicly.

"There are several ways of looking at this. You could say that mankind is getting smarter, removing itself from superstition and irrationality. Or you could say that human society is denying a basic truth that human beings have verified from the dawn of time, and that in removing themselves from the idea of a Supreme Being, man is moving away from all that is spiritual and moral in the world, all that is spiritual and moral in himself."

"Can't you be a moral person and not believe in God?" someone asked in a tone of annoyance, which did not go unnoticed.

"If there is no God, why shouldn't I rape my neighbor?" Father Joseph said.

The class looked shocked.

"Relax. I'm quoting Dostoyevsky in *The Brothers Karamazov*. That's one argument. We've gotten used to a strident atheism. Some say we should trust in science. They want to root ethics in a naturalistic worldview. Can biologists help us distinguish right from wrong? Nature is awfully selfish! The Bible calls on human beings to 'master the earth and subdue it.' Is that not precisely what religion tries to do? To take the natural, selfish instincts, the animal instinct, and refine it? To help us behave not as animals but as men?"

The discussion continued.

Some argued forcefully that a belief in God was necessary for humans to adhere to moral rules, while others countered by saying that religions caused misery and slaughter.

A tall, handsome jock in white shorts raised his hand. "I read this on the internet: 'Religion is an insult to human dignity. With or without it, you would have good people doing good things and evil people doing evil things. But for good people to do evil things, that takes religion.'" He looked around the room, a smirk on his face. A fellow jock high-fived him.

Father Joe grinned. "What is good, and what is evil?"

People shifted uncomfortably in their chairs.

"Islam says good is doing whatever Allah has decreed is good. Evil is the opposite. Hinduism talks about ignorance that causes one to err and those errors are the karma of past lives that hurt one in the present. Not only is evil inevitable in creation, but it is said to be a good thing, a necessary part of the universe, the will of Brahma, the creator. If the gods are responsible for the existence of evil in the world, they either create it willingly—and are thus evil themselves—or are forced to create it by the higher law of karma, which makes them weak.

"Buddhism disagrees. In fact, the whole of life for the Buddhist is suffering that stems from the wrong desire to perpetuate the illusion of personal existence. The Noble Truth of Suffering, *dukkha,* is this: 'Birth is suffering; aging is suffering; sickness is suffering; death is suffering; sorrow and lamentation, pain, grief, and despair are suffering; association with the unpleasant is suffering; dissociation from the pleasant is suffering; not to get what one wants is suffering—in brief, the five aggregates of attachment are suffering.' Samyutta Nikaya 56, 11. According to that belief, good is the complete abolition of personhood, because that is what ends suffering.

"The monotheistic religions go another route. Now listen to this:

"'When you reap your harvest, leave the corners of your field for the poor. When you pluck the grapes in your vineyard, leave those grapes that fall for the poor and the stranger. Do not steal; don't lie to one another, or deny a justified accusation against you. Don't use My name to swear to a lie. Don't extort your neighbor, or take what is his, or keep the wages of a day laborer overnight. Don't curse a deaf man or put a stumbling block before a blind man. Don't misuse the powers of the law to give special consideration to the poor or preferential honor to the great; according to what is right shall you judge your neighbor. Don't stand by when the blood of your neighbor is spilled. Don't hate your fellow man in your heart but openly rebuke him. Do not take revenge nor bear a grudge. Love your neighbor's well-being as if it were your own.'

"And overarching all these commandments is the supreme admonition not to be good but to be holy, 'because I am holy.'"

The class looked stunned.

"Pretty specific, no?" He smiled. "Especially in contrast to the detachment from life of the Eastern religions. In this, we find perhaps the greatest piece of moral education and legislation ever given to mankind in all human history. Do any of you recognize the source?"

"Gospels?" someone guessed.

"It's from the Old Testament of the Jews. From the book of Leviticus. We Christians have been envious of that heritage for thousands of years and have done our best to both assimilate and plagiarize."

The discussion continued, but from that moment on, Leah couldn't hear anything else. The Jews! Her own religion! Something noble and true to be envied! Never once in her life had she fully understood this. Judaism wasn't cutting out felt menorahs. It was this. Of course, everyone had heard of the Ten Commandments, but these things, so much subtler, so embedded in the stuff of everyday human life and human interactions—this was the ultimate goal of all Jewish life: justice, kindness, charity. Holiness. This was the Divine wish of the Jewish God. So small in its way. So human. She felt overwhelmed by its beauty, its amazing depth of psychological insight into the raw matter that made up the human condition. The God who had created man knew exactly what kind of creature He was dealing with and what his limitations needed to be. For the first time in her life, she felt proud to be Jewish and deeply ashamed of her ignorance.

How was it she had not known anything as simple and basic and profound as this?

Father Joe smiled at the jock. "Who were *you* quoting?"

The jock looked down at his notebook. "Someone called Steven Weinberg in 1999."

Father Joe shook his head, smiling. "Why am I not surprised? I wonder if he ever came across what I've just read you from his own religion? But let us all thank Mr. Weinberg for giving us this most interesting and provocative statement as a jumping-off point for our next class. In the meantime, I ask each of you to study your own religion and to come up with a summary of its tenets for good and evil and a life well lived. By then, I will have read your essays, and we should be well on our way to understanding something about the similarities and differences in our religious and moral heritages. Class dismissed."

Class dismissed. But it never was. It had gone around and around in her head ever since, eventually sending her forward on a long, stumbling search for truth that had finally, strangely, brought her here.

8

Leah climbed the stairs of the old apartment house searching for the door to Yaakov Lehman's apartment. She knocked softly. A pretty young girl opened the door slowly. Leah watched, appalled, as the girl's narrowed eyes took her in from the top of her blondish-red, impossibly curly hair down to her worn running shoes, passing fierce, unrelenting judgment on everything in between and obviously finding her guilty.

Another Gittel Ruchel, Leah thought, exhaling. What was it with these snobby kids? She forced herself to smile. "Hi, I'm Leah Howard. Your grandmother—I mean your bubbee—arranged with Rebbitzen Basha for me to babysit this morning."

The girl continued to stare. If anything, her hostility went up a notch.

Next to her, Leah thought, Gittel Ruchel was a bubbly Chabad out-reacher.

"I don't know you," the girl finally said. "I can't let in a stranger to take care of my brother and sister."

Leah shifted nervously from foot to foot, unsure what to do next. "But you know Rebbitzen Basha, right?"

The girl nodded reluctantly.

"So why don't you call and ask her? Or call your grandmother? I'll wait outside."

The girl nodded, only too happy to shut the door in her face. Leah sat down on the steps, all her good feelings suddenly draining away. She felt chilled. Love your neighbor as yourself, even if he treats you like dirt when you are trying to do him a favor. Then the door suddenly cracked open. Leah hurriedly rose, looking inside. While the scowl had disappeared, the girl's expression could hardly be mistaken for anything remotely welcoming. Seeing the door open just wide enough for a human being to pass through, Leah quickly squeaked inside the motherless home.

"The baby likes to have his chocolate milk warmed up. He can drink it from a cup, but if he doesn't know you, he'll want a bottle," Shaindele instructed her, ushering her into the kitchen. "Chasya is playing with her dolls now, but she is throwing up. She sometimes doesn't make it to the bathroom, so here is a pail. Bring it to her quickly if she says her stomach hurts. And here is her medicine. She needs a spoonful every two hours."

Leah looked over the determined young girl giving orders like somebody's disgruntled mother-in-law. *She looks barely twelve,* Leah thought. But if she was wearing the school uniform of Bais Yaakov High School, she must have been at least fourteen, fifteen, maybe older. She was pretty, plump, and pink-cheeked. *If she'd only smile, she'd be adorable,* Leah thought, exhaling, pushing herself to look beyond the abrasive posturing to the heart of a kid who had recently lost her mother and whose life was obviously in turmoil trying to take up the slack. "Thank you for the information."

The girl could barely stand to look at her. "I don't like to leave them with strangers," she repeated, her chin trembling.

Oh, my goodness, she's about to cry! Leah thought, her heart melting. She reached out gently, touching the girl's shoulder. Shaindele flinched as if she'd been smacked. Quickly, Leah's snatched back her hand as if from a glowing coal.

"I'll show you where the diapers are, and the snacks for Chasya."

Leah followed her silently down the hallway. Suddenly, a little girl appeared.

"Go lie down!" Shaindele ordered her.

The child looked up with dull indifference, her pale little face illuminated by two bright, feverish spots. Then she suddenly screamed, "Oy, my stomach hurts!" Shaindele ran to fetch the pail from the bedroom, but it was too late.

"Now look what you've done!" Shaindele screamed, shoving the child hard toward the bedroom. "Didn't I tell you to stay in bed! Now I'm going to smell like vomit, and I'll be late for school! Why can't you ever listen!"

The child stumbled forward, then turned around, looking over her shoulder at her sister, her little eyes aflame with hatred. "Go away! You're a *rosha*. I don't like you. *Meshuganah!*" she screamed before bursting into tears.

Leah listened in astonishment. It was more like an exchange between kindergartners than a child-minder and her charge. She saw Shaindele throw her a quick, embarrassed glance before picking up Chasya and carrying her into the bathroom. Concerned, Leah followed.

It was not lost on her that Shaindele deliberately left the bathroom door open, cooing to the child with unconvincing sweetness as she washed her face. Chasya, unimpressed, continued to sob.

"The lady is going to play dolls with you and do puzzles. You'll have fun!" Shaindele told her theatrically as if practicing for an audition. At this, Chasya pushed her body away from her sister's embrace with both her little hands, craning to look at Leah.

Leah nodded, smiling. "Would you like to come and play with me, Chasya?"

The child looked down, wary.

"We'll be all right," Leah assured Shaindele. "I'll manage. You'd better go, or you'll be late for school," she said, trying to demonstrate a competence she didn't feel while expressing a loving-kindness she sincerely did.

"I don't know. I'm the only one she trusts," Shaindele informed her, only to have Chasya wriggle out of her arms and run away. The older girl's face reddened. "She's overtired. I'll lay her down for a nap." Her face clenched in grim determination as she searched for the child, whom she found hiding behind the couch. Pulling the child's flailing little body roughly into her arms, she held her fast. "You," she ordered, pointing at Leah, "wait here."

Leah didn't argue, listening to the two sisters as they fought, surprised at the venom of the exchange, which left the little one wailing. A door slammed shut, and then it was suddenly quiet. As instructed, she waited. Wandering around the living room, a tableful of photographs caught her eye. There were sepia portraits of family gatherings in which children of all ages crowded around bearded men in large black hats seated next to women in elaborate hair coverings, everyone's faces serious, even somber, as if they could foresee the tragic future of the European towns and villages their families had lived in for centuries. Then there were the recent photos: school portraits of maturing young yeshiva boys; a slightly younger Shaindele, her expression gentle and sweet, in a frilly blue blouse with blue bows in her long brown hair; a wide-eyed, smiling Chasya; and finally a gorgeous, blue-eyed baby.

But the photo that made her eyes linger was a formal wedding portrait. She picked it up, studying the faces. The bride seemed only a little older than Shaindele, with the same pretty, plump face and large, brown eyes. The dead mother, she realized, chilled. She was so young, her soft, fragile lips curled in a hesitant, almost confused smile, her tiny body swathed in a voluminous white dress that made her seem like a child playing dress-up.

In contrast, the groom's smile was an unselfconscious beam of pure delight. He was tall, youthful, and extremely handsome, with shoulders so broad they seemed to stretch the fabric of his dark suit. His forehead was wide, glistening with youth, hope, and intelligence, and his large, blue eyes gentle. He had a fine, straight nose but one that gave character to a person's face, the kind she imagined would wrinkle in amusement or snort in contempt. His lips were well formed over strong, straight, white teeth. His hair and short beard were a dark blond, calling to mind the sun-lightened hair of backpackers she'd come across on nature treks, those tall, tan men with their long, supple limbs. He seemed lighter, sunnier, less somber than the other men she'd come across in Boro Park, men who always seemed a bit bowed as if they were carrying the weight of the world on their shoulders. She couldn't take her eyes off him. Only when she heard approaching footsteps did she hurriedly replace the photo, embarrassed.

"She won't nap. She's playing now. Try not to upset her," Shaindele instructed, striding into the living room. "I'll get home as soon as I can."

"What about the baby? Does he also need medicine? And what do I feed him when he gets up?"

"Mordechai Shalom has taken all his medicine. If he gets up, you'll probably frighten him, so don't get too close. You can make him a bottle of warm chocolate milk and hand it to him while he's in his crib."

"No problem," Leah said as pleasantly as she could. Frighten him! The little witch!

Shaindele put on her coat and went to the door, turning to look at Leah doubtfully. "If you can't manage, knock on Mrs. Kornbluth's door one flight up. She'll help. The children know her." Without another word or any pleasantries of farewell—not to mention a "how nice of you to help us out"—the girl opened the door and left.

"Have a great day!" Leah called out after her as she went to lock and double bolt the door. "Try not to enter any personality contests!" she whispered to herself, exhaling, relieved to finally be alone. She wandered through the quiet rooms. There was a picture of a bearded rebbe, and one of the Western Wall, both garish and poorly executed in ugly shades of brown. But then there were other framed pictures: flowers, the sea, laughing children at the beach. She walked up to them to take a closer look. Why, they were jigsaw puzzles that had been laminated, she realized. How strange. But original, too, and sweet.

It was a nice-sized apartment, but the furniture was worn, the carpets frayed from too many vigorous vacuum cleaner sessions. A damp, wretched odor of unwashed clothes in overflowing hampers seeped out from the bathroom. Everywhere, clothing littered the floors, competing with the toys. In the kitchen, unwashed dishes were piled high in two separate sinks, and used pots cluttered the counters.

She peeked in on the children. Chasya was playing quietly with her dolls, and the baby was still asleep. She closed their doors gently, tiptoeing away. If they were happy, she was happy.

She picked up the scattered clothes, adding them to the hampers, then separated the laundry into darks and lights, putting in a load. She estimated there were at least four more to go. Finding an apron, she pulled it over her head, then washed all the dishes and pots. Only when she was done did she realize there were two dishwashers, obviously one for meat and one for milk dishes. She opened them, but they too were filled with unwashed dishes. She put in little packets of soap she found underneath the sink, putting up both loads to wash. Above the noise of the machines, she suddenly heard a baby call out.

He was standing up in his crib, his wheat-colored hair in spikes, the bangs drifting into his large, blue eyes. His cheeks were red and flushed, but he had a big grin on his face, which immediately turned to a frown when she walked in.

"Hey, little one!" she said softly, not moving too close. She had experience with little kids from being a counselor and then an au pair. They hated anything sudden, especially aggressive affection from strangers. At a safe distance, she covered her eyes with her hands. "Peekaboo!" she said.

The baby looked at her, startled, trembling, but the frown was gone, replaced by curiosity. Then he saw her hands go down and her warm, wide smile. It was such a relief that he giggled, the way people laugh after the plunge of a roller coaster when they are safely still and at the bottom. Encouraged, she tried it again. This time he laughed outright, the infectious, miraculous, joyous laugh of a baby having fun.

She put out her arms for him, and he reached out toward her. Only then did she approach him, lifting him gently into her arms. His silky hair tickled her chin, and his warm, soft body seemed to melt into her chest. *This is why women have breasts,* she thought, glad she had a soft place for a little person to land. He clung to her, and she clung back with a longing that surprised her.

"Mordechai Shalom," she murmured into his little head. "Such a big name for such a little person. Well, we'll have to find something a little more appropriate to call you, won't we? Let's see." She gently twirled around the room with him, and he laughed. "It's those cheeks you've got! World-class cheeks," she told him. "Like pieces of sweet, pink marshmallows. Let's call you Cheeky, shall we? No one has to know, just the two of us, okay?" She looked into his face, smiling, and he smiled back.

"I don't want to offend you, sir, since you seem such a nice fellow. In fact, you are lovely. But the truth is, you smell. Terrible! Why don't we fix that?" She laid him down on top of a changing table, softly tickling his stomach and tenderly kissing his belly button. He rocked with laughter. "Cheeky, Cheeky, Cheeky," she whispered, laughing, pulling off his diaper. It was disgusting. She did the best she could to fold it so it wouldn't soil anything else, then wiped the child clean with baby wipes. But it was no use. He needed a bath.

Taking off his wet undershirt, she carried him naked into the bathroom, hoping he wouldn't pee all over her on the way. "You wouldn't do that to me, Cheeky, would you? No. Such a sweet little fellow like you?" she crooned, laughing. Filling the tub and testing the water temperature, she gently lowered him down. He was immediately ecstatic, splashing around and giggling, completely cooperative.

Gently and in great happiness, she soaped his round, soft, beautiful behind, his plump, kicking legs, and firm little back, until his pale skin glistened with fragrant bubbles. When it was time to rinse him off and take him out, she looked around for a towel. The only one she saw was hanging limply from a hook on the bathroom door. Like everything else in the house, it didn't look very clean. She couldn't very well leave him alone in the bathtub to look for a better one. For a moment, she considered carrying him dripping wet through the house, but she abandoned the idea. It would leave her own clothes soaking wet and muddy the already dirty floors. Besides, given the state of the house, there probably wasn't a clean towel to be had. Unhappily, she reached for the one on the door, then pulled out the bath plug. From experience, babies were much more likely to agree to come out once all the water was gone. Indeed, he didn't resist when she lifted him out, wrapping him snugly but uneasily in the towel, hoping no one in the family had a skin disease.

The entire time, he was sweet, smiley, and adorable. *He's used to strangers taking care of him,* she thought sadly, wondering how many he had seen come and go since his mother died. She felt her throat ache at the thought. *Poor baby! Poor, poor baby.*

She kissed his sweet-smelling, newly shampooed hair, rubbing her cheek against his. His face was radiant, pink and warm and delicious. *Such a miracle, a baby,* she thought. A creation more beautiful and wondrous than the greatest mountain range or the most sublime sunset, not to mention all the works of man, which paled in comparison. *I love the God who created this baby,* she thought. *Love and worship Him.* Unexpected tears suddenly flooded her eyes.

Almost reluctantly, she loosened her grip, laying him down in his crib and going off in search of some clean clothes. After a lengthy and unsuccessful rummage through closets and dresser drawers, all she managed to come up with were a mismatched pajama top and bottom, both a little too small. They'd have to do. She shrugged.

"I apologize, my friend," she told him as she dressed him. "You certainly deserve better. But not to worry, we are washing you some clothes, Cheeky, and we'll have you dressed up like a regular Boro Park gentleman in a jiffy! Even Shaindele might look at you and lose her grumpy frown! But in the meantime, why don't we get you something to drink?"

She carried him into the kitchen. If he had a stomach virus, chocolate milk was about the last thing he needed, she thought, remembering her own stomachache days. "Why don't we get you some sweet chamomile tea? And maybe some dried crackers with jam?" She strapped him into his high chair carefully, then gave him a wooden spoon. Happily, he banged it against the plastic tray like a pro.

From the corner of her eye, she saw Chasya appear.

The child was a fierce and miserable little thing, unhappiness pouring through her eyes like dark light. It was not a normal child's misery that comes as swiftly as a summer shower and disappears with a shining forgetfulness in a burst of sunshine, Leah thought. It was ingrained like an adult's and had been there for some time, etching the sad little corners of eyes that looked out with suspicion and yet an odd hopefulness. That was the child in her, that hope, despite disappointment, Leah thought. She could see it, darting out of the dark eyes like a little kitten who crawls beneath a sofa and carefully surveys the dangers before emerging. *If only I could coax it out,* she thought.

"Chasya, sweetie. Come here. I'll bet you're also hungry. But first, let's get you your medicine." The child drew closer. To Leah's surprise, she opened her mouth eagerly. Apparently, she liked the taste of it! Leah spooned the dosage into her mouth.

"More," she begged.

"Oh, I don't think so. But what about something else?" She opened the fridge, examining what was on offer. Huge, anonymous plastic containers took up most of the shelf space. She felt like an archaeologist. Until she figured out what was in them and what was still edible, it was going to take a while. She searched the freezer. With relief, she spied a package of mango ice pops. She hesitated, then decided they couldn't be worse than the chocolate milk their sister had been feeding them.

"What about one of these?" she offered Chasya, waving the orange-colored treat in front of her.

"That's for oneg Shabbos," the child said, shaking her head as she rejected the offer with surprising self-discipline. Leah was flabbergasted.

"That's okay, honey. These are special circumstances. I'm sure your tateh wouldn't mind. Besides, we can always buy more." She held it out to her.

Chasya hesitated, then took it soberly, like a shopper making an exchange, wanting to ensure they weren't being cheated.

Leah watched as she carefully rolled back the wrapper, then took long, slow licks, obviously in heaven.

"We should give you a nickname, too. Let's see, your brother is Cheeky . . ."

Chasya giggled.

"Thank you. I agree. Great choice. I'm a genius. And you can be—"

"Ice cream!" the child proclaimed.

"Okay, not bad. But what about Icy?"

"Icy," the child repeated, laughing.

"Icy, why don't you come and set a while, as my neighbor in San Jose used to say." She smiled at the child, patting the chair next to her. Shyly, Chasya smiled back, approaching gingerly and then slowly pulling herself up into the chair with her one free hand.

"Of course, now that I've given you ices, I'll have to give one to your brother. And if I give one to him, then why should I be Cinderella? I might as well have one, too."

She sat there in the unfamiliar, crowded kitchen, listening to the noise of two dishwashers and the sloshing, whirring sounds of an overworked washing machine. The children chattered contentedly, their sweet little voices rising and falling as they slurped their ices. For no reason at all, she felt her heart suddenly fill with unreasonable hope. How strange, she marveled, licking her ice pop, feeling more alive than she had in years, perhaps ever.

She thought of the young man and woman in their wedding photo, the kind, devout couple who had given birth to these children. Such a tragedy! And yet, the vibrancy of these young lives were even now carving channels into the raging sea of chaos and despair that had engulfed them. Their needs were set and must be met, their very neediness creating order.

She touched Cheeky's little face, pushing the hair out of his eyes. She pushed in Icy's chair so that her ice pop would drip over the kitchen table rather than her nightgown. Every tiny act made her feel competent and useful. Suddenly, and quite unexpectedly, the little girl raised her arms to be held. Leah reached down to her, lifting the child into her lap. Chasya leaned back blissfully, sinking into the unfamiliar softness of the stranger's womanly body, so different from her sister Shaindele's impatient, angular, young limbs, sighing softly with pleasure.

Leah rested her chin gently on the child's head, holding her close, flooded by an unexpected and overwhelming feeling of love. She wanted so much for only good things to happen to this family, for them to know no more sorrow. *May God bless all of you,* she prayed silently, hoping Shaindele wouldn't rush home.

9

The moment Yaakov agreed to go out on shidduch dates, his phone rang nonstop, until finally he begged them to call his mother-in-law instead.

"How will I learn? How will I finish the work for my accounting classes if every two seconds the phone rings?" he begged Fruma Esther.

She agreed happily, delighted to take all the information and to share it with him at a time of his choosing. What she didn't tell him was the number of suggestions she took it upon herself to reject on his behalf without discussing it with him at all.

"Too old," she would complain about the forty-one-year-old widow with three children. "Not educated enough," she would scold concerning the thirty-nine-year-old Bais Yaakov graduate working in a clothing store on Fourteenth Avenue. "Not enough *yichus*!" she'd shout when a thirty-five-year-old childless divorcée with her own graphic arts studio was suggested. "Her parents moved to Boro Park only five years ago. She's from Cleveland. Cleveland!"

Only when the entire shadchan community rose up as one against her, refusing to give her even one more name, did she finally relent and agree to hand over some names to Yaakov. "We are doing our best, Yaakov." She sighed. "But you shouldn't expect another Zissele."

Candidate number one was a widow with one child. "She is only thirty-one, very frum, with *yichus,* a very well-to-do family who own an import-export company. The matchmaker says she is a wonderful woman who has had a difficult time but is now ready to make a new start. The only problem is she lives in Monsey."

Honestly, he didn't hear a single thing that interested him about this woman. Rich, important family, frum . . . but was she spiritual? Did she love children? Did she love God? On top of that, Monsey—the haredi enclave near Spring Valley—was an hour and a half drive by car from Boro Park if you were lucky! He shared all these misgivings with his mother-in-law.

She straightened her back, offended. "We are all trying so hard to help you, Yaakov. But you have to help yourself. Take a chance. Nothing is perfect. You have to try."

Chastened, he agreed to borrow a car from his *chavrusa,* Meir, and asked that the shadchan arrange a meeting for Saturday night so he wouldn't have to take off time from kollel or miss his evening classes.

That Saturday night after making havdalah, Yaakov took a shower, drying himself vigorously and putting on deodorant he thought had an especially clean smell; never in his life had he owned a bottle of men's cologne. He examined his face in the mirror, testing out a pleasant smile. *It doesn't look sincere,* he scolded himself, giving up. She would see what was there, the truth: an older man, already the father of many children, no longer a full-time scholar, on his way to becoming a regular *baal bayis.* Nobody special. Despite the vigorous assurances of the schadchan conveyed by Fruma Esther that the woman and her family were thrilled, he couldn't fathom why she'd agreed to meet him at all. He shrugged at the mysteries of matchmaking, running a comb carefully through his hair and beard. Resigned that it was the best he could do, he put on his dark Shabbos suit and Borsalino. Meir's car was in the repair shop, so he had no choice but to rent a car for the evening.

He took Palisades International Parkway north. While he could no longer afford a car, he had been driving since he was sixteen. It was a pleasure to be behind the wheel again, he thought, feeling relaxed and hopeful as he sped along, wondering what God had in store for him.

When he pulled up to the address, he felt a moment of unease. It was a sprawling ranch house with a big backyard and a professionally land-scaped front garden that even in the middle of the winter was free of fallen leaves. He had no experience with such wealth.

To his surprise, a man only a little older than himself opened the door. "I'm her brother," he explained, smiling and welcoming him in. Yaakov, who had expected to pick up the woman and drive to the nearby Hilton Woodcliff Lake, a venue he had found on the religious internet dating site Soon By You (it was either that or a billiard hall or Sport-O-Rama ice-skating—Monsey was pretty far from Manhattan), where they would order drinks in the lobby and get to know one another. Instead, he was startled to find himself escorted to the middle of a living room crowded with relatives.

"Let me take your hat, your coat," the brother offered. Yaakov thanked him, looking around the room in confusion as he tried to figure out who exactly was on offer. "This is my sister," the brother finally said, putting an end to the confusion as he pushed a young woman forward. "Because of the terrible nightmare of her recent divorce—"

"I was told you were a widow," he said, glancing shyly at the woman, who said nothing.

The brother took a step in front of her, nodding as he made a dismissive gesture with his hand. "That, too. Anyhow, her family is naturally concerned. Please, I'll introduce you."

Before he got a chance to exchange two words with the woman, he found himself dragged off into the living room to meet and be scrutinized by her mother and father, two brothers, a sister and sister-in-law, and various other vaguely related people, all of whom inspected him shamelessly, doing everything short of rubbing his lapel between their fingers to judge the worth of the cloth. "I know, I know, it's a bit much," whispered the older brother sheepishly. "But we are a very tight-knit family."

Yaakov swallowed hard. "Of course, I . . . understand," he stammered until he was red, all the while stealing surreptitious glances at the candidate herself.

She had a young face, but one unmistakably etched by years of sorrow, he thought. Her pretty brown eyes were half-lidded and wary, darting nervously. Every few moments, she tugged viciously at various parts of her outfit, including a long, dark wig that she pulled down by the bangs as if trying to cover her face.

"Why don't the two of you go into the kitchen?" suggested the brother, who was obviously running the show and had apparently decided that whatever the others might think, including his widowed/divorced sister, Yaakov was just what *he* was looking for. "Offer him some coffee," he ordered her curtly before disappearing on the other side of the kitchen door.

Yaakov sat down behind the counter of the expensively furnished room. "It's a beautiful kitchen, a very nice house," he offered.

"It's my brother's," she said matter-of-factly. "I live over the garage with my son. My husband—my *second* husband, may God curse him to everlasting hell—walked out, left me with nothing. Until I finally got my divorce, my get, well, the whole family had to cough up the money to pay off that ganef."

He sat there wordlessly, shocked. "They told me you were a widow."

"That, too. I lost my first husband, my beloved Shlomi, when I was thirty. He was born with some kind of heart defect that was never diagnosed. One morning, he just didn't wake up. It was horrible."

He nodded sympathetically.

"He and I never had children. He couldn't, something else the shadchan never mentioned," she added bitterly, then shrugged. "But I guess that was for the best seeing how he wasn't around for long. After he died, my family didn't want me to waste any more time. I wasn't getting any younger. So they pushed and pushed for me to remarry. I felt really pressured, which is how I wound up saying yes to the ganef, may he find Gehenna and move in there."

He felt his face grow hot as he listened to her, but decided to be sympathetic. "You say the family had to pay him off before he would grant your get? That's not right. That was never the intention of the halacha."

She stared at him hostilely. "The rabbis were the worst." She sniffed. "They were the ones who told us to pay him off. I'm sure he greased their palms, too, let me tell you. Criminals. Would you like sugar, a piece of cake?"

He tried to focus. "Yes, a teaspoon. Thank you."

She put the cup in front of him together with a bowl of sugar and a teaspoon, not bothering to measure it out for him. "Milk?"

"Do you have parve? I'm still fleishig."

She opened the refrigerator and took out a nondairy creamer and handed it to him. He hesitated.

"Oh, too frum to take something from a woman's hand?" she snarled contemptuously. "My ex was also very, very, very frum. And from such an important rabbinical family. Or so he said. Related to the Chofetz Chaim himself, but who knows? People say whatever they want. Who's going to check it? My family, on the other hand, everyone knows are direct descendants of Akiva Eiger himself. My ex, the ganef—may the ten plagues of Egypt reach him and a few more besides—was so frum he wouldn't drink water on Passover, in case someone dropped crumbs into the reservoir. He was so frum he made me shave my head before I covered it with a wig. He was so frum he once threw out all the matzo because he found a drop of moisture on the kitchen cabinet door. But that didn't stop him from running off with his shiksa secretary when I was eight months pregnant or extorting my family before agreeing to a divorce." She slammed the creamer down on the counter.

"Thank you," Yaakov said fearfully, pouring some into the now cold coffee. He took a few half-hearted sips, mostly to delay the necessity of saying something. "I can hear the suffering in your voice, and it fills me with sorrow," he said finally, with sincerity. "Too many stringencies and not enough human decency, that is sometimes the problem in our world."

"Oh, so you think our world has problems?" There was no mistake. She *was* hostile.

He was surprised. "Don't you?"

"That's what the *frei* are always saying," she murmured, suddenly not anti-rabbi at all but the *frum-ist* of the frum. He felt dizzy trying to keep up with her.

"If something is true, it is true no matter who says it," he answered, finally annoyed, wondering how he could get his captive hat and coat back and escape.

"What happened to your first wife?" she demanded.

"She died."

"They told me, but you know, I've been on so many shidduch dates, I can't keep the stories straight half the time. What was wrong with her?"

His face went white. "I don't like to talk about it," he murmured. "Listen, it was nice to meet you, but this isn't going to work out."

"What? You sit here for two minutes and already you know?"

He stood up. "Yes, already I know." Opening the kitchen door, he entered the lion's den, where he painfully and uneasily extricated himself and his belongings from a quicksand of insistent and chagrined relatives. Once outside, he felt like *benching gomel*, the prayer said after safely navigating a stormy sea.

When the shadchan called Fruma Esther the next day, she was fuming. "Rude, they said. Ran away, they said. Insulting, they said. What did he tell you?"

"He said her next husband would be serving the jail time for the crimes of her last husband." The shadchan was silent. Apparently, she had heard this before. "Well, let's try again, shall we?"

"Do we have a choice?" Fruma Esther replied.

The next time, Yaakov was far less trusting, insisting on interrogating the matchmaker Suri Kimmeldorfer himself before agreeing. Really, he could find nothing wrong with candidate number two. She was a widow his own age with no extra husband hidden in her résumé, three older children, and an interior design company. Her late husband had died in the crash of a small, private plane on his way to a cousin's wedding in Toronto. She lived in Flatbush.

When he arrived, she herself opened the door, with no lurking relatives anywhere to be found.

"My son is upstairs, so there is no problem with *yichud*," she told him, referring to the religious prohibition of a man and woman being alone together in a private space.

She was a small woman, a bit on the heavy side, who looked closer to fifty than forty. But she had a warm smile, he thought. After all, he wasn't looking for a beauty queen. Just a kind, *heimish* woman who would share his values and love his children.

A beautiful spread of dips and vegetables and quiches was already laid out on the table.

"I thought I would take you out. We could go to Café Venezia on Coney Island Avenue," he suggested.

"What's their *hechsher*?" she inquired.

"Uh, I was told it's strictly kosher."

"But who supervises?" she insisted.

"I think they said Rav Himmelstein."

She shrugged. "I hope you don't mind my asking. My late husband, may his memory be blessed, was a saint. He was very, very particular on what he ate outside the house, and so we hardly ever did. Besides, it's so expensive. I'm very thrifty."

He looked around at the expensive, custom-made gold coffee table, the pristine white sofa and matching chairs, his eyes widening.

"It's a Sete Linen Sofa. I got it on sale. Oh, that's Italian. Very in right now."

"That color." He smiled. "White. How do you keep it so clean?"

"Oh, do you have small children?"

He nodded, perplexed. "Surely the matchmaker mentioned—"

"Yes, certainly, but I guess I blocked that out. I'll tell you very frankly, small children and beautiful furniture don't mix," she said, a small crease forming between her brows.

He nodded in total agreement.

"But my furniture is my life. It's my work. I could never live in a house that wasn't beautiful. Most women feel that way. Your late wife . . . ?"

"Zissele and I were a kollel couple—salt and bread, as they say. We didn't have any money for extras. And with five children—"

"Five," she repeated, the crease deepening as her brows shot up in alarm. "And the youngest is . . . ?"

"Fifteen months."

She was silent for a moment. He could almost see the little wheels turning in her head as she processed this. "It's not a problem," she finally said. "I am a very spiritual person, and I can learn to adapt. Children can also learn to adapt. My own children know not to sit in the living room on the furniture."

"So where do they sit?"

"Why should they sit? There are things to be done, places to go. My children are out of the house in after-school activities or away at yeshiva."

"Now, but when they were babies?"

"I was a very efficient mother when I had small children. They always knew their place. I toilet trained them when they were eight months old, and I had special aprons sewn for them with long sleeves and ridges across the chest that caught the food splatters, so not a drop—not even soup—ever touched a tablecloth. Believe me, it's for their own benefit to grow up that way, everything so clean and orderly. I think of my home as a Bais Hamigdash where everything is consecrated and everything I and the children do is like a ritual to please God. This is why I must have the walls painted every year, so that not even a spot of dirt spoils the purity. Would you like to sit down and eat something?"

Honestly, he had long ago lost his appetite, thinking of what this woman would do when she moved into the little apartment he had shared with Zissele; how his children would be trained and disciplined like little robots; his walls painted, his old furniture dumped. From there, it would only be a matter of time before he himself got the full treatment. He wondered what part of the life he loved would pass her rigid inspection, remaining untouched, unimproved, and undecorated? No part, he realized. It would be a total renovation.

"Tell me, did your late husband, may his memory be blessed, approve of"—he looked around meaningfully—"this?"

Her small eyes narrowed. "My saintly husband—may he rest in peace—was so pious, so pure, he took no interest at all in material things," she said haughtily. "Also, when he was alive, we never had the money. But after he died, the insurance money from the airline left me very comfortable. So I started living the way I always dreamed and started my business on the side. You wouldn't believe how many saintly rabbis' wives I have for clients and how much money they spend on furnishings."

"I wasn't criticizing, *chas ve shalom.* Everyone is entitled to their dreams." He nodded, dreaming of getting up and telling her the truth: that sometimes one person's dream is another person's nightmare. She was his. But mindful of the shadchan's complaints about his abrupt departure from the last date, he reluctantly took a plate and availed himself of the generous spread. He found it spicy and strange, food as fancy and unfamiliar to him as the furniture. When he judged a decent interval had elapsed, he bid her good night.

"You are a very fine man, Yaakov, and have come highly recommended to me," she said. To his horror, she sidled closer, staring into his eyes long and hard with brazen intimacy. "I look forward to our next meeting," she called after him as he adjusted his Borsalino and hurried out the door.

All night, he suffered from heartburn. When the shadchan called the next day, he merely said, "It's not *shayich*. Not her, not her furniture, not her *derech* of educating children." No, there wasn't going to be a second date, he said firmly as the matchmaker did her best to pressure him into keeping an open mind.

"If you were a woman," the matchmaker told him, "by now I would be refusing to help you. I have an instinct for who is serious and who isn't. I don't have time to waste."

"My dear lady, I ask *mechila* if you think I've wasted your time. Maybe I haven't been clear enough. So let me be clear now: I want a *heimish* person. I don't care about looks. I don't care about money or *yichus*. I want a good person with a good heart who loves children and is not filled with *gashmiyus*. A person who will be my partner in *ruchniyus*, who will help me raise my orphaned children with good *middot*. Someone who will help me with *parnosa* until I finish my course and begin working full-time as a CPA. A woman whose *neshama* is not bitter or broken or old. A woman who loves life and is ready to open her heart to me."

"Your mother-in-law, may she live and be well, *dafka* gave me a very different impression." She sniffed. "Nu, so I'll try again."

She tried and tried and tried. And when Suri Kimmeldorfer finally gave up, an army of other eager shadchanim willingly moved in to take her place. They also tried and tried: widows with and without children. Women of all shapes and sizes, some with piously scrubbed faces who forced him to eat their homemade cakes while discussing to which yeshiva they would send the children they would have together. Women who wore red lipstick and mascara who walked a little too close beside him on the way to restaurants and hotel lobbies. Divorcées with hard-luck stories who inexplicably couldn't wait to plunge right back in again. Women who had hidden agendas, expecting to be supported, to have their own children lavished with fatherly care while viewing Yaakov's children as a burden, an unwelcome part of the deal. Worst of all, not a single one tugged at his heart. They were strangers, and he was only too happy to keep it that way.

That was, until he met Rachel.

10

"I have someone very special in mind for you," the shadchan told Yaakov. Which shadchan it was exactly, he didn't remember. By now they had all blurred into one person with a nagging voice who interrupted his studies and his peace of mind at regular intervals.

He wanted to say, "That's what you always say." But he already had a reputation for being difficult, he knew. If he hadn't been a Torah scholar from an esteemed family, a member in good standing of a community in which marriageable men in their forties were as rare as unicorns, all the matchmakers would have long ago given up. So instead, he took a deep breath and said mildly, "Can you tell me something about her?"

"She's not a widow or a divorcée. She's young, twenty-nine, a rabbi's daughter, who has never been married."

A single girl. A virgin. It was too good to be true. "What does she want with me?"

"She doesn't, believe me. But I convinced her to give it a try. What does it hurt, I told her. You think thirty-two-year-old single yeshiva boys from good families are out there just waiting around for you to turn thirty? So you need to compromise, to be a little flexible."

"She agreed?"

"I showed her your picture, Yaakov. She agreed."

"Well, if she's seen my picture, I want to see hers."

"Not a problem. I have a picture and a résumé. I'm sending it to you by email right now."

It appeared like magic in his in-box moments later. He enlarged it, studying it in detail. Her hair was dark, like Zissele's, straight and very long. She wore it simply with just a headband, not braided or in a pony-tail like a teenager or in a bun like an old lady. She had big, blue eyes that stared at the camera wide-eyed, innocent, and tender, serious young lips that didn't smile. She looked young and intelligent. She looked young and pretty. She looked young. He looked in the mirror. *And I look old.* He plucked at the random silver in his dark gold beard.

Her voice on the phone was also young, he thought, filled with friendliness as they made arrangements to meet. All week, he felt a growing sense of excitement as Saturday night approached. As much as he tried not to get his hopes up, he couldn't help it.

Even Shaindele noticed. As much as she resented the idea of another woman taking her mother's place, she felt a solidarity with her father's hopes and did not want him to endure any more disappointments. "Maybe you should wear the blue tie," she suggested. "The one Mameh bought you for Rosh Hashana."

"You think so, Shaindele?" he answered, ready to take any advice of-fered.

She nodded, quickly going through the closet and finding it. "I'll put it on the bed. And this week, Tateh, I have exams on Tuesday afternoon, so we need a babysitter for the children."

"We want Leah," Chasya blurted out.

"La . . . ya," the baby repeated with a smile.

Shaindele frowned.

"Who is this?" Yaakov asked, busy putting on his tie.

"No one. Just a convert living with the Blausteins. She's come over a few times to help out."

"A convert?"

"Or one of those *baalos teshuva* from Rabbi Weintraub's program. She's not *shayich.*"

"How much does she charge an hour?"

Shaindele hesitated. "She doesn't charge."

"She babysits for nothing?" He stopped fiddling with his tie and looked up, surprised. How long had this been going on in his home without him knowing a single thing about it?

"She says it's a *chesed*. To help out."

He had vaguely noticed of late that the house had been in better order, his closet and the children's filled with clean clothes. "How often does she come?"

Too often, Shaindele thought irritably, but she said, "Whenever I can't be home and Bubbee can't make it."

"That is very nice of her! We should buy her a present," Yaakov told his daughter, who was silent.

"I don't want her to come anymore," Shaindele burst out.

"But why?"

Her young siblings had grown close to her and were now asking for her all the time. It was "Leah did this" and "Leah said that." Constantly. "Because who knows what she's teaching them, if she's bringing in food without the proper *hechsher*? I said, she's not *shayich* "

"I think a person who does such a *chesed* and doesn't ask to be paid is very *shayich*," Yaakov scolded her gently. "We should all have her *zchus* in mitzvoth. As it is written: *Where a true penitent stands, even the greatest tzaddikim cannot.*"

"Because of the smell," she murmured. It was an old joke that everyone had heard.

Yaakov's face grew serious. "I don't ever want to hear you say something like that again, Shaindele. It's wrong, and it's disgusting."

"Tateh, I didn't make it up!"

"Tell me, Shaindele, was our father Isaac greater than Moshe?"

"Of course not, Tateh. Moshe was the greatest prophet of all, and closer to God than any human being."

"And yet Moshe grew up in the idolatrous house of Pharaoh and only learned to love God and keep His commandments when he was old, while Isaac grew up in the holy house of Abraham. Never, ever shame a *baal teshuva* or a convert. This is a direct commandment from the Torah: *You shall not abuse a stranger and you shall not oppress him, for you were strangers in the land of Egypt.* This is a very serious prohibition, Shain-dele."

She hung her head, ashamed, unaccustomed to such harsh rebukes from her father. "I'm sorry, Tateh."

He relented, caressing her young, flushed cheek. And as he did so, he couldn't help but think of the young woman he was about to meet and the night to come. His voice softened. "Think of something nice we can do for this person to thank her, all right, Shaindele?"

"Yes, Tateh. Now go. And it should be in a good hour."

A good hour. It's what you said about weddings, he thought, smiling at his daughter, who smiled back.

He felt a little frightened as he approached the brownstone in Flatbush that night, something that he had not felt before in meetings of this nature. Before he had felt anticipation, nervousness perhaps, but not fright. *I am terrified,* he thought. *Of being turned down. Of being seen for who I am, a man who just turned forty, whose best years are behind him; a Torah scholar who has abandoned his studies to become a CPA; a failed husband who could not prevent the tragic death of his beloved young wife.* Only a strong sense of discipline and the thought of the phone call from the furi-ous shadchan stopped him from turning around and fleeing.

He rang the bell. A woman answered. His face fell. She was not young, and her dark hair was tied back with a kerchief. Wrinkles were beginning around her eyes. *I should have known,* Yaakov thought, swal-lowing his disappointment. *Another shadchan story. They said two words, and three of them were lies.*

"You must be Yaakov. I'm Rachel's mother. Welcome. Please come in-side. She'll be down in a moment."

Rachel's mother! He stepped over the threshold, almost stumbling in relief.

"Please meet my husband," she said graciously, introducing him.

The father, too, looks young, not much older than I am, he thought, even though he knew that was impossible. He was only eleven years older than Rachel. Still, he, too, had children who were not far from marriageable age. The father shook his hand and offered him a chair around the dining room table, where he himself had been sitting, an open Talmud before him.

Yaakov looked into the book. "You're learning *Baba Basra*." He nodded.

"Yes," Rachel's father said. "And it's very *shayich*. I'm just now talking to my neighbor about building a fence between our properties."

"With round stones or rough stones?" Yaakov smiled, referring to the dispute in the Talmud over how to equally divide the contribution of land between neighbors for the purpose of building such a fence.

"Well, as a matter of fact, it's interesting you mention, as the Talmud says—"

Just then there were footsteps.

"Hello," Rachel said.

She was even more beautiful than her photograph. And so young!

He felt tongue-tied next to this tall, slim, pretty girl.

"I was just discussing *Baba Basra* with your father," he said.

Her brow creased in confusion.

"I guess we should go," he said, looking away, feeling like an idiot.

"I'll get my coat," Rachel answered, disappearing.

A light rain was falling. The contrast between the warmth of the house and the damp cold of the still wintry streets was startling, but he hardly noticed. He was glad he had rented a car, even though she lived not far away. He wanted to create an intimate space in which to talk to her as soon as possible.

"I thought we could go into Manhattan. Is there someplace special you'd like to try?"

Rachel smiled. "It's very nice of you to ask me. I've been on so many shidduch dates I've probably seen everything. But if you haven't been, then the Marriot Marquis on Broadway has this revolving lounge. The view of the city keeps changing. It's fun. But if you don't want to travel so far, we could go to Court Street in Brooklyn to the Barnes & Noble. They have a nice place to get coffee."

"No, let's go to Broadway," he said magnanimously, pulling out into traffic. "I wanted to thank you, Rachel," he said, keeping his eyes straight ahead.

"For what?"

"For agreeing to go out with me. A widower with five children."

She was silent for so long that he took his eyes off the road and gave her a worried glance.

"I'm sorry." She shook her head. "This isn't easy for me."

"What?"

"Being twenty-nine and unmarried."

"Oh."

"You have no idea how horrible it can be for a woman. Every time I go to a simcha, I feel this hail of sharp little stones thrown in my direction, every cliché in the book. If I had a dollar for every time someone has said to me, 'God willing by you,' 'You just have to make it work,' 'Send another picture,' 'Maybe you really don't want to get married,' 'Don't be so smart; you'll scare him off,' 'No one can steal your *bashert*,' 'Your time will come,' 'He'll come when you least expect it,' 'You have to put yourself out there . . .'" She grew hoarse and finally silent.

He glanced at her in the dark. Were those tears glistening on her cheeks?

"We—I mean, we men—don't realize."

"No. I think it must be easier for men."

No, he thought but didn't say. *It isn't.* But why start a misery competition? Instead, he asked with all the genuine kindness and sympathy he felt toward her, "What's a lovely girl like you doing in a situation like this?"

She shrugged. "I've asked myself that question so many times. Like everybody else, I spent a year in Israel in seminary and started dating when I got back. I was nineteen. Before they would even agree to take me on and introduce me to the best prospects, the shadchanim demanded my parents promise $30,000 up front and seven years' support so the boys could continue learning. How could they afford it? I'm not an only child, and my father is a *maggid shiur,* not a businessman. For most of his life, my father was also learning full-time. Where was all this money supposed to come from? So we tried through friends and neighbors and relatives. But the boys I wanted, the learner-earner types, the ones that were pious but also had a head on their shoulders; someone ambitious to secure a future for his family so he didn't wind up like my father who can't meet the demands of the shadchanim, those kinds of boys are few and far between.

"If I'd only wanted a learner, I could have found. If I'd only wanted an earner, I could have found. I wanted both. So the years passed. I was working, teaching. And each year, my offers were fewer and fewer, and the number of younger girls coming of age more and more. The best boys went to the eighteen-year-old girls with rich fathers. The boys that were left behind also had something keeping them from finding their *bashert,* some problem with the reputation of their family or bad reports from the yeshiva about the boy himself. Physical handicaps. Mental problems. The older I got, the worse the selection."

"And so now you are here with me, a forty-year-old widower with five children."

She nodded. "'Think out of the box,' they are telling me now."

A stone fell on his heart when he thought of this date from Rachel's point of view. He was sad for her, that she had come to this.

"I understand," he said softly. "And really, I was surprised that a girl like you agreed to meet me. But excited, too. When I saw your picture, Rachel, I felt happy. And I haven't felt that way in a very long time."

"What about me made you feel that way?"

"I've also been on the shidduch treadmill. Maybe not as long as you, but I'm sure we could trade horror stories."

She laughed, twisting in her seat to face him.

"I only ever wanted to be with one woman, my wife, Zissele, may she be remembered with blessing."

"Do I remind you of her?"

"No, not really. She was tiny and plump with short hair. But when I saw your picture, it reminded me of how I felt when I first met her. That same excitement and joy."

"Really?"

"Really."

They parked in a paid lot and walked the short distance to the hotel. The wet streets glistened in the halo of streetlamps. He longed to usher her safely through the crowds by holding her hand, or giving her his arm, all things strictly forbidden, as was any physical contact between men and women who were not intimate family members. Most religious men would not even agree to a polite handshake with a woman at a business meeting.

They followed the hostess to their table in the bustling lounge. For a few moments, they were silent, taking in the bright lights of the New York skyline as the whole room slowly swiveled on its axis. It was wondrous. When their modest order of nonalcoholic drinks was put in front of them, they sipped slowly, shyly.

"Tell me about yourself, Rachel. What are your hopes, your dreams? What do you want out of life?"

Eagerly, she answered him.

There was nothing special about her answers, Yaakov thought, nothing he could not have thought of himself as the goals of a religious girl from their community. A Jewish home filled with hospitality. Children raised to be good, God-fearing Jews. Perhaps a chance to go back to school to learn graphic arts. But as he watched her speak, her young face so animated and vital, he felt entranced.

"And what do you want, Yaakov?"

"All those things. But most importantly, a partner to share my life, to help me on my journey. Someone to love and help my children on theirs."

She listened, her face serious and intent.

"When did your wife die?"

"Thirteen months ago." *Five days, six hours, seventy minutes.*

"What happened?"

As usual, he froze at the question. "I really don't like to talk about it. It was shocking and sudden. The doctors did all they could to save her, but it was no use." He hoped she wouldn't probe. This kind of investigation had put an early end to more than one shidduch date.

Thankfully, she changed the subject.

"How old are your children?"

He answered her eagerly, talking briefly about each one, trying to help her picture how special and wonderful they were. "The baby is already climbing out of his crib."

She smiled. "And how are you managing day to day?"

"My mother-in-law and oldest daughter are a tremendous help. And we benefit from the *chesed* of our friends and neighbors. It was very hard at first; I felt lost. But now I am more hopeful." He looked into her eyes. She blushed and looked down.

For a moment, he had the mad thought of reaching across the table and taking her soft, gentle hand in his. He put his hands firmly into his pockets.

"How would you feel about more children?" she asked him.

"It would be a blessing!" he answered without hesitation. "I would want you to have everything you want in life, Rachel. Everything that is in my power to give you."

She said nothing, glancing at him, then looking out at the dark night and the twirling lights of the big city, so rich and varied and confusing.

The next day, he waited for the call from the shadchan. When it came, he dived for his phone.

"What did she say?"

"Hello to you, too, Yaakov. What did *she* say? What do *you* say? Do you want to take her out again?"

"Of course!"

"You say that like it's something I shouldn't even have to ask. But my dear Mr. Lehman, if you remember, in the past you sang a different tune."

He was beginning to remember who this shadchan was. It was Suri Kimmeldorfer.

"What does the past matter now?" he said impatiently.

"So, you are willing?"

"Yes. But is she?"

"I had a talk with the young lady. She said definitely yes. She will go out with you again."

A burst of joy lit up his heart.

All week, he floated on air, an untied helium balloon, hardly hearing a word Meir uttered, unable to concentrate on the delicate nuances between various Talmudic commentators. During his evening classes, he found the tables and calculations confusing and strangely detached from context, often wondering what he was doing and why. He found himself filled with longing to escape, to feel young and alive again. To be with Rachel.

"God help me to find my *bashert* again," he prayed, feeling overwhelmed with a strange gratitude, as if he and God were colluding and help had already arrived.

They went out for three weeks, finally dropping the shadchan and calling each other directly, freely, to make plans and take up conversations where they'd left off. They went unusual places together: the Metropolitan Museum of Art, the Frick, the Cloisters. The depth and breadth of her knowledge and curiosity enthralled him. "I took an art class in Israel, at the Israel Museum. I wish I could be a painter."

Shyly, she showed him some pictures she had drawn and colored with pastels—garden scenes and the hands of an old woman holding a siddur. He found them enchanting. She had so much talent!

"You should continue, Rachel. It's a gift."

She shook her head. "It takes free time. It takes money for supplies."

The words hung between them like rancid smoke from a burned pot. If she became his wife, she would have neither, they knew. All her days would be spent in housework, as well as in some tedious teaching job, when she wasn't caring for another woman's children and then, God willing, her own. She would always work harder than other women her age. She would always have less money than they did.

Finally, the time came for a decision. "I need to meet your children," she told him.

Fruma Esther was recruited to help tidy the apartment and dress the children. Rachel walked through the door with Yaakov at her side. Shaindele stood by tensely, holding Mordechai Shalom in her arms as he squirmed to be set free. Chasya sat on a little two-wheeler, riding through the rooms, while the two older boys, Elchanon Yehoshua and Dovid Yitzchak, who had made the trip all the way from their yeshiva in Baltimore, stood at awkward attention.

It went very well. Everyone said so. The children were friendly and courteous. Even the little ones smiled and shook hands.

But Yaakov, who stood behind Rachel, suddenly saw his home through her eyes: the distempered walls, the shabby, neglected furniture and carpets, the crowded spaces. Most of all, he saw his children through her eyes, five other partners in their marriage with demands on his love, his time, his attention, and his income; offspring of a mother who was no longer there to care for them and so needed to be cared for by a stranger, someone who must be willing to dedicate her life to them, even though they would never feel about her the way they felt about their mother. To be his partner, she would have to risk getting lost in the crowd. And there was absolutely nothing he could do about that.

They went out only once more. He already knew what her decision would be. There were no surprises. Honestly, he was happy for her that she had made the choice to find a better and easier life for herself than the one he could offer her. She was still so young, he thought, wishing her every blessing. When he dropped her off at her house, she turned to look at him. He drank her in for the last time, like a rare wine.

"I've enjoyed getting to know you, Yaakov. If things were different . . . maybe if I were older . . . I'm just not ready to give up yet on finding a *bashert* that is still single so we can start our family together."

"Rachel . . . I think . . ."

She looked at him intently, waiting for what he was about to say.

"I think you made the right decision."

She exhaled. "You are a wonderful man. May God bless you and your family and give you the partner you need and deserve. Goodbye, Yaakov."

"Goodbye, Rachel. May God give you what you pray for." He got out of the car, opening the door for her.

"Please, don't walk me to my door. My parents will be waiting; I don't want them to think . . ."

He nodded with understanding, getting back inside. Then he sat in the darkness without moving, watching as she rounded the corner and disappeared.

11

After three months in Boro Park, Leah decided she needed an apartment of her own. Luckily, money wasn't going to be a problem. Her work for Rabbi Weintraub had been so successful that she had been besieged by local businesses and a number of other institutions to do the same for them. As a result, she had actually been to a lawyer and tax consultant and set up her own independent marketing firm. The biggest advantage was having flexible hours she chose herself, which meant even more time available for good works, like helping out the Lehmans. The children were always so happy to see her, and even Shaindele's sour expression had been modified, if not sweetened. The bottom line was she no longer had the door slammed in her face.

She found a one-bedroom with hardwood floors on Fiftieth Street for $1,500 a month, less than half what she'd been paying on the Upper West Side of Manhattan. She thanked Rav Aryeh and Rebbitzen Basha profusely, buying them a beautiful silver cup for ritual handwashing as a parting gift. Rebbitzen Basha kissed her warmly. "Now, maideleh, it's time to find a husband."

"I wouldn't know how to begin."

"I'll help you."

Rebbitzen Basha made some calls, but finally—a little shamefacedly, Leah thought—admitted defeat. "It's better if you call them yourself. Once they get to know you, as we have, I'm sure they'll be able to find a person on your level."

She hesitated. "They hear thirty-four plus and it's already a story. But then they hear *baalas teshuva,* and they won't cooperate no matter what I tell them." She sighed.

"Leah-le, just, when you talk to them, be flexible. Show that you are open, cooperative. That you'd be willing to relocate. That you'll go out with other *baale teshuva* and even converts. That you love children—which I know is the truth if you could love our Shabbos meals with all the screaming grandchildren! And Leah-le, I know you have a difficult relationship with your mother, but never tell them that, or that she doesn't support your decision to become frum."

"But it's unfortunately true."

"So what? It's none of their business, and what does it have to do with you? You are you, and she is she."

Leah nodded, confused, wondering why it was necessary to omit these things that were part of who she was. What was there to be ashamed of?

"And Leah-le, when they ask you how long you've been frum, count from the time you first started thinking about it, not from when you moved here."

"Why?"

"Because people worry that *baale teshuva* will go back to their secular lives when they realize that our world has prob—well, it is wonderful, but it's not perfect. The longer you are here, the more you will see."

"Nothing's perfect," she answered cheerfully, not really understanding.

Rebbitzen Basha gave her a list of names and phone numbers, and Leah started setting up appointments with the matchmakers.

The first one was on the fifth floor of an old building with no elevator. She was still catching her breath when she found the right door. Because the button for the doorbell was hanging by a loose wire, she had no choice but to bang on the door.

"It's open," she heard faintly.

Inside, she found a heavyset Chassid with a long gray beard, whose black satin waistcoat hung sloppily unbuttoned over a white shirt that looked not only as if it had been slept in but had not been changed for at least a week. He seemed glued to the chair.

He didn't ask her to sit down. He simply stared at her intently, his beady little eyes roaming over her from head to toe until finally making a crash landing on her hands.

He turned his face away. "There is a lid for every pot, but you are a difficult fit. I'm sorry. I have no one for you."

She left without saying a single word, deeply humiliated, wondering what it was she had done wrong. She had worn only minimal makeup— afraid of appearing too modern—a long, mid-calf skirt, and a high-collared blouse that covered her elbows, both purchased on Fourteenth Avenue in a clothing store that catered to Chassidic women. Her thick, curly hair was braided and held back by two hair clips. It couldn't have been what she'd said, she thought, or even her California twang, because she hadn't opened her mouth. Yet the rejection had been immediate and absolute.

She trembled, feeling as if she'd been mugged.

She had always known singles her age in Boro Park were rare, much rarer than in other modern Orthodox enclaves, or even in Israel, where young religious Jews were following the trend to postpone marriage and childbearing to their midthirties. Here, the boys married at twenty-two, twenty-five at the most, and the girls even younger. There was even a lively debate going on about the year-long programs in Israel for graduating high school girls. Why did they need to be so far from home? the rabbis complained. Unsupervised. Besides, by the time they got back to Boro Park, they'd have wasted a year of shidduchim, and everyone knew a girl of nineteen or twenty was practically over the hill. Not all agreed with this viewpoint, and the girls were still signing up for the year programs. But the idea that some in the community considered a twenty-year-old less desirable because of age chilled her heart.

But most disappointing was that this person, the shadchan, who dressed the part of a religious Jew, nevertheless exhibited none of the qualities she had so come to value. A decent person, let alone a religious person, could never have treated a vulnerable young woman like herself that way. The whole thing smacked of phoniness. And yet, she had been advised that he was one of the best matchmakers for the newly observant.

She tried not to be judgmental, but obviously someone had made a serious mistake in recommending him to kind Rebbitzen Basha.

She had more luck contacting a shadchan over the phone. Now, finally, she had found a woman who promised to help her. She tried to think what she could do differently to avoid being thrown out again but couldn't. Then she thought, *Maybe my stockings weren't the right color or weren't thick enough, modest enough.* So she went out and bought 40 denier black tights.

Faigie Klein turned out to be a tall woman with a sharp, angular face whose lopsided smile—almost that of a stroke victim—didn't reach her eyes.

"Very nice to meet you," she said in a way that Leah took to mean the very opposite. "If you wouldn't mind, can I ask how you got my number?"

"I was given your name by Rebbitzen Basha."

"Ahmm." She nodded approvingly. "A real *tzadakis*. She's helped many of the girls from Rabbi Weintraub's program, although not as many as I have. I'll be happy to help you, too, but I can't do nothing if a person doesn't cooperate. It's up to you." She shrugged as if already facing great obstacles.

"Yes, of course. I'll cooperate."

"So take off your coat and hat, and let me take a look at you," the woman said, waving her into a living room chair while she herself sat opposite on the sofa, her back straight, her hands clenched defensively in her lap as her myopic eyes peered out severely behind enormous horn-rimmed glasses. Leah shifted uncomfortably.

"First off, you should stop dyeing and curling your hair."

Leah's hand went protectively to the top of her head. "This is my natural color."

The woman looked skeptical. "Nobody has such a color naturally. And all those curls. It looks wild."

"I've tried to tie it back, but it's difficult. I could cut it short."

"No, no, men don't like short hair." She sighed as if already defeated. "Maybe have it straightened and dye it a nice, normal-looking brown?"

Leah felt her jaw clench. "I prefer to remain as HaShem made me. Besides, it's expensive."

Faigie Klein couldn't argue with that. She shrugged. "So, we have to live with it. Anyway, after the wedding, you'll wear a wig. But you could lose ten pounds. A size fourteen is a hard sell."

"I'm a ten," Leah said, almost choking.

"Oy, so maybe a more flattering style, then, something that pulls you in at the waist. Men are so picky these days. They want skeletons. Even a size six is not good enough for them. Six, they say, is on the heavy side. And you could dress a little more expensive. As I always tell you girls, you can't afford *not* to. Also, a better bra, with more lift. You know, most girls have no idea what their bra size is. But if you go to Lord & Taylor, they'll measure you and bring you exactly what you need. It costs, but it's worth the investment. And maybe try a little higher heel? I'm not talking *prutza,* but a nice heel gives a woman a good posture and also a good shape to the leg, as much as we're allowed to show. And what's with the black tights? You're not a Chassid, are you? It gives you heavy calves! The men, they hate that, heavy calves. And another thing . . ." She hesitated.

Leah felt a sickening wave of dread. What could possibly be so bad it gave even this awful, insensitive, and tactless woman pause?

"Your hands. You might consider waxing them to remove the hairs."

Leah felt her blood rising and her legs doing the same. She itched to flee this incredible yenta with her litany of insults. Where, after all, was the much-touted Orthodox value of not treating women as sexual objects? Of appreciating a person's spiritual attributes and inner beauty? All that emphasis on modesty, on wrapping a diamond to protect it, on the "all the honor of a king's daughter" lying within, yadda, yadda, yadda? Looks—and only looks, it seemed—were the key to happiness for women in the Orthodox dating game, just like everywhere else. She exhaled, allowing herself to be disappointed as she turned her hands over, examining them for nonexistent hairs.

"Oh, God help us!" the woman suddenly shrieked, pointing. "Tell me that's not what I think it is!"

Leah followed her accusing finger. She was pointing at two tiny, winged birds on the inside of her wrist. Her first and only tattoo. So that explained the fat Chassid throwing her out of his office.

"You'll have to get rid of it immediately!" she shouted. "No religious man will go out with a woman who has an abomination like that on her skin! As it is written—"

"*Do not cut your body for the dead, nor make any tattoo marks,*" Leah interrupted her. "Leviticus, chapter 19, verse 28. I know, I know. But I got it many years ago, with someone who was very close to me. We were in college. Everybody was doing it. Look, Mrs. Klein, I haven't hidden the fact that I am a *baalas teshuva*. I can't help it that I did things then I only now know are forbidden. The ham sandwiches and cheeseburgers I ate—"

"God help us!" Faigie Klein clutched her heart.

"—were digested long ago. Besides, Rabbi Weintraub taught us that the Torah specifically forbids oppressing the convert by reminding him or her of their past sins. Surely you've heard of that, a pious woman like yourself?"

Faigie Klein closed her mouth like a fish but quickly recovered. "Get rid of it! The minute a God-fearing man and his family see it, you are done for, and my reputation will be ruined!"

"I don't want a man or a family who don't observe the Torah," she answered levelly. "If they find it in their hearts to oppress me for my past, they are neither God-fearing nor observant but vicious sinners who ignore God's commandments."

The woman sank back on the sofa into a thoughtful silence. "People are weak, and you must help them. Don't wave a red flag in front of a bull. Get rid of it."

Leah shook her head. "I'm sorry. I can't . . . I won't . . . do that."

The woman rose. "Then, I'm sorry."

Be flexible. "Please," Leah begged. "It's . . . the other person . . . he was my fiancé, and he died, very tragically, soon after we got these tattoos. I am *never* going to take it off. It would be like erasing him from my life."

The shadchan sat down. "Listen to me, maideleh, you'll at least cover it with a Band-Aid when you go out on a date. Understood?"

"Of course," she agreed, relieved. Beggars could not be choosers. Faigie Klein was purported to be the only shadchan blessed with success in "difficult" cases. Also, more importantly, one of the few willing to take on an interesting *baalat teshuva,* when most of her colleagues limited themselves to boring, cookie-cutter Bais Yaakov–Lakewood matches. As a result, the woman had a long roster of unmarriageables and undesirables and desperates in her Rolodex. *People just like me,* Leah thought wryly, gritting her teeth and planting her behind firmly in the chair.

In the end, the matchmaker asked Leah to write up a page listing her education, background, employment, family, likes, dislikes, interests. What were her absolute red lines as far as age, appearance? Would she accept converts or the newly Orthodox? How long had she been Orthodox? It was sort of a shidduch résumé, except that instead of a headhunter, this woman was a womb-hunter.

She answered the questions truthfully for the most part, while increasing her time as an observant Jew to include everything that happened after Josh's death.

This material would be Xeroxed and placed in the wrinkled, determined hands of numerous other local matchmakers, maybe even emailed to them as far away as Baltimore and Jerusalem. Hopefully, the network would be able to find in some remote outpost a person who was looking for a thirty-four-plus-year-old woman from beyond "the Wall" with a Band-Aid–covered tattoo, born out of wedlock from a one-night stand to a mother who dressed like a biker chick and who was now shacked up with a lapsed Sikh.

Or not.

When she got home, she poured herself a large gin and tonic. Nursing the glass, she studied the two little birds, remembering.

12

They had started out as part of a group of runners who met every morning to jog through the campus and then collapse on the lawn. Each morning, they ate breakfast together. She, Laurel, Carla, Morris, Arsenio, and Joshua.

But it was always Joshua and she who wound up running side by side for some reason, whether by accident or because he (or she?) measured their steps to keep in stride. She loved the way he moved, powerfully yet with surprising grace for such a large man. He was at least six three. She would have expected him to be a jock—basketball, even football, material. Goodness knows, Santa Clara never stopped trying to recruit him. Jesuit Catholic or not, it was a sports-crazy institution. But he had no interest at all in competitive sports: "The only person you need to compete with is yourself." He shrugged.

And he did, challenging himself with a double major in biology and comparative religion. "I want to be a doctor, or a writer, or both, like Maimonidies," he said, only half-joking. "What's the point of saving a life if it goes morally to waste?"

His father was a doctor, and he had an uncle who was a conservative rabbi in New Orleans. He was deeply involved in the campus Hillel.

Because of him, Leah also got involved. She helped organize a charity fashion show whose proceeds went to Israeli victims of terror, and a Passover seder for local Jewish high school students.

She gave him all her papers to read for Father Joe's class, which inevitably led to deep, wide-ranging, and—more often than not—consuming discussions about eternity, the existence of angels, the Messianic age, and if man was born good or evil.

Josh believed passionately in the innate goodness of human beings.

"Even after the Holocaust?" she'd question him.

"There were good people even then. Look at Yad Vashem's list of Righteous Among the Nations—very ordinary people who took enormous, life-threatening risks to save strangers. Granted, they were a handful, but it shows that man even under the worst of circumstances has an innate goodness nothing can destroy."

"You could also say it proves the opposite. The fact that so few had the courage to help shows the majority were innately evil."

"No. It only proves that human beings are born with the capacity for both. It's leaders who create conditions that allow the good in men to blossom or—like Hitler—the worst. That's why the most noble thing you can be is a good leader. That's why Moses was the prophet closest to God, because he was shepherding a people, trying to talk them out of the evil inclinations in their souls, to lead them out of a wasteland to the golden promised land where they would become a nation of priests and a holy people."

"So, you want to be Moses?" She laughed.

"I want to be Joshua."

"The prophet Joshua, who replaced Moses? Or my running partner Joshua?"

"Your running partner." He grinned.

"I don't understand."

So he told her a story his uncle had told him. "One day, a great Chassidic rebbe came to his followers. He had tears in his eyes, and his face was as white as a ghost. Everyone crowded around him. 'Reb Zusia,' they asked, 'what's wrong?' 'I saw the moment of my death,' he told them. 'There I was passing to the other side, surrounded by angels who lashed me with questions I couldn't answer.' 'But, Rebbe,' his disciples asked, 'what do you have to be worried about? Of all of us, you are the most pious, learned, and modest. Every one of us has been taught and uplifted by you. What could the angels possibly ask you that you couldn't answer?' He looked at them sadly. 'If they would have asked me, "Why weren't you a Moses, leading your people out of slavery?" or "Why weren't you a Joshua leading your people to the Promised Land?" I would have had an answer. I could easily say, "Prophecy was not given to me, nor strength and wisdom of leadership to bring an entire people into their inheritance." But they didn't ask me that. "Zusia," they said. "There were many kinds of men you could truthfully say you did not possess the talent or wisdom to be. But there is one thing for which you have no excuse and that no power in heaven or earth could have prevented. Zusia, why weren't you Zusia?"'"

She'd never forgotten that story. It was so Josh.

He'd grown up in a large, warm family. His Jewishness was like a second skin. It wasn't a burden or a discussion. It was Josh being Josh. She envied that so much, the naturalness of it, the lack of struggle and temptation. They had made the slow journey from acquaintances and running partners, to friends, until one day it had grown into something more. And that, too, had been natural and effortless.

She remembered the moment it happened. A rainy day in November when almost everyone had already left for Thanksgiving. It was just him and her on the running path. Halfway through, it started to pour. They laughed, shouting at each other that they were completely nuts as the rain pounded through their thin hoodies, soaking their shirts and running pants and making their running shoes squish every time their feet slammed against the wet pavement.

"Come on, don't chicken out!" he kept calling out over his shoulder, and she pushed herself to keep up until, miraculously, she overtook him. By then, they were both exhausted and soaked to the skin. Her dorm room was closer, so she motioned him to follow her.

"What about your roommate, the born-again Christian?"

She smiled. "She's gone for the holiday. Here, take this," she said, throwing her ratty old terry cloth bathrobe at him as she dashed into the shower. "I'll just be a second."

She would never remember a more delicious shower, the hot water neutralizing the chill, turning her skin a bright, warm pink. She wrapped herself in a thick bath towel, then hurried out, leaving the door open for him. She had to laugh. He looked so funny, his broad shoulders pinched by the tiny sleeves leaving most of his broad chest exposed, and only just barely covering his groin and behind. His long, solid legs were covered with dark hair. He smiled, pursing his lips, giving her Kim Kardashian poses, making her laugh until she cried. Then she remembered how cold he must be. She rummaged in her closet for a bath towel, throwing it at him. "Go!"

While he showered, she rubbed herself dry, putting on soft, dry clothes. "I have absolutely nothing that will fit you," she called out to him. "I'm taking your wet things downstairs to the dryer." When she returned, he was sitting on the bed, the towel around his slender waist, his chest bare.

He was so beautiful, she thought. She didn't think beyond the need to touch him, to feel the muscles beneath his skin. All the things that she loved about him, his sincerity, his modesty, his self-deprecating humor, his joyful ambitions to make a better world, were all contained in this beautiful package. This was a whole human being, she realized, every part of which she loved.

She sat down next to him and put her arms around his neck and pulled him toward her. "I love you," she said, shocking herself. How had this slow growth, the unfolding of petal after petal, finally produced this amazingly wonderful full bloom?

He said nothing, his lips widening into a smile. Then he pulled her toward him, his big hands warm and gentle, his whole body responding to hers, both of them moving to a rhythm that was ancient and godly and as human and natural as breathing.

Afterward, both of them had felt only joy without a single taint of guilt or regret. How could that have been? They were like Adam and Eve before they bit into the apple and were polluted by the knowledge of good and evil.

She loved this man, and he loved her.

The way the sky transforms in reflecting the different rays of the sun, so was time colored by her love for Joshua. Every day, every hour, every minute they were together was like dark earth in the spring, new feelings, new ideas budding into life under the fertilizing rain of their connection.

To be that close to another human being, to know what they are thinking when they uttered certain words, or were confronted by a particular view, was to lose that existential loneliness we are all born with. It was magical, filling life with freshness and wonder.

She had never known what kind of thing her heart could be, how changeable, how flexible, expanding without end and shrinking almost to nothing, completely dependent on their closeness or distance. She hadn't known she was capable of such joy, such despair, the highs and the lows. Through knowing and loving him, for the first time, she came to know herself, what she was capable of being, of feeling, her limitations and weaknesses, her strengths. He brought out in her the deepest, clearest, most compelling version of herself she had ever known.

They did not agree on everything. In fact, they disagreed, sometimes vehemently, all the time, each one of them fiercely maintaining their own views, refusing to budge about politics, the environment, women's rights, organized religion. It would reach a crescendo of conflict, of passionate, furious disconnection. And then, for no reason at all, the barriers would melt like ice in the sun. No one changed their mind. The climate changed. It was as if they'd been asleep and suddenly awakened. What did these things matter, these silly, petty disagreements? What did they really care, after all, who won the election, or if the government should raise the minimum wage, or whether or not illegal immigrants should be allowed to vote, when they had each other, when they were building a future together?

That future, it was everything. Whatever they did, it shone in the near distance, palpable, life affirming: the home they would buy and furnish; the children they would cradle and nurture. They envisioned their hair growing gray and their bellies slack, surrounded by the family they would create—children and grandchildren—warmed by the knowledge that they would invest their lives in making the world a better place not only for their offspring but for all future generations.

Lying in the crook of his strong, tender arm, all things seemed possible. He would be a wonderful doctor. And she would show him how to turn his lifesaving ideas into a program that would touch and better the lives of millions. It would be more than a business. It would be a calling, and they would be in it together. How often did they whisper their plans to each other watching the setting sun go down over the hills of Northern California, filled to the brim with hope and joy?

He proposed the summer of their senior year in Yosemite during a hike along Glacier Point Road. As her head swam from the dizzying heights and the otherworldly views of the mountains at sunset, he threw down his backpack—that ugly orange-and-green frayed piece of baggage with all the sewn-on souvenir patches that had seen him through all his adventures—getting down on one knee and taking her hand in his. Their lives together would be one beautiful trail after another, he told her. They would help each other when they got tired and encourage each other to go ever further. Together, they would see God's creation.

"Joshua, look!"

He turned, and there, flying over the mountain into the blazing fire of the setting sun, were a pair of eagles. They watched, mesmerized, as the birds swooped and dove and rose, playing with the air, companions, adventurers, lovers.

On the way back, delirious with happiness, they passed a tattoo parlor that had in its window two eagles in flight.

"Let's do it!" She laughed.

"Well, you're not really supposed to." Josh shook his head, smiling.

"Just a tiny one, inside our wrists," she pleaded, insistent for some reason she could not even explain to herself.

He'd given in, laughing, and they'd sat there as the tattooist promised them both exactly the same tiny tattoo in exactly the same place inside their wrists. "Right above your ulnar artery," he said.

"That's our main blood vessel, so be careful," Josh teased.

"That's why we do it, man. Very romantic," said the artist, an obese slob in a leather biker vest with no shirt on. She thought he was disgusting. But she loved the tattoo. It marked the moment she went from being single in the world to being a couple, banishing loneliness from her life forever. It was the end of the miserable childhood that had been thrust upon her, the beginning of a new life, *her* life, freely chosen.

They planned the wedding for the following June. He'd just been accepted into Stanford School of Medicine. She wanted to go on for an MBA. She didn't have the grades for Stanford, and even if she had, the tuition was about three times that of San Jose State—and even that wasn't cheap. They moved in together right after graduation: a perfect, roomy, two-bedroom apartment in Sunnyvale, halfway between the two schools.

A few weeks before Thanksgiving break, Josh came up with the idea of hiking Zion National Park. He'd been there with his family when he was a teenager, and he wanted her to see it. "It's God's cathedral. The red stone cliffs, the canyons and waterfalls. You cannot believe how beautiful it is," he told her.

For some reason, she resisted. "I don't know, Josh. We've got so many expenses right now with tuition and the wedding," she hedged.

In response, he took her into his arms. "I don't want to have that kind of life, where you are always putting off what you want to do because of something else you want to do. Look, it doesn't have to be expensive. We can drive there. It'll take about eleven hours. So we can do it over two days and spend one night with my friend, who lives in Bakersfield. Afterward, we can go visit my uncle in Las Vegas for the weekend. It'll be a blast! Besides, I'm so tired of school. I need a break."

"But won't it be cold and rainy in November, no good for hiking?"

He thought about that. "Yes, probably. But it's worse in the summer. I prefer the cold to the heat. And we'll be careful."

How many times had she gone over this conversation in her mind? A hundred? A thousand? Ten thousand? She could not help but blame herself. As with any tragedy, there was always the "if only I hads" that tortured you. Why hadn't she just refused, said no, put her foot down? But in the end, she finally knew that the true answer was because she had wanted to please him. This is what they did. They pushed each other forward to do amazing things, things other people didn't have the brains or the guts or the vision to do. Why not go to one of the most beautiful places on earth and spend some time there when there were no crowds and no oppressive summer heat? Why not? After all, they weren't afraid of a little rain, were they? They leaned on the "we'll be careful" as if it were solid, stainless steel, not a rickety bridge of twigs; as if saying it meant that you could somehow control the unpredictable forces of life and nature.

The day of the hike, he was so happy, shouting the words of Walt Whitman as he walked along the trail:

Afoot and light-hearted I take to the open road,
Healthy, free, the world before me,
The long brown path before me leading wherever I choose.
Henceforth I ask not good-fortune, I myself am good-fortune,
Henceforth I whimper no more, postpone no more, need nothing,
Done with indoor complaints, libraries, querulous criticisms,
Strong and content I travel the open road.

They had already been to the Court of the Patriarchs, those beautiful peaks named Abraham, Isaac, and Jacob. And now they made their way up to the Emerald Pools. A light rain had begun to fall.

"It's okay. The rain is only dangerous if we are going inside the Narrows, which we aren't. There could be a flash flood. What we are doing is perfectly safe."

Yes, she thought, reassured, her growing doubts as her steps grew slippery on the rocky slope fading away for the moment as she concentrated on the magnificent view. They were being careful, she told herself as they began the trail from Zion Lodge across the bridge and up the paved road to the lower Emerald Pool. It was an easy hike, she reassured herself, watching people holding their children's hands, carrying babies on their backs. Past that, the hike was on rockier terrain. They took a detour to the second Emerald Pool. Sitting by Heaps Creek, they dangled their feet in the water, eating apples and taking photos of each other and the marvelous scenery.

"Smile," she told him.

"Wait, I'll do this standing up."

He pulled himself up.

And then it happened.

His foot slipped on the algae-covered rock. He fell heavily to his side. She thrust out her hand to him, but he didn't take it. Before she could even react, his body slid over the rocks to the canyon one hundred feet below.

She sat there, numb, unable to move. Was she dreaming?

All the rest of it was a blur. She remembered lifting his backpack and lugging it down along with her own, then abandoning it on the way as she realized it was impossible to carry the weight for both of them. Her next memory was collapsing into the arms of the park rangers as they began to question her.

"It's my fault," she'd wept. "If I had just grabbed his hand faster, I could have saved him."

They shook their heads. "If he had taken your hand, you would have both gone over. There was nothing anyone could have done."

She never believed that.

She sat vigil with his body at the ranger's station until his uncle arrived, and then his parents. And all the while, she kept thinking, *Maybe he will wake up. Maybe some doctor will come and say, "It's not as bad as they are telling you. I have this pill . . . this shot . . . this operation . . . that will cure him."* And all night long, she stared at the tiny eagles on her wrist until she could almost see them fly away.

13

This was the routine. Faigie Klein would call her after she'd spoken to the prospective date and gotten his approval. She'd preface her remarks by saying, "He's a good-natured person who is very anxious to get married. He wants to meet you."

The first time, Leah was filled with hope, happy and grateful to the matchmaker. It was like being in seventh grade again and having one of your friends be the go-between when you got a crush on a cute boy, doing all the difficult, embarrassing work. He was going to pick her up at eight, then drive her to a hotel lobby in Manhattan, Faigie Klein explained over the phone. "Dress nice," the matchmaker exhorted her.

Leah dressed carefully in a new, expensive dress with a cinched waist, wearing the perfectly fitted bra that had cost her close to a hundred dollars in Lord & Taylor. She had lost a little weight but was far from feeling thin. Once a runner stopped running, the weight was impossible to dislodge, she thought.

The intercom rang and she answered it, buzzing him in.

When she opened the door, she felt herself go suddenly breathless. She tried not to gasp as she took in the person who stood before her: 250 pounds on a five-foot-seven frame, with a stomach so enormous he struggled to carry it, touching the walls as he walked. He was gray-haired with glasses, his eyes sunk so deeply inside rolls of fat you needed to be an archaeologist to find them, she thought, horrified. He was wheezing as he spoke, even though it was an elevator building and she was only on the second floor.

Am I really going to have to go out in public with this creature? she asked herself, mortified. But to reject him outright would be both unkind and insulting. Certainly the matchmaker would see it that way. Steeling herself by imagining all the ways she was going to murder Faigie Klein, she put on her coat and waited by the elevator. There was hardly room for both of them, she realized. "I'm going to walk down," she announced with a smile. He didn't protest.

Sitting in the car, his seat pushed back to the limit to make room for his stomach, his short arms barely reaching the wheel, he tried to make conversation. He told her about his wine-importing business, and the nice house he had, a two-family he'd converted into a one-family that even had a driveway. No one in Boro Park, he told her, had a driveway. Every so often, he took out an asthma inhaler, spraying some mist into his lungs.

Was she put off by his weight? he finally asked.

What could she say? "A bit," she admitted.

He nodded understandingly. His plan, he told her, was to have his stomach stapled. Then the weight would just melt away, he'd been told. He'd be thin in no time. His problem was willpower. He had none at all when it came to the good things in life, all of which he could afford in abundance, he assured her. "Sirloin steaks, prime ribs, mashed potatoes, French pastries . . ." His eyes lit up, and he smacked his lips.

"You know, if you have your stomach stapled, you can't eat those things anymore. The staples will burst, and you'll be very ill," she pointed out, trying to be helpful.

He seemed astonished to hear this. "You mean, after the operation, there will still be a *diet*?" He pronounced it like a curse word, his tone one of outrage. "Then what's the point?"

From then on, his mood shifted from cheerful self-promotion to morose discontent. When the traffic into the city turned bumper to bumper, he shifted in his seat and turned to her. "Would you mind," he asked abruptly, "if we called it a night? I'm not feeling very well."

Silently, she said a prayer of thanksgiving. She didn't have to politely urge him not to see her to her door. He had no intention of even loosening his seat belt. "I wish you every happiness!" she shouted through the closed window on the driver's side. He grunted, driving off.

The conversation with Faigie Klein the next day should have been recorded as a comedy routine, she thought.

"So how did it go?"

"Mrs. Klein, why would you send me an old man who is so obese he can hardly breathe?"

"He's getting his stomach stapled! And he owns a house in Boro Park with a driveway! Besides, you're not exactly a size four yourself."

Fury took her breath away, and tears came to her eyes. But before she could tell the woman off, Faigie Klein changed her tune.

"Perhaps you are right. He is a personal friend of my family, and he seemed so anxious to meet you. Sometimes, I'll admit, I let the men's dreams sway me. So we'll try again. Luckily, I have another prospect for you. Someone tall and slender with a full head of hair. A professor of mathematics."

Leah was wary. "How old is he?"

"He's forty-two."

"Is he single, divorced, widowed?"

"Single, from a very respectable religious family in Flatbush. He teaches at Brooklyn College. Some kind of genius. And he smiled when he saw your photo. That doesn't happen very often."

Leah, who was going to tell Mrs. Klein she hoped she'd burn in hell, softened. Perhaps the first one *had* been a fluke, an honest mistake. Perhaps the woman really did have her best interests at heart.

"Well, okay. And thank you."

"Don't thank me now. Thank me at the engagement ceremony." She didn't hang up.

"Yes?"

"Well, this date is going to be a little different. Tuvia—that's his name—doesn't like to make dates on the phone. He wants you to send him all the possible dates and locations and times you can meet him through email. I'll send you his address."

"Isn't that a bit odd?"

"A bit. But you know. Professors can be absentminded."

She hung up, trying to think positively. She sent the email and got back one that said: "When you say 'go out,' does that mean leaving the premises? Does it mean walking, or taking a car, or a train or bus? Could you be more specific?"

Well, at least he has a sense of humor, she thought hopefully.

"Whatever you decide is fine with me," she texted back.

"I will come to your house at 7:22 on Sunday evening, and I will bring a car so we can go out."

At 7:21 and twenty-two seconds, he rang the bell.

"I'm a little early," he said.

She smiled. "I don't think so. I think you are exactly on time."

He didn't smile back. He seemed confused, checking his watch. He shook his head. "No, I have another forty seconds to go."

Was he for real? She looked him over. He was nice looking—kind of cute, actually—with thick, curly, sandy-brown hair that had been left a bit long, which was not usually the custom among haredi Jewish men. His eyes were a wide, innocent blue. On his head, he wore a black velvet skullcap, and he was dressed immaculately in a yeshiva boy's black suit.

"Well, since you are 'a little early,' why don't you come in for a few minutes? I'm almost ready."

He stood there uncertainly. "But we said at 7:22 we'd go out. If I come in, it will be 7:23 or 7:24 until we go out."

"Maybe even 7:30." She smiled, trying to keep positive.

"And that would be all right?" he asked.

She was beginning to wonder if this *was* a joke. If it was, it was wearing thin.

"You know what? I'll get my coat."

He drove a nice, midnight-blue Toyota that was so clean it shone.

"You take great care of your car," she complimented him. "I wish my house was as clean."

"It isn't," he told her matter-of-factly, with no trace of irony or embarrassment. "I wash my car every day. Do you wash your floors every day?"

"No," she admitted. "Usually just on Fridays, before Shabbos."

"You aren't as clean as me," he said humorlessly, snapping in his seat belt.

Mortified, she sank down silently into the spotless seat.

"Are you insulted?" he asked after they'd been driving close to twenty minutes without a word being said. He didn't seem upset by the idea, just curious. "I find it hard to tell when people are upset with me. When I am upset, I usually make a sad face, like this." He turned to her, the corners of his mouth stretching down in an exaggerated mime of sadness. "And when I am happy, I do this." He broke into a clown-like smile that stretched across his face.

She stared at her hands, horrified.

He parked the car and very politely opened the door for her. The lobby was packed with conventioneers.

"Would you mind if I held your arm so you don't get lost in this crowd?" he asked.

"I don't mind," she told him, pleased at his consideration.

He pinched her arm between his thumb and forefinger.

"Ouch!" she pulled away.

"Was that too hard?" he asked. "I can pinch you softer, but then we wouldn't be connected as well and could lose each other."

She rubbed her arm. "Why don't we just sit down and talk for a while."

"How long is 'a while'?"

"What about twenty-two minutes and forty-three seconds?" she answered.

He glanced at his watch.

"So, why did you want to go out with me, Tuvia?"

"My shadchan told me that you were a pretty, kind girl who was religious now but not before."

"So, what about that made you interested in me? That I was pretty, or kind, or religious?"

"I am not interested in you."

She bit her lip. "Then why are we on this date?" *In twenty-three and a half seconds,* she thought, *I'm going to sock him.*

"The rabbis are interested. The halacha is that a man must have children. Two boys and two girls. My mother is interested in you. Also my father. You can't have children without a wife. How many children should we have?" he asked her.

"Why would you want to have children with someone you aren't even interested in?"

"Biologically, a male and female don't have to be interested in one another to reproduce. They only have to get close enough to copulate. Would you like to order from the menu?"

"Thank you, but there isn't enough time. We only have twenty-one minutes and forty seconds left."

He seemed to find that perfectly reasonable. "Maybe the next time we go out, or after we are married and have copulated a number of times." He got up, ready to usher her out.

"Don't touch me!" she warned him. He seemed surprised. "Sit down and wait here; I'm going to the ladies' room."

"When will you be back?"

"When my feet are on the floor in front of you," she replied, pointing down to the ground. She could see that far from being insulted, he was relieved.

He sat down.

She stood in front of the mirror in the ladies' room, her elbows digging firmly into the marble countertop to keep her entire body from trembling.

"Is yours going as well as mine?"

She looked up. A pretty brunette with a model's slim figure dressed in the impeccably modest style of the Boro Park *kallah moide* flashed a sympathetic smile at her.

"Only if yours is autistic," she replied.

"Mine is partially deaf. My shadchan said he was forty-two. But when he opened his wallet to pay the bill, I saw his driver's license. He's fifty-four. I'm thirty-five."

They stared at each other, then erupted in laughter that made their stomachs shake and formed tears in their eyes. They couldn't stop. Finally, they wiped their eyes and adjusted their makeup.

"I'm Shoshana Glaser," the woman said, holding out her hand.

"I'm Leah Howard." She shook the proffered hand gratefully. "I'm a BT, and that doesn't mean bacon and tomato! I'm also too old, too fat, and have a tattoo."

"Really? Let me see."

Leah held out her wrist.

"Cool," Shoshana said.

"The shadchan wants it removed pronto."

"And if you agree, she'll turn all the mice into horses and the big, fat pumpkins into coaches?"

"All I want is for the prince not to turn out to be a frog *all the time*. Is that too much to ask? What is wrong with me that I am getting fixed up with the biggest misfits and losers on the planet?"

"I don't know, but after you get them, I'll get them. Or vice versa. I can tell you what's wrong with me: I'm a doctor. You'd think that would be a plus, but in our world, it's a badge of shame. Like I went off the *derech*. The men have to have the upper hand in our world, and my being a doctor makes that hard for them. So to punish me, they set me up with these losers. I only give in to keep my parents happy. They aren't well, and this is their heart's desire, to dance at my wedding."

"You are so beautiful and slim. How do you do it with all that Shabbos food?"

"I Rollerblade," Shoshana said. "You should come with me. There's a group of us. A swimming instructor, a rabbi's wife, and a librarian. We have a blast. Monday nights at the Aviator Sports and Events Center on Flatbush Avenue. Seven o'clock. Well, I guess I should get back and put him out of his delusional misery. It was so nice meeting you, Leah. Hey, don't give up. I know my *bashert* is out there. So is yours."

"You can't imagine how much this night has been ransomed from despair by meeting you."

"Monday, seven o'clock. And bring skates."

When she went back to Tuvia, she saw that he was staring intently at the floor at the spot she had indicated. She moved her shoes into his line of vision. The moment that happened, he looked up, giving her his widest, most clownish smile. A perfect end to a perfect evening.

"He said it went very well," Faigie Klein insisted the next day.

"He's certifiable!"

"That's unkind! I admit, he's on the spectrum, but he functions at a very high level," Faigie Klein pleaded. "The right woman could make gold out of him."

"Yes, in a hundred years, four hours, and thirty-five seconds."

"What?"

"Never mind. Obviously, I'm not the right woman."

"All right, all right. Look, I first wanted to try to get you local people from very respectable families, but if you are willing to go out with a convert, that will open the possibilities."

Why would you trust this woman again? she berated herself silently. But what other choice did she have? "But this time, tell me everything, and I mean *everything*."

"He's forty-four. He has a very successful store selling African art in Manhattan. He's a convert. He really wants a serious relationship and marriage. In fact, he's a bit desperate."

"Any mental problems or physical illnesses or handicaps?"

"I swear on my life that he is perfectly healthy in all ways."

"Is he a midget, seven feet tall, obese, ugly, bald, deformed?"

"No, not at all! A handsome man in his way. Totally normal looking."

"Then what's the catch?" she asked.

"Why does there have to be a catch?" the woman replied innocently.

The truth was that from the moment Faigie Klein had called her back with a date and time, she was filled with dread. She tried to talk herself out of it. It couldn't be that Faigie Klein didn't have a single, normal man in her Rolodex. It was like going to a real estate agent, she told herself. Every new client got shown the worst, most unsaleable properties—the decrepit old houses with the dingy, small rooms on the dangerous side streets, the ones that were overpriced and in terrible repair—before the agent showed them the newer, more desirable properties. That was just business. But perhaps now, after she'd made it clear that she wasn't buying, Mrs. Klein would finally send her a reasonable prospect.

She put on the new bra, again. She put on the new dress, again. She even put a Band-Aid over her tattoo. If it didn't work out, she wanted to be blameless.

The buzzer sounded, and she once again opened her front door to possibilities. But this time it was no use; her mouth fell open in astonishment she could not hide. The one thing she hadn't thought to ask, and of course Klein hadn't volunteered the information.

She did not answer her phone the next day. Instead, she had the number changed and spent the morning sending the new number to all her clients. When she was done, she went out and bought a pair of the most beautiful, expensive Rollerblades ever manufactured. At seven o'clock on Monday, she waited inside Aviator Sports and Events Center on Flatbush Avenue.

Dr. Shoshana Glaser was right on time and delighted to see her, introducing her to three other friends who all looked like typical Boro Park matrons, except that instead of being overweight, they were athletic and slim. She pulled the laces tightly, then rolled onto the ramp inside the arena. In no time at all she was whizzing around, laughing. While she never got up to Shoshana or her friends' speed, she only fell twice.

"So, what's the latest on the shidduch battlefield?" Shoshana asked her as they sat side by side changing back into their shoes.

"He was a convert from Nigeria; an African with sidecurls, a black suit, and a black Borsalino."

"Did the shadchan mention . . . I mean, she should have prepared you—"

"No, not a word. Because it was the one thing I forgot to ask her!"

"What happened?"

"After I closed my mouth, I invited him in. 'Would you mind if we didn't go out just yet?' he said, closing the door behind him. I didn't mind at all. My feet were shaking. So, I offered him coffee, but he said he preferred bottled water. I tried to explain that New York city tap water was perfectly safe to drink, but he waved that idea away. He told me that only Africans were aware of what was in water. That we Americans were naïve. 'Do you have tea, or orange juice? I love orange juice,' he said. So I brought him orange juice. He sat over that drink for half an hour, inching his way closer to me on the couch. I got up and opened the front door. I explained that according to Jewish law, a man and a woman couldn't be in an enclosed space together if they weren't married or close relatives. He said he'd learned all about that, but that it was one of the things he found very hard to get used to. Africans were very warm and friendly people. He patted the seat next to him on the couch. I stood up and kept standing. 'You've had an amazing journey,' I said to him, trying to be nice. He agreed, explaining that he'd been a Christian, but after learning the Bible, he had come to understand that really, he must be a Jew; one of the members of the 'lost tribes' that had wandered off across the River Sambatyon. 'As soon as I realized that,' he told me, 'I knew I had to convert. But my wife—'"

"Wife?" Shoshana gasped.

Leah pointed to her face. "Exactly what my face looked like, exactly what I said. 'What, you have a wife?' Well, not legally, he explained. She was a woman he had been living with. She wouldn't hear of converting. 'She loved Christ too much'—he shook his head—'and she was afraid it would be too confusing for the children.'"

Shoshana tried hard to keep a straight face. "The children?"

"There were apparently six of them. 'Where are they now?' I asked him. He looked at me as if it were a ridiculous question. In Nigeria, of course. They were all good Christians. *'You've got a wife and six children you left in Nigeria?'*

"'Well, maybe technically,' he admitted. Then he explained to me how a convert is born anew. 'You have no mother, no father, no wife, no children. I'm ready to start anew. I'm a new man!' Then he looked at me suggestively and patted the space on the couch next to him a few more times. Then suddenly, he stood up and his hands were all over me. I don't exactly know what happened after that. All I can remember is seeing red, literally. Also snippets of myself screaming that I was going to assassinate Faigie Klein; I was going to drown her in the mikvah, put strychnine in her cholent. And then I stood by the door and told him to get out."

By this time, all Shoshana's friends were crowded around listening. *Ahhs, oohs,* and *oys* filled the room.

Shoshana covered her eyes with her hands and shook her head.

"And he said, 'Excuse me?' and I screamed, 'Leave!' So he picked up his black hat and settled it on his head. But before he walked out, he turned to me. 'Maybe you have a younger sister?'"

"Put those skates back on!" Shoshana demanded. "Put them on. All of us. We are taking you home."

All along the route, pious people stood in shock by their windows discussing the halachic permissibility of five pious women—some even wearing wigs—linking arms and Rollerblading down the streets of Flatbush all the way to Boro Park.

14

"I am sorry. I never want to talk to a shadchan again. They are all *dreykops,* dishonest shysters. And the shidduchim! I never in my life met such people!"

There was a moment of silence as Fruma Esther Sonnenbaum tried to recover from her shock. Never in her life could she have imagined such venomous words coming out of the mouth of her pious and circumspect son-in-law. With strenuous effort, she finally gathered herself together, swallowing hard and clearing her throat. "My dear Yaakov," she began slowly, choosing her words with care lest he turn his fury in her direction. "This is not like you. I won't say you're wrong, but you know you must keep going. For the children's sake," she pleaded. "How else will you find your *bashert*?"

"Forgive me, Bubbee Fruma, but if you knew even a tiny portion of what I've been through . . ." He shook his head vehemently. "I just . . . can't. I *must* have some peace. I will pray to the Almighty to help me. After all, it is He who blesses man with a helpmate."

"As it is written: *Do not put your faith in miracles,*" she countered with rising indignation, her courage returning at his mild response. "Effort must be made, my son!"

He shook his head decisively. "Tell them to leave me alone! Tell them Yaakov Lehman is finished with their scheming, their false advertising." He was furious again. "Finished being their little experiment! I've put it in God's hands." He had tried six more times after the disaster with Rachel. Enough. It was better for him to remain single the rest of his days than to endure another hour of such torment!

She pulled her handbag close to her chest, rising stiffly to her feet. "It's not my business to tell them any such thing! I wash my hands of it. God have mercy on you," she said over her shoulder as she firmly closed the door to the apartment behind her.

He felt remorse at having offended her. As for the matchmakers—those criminals!—who for months had played havoc with his life, introducing him to aging, demanding, silly divorcées and sour widows eager to trap him into matrimony for their own selfish ends, he owed them no apology for stating the facts.

For a little while, he got his wish. The phones ceased to ring, and the grasping, scheming hordes of women disappeared. Slowly, he felt himself recovering, a smile finding its way to his lips slightly more often. But six weeks after his last disastrous shidduch date, and a month after his conversation with his mother-in-law, he began to feel a bit dispirited, as if the sameness of his days were a groove in the mud that deepened with every step he took, making it impossible for him to move forward.

Sometimes, when he went to sleep alone in his narrow bed, he thought of Rachel, her face, her sweet smile, her young voice. He missed the tingle and glow of possibilities that their meeting had brought back into his staid existence. He felt like an ox in harness, pulling the heavy plow of his obligations behind him as his conscience cracked the whip. He was grateful for the gradual numbing of the sharp pain of loss brought about by the passing of time, but he wanted more than that. He wanted to feel alive again! To feel hopeful about his personal future as a human being living out the rest of his days on God's earth.

The only things that brought him true happiness were his children. They were everything to him now. And so when Shaindele came to him with her sad face, he was more than eager to help her.

"What is it, my child?" he asked her, stroking her dark, soft hair from her forehead. She stood stiffly, smoothing down her skirt. She was almost sixteen, yet not much more than a child, and already she behaved like a matron twice her age. This pained him, but what could he do about it? As the oldest child living at home, and a girl, so many of the household responsibilities had naturally fallen into her lap. He was grateful she had taken them up without complaint. But with the shouldering of tasks that would not have been hers had her mother lived, her sunny personality also transformed. She was constantly making faces or rolling her eyes in disapproval at one thing or another, finding fault with her friends and neighbors for their insufficient piety, the hemlines that in her view fell too short, the sleeves that left a shocking gap between elbow and wrist. Sometimes, with her litany of dissatisfactions and complaints, she sounded more like an old yenta than a teenage girl.

"Tateh, something happened."

He was immediately concerned. "Is it Chasya or Mordechai Shalom? Are they hurt?"

"No, no, nothing physical . . . but yes, I think they've been hurt, but you refuse to do anything about it."

He took his hands from her hair and leaned back. "Disrespect to a parent is a worse sin than short sleeves, Shaindele."

She bunched up her lips in that prim, old-lady way she had lately taken on and that he couldn't stand. "Taking care your children don't go off the *derech* is the same as keeping Shabbos."

"Go off the *derech*?"

"Yes! Bringing someone into the home that's teaching them *goyish narishkeit*. It's that woman. That Leah."

"Leah, the woman who's been cleaning our floors, washing our clothes, and babysitting the little ones so you can go to school and I can go to kollel? The woman who has never asked to be paid or even for thanks? *That* Leah? You are complaining about *her*?"

Her self-confidence slightly deflated, she nevertheless plowed defiantly ahead. "Yesterday, Chasya drew birds on her hands with black magic marker. It was impossible to wash off! When I asked her why she did it, she said she wanted to look just like Leah."

He looked at her blankly.

"She has tattoos, Tateh! Just like the goyim! And now Chasya also wants tattoos!"

Tattoos. He was shocked. The prohibition was written specifically in the Torah, the words of God Himself! He'd been aware Leah was newly observant, but tattoos! Only the most depraved secular people defiled their bodies with tattoos. Or so he'd always been led to believe. Shaindele had been coming to him for months with complaints about the volunteer, to which he'd responded with biblical verses demanding the stranger be treated with love and respect. But now a small doubt crept into his heart, wondering if he'd allowed material considerations to cloud his judgment.

On the days she was there, he came home from night school to find the laundry neatly folded, the dishes done, the younger children washed and, most importantly, happy. When she wasn't there, the place went back to its usual chaos, with Shaindele running ragged to do the chores as well as her homework. Yaakov appreciated that his young daughter was trying her hardest to manage, but the simple fact was she just couldn't. Often she lost her temper, especially with Chasya, whom she bossed around mercilessly, punishing her left and right for every little thing. Too many times, he came home to find the child wailing in her bed.

But that was neither here nor there. A father's responsibility was first and foremost to protect his children from destructive outside influences. Nothing was worse than the wrong education.

"I will look into it, Shaindele."

"When?"

"Behave yourself! I will take care of it!" he shouted, guilt making him react more harshly than he would have under normal circumstances. As was written in Talmud: *Do not be angry and you will not sin.*

She is right, and you are wrong, he admitted to himself remorsefully. He should have met this person who was coming into his home, interacting with his children, months ago.

He meant to. He wanted to. But their schedules conflicted. She came when he had already left for morning prayers and left before he came home after his evening studies. It would have required taking time off from yeshiva or his night classes, neither of which he felt he could afford. And then, of course, he'd been busy with all the phone calls, all those horrible and disappointing shidduch dates. But now he had no choice and no excuse. He had been pushed into a corner and exposed as the derelict father he was.

Leah. What did he know about her, really? Only that she had come into the neighborhood through Rabbi Weintraub's religious studies program for *baalos teshuva* and had been living with Reb Aryeh and Rebbitzen Basha, who had contacted Fruma Esther suggesting she might be willing to help out the family in her spare time as a *chesed*; only that she had done a marvelous job and that Chasya and Mordechai Shalom loved her, and Shaindele couldn't stand her.

He didn't even know what she looked like or even her last name! But Shaindele had been with her every day for months. He had no reason to doubt that what his daughter was telling him was true. Given that, he was left with no choice but to ask this kind, giving person to whom he owed so much to leave and not to come back.

A sickening ache filled his heart at the thought. But his hands were tied. As head of this household, responsible for safeguarding the innocent young souls entrusted by God into his safekeeping, he had no choice but to see that this danger to them was removed. He had left it too long, and now there would be hell to pay.

He called his mother-in-law. "Please call Rebbitzen Basha. Tell her how much we appreciate everything the volunteer Leah has done for us over the last few months but that now we can manage on our own. Tell her we've made other arrangements."

There was a short silence. While Fruma Esther had nursed her own doubts about how close her grandchildren had become to that redheaded *baalas teshuva* who spent so many hours alone with them, there was no question she was a big help. The house had begun to function again; you could walk through the living room without breaking your head over toys and clothes; the dishes were clean and put away; closets and drawers were once again filled with clean, ironed clothes. Had they found another volunteer, perhaps, someone more suitable? Her son-in-law was certainly in no position to hire anyone. "You want we should tell her to stop coming?"

He felt his stomach somersault with misery. How would they manage now? "Yes, tell her not to come anymore."

For months, Leah had plowed through her days trying not to think about the future. She had more work than she could handle, and every day more clients called wanting her to help them set up mailing lists and create flyers or websites. But whatever her workload, she left part of her time open for the Lehman children, and the rest for classes or rabbinical lectures she needed to strengthen her faith. It was shocking how quickly she forgot sometimes not only all the complicated rules of her new life but also her motivation.

She had entered into religious life for one reason: to fill her empty heart. Once, beautiful sunsets and stunning scenery were all she'd needed as she sat next to the love of her life. But without him, it almost hurt to take in the splendors of nature. Worse, it was meaningless. It gave her no answers to the questions tormenting her, tearing at the core of her being: Why was she on this earth in the first place? Why did good people die for no reason? What was the meaning and purpose of all man's misery, all his joy, his attempts at goodness and kindness?

A belief in Judaism had given her some good answers.

"What is your God asking of you, really?" Rabbi Weintraub would say. "Not to hurt anyone, or cheat them? To be honest? To be charitable? To love God? He gives you the sun, and all He asks is that you light a little candle. Is that too much to ask?"

She didn't think so.

Many people took the option of believing in nothing, doing nothing of value, choosing instead to self-annihilate in a million different ways through drugs, alcohol, promiscuity, money lust, status-seeking, fame, or obscene material excess, anything to blunt the inescapable reality of emptiness, of waking up every morning to a new day that had to be gotten through one way or another, until you died. And to obtain these things, some people were ready to lie, cheat, steal, murder, and rob other human beings of their happiness and sometimes their lives. And after they'd done all that, would they be happy then? Could they look themselves in the mirror afterward and think *Wow, what a great life!*

She thought about Andrew, her boyfriend for five years, who had brought her into PureBirth, about Juliana Hager, CEO and founder of the company, and wondered what had happened to them. Even if they weren't in jail, were they happy? Could they ever be, considering the lives they'd ruined, the misery they'd caused? And all for what? That big Manhattan apartment with designer furniture? The fancy car? The clothes? She, at least, hadn't been sure of the truth. She, at least, was sorry.

But most people weren't like Andrew and Juliana. Most people were good, intelligent, responsible human beings struggling to live decent, useful lives. Why was it so many of them found that almost impossible? Was it because there were just no rules anymore, people making them up as they went along? From her own bitter experience, she saw that most good people were simply lost, bobbing around like castaways in a moral wasteland flooded with debris and ugliness, waiting to be rescued and placed on solid ground.

Her own solid ground, the way she had chosen for herself, was often difficult. Keeping the laws of the Torah was called a yoke. Sometimes, it hung heavily around her tender neck.

She missed the freedom and spontaneity of wearing whatever she wanted—long sleeves were so hot in the summer, and mid-calf skirt lengths were absolutely dowdy! She missed hopping over to a McDonald's for a cheeseburger. She missed having a whole weekend to herself where there were no rules, no don't-do-this-don't-do-that. She missed dancing in public and going to rock concerts. And if and when she ever got married—God willing!—she knew she was going to absolutely hate covering her hair.

But there were also so many things she loved.

Despite the rigidity, she loved Shabbos, turning off her phone and disconnecting from the internet, being motivated to take time to contemplate a higher meaning in life. She loved having a sense that God was a real presence in her life, hovering nearby when she prayed, smiled at a child, wrote out a check for charity, or saw a sunset. All that pent-up love for the father she'd never had, she now channeled to God. And was He not the most wonderful Father of all?

As for a woman's place, despite her mother's dire predictions, as far as she could see, it wasn't all that different from the world she'd known: if you showed initiative and talent, people respected that, and if you were a sheep, they accepted that, too, and treated you accordingly. It was always hard for a woman to spread her wings.

But what she loved most of all was the time she spent at the home of Yaakov Lehman. That, above everything, strengthened her resolve, reminding her of why she had changed her life so radically. Those children! How she loved them! They were so funny and affectionate and kind. And so smart! Why, little Chasya could already recite all the blessings over food and say grace after meals by heart! Once, when a deafening clash of thunder and lightning filled the sky, instead of running away in fright, she had recited some prayers. Leah caught one of them: *Blessed O Lord, King of the Universe, whose power and glory fill the earth*. But a few days later, when there was more thunder, to her surprise Chasya ignored it.

"Chasya, what's wrong with you! You forgot to say the bracha on thunder," Leah teased her.

She answered very seriously, "But I didn't see any lightning. There has to be lightning."

"Why?"

"How do you know it's thunder and not another noise? It could be a *bracha levatala*."

Leah was flabbergasted. She picked her up and swung her around the room. "You are the smartest five-year-old on the planet! I hope when I'm ninety, I'll know as much as you, Chasya."

The child squealed in delight.

As for Mordechai Shalom, she thought about him all the time: his beautiful head of silky blond hair, his chubby thighs and soft, adorable little fingers. He was constantly singing real or imagined tunes that sounded like the songs around the Shabbos table. He was very easygoing and loved to laugh. And then there were those precious moments when he wrapped his little arms around her neck and nestled against her breast. Often, the feeling stayed with her so that even at night when she was alone in her bed, she could feel his warmth, hear the beat of his heart.

"You're in love," Shoshana warned her.

"Hopelessly," she admitted, not wanting to think what would happen when the situation changed, which she was sure it would.

She knew Yaakov Lehman was looking for a wife. She had heard his mother-in-law talking to Rebbitzen Basha about it. And it was not going well. This surprised her. She'd assumed that if only she'd been a man, a yeshiva bocher, from a respected family in the neighborhood, there would have been no impediment to a swift betrothal with any number of willing and worthy candidates. But apparently, that was not so.

Often she looked at Yaakov's wedding portrait, studying his eyes, his dark blond hair, his broad chest and slender waist, wondering how he looked now. Perhaps he had gained a lot of weight. Yeshiva boys tended to do that soon after the wedding. It was the sedentary lifestyle, and traditional fat-filled Jewish cooking—not to mention marathon gorging events like a two-day New Year's celebration that ran directly into Shabbos, which made it virtually impossible for even the most careful eaters to avoid piling on the pounds. She knew he was in yeshiva in the mornings and in night school in the evenings. Not likely he was going to a gym in between. By now, he had also probably lost his hair and had bad teeth.

She tried to imagine him grossly overweight, balding, with crow's feet around his eyes and a double chin. Add to that five kids and no visible income, well, *yichus* or not, he wasn't exactly a catch. She was surprised Faigie Klein hadn't thought of him! Still, an FFB always trumped a BT no matter his looks or circumstances. That was just the way it worked in this world, she understood without rancor. More women would be willing to marry him than there were men willing to marry her. Still, she dreaded the day she'd learn another woman would be moving into the home to care for Chasya and Mordechai Shalom, making her presence there unnecessary.

She must not give up hope, she kept telling herself. One day, she could have her own children to care for and love. How this was going to happen, though, was as yet a mystery. She had given up all hope of achieving this through local matchmakers. It had been a humiliating experience. Instead, she increased the frequency and intensity of her prayers.

Sitting in the synagogue, she would close her eyes, imagining standing at the foot of the Throne of Glory enshrouded by thick, white clouds. She opened her heart to the compassionate Ruler of the Universe, but most especially to her Father. And because the ancient, scripted words of the daily and holiday liturgy did not express what was inside her, she used her own words, speaking to God as if He were sitting next to her at a lunch counter.

"Listen," she'd say, "I so much appreciate You taking Your valuable time to hear me out. I want You to know, I'm so incredibly grateful for everything You've done for me. Bringing me here to this place, to these people. Getting me out of San Jose. Giving me my healthy body, my good eyesight, my excellent hearing, my good head. But can I admit to You I'm not doing very well lately?

"It's not because I'm not trying. I am. I've made so many changes in my life, gone in a completely different direction. I'm trying so hard to make my life something You can be proud of. Correct me if I'm wrong here, but I want for me what You want for me: a husband, children, a deep, spiritual life. But You've got to help me out here! I'm so tired. I don't have to tell you some of the stuff I've been through lately! I just want a break. A little break. A little sunshine coming through the clouds. Some sign from You that you are here with me. Nothing grand. No splitting the sea or stopping the sun from setting, just something, anything, to give me the tiniest bit of hope.

"I want with all my heart to be part of these people, part of this world. But honestly, a few of them are not very nice, not very honest, and I could name names, which I won't because that would be *loshon hara*. Anyhow, I guess You don't need me to tell You. You've seen it all, literally. Please, dearest God, dearest friend, my Father. Give me a miracle. A teeny, tiny, almost unnoticeable, barely there, you-could-always-explain-it-away miracle. I mean, I don't expect You to send the right man to my door with a red ribbon around his neck (although that would be nice and would save me a lot of grief), and I don't expect to trip over him in the street. But maybe You could see Your way clear to ever-so-slightly pushing him in my direction? I would be forever grateful. Thank You so much for listening!"

When she opened her eyes, her cheeks were wet with tears, which she wiped away smiling, her heart irrationally eased, even though nothing had changed. And even though she fully realized that if anyone she knew had heard her private prayer they'd be scandalized by its familiarity, she didn't care. She could feel her words going straight to heaven, certain they had been heard.

The next morning, the phone rang. It was Rebbitzen Basha.

"Leah-le, how are you?" she began with her usual warmth. But something was off. Leah noticed it at once. As hard as she was trying to hide it, Rebbitzen Basha's voice had a Tisha B'Av undertone.

"What's wrong, Rebbitzen?"

"Nothing, nothing, maideleh. My dear Leah. Rebbitizin Fruma Esther called me just now. She says her son Yaakov has good news. The family is finally on its feet. They are able to manage on their own. She asks me to thank you from the bottom of all their hearts for your *chesed* all these months. They couldn't have managed without you." She paused, clearing her throat. "They won't be needing your help anymore."

Leah felt as if someone had kicked her in the stomach.

"Leah?"

She cleared her throat. "I'm here. Yes, well, I guess that is very good news," she said, the way she would have said, "I really wish I were dead."

"You will have more time now to find a husband and start your own family. May your good deeds stand before God and heaven and plead for you. And if you find you have extra time, I can suggest many worthy causes that would love your help—"

"Thank you, Rebbitzen Basha. Yes, of course. I'm a bit busy right now. But I'll call you soon to set up something else."

She put down the phone, dizzy. She put on a sweater and went out into the street, walking toward the little park. Although it was unseasonably cold for spring, she sat down on a bench, closed her eyes, and tried to pray. Somehow, it wasn't working. The words wouldn't come. Her mind was blank, an icy, glacial mass. She could find no signposts, no meaning.

She had never in her life felt this way. It was frightening. Was she losing her hold on her faith? Or perhaps some sin she had committed and had not repented was blocking the flow of her soul to God? She searched her brain but could think of nothing.

"Oh, King of the Universe, I know that I am a lowly creature, less than nothing in Your vast universe, and I guess You get trillions and trillions of prayers heading Your way at every second, so why would I think mine would interest You? But I need to know: Is it that You have not heard my prayers? Or have You heard them and said no?" She stared at the vast, blank sky, which stared back indifferently.

Chilled to the bone, she finally got up and walked slowly toward home. Shivering, she put on the kettle, desperate to put her hands around a warm cup of some comforting liquid. The whistle of the boiling water was loud and for some reason, at that moment, unnerving. Thinking only of stopping the screeching, she hurriedly reached for the kettle, forgetting to get a pot holder.

"*Ow, oh my God!*" she screamed, burned, letting it go. It fell to the counter, its boiling contents splashing all over her hand.

She screamed in pain, almost breathless in agony as she held up her hand to examine it. The skin was already a vicious, blistering red. She turned on the faucet, watching as the cool water cascaded over her ravaged flesh. The burn, she saw, was right over her precious tattoo, already distorting and erasing it.

"*No!*" she cried out loud. "God, I asked for Your help! Why would You do this to me?"

The cold water wasn't helping. She put on her coat and hurried to one of the numerous private urgent care centers that inexplicably dotted the streets of Boro Park, indicating that God's chosen knew better than to trust in miracles.

"You have second- and third-degree burns," a friendly doctor told her, cleaning the wound and applying antiseptic. "What are those little black dots over your wrist?"

"My birds," she whispered, devastated.

He shrugged with incomprehension. "Anyhow, whatever it was, it's nearly gone, and what's left will fall off soon. Keep the area clean and come back to get the dressing changed. In a week or two, you'll be fine," he promised.

That afternoon, Yaakov came home early, something inside him hoping his mother-in-law had forgotten to convey his message to Rebbitzen Basha and he would find Leah at his house and have a chance to behave more decently. But it was Fruma Esther who answered the door, squeaking toward him in her orthopedic shoes, only too anxious to put on her coat and hurry home. Chasya ran to him, her hands sticky, while the baby looked up at him eagerly crawling half naked on the worn carpet, his diaper drooping and moist.

"Leah didn't come!" Chasya told him. "We waited for her. We were going to make more cupcakes, with green icing."

He picked her up and held her in his arms, kissing her sticky cheeks, her fragrant, tangled hair. Clothes were strewn all over the floor, along with the flotsam and jetsam of games out of their boxes and half-broken toys. The kitchen was piled with the remnants of last night's supper and this afternoon's lunch. He didn't even know where to begin.

"I'm sorry I couldn't do more. My back . . ." his mother-in-law apologized. "Tell Shaindele to clean up when she gets home from school."

"You do so much, Bubbee Fruma," he said, his heart heavy. Aside from being physically present, his mother-in-law had obviously done nothing.

As usual. "Tell me, the thing we spoke about . . . did you call Rebbitzen Basha?"

"What, you changed your mind?"

"No, no, nothing like that. I just thought, if she were here, I'd say thank you."

"Not necessary. Not to worry. The matter is taken care of. And I must say, Yaakov, it was the right decision."

He looked at her, surprised, hoping there was some substance to her statement that would help to ease his aching heart and bad conscience. "Why do you say that?"

"I've heard things."

"What things?"

"Mrs. Kimmeldorfer said her friend Mrs. Klein, who is also a shadchan, heard that Leah was seen in roller skates . . . roller skates, God help us! She was flying down the streets of Boro Park like a hooligan. God watch over us!"

He wanted to laugh. He wanted to lay his head down and cry. Oh, how he wished he'd seen that!

As soon as the door closed behind her, Yaakov took off his hat and jacket and rolled up his sleeves, trying to care for his children and make a dent in the housework. He was not even half done by the time Shaindele came home from school.

She found him lying on the couch while the children climbed all over him. He looked exhausted. "Tateh, why are you home so early?"

"I came because Leah won't be coming anymore. I will try to make other arrangements. But in the meantime, you might have to take some time off from school. I can't miss any more kollel or any of my night classes."

"But I have exams!"

"I'm so sorry, Shaindele. But this is the situation. If I don't come to kollel or finish this course, I can't support our family."

Shaindele was silent. He tried hard to read his daughter's face. It was nothing simple he saw there—not anger or glee or satisfaction or even disappointment. It was more having your way and regretting it. This puzzled him. But at that moment, he could not think about anything. He closed his eyes, ready for sleep, the only escape he had all day from the chaos of his life and its awful choices.

15

⊸⊷

The week after Shaindele got her wish and Leah Howard stopped coming, the baby woke up with a fever. Soon enough, she found out her bubbee wasn't going to be any help; she had an optometrist's appointment in the city. So Shaindele had no choice but to stay home herself, missing school.

After carrying him around the apartment as he cried nonstop for two hours, she noticed his eyes were finally closed. Laying him down gently in his crib, she slid down onto the couch, wanting nothing more than to join him in a long nap. But it wasn't going to happen, she realized, glancing at her watch. In three hours, she had to pick up Chasya from kindergarten, but before then . . . She looked around. The house was a total disaster. She couldn't let her father see it this way, casting in fine relief the before and after of Leah's presence.

Her back against the kitchen wall, she confronted with bitter resentment the tottering piles of dirty dishes and pots that stared back at her from the counters and sink. As she rolled up her sleeves, she thought of her classmates. Just about now, her friends would be sitting in Rabbi Feldstein's chumash class, learning about the tithes due the Levites and the priests during harvest season in the Land of Israel. Soon they would be sitting around the courtyard, opening their lunch bags, sharing treats and the latest gossip. She wondered what they would say about her.

Ever since her mother died, she'd been terrified of gossip, afraid the word would have gotten out and that people would see the terrible truth in her eyes. If that happened, there would be no atonement for her, no redemption. The only reason she could still live in the world was that no one suspected. The opposite—they felt so sorry for her that they would never have dreamed of asking questions, investigating the role she had played in that disaster. But one day, she told herself, frightened, the time would come when some clever girl put two and two together, laying bare everything she was intent on hiding.

Even without that, though, any family singled out by fate for tragedy had its sterling reputation tarnished. That was true despite the book of Job, specifically included in the holy canon to counter just such an idea, emphasizing that bad things *could* happen to even the worthiest and most God-fearing. Still, no one really believed that. Eager to find comfort and protection, most still whispered knowingly that tragedies were a punishment from God and that God didn't make mistakes.

She worried constantly that such an idea would ruin her chances of finding a proper shidduch. Like all her girlfriends in Bais Yaakov, that was uppermost in her mind, the most urgent wish of her heart. Despite her youth, like all her girlfriends, she dreamed of very soon being noticed by the matchmakers and offered the top Torah scholar in the top yeshiva, someone who would one day rise to rabbinical prominence and influence—a scholar and a saint.

For a bridegroom with such potential, she was only too aware that matchmakers never even considered girls from families touched by scandal or girls about whom there was even the slightest negative feedback. Such trivial things as giggling during chumash class in eighth grade or rushing through prayers or even wearing a loose, ankle-length denim skirt after school hours were enough to ruin your chances. The matchmakers and the boy's parents even went so far as to speak with a girl's elementary school teachers!

That in itself didn't worry her, nor—ironically, given her family's dire financial situation—was she anxious about coming up wanting concerning the question of dowry. Like everyone else, she had heard the horror stories of boys' families extorting potential in-laws for an apartment, a car, and thousands of dollars in annual support. But she just couldn't believe it. A truly religious man would not—*could not*—reject an excellent girl with wonderful middos from a pious family with *yichus* because of money! But if her name or reputation were sullied, that was quite another matter altogether; then God Himself would not be able to help her.

As she thought about it, her hand automatically reached up into the kitchen closet for a bag of cookies. All they had left were some dry almond biscuits. She didn't even like the taste. Still, she sat down at the kitchen table and morosely, one by one, finished them off.

She was gaining weight, she knew. But she couldn't help it. Sometimes sweets were the only thing that lifted the dark cloud over her head, the burst of sugar on her tongue giving her the only moments of happiness she experienced all day long.

If only there weren't so much pressure to be thin! Why, even her friend Gittel, who was a size four, was on a diet! Every day, Gittel brought only one apple, cutting it up into six pieces and eating each one slowly throughout the day. Her friends were always buzzing about how the shadchanim had warned their older sisters about their weight. It was a well-known fact that fat girls couldn't be matched with anyone except sloppy, lazy, stupid boys. Everyone, including herself, accepted that a worthy Torah scholar—even if he was himself fat and nothing to look at—deserved a beautiful wife.

After all, hadn't all the matriarchs been stunning beauties? Sarah was such a stunner that Abraham had to hide her from Pharaoh, pretending he was her brother. And that was when she was in her eighties! But Pharaoh took her anyway and only released her when God covered his body in boils, giving him bad dreams in which the truth was revealed so that he hurried to return Sarah to her husband. Isaac had done the exact same thing with Rivka because of Avimelech's roaming eyes. And the Torah came right out and said Yaakov fell in love with Rachel because she was "fair of face and fair of form." This was a pious scholar's just reward. The opposite was true of women, for whom an interest in physical appearances showed a petty and materialistic nature. Still, she secretly admitted to herself she wanted someone tall and slim and handsome like her father. But also, and of course, someone who was a brilliant scholar and pious as well.

Throwing out the empty bag of cookies after digging out the last remaining crumbs with a moistened finger, she went into her parents' bedroom to look at herself in the full-length mirror. Touching her round, pink cheeks and patting her tummy, which slightly protruded under her close-fitting skirt, she felt disgusted. Just one word from her father would have helped her stave off these sweet binges, she told herself bitterly. All he needed to do was look at her with his kind, sad eyes and shake his head and say, "My dear, pretty daughter, you must stop eating so many sweets!" But her father was never around, and when he was, his eyes seemed vacant and unfocused as if he didn't actually see her.

She tried hard to excuse him. What really pious man would notice such a petty, physical thing like that? Besides, it was more important what other women thought of you than what the men thought. After all, when you went to a wedding, wasn't there an impenetrable mechitza separating the hall into men's and women's sections, so no man or boy could see you? The pains you took with your appearance weren't to catch the eyes of the men as much as to impress the bewigged matrons who ruled the shidduch world. The best you could hope for was that somebody's aunt or grandmother would turn their sharp little eyes on you and make inquires. Sometimes, local yentas would single out a particularly attractive girl and make the matches for free, in line with the cherished belief that arranging three successful matches ensured one's place in heaven.

It was so important not only to lose the extra weight but to know exactly what to wear, how to do your hair, and how to use makeup to gently coax the best out of your features without appearing like a *prutza*. To navigate all these things, she desperately needed her mother.

Mameh. She glanced at the empty, unwrinkled sheets on the twin bed in her parents' bedroom that now did nothing more than take up room. *She* would have noticed that the zippers on her Beit Yaakov pleated skirts could hardly be closed. *She* would have sat her down and given her so much mussar that she would never again have even looked at a rugelach. How she missed her! She needed her hugs, her kisses, her advice, her *presence*. She had no one to talk to, no one to teach her what she should believe, what she should be doing, how she should behave in the world. With her absence, the house had stopped feeling like a home. It was an empty space, she thought, where she ate and slept and worked her fingers to the bone. She felt so alone.

The few shy attempts to share some of her feelings with her bubbee had been disastrous. "*Az m'veint, veint men alein; az m'lacht, lacht di gantzeh velt mit.*" "Cry and you cry alone; laugh and the world laughs with you," the old woman had said. Or "There is no reason for you to feel so discouraged." Or "*Az m'bt zich gut doh, ligt men gut dort*" (He who prepares his bed here, in this world, will lie comfortably there, in the next world). To open your heart and be met with clichés and belittlement and holier-than-thou piety was infuriating. She didn't repeat her mistake.

As for her father, he was never around or available. Besides, something inside her froze when she thought of sharing her feelings with him; so many of her questions involved him. Where had he been when her mother needed him after Mordechai Shalom was born? Why had he left for yeshiva every morning as if nothing were wrong? Why had she heard her mother crying behind closed doors? What had happened once the ambulance picked her up? Why hadn't they been able to save her? And underlying all those questions, the unfathomable mystery at their heart: How could a healthy young woman, still in her thirties, suddenly die? What had really happened to her mother?

It wasn't natural.

It wasn't fair.

No one had ever spoken openly about it. That in itself, Shaindele thought, was not unusual. People in their world never spoke about fatal illnesses, and the C-word was never spoken out loud. It was called "a difficult sickness," whether from superstitious dread or traditional reticence to talk about tragic subjects.

At first, she had made every effort to absolve her father. He had, after all, been a good husband, a kind father. Part of her heart sincerely went out to him. She could see how lonely and sad he was. But her mother's death had left a minefield between them that couldn't be crossed. Each time she tried, little explosions left her with festering wounds that she knew would never heal until there was a full, open reckoning, exposing them to the fresh air and sun of truth.

Most infuriating was that no one seemed to even realize how deeply she was wounded, how traumatized, how utterly unready to be thrust into the role of housekeeper and mother-substitute. Brokenhearted, she had done her best to undertake her new responsibilities, but it was hopeless.

Without someone to guide and teach her, she burned the challah and over-salted the soup, which was tasteless and thin anyway, nothing like the rich broth with floating vegetables she remembered from her childhood. The laundry especially overwhelmed her. She was always accidentally leaving in some colored cloth among the white load that turned all her father's white shirts pink or blue; or forgetting sweaters in the dryer until they shrank so small even Mordechai Shalom couldn't wear them.

Everything she did, she did poorly, she thought, not to mention those things she didn't do at all, like the ironing. They had an old iron that took forever to heat up and had no steam. Week after week, the ironing piled up, untouched and ignored, until her father went looking for a clean shirt and couldn't find one, or she tried to lay a Shabbos table with a cloth so hopelessly wrinkled the dishes wouldn't lie flat and the cups tipped over. She promised herself that at the very least, every day she would iron at least one blouse for herself and for Chasya, and a shirt for her father. She didn't always succeed.

But what she was most ashamed of and wanted to hide was how she treated her younger siblings. Before her mother died, they'd always gotten on so well! She loved them. But now, they were acting out. Every time she told Chasya to pick up her toys or wash her hands, the child stubbornly refused. And if she lost her temper and yelled at her and (to her shame) smacked her, Chasya immediately started to weep. "I want my mameh!" she'd cry, which tipped Shaindele over the boiling point.

"I also want my mameh!" she'd shout at the child, smacking her again even harder. "But she isn't coming back! I'm all you've got, so you'd better listen to me and behave yourself!" Afterward, hiding in her bedroom, she'd want to scream and cry and hit herself for her stupidity and incompetence.

She had no idea how to comfort herself, let alone the little ones. She was, after all, not that much older. With each passing month, instead of getting more experienced and better at her chores, she felt she was getting worse, her patience stretching thinner, her temper more brittle, breaking through red lines more easily and with greater explosiveness.

Every day, she asked herself why she wasn't the person she wanted to be. And what she hated most of all was that she could never stop pretending, never admit failure or ask for help. She could never be herself. "Be strong," everyone told her at the funeral. "You must be the mother now," they demanded. Good little yeshiva girls did as they were told.

Lately, thoughts about death and the fragility of life obsessed her. When she was invited to a simcha—a wedding or bar mitzvah—she looked around the crowded catering hall at the guests, wondering, *Who among you will be dead by next year? In five years?* She wanted to shout at them, "How can you smile, dance, talk about silly things when the executioner is coming for you?"

She was sure no one had ever felt this way before, and so there was no point in sharing her feelings, which she was convinced were shamefully freakish, even insane. She lived in terror of someone finding out the truth about sweet little Shaindele Lehman, particularly her father.

Leah Howard was her nightmare. An outsider who could see and report everything that went on inside the house when the adults weren't there; who would hear stories from Chasya and see her bruises. Who would see day by day how the housework was being neglected, the ironing piling up, the dishes and pots left unwashed. If it had been up to her, Leah Howard would never have set a single toe over the threshold.

Now it was too late. Just as she'd feared, ever since Leah started, it was clear what a difference her presence had made. Where disorder and dirt had reigned, neatness and cleanliness had taken over. Where the children had gone unbathed and unfed and unhappy, there had been not only a schedule but a new joy of expectation. They waited for her by the door on the afternoons she came. "Leah doesn't do it like that" was Chasya's new mantra. Leah knew how to brush out the knots in her hair so gently that it didn't hurt. Leah knew how to make beautiful French braids and draw funny pictures. Leah knew how to bake delicious cookies and whip up pink icing for cupcakes. Leah knew how to wash hair without getting soap in your eyes; to iron dresses so that there were no ugly wrinkles.

The adults were less forthcoming, but she knew her father and grandmother and the neighbors who visited must have also noticed the difference. While they politely pretended to attribute the better conditions in the house to her, praising her hard work, each time she got a compliment she knew it belonged to the interloper and that if people ever knew the whole truth, they'd be disgusted and horrified with her. The longer Leah stayed, the more this kind of exposure was inevitable.

Thus, even though having Leah Howard coming three times a week had saved the household from total collapse and herself from exposure as a failure; even though it had allowed her to keep up her studies and had even improved her relationship with Chasya, who was no longer wetting the bed and crying herself to sleep every night, she had been determined to get rid of Leah. At first, her father had ignored her complaints, even giving her pious lectures. But the moment she'd seen the tattoos, she'd recognized victory was at hand.

She had not been mistaken, she thought, allowing herself a little smile of triumph, which soon faded as she returned to the kitchen and surveyed the chaos. Plunging her soft, young hands into the hot, dirty, disgusting dishwater, she cringed as the Brillo Pads scratched her tender skin, ruining her nails.

Had she been a modern girl brought up in the usual way, she might have thought, *If only I had been born a boy!* She might have cast her mind on the incongruities between herself and her elder brothers, Elchanon Yehoshua and Dovid Yitzchak, both safely ensconced in yeshiva in faraway Baltimore, coddled as Shabbos guests by their generous uncle and aunt, with no one expecting them to change *their* routines, to give up *their* studies to help out the family! No one, including herself, would hear of them changing yeshiva to move back to Boro Park where they'd be able to help out, at the very least with occasional babysitting, not to mention part-time jobs to alleviate the family's dire economic situation. Her entire life, she had been led to internalize the idea that learning Torah was not only her brothers' right but their obligation, overriding all other responsibilities. Keeping their behinds glued to their seats in yeshiva—even as their family fell apart—was deemed both fortunate and worthy.

Outwardly, she accepted this idea with meekness and humility. But inwardly, she raged with inchoate fury, her heart a frothing cauldron of hatred that blackened her soul. She flailed, looking for someone to blame, someone to hate, without going against her upbringing and cherished beliefs. And then, one day, Leah Howard walked into her life, giving her the perfect target, a person she could find a million pious reasons to despise. So what if she was only trying to help and had made Shaindele's life so much easier?

"I don't need anyone. I don't want anyone!" she fumed, scrubbing away.

She would survive her horrible secret guilt, the tragedy of her life, this mess, all these people who had abandoned her. And one day, she, too, would escape, she thought, smiling with grim pleasure as she savagely scoured the burned-on grease off yet another huge pot. She had her own plans. She would surprise them all, and they wouldn't be able to do a thing about it.

Until then, being shown up by Leah Howard as an incompetent wasn't in the picture. At least with that, she had finally succeeded brilliantly.

16

Leah watched the doctor unwrap the bandages from her wrist. The ugly blisters and brown scab were gone, along with her eagles. Not a trace of them remained. She choked, feeling her lungs deflate as if the living breath had been sucked out of them.

It was, she thought, almost like having a limb amputated.

She had lived with them for so long. They'd been such an important part of Lola the college coed with the long, golden-red hair; Lola the runner and biker and fearless hiker who wore shorts and stomach-baring T-shirts. It wasn't just the tattoo that had shriveled and died; it was Lola herself. And who had taken her place? she thought, looking down at the dull skirt that hung loosely from her well-padded hips to mid-calf. A stranger. A person the old Lola would never have noticed in a crowd except to pity.

She thought about Icy and Cheeky. How she missed them! She wondered what they had been told and if she had done the right thing staying away. Would they be angry at her absence? Or had they forgotten all about her over the last two weeks? Kids had such short memories. She was determined to at least visit them one last time to say goodbye, even though no one in the family had invited her or suggested it (rudely, she thought). The family owed her that at least after all her hard work. She'd postponed it until her hand had healed and the bandages were removed. Icy, she knew, would have been upset seeing her bandaged up, and that dear, sweet kid had been through quite enough.

"I'm sorry, am I hurting you?" the young doctor said, watching her wipe away a tear.

She shook her head. "No, it's fine."

She stared at the slightly reddened new skin, as smooth and featureless as a newborn's, underlining the fearsome reality of the revocation of her old life. It was terrifying and sorrowful, and yet—dared she hope?— filled with new possibilities. A rebirth.

Whatever the case, she needed to see the children. She looked at her watch. It was only a little past eight in the morning. She wondered if the toy stores in Boro Park opened that early.

It was early spring, a cool, damp day of filtered light that passed through thick clouds. She pulled her raincoat closed, shivering.

While the sign hanging at the entrance to the largest toy store on Eighteenth Avenue indicated nine as the opening hour, Leah noticed a woman was already ensconced behind the cash register. Tapping gently on the glass to get her attention, Leah smiled gratefully as the woman walked toward the door, unlocking it and gesturing her inside.

"Thank you so much!"

"A toy emergency?" The woman laughed, locking the door behind her.

"You could say that." Leah smiled.

"Need help?"

"No, thanks, I'll just look around. I have some ideas."

She wandered down the aisles, looking over the piled-high box games. Some were familiar—Monopoly and Clue—but others had Hebrew lettering or transliterated Yiddish words. There was Mitzvah, Blik, and a card game called Old Maid depicting amusing ultra-Orthodox cartoon characters—men with skullcaps and old women in wigs. Another was called Yiddishe Kop (Jewish Mind) and Uber Chochom (Great Genius). She'd be no help in showing the children how to play such games, she realized, troubled. It was just then she saw the jigsaw puzzles. She imagined spreading out the pieces on the big dining room table as the children sat around watching. Mordechai Shalom would be sure to taste them, destroying whatever they managed to put together. But it would probably bring back good memories for Shaindele of Shabbos afternoons and holidays with her mother, fitting together the pieces to the pictures that now hung, laminated, on the walls.

Not that Shaindele deserved a present, she argued with herself. But soon she relented. She was just a kid—a stupid, arrogant, snobby kid—but still, just a hurting child who was suffering the loss of the most important person in her life. Leah understood that kind of loss. Impulsively, she picked out a beauty, a Ravensburger with eighteen thousand pieces! If they ever finished it, it would look lovely laminated and hung on the wall. For Chasya, she found a doll dressed up exactly like a Boro Park matron, with long sleeves, a long skirt, and even an elaborate head scarf. It was a riot! As for Mordechai Shalom, a soft ball that lit up in different colors and made barnyard noises when it was jiggled seemed perfect.

She was happy when she got home, laying her bundles on the table, anticipating the children's joy when they opened their presents. Even Shaindele might crack her face with a smile! But that would have to wait. After two weeks of not being able to get her bandages wet, she couldn't wait another second for a shower.

Quickly stripping off her clothes and turning on the water, she cautiously tested the temperature with a newfound respect on her undamaged hand. It was perfect. How lovely, she thought, luxuriating under the warm flow, using up the last of her expensive European shampoo to lather her hair with gusto. It had gotten so long again. She desperately needed a cut and blow dry, but in Boro Park, it was next to impossible to find anyone who worked with hair that was still attached to a woman's head. Most women stayed home and just sent in their wigs. Hairdressers were used to dealing with Styrofoam head forms instead of human beings.

She was only halfway through rinsing off when her cell phone began to ring. It rang and rang and rang. Probably that new customer, Herschel the butcher, who always wanted everything done yesterday. She ignored it, annoyed. He and his glatt kosher chopped meat and brisket would just have to wait.

When she was done, she reached for her thick, lavish robe—another remnant from her old life—relishing its warmth and softness. The phone was still trilling like a madman, almost hopping off the counter.

"Okay, okay, Herschel. Keep your pants on," she told it, reluctantly picking it up.

But it wasn't Herschel. It was Rebbitzen Basha.

"Chasya is in the hospital. She hasn't stopped calling for you. Please go quickly!"

Leah caught her breath, trying to voice some basic questions: What happened? Which hospital? When are visiting hours? But she found herself struck mute with terror, allowing the phone to drop to the floor as if it were molten lead.

She swooped with a mad urgency to retrieve it. "Okay, I'm coming," she said, hurriedly hanging up.

She grabbed some clothes from the closet, hardly noticing what she put on, towel-drying her hair. There was no way she could spare fifteen minutes to blow-dry it. She searched for a hair tie but couldn't find one. Desperate, she took a rubber band off a bunch of asparagus on the kitchen counter, forming a messy ponytail that reached halfway down her back. She grabbed Josh's vintage orange-and-green backpack, stuffing in her phone and wallet, and only as an afterthought remembering her raincoat. She was halfway down the stairs when it struck her that she had left Chasya's new doll behind. Racing back up two steps at a time, she shoved it into the backpack. Only halfway down the block did it occur to her that she had no idea where she was going.

She called Rebbitzen Basha back, writing the address on the back of her hand, hurrying. The skies had darkened, and a light drizzle began to fall, frizzing her already damp hair into a million curls that formed a halo around her head. She hardly noticed. Running to catch the bus, she felt her heart beating violently through a combination of exertion and fear. Only when she actually entered the hospital building, did she take her first deep breath. Where to go? She looked at the signs. Rebbitzen Basha had told her Chasya had been admitted to pediatrics. Ignoring the elevator, she ran up three flights of stairs.

"Please," she said, her tone almost desperate as she grabbed a nurse by the arm. "Chasya, Chasya Lehman? Where is she?"

The nurse was about to call security, when she looked into her eyes. "Are you family?" she asked, softening.

"Yes, no, please," Leah blurted out.

"Room 6A, around the corner," the nurse said, pointing. "Hey, she's going to be fine!"

Leah hardly heard her, hurrying forward and almost losing her balance around the sharp turn, resting her shoulder against the wall to stop herself from falling.

The door was open.

She saw Chasya lying there sobbing, her little face as white as the sheets.

"Icy!" Leah called out.

The child stopped crying, pulling herself up into a sitting position. "Leah!" She wept, reaching out with both her small arms.

Vaguely aware there were others in the room, people she did not recognize and had no time for now, Leah threw her backpack to the floor and leaned in, hugging the child, whose sobs subsided immediately into soft hiccups.

"What's wrong, Icy?"

"My stomach. It hurts so much!"

Leah held her close, patting her back, kissing her pale, sweet cheeks. Another stomachache? And now she was in the hospital. A frisson of fear made her spine go rigid.

"I'm sorry, but you'll have to leave now," a nurse told her.

"No, wait. Can I just—?"

"Leah, don't go!" the child wailed.

Yaakov stood up shakily from the chair he had been glued to all night, watching the scene in amazement. "Are you *that* Leah, the volunteer?" he asked her, although he already knew the answer.

Leah looked around in surprise. It was him, the man from the wedding photo! But he wasn't fat and bald and old. He was slender and young, and if not for the weary wretchedness of his expression, as handsome as ever. Only the eyes, she thought, those big, blue eyes, were different. Instead of gentleness and hope, they had narrowed into pools of unfathomable misery.

She felt suddenly shy. "That's me," she told him, nodding, overcome by a small, panicked thought as to what she must look like to him.

Leah! The kind woman he had treated so badly! Instinctively, he looked at her hands, searching for the tattoos. But all he saw was some ink on the back of them.

Leah followed his gaze, embarrassed. "I was in such a hurry, I called on the way to get the address. I didn't have any paper." She rubbed the ink off with a moistened finger.

He felt overwhelmed by his sins. There was nothing! Shaindele had lied. And he had fallen for it. He had raised a gossiper and slanderer, a child who had violated serious commandments from God Himself. As it is written: *Do not be a talebearer among your people.* It was a sin whose punishment was the death of the soul. But instead of reprimanding his child, educating her, he had listened and believed her, and even acted upon the slander. According to the Code of Jewish Law, his sin was the more grievous.

The Torah forbade a Jew from listening to *loshon hara* even if what was being said was true and accurate. This included discussions ranging from criminal misconduct to lackadaisical Jewish observance, such as not keeping kosher or not giving charity. Having a tattoo certainly fell into that category, as did using roller skates. And it didn't matter if the information was conveyed verbally, in writing, or just silently implied. And it didn't matter how exalted the gossiper was, if he or she were one's parent or even one's rav. It was an inexcusable sin. This was also true concerning factual information. How much more infinitely damnable, therefore, was spreading slanderous lies?

Now he understood why his shidduch dates had gone so badly, why his child was suffering, and why God had brought him back to the blank walls of the hospital where his life's tragedy had unfolded, a place he had never wanted to see again as long as he lived.

"Please, let her stay," Yaakov said to the nurse.

He saw her glance shift between himself and Leah—curious, questioning—and felt a sudden blush ride up his neck.

The nurse shrugged. "The doctors are making rounds now. You're both going to have to leave for a few minutes."

Chasya moaned, clutching Leah tighter.

"It's okay, honey," the nurse crooned, patting the child's arm. "It's just for a few minutes. Your dad and . . ."

"Leah," Yaakov said.

"And Leah will be right back."

Leah pried the child's hands gently from her neck, holding them in her hands and kissing them. "Your tateh and I will be right outside the door, Icy. And when I come back, I have a big surprise for you. Something nice, okay, honey? Can you be very, very brave for me?"

The child nodded, smiling through her tears, lying quietly back on her pillow.

Yaakov and Leah sat down awkwardly side by side in the only chairs available in the hallway, watching as the battery of doctors entered, closing the door behind them.

He shifted his weight, stiff and uncomfortable, lowering his eyes. What could he say to her? He was so ashamed. Should he try to explain, to apologize? But that might embarrass her even more, knowing that she'd been the subject of gossip. She might suspect that she'd been willfully discarded and not—as he hoped had been respectfully conveyed to her—reluctantly and gratefully parted from now that the family was back on its feet, thanks to her *chesed*. He tried to decide.

Compounding the problem was the fact that he had no idea how to talk to young women who were not family members. His only experience had been the formally arranged and carefully orchestrated shidduch dates. And look how they had turned out! And this woman—he glanced at her shyly—looked nothing at all like those women.

He had never seen hair like hers—so thick and massively curly, the very color of sunrise. It was like a crown, he thought. No woman in his world had hair like that, or if they did, they'd probably chop it off or torture it into some tight braid, or imprison it with hairpins until it was small and neatly tucked away and out of sight. Certainly the rabbis would never allow a married woman to fulfill the commandment of covering her hair by wearing a wig like that! She'd be ostracized, condemned for immodesty. Her husband would divorce her.

But this woman wasn't married and didn't have to cover her hair. And although he was no expert, it didn't seem to him to be artificial; it was simply too wild to be the creation of hairdressers from a Boro Park beauty parlor. God himself had given her that hair. No artifice was involved. Even the band she'd used to hold it back was the commonplace kind found wrapped around newspapers. It was unequal to the task, he noted, threatening at any moment to burst under the strain. As it was, so many tendrils had escaped. They were lovely, trailing down her back, framing her long, white neck, her forehead and cheeks. He looked down at his shoes, mortified by where his mind was wandering.

Leah spoke first. "What's wrong with Chasya?"

He shrugged helplessly, not looking up. "It started yesterday. Vomiting, stomach pains. We thought it was another virus, but then it got worse. She couldn't hold anything down."

"How is Cheeky? Uh, I mean, Mordechai Shalom."

For the first time, he relaxed, a little smile playing on his lips as he looked up to face her. "Cheeky?"

"It's what I call him. His cheeks are like big, pink marshmallows."

"Yes, they are." He nodded. His beautiful baby boy. "My mother-in-law is watching him. He is also upset. The house is in turmoil."

"Shaindele is at school, right? Her midterms?"

He nodded, surprised.

"And you are missing kollel and your night classes. It must be hard."

He was amazed. She knew everything about him and his family, this woman he had never bothered to meet and thank, while he knew next to nothing at all about her except for the ugly gossip and lies that he—to his everlasting shame—had allowed himself to be fed. He stared down at the floor again, mortified.

Leah took that as the usual religious man's sense of modesty that did not permit him to look at a woman. She used the opportunity to study him.

His forehead, so broad and intelligent, was wrinkled in concentration, the expression on his handsome face almost rigid with fear. His generous lips were pinched together anxiously. And those eyes, those big, innocent blue eyes so like his son's, were miserable. Without willing it, her heart went out to him in a primal and motherly way, disconnected from any sexual feeling. She wanted to wrap him in softness and comfort, the same way she had so often embraced his little boy.

"Maybe it is just another virus," she suggested. "Or maybe it's psychological. She's had a hard year. The mind-gut connection, you know?"

"God should help us, if only! I pray it's nothing serious. In fact—"

Her phone rang.

"Sorry, I have to take this. It's my customer." She got up and walked down the hall.

He followed her with his eyes, catching a glimpse of the long, flowery gypsy skirt and crisp white blouse that winked beneath her open coat. It was shockingly summery for such a day, he thought. And rather girlish. He remembered the women on his shidduch dates, their heavy bodies squeezed into tight girdles and covered with dark, heavy material that was no doubt as expensive as it was tasteless. In contrast, she seemed unfettered, carefree, her natural plumpness reminding him of his young daughter's.

Instead of a purse, she had an old backpack slung across her shoulder. It was a strange color—orange and green—worn and scruffy, the kind young people off on adventures all over the world carried with them. How he had always envied that! The freedom to wander and discover the *bri'ah*!

From his earliest childhood, he had never had the opportunity—nor, honestly, the desire—to stray from the straight-and-narrow path so clearly marked out for him by his parents and his rebbes. In his world, to go off that path, that *derech,* was deemed a tragedy worse than death, a rejection of all that was holy and good.

This idea had always kept him in place, a horse in harness pulling behind him the heavy load of his responsibilities and others' expectations as he struggled down the well-rutted trail that had been carved out thousands of years before by others just like him. His sons and his future sons-in-law were already in harness and would do the same.

She leaned against the wall, continuing her phone conversation. As she spoke, he drank in the lively timbre of her womanly voice, the way she stopped to laugh, going silent for a few moments until the sound broke out, catching up with the look in her eyes and the upturned corners of her mouth. How blue her eyes were! The color of a summer lake in the Catskills. Her mouth was generously curved with a soft, pillowed lower lip, which she gnawed at in a way that somehow touched him with its concentration and uncertainty.

When she put away the phone and returned to her seat, he smiled at her.

"You have a nickname for Chasya also? Icy?"

She smiled back. "Yes. That first time, we bonded over mango ice pops. I also love them." She looked down, squeezing the sides of her chair and dangling her feet off the ground. "How is the new arrangement working out?" When he didn't immediately answer, she gave him a furtive side-long glance.

"The new arrangement?"

"I understood that you don't need volunteers anymore. That you have made some other arrangement."

"Oh, that." He nodded, ashamed. "I'm not sure . . . not so good."

She raised her head, her heart leaping up in secret joy. "Really?"

"Yes, you know, we didn't like to take charity. People were so kind. You especially were coming, donating so much of your time to us. I understand you have your own business now?"

When had he been told about her business? That couldn't have been the reason he'd found someone else to care for the children, could it? "I was working with Rabbi Weintraub, helping to create a website and mailing list online for the yeshiva. That's what I do, marketing. It did well. And then other people heard about it and wanted the same thing, and now, *Baruch HaShem,* it's my job."

"How is it for you?"

"I'm lucky. I have a good income, flexible hours, and most of the time, I can work from my apartment. I have plenty of time to volunteer," she stressed. She paused hopefully, allowing him to take her up on it. To her bitter disappointment, he didn't. While she was mentally licking her wounds, the door opened. The doctors and nurse walked out. They gestured toward him to join them.

She wanted to join, too, desperate to hear the diagnosis, but she had no right. It wasn't her place. "Can I go back in?" she asked the nurse, who nodded.

"Thank you, Leah," Yaakov said, hurrying after the doctors. He, too, wished she could join him. He didn't want to hear this alone.

There were three doctors. One he recognized—the young intern who had admitted them to the emergency room—and two other important-looking men with graying hair. They introduced themselves as the head of pediatrics and gastroenterology.

"We've done a number of tests. We've ruled out her heart, her lungs, her liver, her kidneys. Her stomach is normal. Her blood tests are normal. Her pain isn't coming from her appendix. It's over her belly button. We understand she has been having this off and on for about a year?"

"Yes, but never this bad. We thought it was a virus. But she wasn't getting better."

"And the symptoms are always the same?"

He nodded. "Vomiting, stomachache . . ."

"Diarrhea, constipation?"

He racked his brain. "I don't think so."

The two doctors consulted with each other, including the intern in their conversation. Then they turned back to him. "It doesn't seem to be anything serious. For some reason, she seems to be feeling better now."

A weight the size of a bulldozer rolled off his heart. "What is wrong with her, Doctor?"

"We think it's an abdominal migraine. It's fairly common among children."

"Migraine? I thought that was when your head hurt. My late wife, she had migraines."

This information was greeted with knowing nods among the doctors. "There might be a genetic component, then. What we think your daughter has is similar, but in the stomach area. It presents with exactly the symptoms your daughter has and can be triggered by stress. We understand she lost her mother last year? Did anything happen recently that might have put her under stress again?"

He thought of his daughter's face as she sat up in bed and held out her arms to the young woman he had ripped from her life with no thought at all as to how it might affect her.

"Her babysitter hasn't . . . couldn't . . . be with her for the last two weeks."

"Well, yes, that could certainly have done it. Look, we will keep her for another day, do a few more tests. But in our opinion, the child is suffering from an overload of stress. If it continues, she might need counseling. In any case, did she have any attacks with this particular caretaker?"

"None at all," he realized.

"Can she, the caretaker, return to work now?"

"I . . . don't know."

"Well, if she is available, it would be best for the child. And if she has to leave, it should be done gradually, nothing abrupt that would remind her of losing her mother."

I am an idiot, he thought, appalled that he had not made that connection. Of course!

Chasya wrapped her arms around Leah, lying her head on her shoulder. "I missed you so much. Why did you go away?"

Leah felt tears come to her eyes. "I also missed you so much. Wasn't your new babysitter nice?"

"No one came to take care of us. Only Shaindele." The child's eyes filled with tears. "She's mean. She hits me and yells."

Leah sat up straight. So, the minute no one was watching, she thought she could get away with it again.

"Please come back, Leah!"

"I will talk to your tateh. But now, look what I have for you!" She opened the backpack and slipped out the big box with its cellophane wrapper. The child's eyes grew round with awe. Leah helped her ease the doll out of the box, unpinning her plastic body from the packing materials.

Chasya took off the head covering and patted the hair. Then she ran her hands over the eyes, opening and closing the lids. She unbuttoned the long-sleeved shirt. "She is a frum doll?"

Leah nodded, trying to keep a straight face. "She is very, very religious. She prays three times a day and only eats glatt kosher food from Herman's deli."

Chasya hugged the doll, kissing it. "It's so beautiful I should make a bracha," she said with a big smile.

Leah smiled, touched. "What bracha is that, Icy?"

"I could make a *shehechiyanu.*"

Oh, Leah thought, *the blessing for some new and wonderful experience, for firsts. Blessed are You, Lord our God, Ruler of the Universe Who has given us life, sustained us, and allowed us to reach this day.*

"Or I could say, 'Baruch she'bara brios naos b-olamo.'"

Blessed be He who made wonderful creatures in His world, Leah translated with tears in her eyes. She loved this so much about Judaism, that people stopped to express gratitude to God when they were filled with joy. How lovely that at such a young age this lovely little girl already grasped this. "Maybe I should make a bracha on you, Icy. The doll is pretty, but not as beautiful as my Icy."

The child threw off her covers. Clutching the doll, she crawled into Leah's lap, lying her head on her breast. They rocked together blissfully. It took Leah a while to realize Yaakov was standing in the doorway watching. He, too, had tears in his eyes.

Oh, hell, she thought, unable to wait another second. "If you need me to come back for a little while, I'd be happy to do it."

He nodded gratefully, trying to hide his bottomless relief, the embarrassing depth of his neediness for fear it might frighten her away. " But you have your business to run. I couldn't ask you to do it for nothing. I'd want to pay you at least something, but I don't know how much I can afford—"

"Please!" she interrupted him. Then, almost under her breath, "I miss the children so much."

There it was, out there. A stranger, a young woman, who loved his children. He looked at his little girl, curled up in Leah's arms, her pale face already getting some color. The feeling, he saw, was mutual.

He sat down abruptly, something breaking inside him, making it impossible for him to continue the pretense. "Everything is falling apart since you left," he told her frankly, forgetting his pride, all his reasons for hiding the truth. "If you could, it would be a tremendous help. The children would be so happy."

He said this in all sincerity, giving only a fleeting thought to Shaindele. She would be furious, but it could not be helped. She was a troubled young woman, he realized. She had crossed the forbidden boundary, lying and slandering this good person simply to get her own way. What possible benefit had she gotten from it? Her machinations had only served to make everything more difficult and unpleasant for everyone, especially herself. Even now, she was struggling to catch up with her schoolwork. And Chasya had wound up in the hospital. He found it hard to fathom her motivations. Her actions had been simply irrational and self-destructive. Then it suddenly struck him: Zissele, haggard and wild-eyed in her blue nightgown. A cold stab of icy fear pierced his heart.

17

As soon as Shaindele got to school, she was surrounded by girls. "We heard your sister is in the hospital, *HaShem yishmor!*"

"Your poor family," Freidel Halpern said, clutching Shaindele tightly by the shoulder and peering deeply into her eyes. "First your mother, now your sister. Such a *rachmones,* HaShem should watch over you."

Shaindele froze. Freidel with her perfect blond French braid and polished clean face, on whom even the horrible uniforms of Bais Yaakov looked chic, was two years ahead of her and the daughter of Rabbi Shlomo Halpern, principal of their school and a most respected and praised Torah scholar. Freidel was one of seven sisters and four brothers, all of whom were Boro Park royalty. Often, Shaindele dreamed of the handsome Halpern brothers. Just to be friends with Freidel raised your reputation. And to be pitied by her did the opposite. Everyone would now heap praise on Freidel for her kind concern, but the object of her pity would be labeled one more unfortunate suffering Godly disfavor and requiring prayers and rescue. There was no lower status.

"Who is watching your baby brother?" Freidel investigated.

"My bubbee," Shaindele answered, already feeling the flames from the upcoming inquisition licking her aching heart.

"Not the *baalas teshuva* with the wild red hair? We heard she practically lives in your house. A young unmarried woman. Is it true?" Friedel asked sweetly, her eyes narrowed.

"No, no, she's not there anymore," Shaindele breathed, grateful that at least about this she didn't have to lie. "She only came for a few weeks, and her hair was more blond than red—"

"We heard months," Friedel's sidekick, the plump Gnendel, interrupted relentlessly.

"A little while, to help out, so I didn't have to leave school so often. Reb Aryeh and Rebbitzen Basha recommended her. And my bubbee, Rebbitzen Fruma Esther Sonnenbaum, would be there with her. It was a *chesed* to help a *baalas teshuva*, everyone said."

"So, now she's gone?" Freidel demanded.

"Yes, yes, my tateh told her not to come back."

"Why is that?"

"Just something I saw. I told my tateh she wasn't *shayich*."

"What did you see?"

"It's . . . *loshon hara.*"

"Not if she is in the neighborhood and people need to be warned about her. It's a mitzvah," Freidel wheedled.

Shaindele hesitated, wanting to supply the goods Freidel wanted but knowing it was wrong. "She had a tattoo!" she finally burst out, unable to resist.

"*HaShem yishmor!*" all the girls gasped.

"On her wrist, two birds."

"And the little ones saw it?"

Shaindele sighed. "How could they help it? She was there all the time."

"And your tateh never noticed?"

"My tateh never met her. He was learning, and then in night school."

"I heard your tateh dropped out of kollel and is learning to be an accountant. That must be hard," piped up Gnendel, who was no genius and no beauty but did have four older brothers who were all in a top yeshiva in Lakewood.

"He hasn't dropped out of kollel!" Shaindele protested weakly.

"I think about your family often, Shaindele," Gnendel continued, ignoring the interruption. "My father says accounting is a very good profession for those who drop out of kollel. He himself tried it, but my mother wouldn't hear of it and made him go back to learning full-time. So sad, *nebbech*." Gnendel's father was now the head of his own kollel, a small, minor one to be sure, but still. Her future was assured.

Shaindele thought of her father. He could have gone in the same direction, and then her future, too, would have been safeguarded. But instead, he had started night school and was well on his way to dropping out. So, everyone was talking about it. First her mother, then her sister, now her father. Oh, the disgrace of it!

"Yes, such a *rachmones*," Freidel agreed, commiserating, her eyes alert for Shaindele's reaction.

"If you only knew what a wonderful Torah scholar my father is," Shaindele said defiantly. "He is still in kollel. But yes, it is a *rachmones*. Since my mama's *levayah* . . ."

Even Freidel Halpern shifted uncomfortably at this reminder of the poor, dead woman, as did Gnendel and all the other girls who had pushed together to watch this scene unfold.

"God bless you, Shaindele. You did the right thing to tell your father about the tattoo. It's a mitzvah. May HaShem help your family and watch over them," Freidel said piously, quickly changing the subject now that the ghost of that unfortunate woman had been invoked and was hovering over them. Needling an orphan was beyond the pale, even for her. Later, perhaps, when the air had cleared, she could corner Shaindele alone. She had lots more to say to the girl with her pretty pink cheeks and lively brown eyes, granddaughter of the great Admor Yitzchak Chaim Sonnenbaum. It never hurt to tear down possible rivals, but not when there were so many witnesses.

Shaindele nodded, sweat breaking out on her forehead in relief as she watched Freidel, Gnendel, and their friends turn to go.

She was weary when she got home, and worried about Chasya. She felt guilty about the child and the huge fight they had had just before her little sister got sick. But it wasn't her fault! Someone had to discipline that child. She'd come home from kindergarten with her white tights covered in mud.

"Who do you think does the laundry? You do it on purpose to aggravate me, you little *machashefa!*"

Chasya threw a shoe at her, which hit her right in the middle of her shoulder, muddying her newly ironed blue school blouse. Shaindele saw red. She didn't even remember how long or how hard she spanked her sister. She only stopped when Chasya began vomiting.

"Aach, all over the floor! You did it on purpose! I hate you!" she screamed at the child, who cowered in the corner, vomiting again until she fainted.

Shaindele thought at first that she was faking but then realized something was really wrong. She lifted the child in her arms and rushed into the bathroom, wetting her face with a washcloth. Slowly, Chasya opened her eyes. She was terrified, flailing, pushing out of her sister's arms. It was then Shaindele called her bubbee, who rushed over and took the child to the emergency room in a taxi.

"Is anybody home?" she called out.

She heard footsteps then saw her father standing in the living room, his arms folded tightly across his chest. "Shaindele," he said, his tone strangely blank. "Come sit down."

Her heart sank. "Where is Chasya?"

"Your sister is going to be fine. She is coming home tomorrow. Tell me, what happened yesterday before she got sick?"

She lowered her eyes. "Nothing. I don't know. She said her stomach hurt. She started vomiting. Then she passed out. I called Bubbee."

"She passed out?" This was news to him.

"I washed her face with cold water, and she opened her eyes. Then I called Bubbee."

"And that's all? Are you sure? Be very careful to tell me the truth, Shaindele, because you don't always do that."

She was shocked. Her father had never in his life spoken to her this way. She was rattled, mortified. "Tateh, of course I do!" she protested weakly.

"No, Shaindele, you don't."

"What do you mean?" Her heart began to beat with ferocious speed.

"You told me that Leah Howard has a tattoo."

She exhaled, confused. "But that's the truth!"

"I met her. She came to the hospital. She has nothing on her wrists. Nothing. Why would you lie to me?"

"I swear I'm telling the truth!"

"Don't swear, it's a sin! I also asked Chasya if she had drawn birds on her hands because Leah had birds on hers. I told her you said it was hard to wash off. Chasya said it wasn't true, that you just don't like Leah, so you make up lies about her. Is that true?" His voice was harsh.

She felt like a cornered animal, confused at how to escape this amalgam of lies and half-truths. "Of course Chasya said no. She hates me."

"Shaindele!"

"It's true! She blames me for what happened to Mameh." This wasn't true, but in her heart, Shaindele felt it could, maybe even should, be.

Yaakov unfolded his arms and sank into a chair. Wearily, he covered his eyes with his hands. "This has been so hard. For all of us. I know."

Shaindele sat down opposite him. She nodded, tears coming to her eyes.

"I don't know why you would make up such things about a pious *baalas teshuva* who has done nothing but help us. The doctors think your sister's illness is because she's upset. She was very close to Leah, and I asked her to leave because of a lie you told me."

"It wasn't a lie! And they are not so close!" Shaindele shouted in panic, afraid where this was going.

"Shaindele, she came to the hospital. I saw them together."

What could she say? She was silent, fidgeting with the fringes of a couch pillow.

"I've asked her to come back."

No! 'Tateh, you can't!"

"Why not? Why are you so against her?"

"You don't know . . . you don't understand . . . in school . . . the girls . . ."

"What?"

She hesitated, thinking about the consequences of telling her father the truth, that their family was under scrutiny because of her mother's death; that they were being examined and talked about. She would have to admit that she had told Freidel about Leah's tattoo, making herself look good at Leah's expense. All these things were hurtful and shameful.

Knowing her pious father, he would be outraged both at the girls in school and at her for wanting such friends. So she said nothing.

He exhaled deeply, resting his elbows on his knees and steepling his fingers under his chin. "Shaindele, let me tell you a story. There once was a very wealthy man who had a successful soap factory. This man, who considered himself very smart, had thrown off the yoke of the Torah, telling himself that there was no Law and no Judge. One day, he was walking around town when he met a rav. 'Rav,' he said arrogantly, 'your Torah is useless. It simply has no effect. Just look at all the nasty people in the Jewish community. I really can't understand why you continue to teach it.' This is what the rav answered: 'My Torah is perfect. It is your soap that is useless. If I were you, I would get out of the soap business.'

"'What are you talking about? My soap is the best on the market.'

"'Well, why don't we take a walk and discuss it further,' the rav suggested. Soon they passed a playground where children were in the sandbox covered in dirt.

"'Just look at those children!' the rav exclaimed. 'They are so messy and dirty. Obviously, your soap is useless.'

"'How can you say that? My soap is the greatest. It's just that those kids haven't used it yet.'

"'My Torah is also the greatest,' said the rav, 'but those who are mean-spirited have yet to use it.' Do you know what Rav Yermiyahu used to say in the Talmud? 'Even a non-Jew who keeps the Torah is to be regarded as equal to the high priest.'"

He saw Shaindele's eyes light up in confusion and anger. He ignored it. "As it is written in Isaiah: *Open the gates so that the righteous nation that keeps faithfulness may come in.* It does not say so that 'priests, Levites, and Israelites' may come in. Every person, even a non-Jew, who keeps the laws of the Torah is equal to the high priest."

He looked at his daughter, his eyes worried but compassionate. "I don't know what is going on with you, Shaindele, but if people are unkind to you, if they talk *loshon hara,* they are not God-fearing Jews who keep the Torah. You must be stronger than they are, my child. You must let our holy Torah guide you. It's not just words. It's a way of life. Do you know what it means to 'love your brother as you love yourself'? The more you give to your brother, the more you will love him. Leah Howard is a sincere person, a good person, who is a stranger in our midst. How many times have I told you that our Torah tells us we must always treat the stranger kindly? Can you do that, my child? Can you keep the Torah and make me and your mameh proud?"

She hung her head in shame, for the moment more afraid of his bad opinion than Freidel Halpern's. She knew it would not last.

18

The only cure for grief, someone had once told her, was love. Only now, reunited with the children, did Leah Howard understand what that meant.

She thought of the days following Joshua's death, the despair, almost suicidal, the spiritual emptiness. She remembered seeking out the young, trendy rabbi who had given the eulogy, sitting down next to him after the funeral at Josh's parents' home.

"Rabbi, tell me why God would do this."

He shifted uncomfortably, trying not to spill his coffee or unbalance the plate of quiche and smoked salmon in his lap. He shrugged. "This is the deck of cards you've been dealt. Now you have to deal with it."

She'd been flabbergasted, almost physically ill. If this was being Jewish, she wanted no part of it! With the same warmth and enthusiasm with which she had once sought out God, now she rejected Him, her bitterness a poison she guzzled, the only casualty herself. She wanted revenge! If He was there, she wanted no part of Him! He could do anything, and He had done this, taken away this precious person and along with him the life she had planned for and counted on. He had taken away the many years of life Joshua, her first love, had coming to him by right of having been born. And why? Why, why, why? The accident was so sudden, so senseless. If there was a God, why didn't His world make any sense?

She raged, rejecting the comfort of friends, resenting the commiseration of family—her own and Josh's. Then she fell into a deep depression. *If only I'd held out my hand to him sooner! If only we'd slid down together!* She wanted to be with him, wherever that was, instead of here, alive and alone. Every tiny reminder of their history together was like a bullet piercing her heart: the large oak tree in the park they had passed on their runs; the corner coffeehouse with its huge carrot-apple muffins and the smell of cappuccino; the familiar Chinese logo on a takeout food box in a garbage can.

She quit school and gave up their apartment, packing up carton after carton and shipping them to her mother. Then she and her cartons, which she had neglected to label, moved back into her old room.

Her mother, trying to be helpful and supportive, only made things worse. "There is a reason for everything." "He wouldn't want you to grieve forever." "It's time to move on." "Be strong." And worst of all: "I know how you feel."

Looking back though, it was probably her mother's absolute incompetence as comforter that drove her back into the world, if only to escape from her unbearable clichés. After four months of crying, gaining ten pounds from eating products that—whatever their catchy labels—were high-fructose corn syrup mixed with palm oil and chocolate, and the nonstop watching of daytime television soaps and talk shows, she finally cracked and did a web search for "master's degree in marketing programs New York City." The East Coast was as far away as she could get. Columbia, ranked number one, was ridiculously expensive. And who wanted to live near that dangerous campus up in Harlem anyway? She settled on the Zicklin School of Business at Baruch College, which was part of the City University of New York. She'd work for six months and save up money for tuition, then apply for federal student aid. The school had an excellent reputation, was reasonably priced, and after a year, she could claim New York State residency and be eligible for a reduction.

"Are you sure you're ready? How are you going to support yourself?" her mother heckled, suddenly changing her tune.

"I'll get a job."

"Rents in New York are sky-high!"

"I'll get a roommate."

"The weather is terrible."

"I'll buy boots."

And finally, "Why do you want to move so far away from me?"

"This is not about *you,* Mom. I'm not leaving *you.* I'm starting my own life. Be happy for me." Her chin quivered. "It's not easy to start over."

Her mother sighed, patting her on the shoulder and lighting up a cigarette.

Leah wrote to Laurel, her friend from Santa Clara who was at NYU. Luckily, she needed a roommate.

"What should I do with all your boxes, Lola?"

She had three choices: open up each one and go through the contents; never look inside again as long as she lived, saving them for her grandchildren; or throwing everything out. She chose door number three, taking only the same suitcase full of clothes she'd come with. "Just drop them off at Goodwill, Mom, okay?"

"And what should I do with the candlesticks from your grandparents?"

"Whatever you want," she said wearily.

The only other thing she took with her besides her clothes was Josh's old, ugly, orange-and-green backpack.

New York City was another world. Fast, dangerous, full of vitality, color, and movement. It made her dizzy. And it helped her forget. For two weeks, she pounded the pavement looking for work, trying to learn to walk and think like New Yorkers, who seemed always to be either rushing toward or away from something. But it was no use. She couldn't keep up, loitering to marvel at the skyscrapers like the out-of-town hick she knew she was.

After growing up in a place that had no sidewalks because everyone— except those convicted of DUI or vehicular manslaughter (and even *they* took buses)—drove, walking everywhere was a new experience. As for running again, she was afraid to, sure if she didn't get mugged, raped, or cut up and put into large plastic garbage bags, she would surely die of lung cancer from inhaling all the carcinogens in the polluted air. Laurel, who often ran along the Hudson River Greenway or did the East River run from the top of Central Park over RFK Bridge to Randall's Island and then to Queens and back, made faces at her and told her to stop being such a sissy. Finally, when she couldn't fit into any of her clothes and couldn't afford anything new, she laced up her New Balance cross-trainers. To her surprise, it was lovely: the fresh wind in her hair, the smiles and waves from the other runners, the beautiful New York City skyline. Taking up running again did something for her spirit, too, reconnecting her to the happiest time in her life.

She improved her résumés, dressed up, got her hair professionally cut and straightened, bought killer heels that got caught in subway gratings and escalators, and went to interview after interview. All of them went something like this:

Smile, handshake. Sit down in front of a desk. Smooth your hair and tug the sensible dark skirt of your good business suit over your knees. Try to look awake and enthusiastic even though you went to bed at midnight, and only fell asleep at 2:00 a.m. Look the interviewer in the eye. Try not to focus on their stubble / bad teeth / cleavage / horrible bra with the stitch lines showing through.

Tell me, Lola, what gets you up in the morning?

TRUTH: The alarm clock.

ANSWER: I'm just an optimistic person who envisions each day as a new beginning with new opportunities. I'm young, and I'm eager to use all the skills I've learned during my academic career. I was an intern at a top Silicon Valley company, Gardis, for two summers, and I have a letter of recommendation from the head of marketing. Gardis just went public.

What motivates you personally and professionally?

TRUTH: Terror of not having my share of the rent by the first of the month.

ANSWER: I'm motivated by the idea that I can be part of a successful team that is building something extraordinary like *(insert whatever the hell their business is selling to the gullible public)* that will take it to the top of the industry. I've read all about *(your product)* and your company online, and I was so impressed by how you've grown. I would love to be part of such a success story, and know I have so much to contribute. My first mentors at Santa Clara University always told us that *(blah, blah, blah, look up something inspiring on the internet and memorize it)*. I keep those words close to my heart.

That part always went so well. Everyone was smiling, flowing. And then came this:

Tell me, Lola, about one of your most challenging experiences and how you overcame it.

TRUTH: Watching my fiancé fall off a cliff. I will never, ever overcome it, but I tried being a couch potato and death by chocolate.

ANSWER: *[Coughing]* Excuse me. I need to use the restroom. *Quick exit. End of interview.*

Finally, running out of money, she went to a temp agency who only asked when she could start. She got placed as a receptionist in dusty Brooklyn offices, or as a typist in factories out in Staten Island. She stopped sending out résumés.

The apartment was on Walker Street, between Chinatown and Little Italy. It was tiny and faced a brick wall on one side and the flashing, seizure-inducing, neon lights of an all-night Mexican restaurant and bar on the other. They had two tiny bedrooms and basically a hall and a bathroom. The "kitchen" was a refrigerator from the fifties and a four-burner gas top with no oven, situated smack in the middle of the hallway.

Most of the time, the house was quiet. Laurel, beautiful, black, with an Angela Davis throwback Afro, was hardly ever home; when she wasn't slaving away on papers for her master's in communications (she was going to be the next Oprah Winfrey), she worked in a sports bar delivering beers to loud, obnoxious jocks. She made up for this by enjoying a busy and rather wild social life on the weekends in which she generously tried to include Lola (thinking of herself in the past, she couldn't think of herself as Leah, who was another creature altogether). But the one time Lola accepted her invitation, she found herself cornered by a horny, drunk, insistent bore at 3:00 a.m. in someone's dirty, crowded living room in Bushwick with no way of getting home without taking her life in her hands on the subway or paying some cabdriver a week's food money. So that was the end of that.

When she felt herself getting weepy and claustrophobic in the tiny apartment, she took long, solitary walks. It was from these forays into the city that she discovered that the loneliest you could ever be was walking down a crowded street in Manhattan teeming with people you didn't know, and with whom you would never exchange a single word. More than once, these ambles had wound up in dangerously ill-lit spaces where strange men leaned against buildings eyeing her as she passed by. In the best case, they sometimes called out ugly, sexual epithets; in the worst, they caused her to pull out her whistle and pepper spray (both of which she had purchased to scare away bears on California hiking trails). She'd only used the spray once. It turned her assailant's face a bright red and blinded him. Unfortunately, it dyed her fingers as well, providing incriminating evidence if the guy filed a complaint. Afraid of being arrested for assault, she dropped the spray and sprinted as fast as she could to the closest well-lit space where she could hail a cab. After that, she didn't go out after dark anymore.

She was actually getting used to living like a hermit when Laurel sat her down. The landlord wasn't renewing the lease. He had cousins coming in from China. They needed to move at the end of the month.

"But where will we go?" she pleaded, panic-stricken.

"Well, actually . . . I'm moving in with Jeremy."

"Jealous Jeremy? The one who follows you like a KGB agent? I thought you were going to take out a restraining order?"

"He's not so bad. We talked about it. He understands—"

"*Laurel?*"

"Okay, he has a beautiful two-bedroom in Murray Hill his parents are paying for."

"Remember that book by Tama Janowitz, *Slaves of New York,* about all those people selling themselves for an apartment in Manhattan?"

"I think we're in love."

Right. You and the apartment, she thought. So that was it. She had one month to find an apartment and a roommate in New York City at a rent she could afford. It was mission impossible. She couldn't even decipher the ads.

"What's 'Tr ld blk'?" she asked Laurel.

"Tree-lined block."

"And what's 'wbfp'?"

"Wood-burning fireplace. Look, I'll help you. We'll go together."

"May God bless you."

Their first foray was to the upper Upper West Side. The building was defaced by graffiti, and overturned garbage cans littered the sidewalks. Two very suspicious men loitered on the front steps. At their approach, one of them turned around and stared, then stood up and slowly moved closer. He had a heavily pockmarked face, a black leather jacket, and numerous gold chains. Laurel reached into her purse, clutching her pepper spray.

"Hi," he said. "You girls come to see the apartment?"

He turned out to be the agent. The apartment itself was about ten blocks away.

He led them to a car that looked exactly like the two dumpsters it was parked between, opening the door and gesturing them to get in. She looked at Laurel, who shrugged. So they got inside, sure they would both make the headlines of *The New York Post* the next morning when their bodies were found. But he actually pulled up to an attractive brownstone on a Tr ld blk. Unfortunately, it was soon apparent that the house had been converted into who knows how many college-student-abused apartments. The one he ushered them into made their present accommodations look like a suite in Trump Tower. When Laurel turned on the burner, an army of black cockroaches scurried out madly in every direction.

"*Aah!*" they screamed, clutching each other, disgusted.

"A spray can of Raid will take care of it." The agent shrugged. "The guy who lived here before was an animal-rights activist."

"How did he feel about rats and mice?" Laurel sputtered, lifting her feet up and checking behind her.

"Never complained," said the agent, avoiding the real question.

The bathroom was worse. Something crawling down the side of the toilet made the roaches look Disney-cute. And a single tiny room with no window at all was presented to them as the bedroom.

They flew down the steps, gasping for air.

"So, are you interested? This is going to go fast," the agent called after them warningly.

"Not as fast as we are," Laurel muttered, grabbing Lola's arm and sprinting away.

They tried a few more times. They saw apartments that had bunk beds, where you could choose top or bottom. They saw apartments in the bowels of buildings you were expected to share with the heater and boiler. They saw apartments with ceilings so low you had to be the height of a five-year-old or crouch the entire time you were inside.

"I may have to buy a tent and bunk in Central Park," Lola wailed.

"No. What you have to do is talk to Rafi," Laurel said decisively.

Rafi turned out to be a two hundred–pound former Israeli commando with a knitted skullcap on his almost bald head who was now studying film. Rafi lived with his roommate, another sabra who had been a paratrooper and was now studying graphic art. When he opened the door to their apartment in Brooklyn, she gasped. It was like something out of a movie set. A newly renovated duplex, it had a white spiral staircase, large picture windows, and a dream kitchen. But that wasn't the best part.

"Tell her how much rent you pay," Laurel playfully nudged Rafi, who grinned. "Go on. Tell her."

"Nothing. We pay nothing," he said, his grin widening.

She knew it. *Drugs,* she told herself. Except, that skullcap . . .

"This is what happened," said Rafi, sitting them down on the sofa and plying them with Israeli halva and Oreo cookies.

"I finish the army and want to go to college, but I don't have the *bagrut*—uhm, this means high school matriculation. So I ask, who will take me? Nobody in Israel takes me. But they tell me you can go to New York, and they even give you scholarship! So, I take out loan for plane, a few dollars extra maybe. Take subway from airport to school. Two months they give me a room. After that, they tell me, you on your own. I meet another Israeli. Same boat. So we go to Jewish neighborhoods, put up signs in Hebrew—'looking for cheap apartment.' We tape them up in kosher butcher shops, glatt kosher delis. Then, we are taping, and a Chassid comes over, reads sign, looks me up and down, looks Yossi up and down—Yossi makes me look small—and Chassid says, 'I got deal for you. Beautiful apartment, no rent, and $200 a week salary.' Me and Yossi we look at each other, then we ask him: 'Who do we have to kill?' But he says, 'I got a hundred apartments. You two go every month, collect rent.' So I'm thinking what if somebody don't pay? But he says, 'They see you and your friend, they pay. If not, you call me. I have friend, policeman. I take care of it. You don't beat anybody up. Against my religion.'"

That was two years ago, he said. Now he'd joined the union and was working as a cameraman, making good money. But he'd kept his first job and the apartment. Yossi was still his roommate. "How can I help?" he asked.

Laurel dramatically repeated all the horror stories of their apartment hunt. "We can't find anything!"

He thought about it for a few minutes. "I have good idea. One apartment leased to two girls. Last week, I went to wedding. Other girl, very nice, needs new roommate. Maybe she takes you?" he said to her.

"Where is it?" she asked.

"Crown Heights."

"Brooklyn. A lot of Chassidic Jews, blacks, and Asians," Laurel explained, chewing nervously on her lower lip.

Rafi raised his eyebrows in mock condemnation. "What's to be afraid? Crime rate 71 percent lower than rest of country. Safer than 72 percent other American cities. No murders, no kidnapping, no rapes. Better than Little Italy. Better than Manhattan."

"Is it a nice apartment?" she asked, convinced.

"Beautiful. I'll show you now. And rent, special rate. Landlord like Orthodox girls."

"But I'm not religious," she protested.

"But you are Jewish?"

"Barely."

"Good enough. Roommate is convert. Orthodox enough for both of you."

"Rafi, you take Lola right now to see that apartment before someone else snatches it up!" Laurel stood up. "But I have class. Are you okay going yourself?" Laurel asked her. Leah nodded happily. Rafi might be built like a tank, she thought, but she could clearly see he was as cuddly and sweet as a puppy.

The girl who opened the door was about her age, with coal-black hair and big, brown eyes. Seeing Rafi, she smiled, swinging the door open.

"Hi, mate. How are you cuttin'?"

"Hi, Dvorah. I bring you new roommate. Lola, nice Jewish girl from Santa Clara."

"Fair play, mate! Come in, come in!" She looked at her. "Isn't this apartment deadly! Are you as delira and excira about it as I am?"

"What language is that?" she asked her.

"Sorry, it's Irish. But don't eat the head off me!" Dvorah laughed, examining her red hair and freckles and blue eyes. "Excuse me gawkin', but out of the two of us, it's me who looks Jewish! You'd fit in anywhere in the Pale. That's Dublin."

Dvorah took her on a tour. The apartment was spotlessly clean, light, and airy. There were two generous bedrooms, a living room, and a real kitchen with whole appliances, a counter, and white cabinets. The bathroom gleamed with polished white tiles and smelled like perfumed soap.

"It's fantastic," she blurted out with unrestrained enthusiasm that she knew was like asking for a rent hike. She couldn't help herself. "But I'm on a very tight budget," she threw in too late, trying to mitigate the damage. "How much are you asking?"

"What were you paying Laurel?" Rafi asked her.

She told him.

He looked at Dvorah, and the two of them exchanged a smile and a nod.

"I think that might work. I'll talk to the landlord."

She put her arms around him as far as they would go and hugged. He seemed embarrassed, like a boy caught out by his friends picking flowers for his mother.

"Well, okay. I go now. You talk. I make shidduch. You decide if you marry. I have television show to film."

They sat across from each other at the kitchen table.

"Is he your fella?" Dvorah asked her.

"Who? Rafi? Oh no. We just met."

"Well, Jews . . . at least the ones in this place, they don't get physical with each other even when they are dating. So that hug . . ."

"Well, I guess I'm kind of a lapsed Jew. My grandparents were observant, but I was raised differently."

"I was raised pretty much a lapsed Catholic. I never gave much thought to God at all. All I ever wanted to do was get married and have children. Of course, I had a fella, a grand one. We met when we were fourteen years old and in high school. I had it all planned out. Even the color of my wedding dress—cream—and the kind of sleeves, sort of Princess Diana puffy-like. I finished high school and started uni, and so did he. Then one day, after six years together, he wasn't around anymore. Just like that. Went around to his place—I thought for sure he'd kicked the bucket—and found him in bed with some slag. But I say *Baruch HaShem* now."

She pressed her lips together to repress a smile at Dvorah's accent. Yiddish with an Irish brogue!

Dvorah laughed. "It's okay. I know it's funny. You should listen to me daven . . . Anyhow, I thought God is giving me a wake-up call. Just imagine if all my plans had come true and I'd walked down the aisle with that ejeet! What a life *that* would have been, huh? So, since nothing I planned was going to work out, I realized I'd try *not* having a plan. I dropped out of school, put on my backpack, and used my waitressing money to see the world. I was in Jordan, and someone told me that I should go scuba diving in Eilat. So I wound up in Israel. I took a job as a chambermaid at this hotel. There was another backpacker there, a Jewish girl from Argentina. And one weekend, when we got tired of the heat, we thumbed it to Jerusalem. I was gobsmacked. To see the place where Jesus walked! And there we are, at the Wailing Wall—although no one was wailing as I could see—and this woman covered up from head to toe asks me friend if she is Jewish, and she says yes. So she invites us both to spend Saturday at this women's seminary in the Old City. Me friend wasn't too keen on it, but I thought it was a deadly idea. I was delira and excira about it. One thing led to another, and I wound up stayin'. Two years later, I was dunking in the water and pronounced a Jew."

"I suppose you are leaving out a lot of that story."

Dvorah nodded, smiling. "Got a few days?"

"How did your parents take it?" she asked, trying to imagine her own mother's reaction if she came home and announced herself a Catholic, a Buddhist—or worse, an Orthodox Jew.

"Me oul fella was a bit of a holy Joe, and me oul dear had a puss on her. But they're okay with it now that they've met me fella. He's also a convert. He's a fine thing." She beamed, then her face turned serious. "Look, I'll be honest. I'm happy to take a chance, and you look nice. But

I think you should know what you're gettin' into. This apartment comes with lots of rules."

"Rules?"

"Like the kitchen. We have two sets of dishes, one for the meat and one for the milk. But since we only have one sink, you have to put down a plastic mat, one for the meat and one for the milk, before you put in the dishes and don't mix them up or we'll have to throw everything out and start over!"

"What if I bring my own dishes?"

She shook her head. "No good. It doesn't matter whose dishes they are; if you put them in the sink, you'll ruin the mats. So you've got to be careful. Also, you can't bring anything into the house that isn't kosher with a rabbi's stamp of approval. And not just any rabbi. There are symbols on food. I can show them to you. It's got to have the right symbol. And the meat has to come from only one butcher shop my rabbi says is kosher enough. Otherwise, you'll ruin the stove and oven and the dishes and the cutlery, and it will—"

"All have to be thrown out . . . I get it." Her head began to throb. "Anything else?"

"Well, on Saturdays and holidays, which start at sundown the night before, all the electric lights are on a timer. You can't turn them on or off."

"But in my room, I can do what I want, right?"

"Not exactly. The whole electrical system is on this same timer. Also, as a convert, I have to prove to my rabbis I am keeping the laws strictly. So if someone hears music coming out of this apartment on Friday night or Saturday, I'd be mortified and it would be murder to explain. But it's not only that, it would ruin the Shabbos for me. I hope you understand. It's nothing personal."

She looked up, feeling this lovely dream of an apartment evaporating like mist, slipping through her fingers, sending her back out into the graffiti-filled, garbage-strewn streets with their tiny, ugly apartments inhabited by aggressive armies of cockroaches, bunkbeds, and boilers. She panicked.

"It's fine, really, Dvorah. I . . . I always wanted to learn more about being Orthodox. I think God has sent me here," she improvised desperately. Many years later, thinking back to this crucial moment, she felt the hairs on her neck rise up, and a chill down her back.

19

After Chasya returned home, Leah returned to her old routine, coming in three days a week to help out at the Lehmans. But then she promised Icy something and had to come in on a day she usually didn't. And then Cheeky wasn't feeling well, so she also came the following day to check up on him. And then . . . and then . . . until finally, except for Friday and Saturday, she was there every single weekday afternoon.

It was surprising what a difference that made.

"If you want to change who you are, change what you want," Dvorah once told her.

Her fierce longing for children had been assuaged by an almost daily encounter with them. Day after day, week after week, that part of her that had been torn asunder by death, loss, and disappointments, leaving her decimated and festering, began to truly heal. Like her burned wrist, the healing had not left her less than she was or more, but different. She was amazed to find that the past, like a snake's skin, could be outworn, shed, and replaced, surprised that her capacity for joy had never been destroyed or even diminished. It had simply been in hibernation, ready to sprout wings and fly again given the right conditions.

Reunited with Yaakov Lehman's young children, Leah realized just how much the world she had lived in close to thirty-five years, the world she thought she knew, had been transformed, and she along with it. It did not happen suddenly one morning but was cumulative.

Oh, the transforming joy of those hours, minutes, seconds! The joy of buying food and cooking a meal for small hungry children, who ate with relish and asked for more. The joy of a child's innocent questions and the opportunity to share with them an answer that left them smiling and breathless. The joy of teaching a child a skill you had to share. And perhaps most of all, the joy of holding a small hand, supporting a small body close to your own, leading a vital, warm, responsive, innocent, sweet-smelling little person to a place that would make them happy—the green grass of a park, the enclosed spaces of a zoo. Oh, the pleasure of hearing their laughter, and laughing with them! It made her feel as if she had never before lived. All the things that she had previously desired—stylish clothes, a big apartment, tickets to the theater and the ballet—seemed faded and meaningless, an adult's puzzled memory of yearning for long-forgotten plastic Christmas toys.

Her days were divided between her computer, her phone calls to and from clients, and then the eager rush to the home of Yaakov Lehman and his children. Now, she went there every day at noon. And if someone got sick, she would sometimes come in the morning as well, bringing her computer with her so that Shaindele wouldn't have to take off time from school.

At first, the encounters with Shaindele had been strained. There was no doubt in her mind that whatever had transpired to separate her from Icy and Cheeky, the girl had played a major role. But now she was extremely polite, whether sincerely chastened or simply giving a good performance, Leah didn't know and frankly couldn't have cared less. It was enough that she seemed grateful—even seeking out Leah's advice about the housework, cooking, and childcare.

Chasya was blooming, her stomach pains a thing of the past. And little Cheeky was growing taller and more adorable every day. His silky blond hair—which, according to custom, would only be cut on his third birthday—hung down his back in a ponytail, long, pretty curls sneaking out of his embroidered velvet skullcap to cascade down his chubby cheeks. She was *addicted* to kissing him.

Gradually, the topsy-turvy mess that had greeted her that first day when, despite Shaindele's best efforts, she managed to slip through the front door inside Yaakov Lehman's home, was gone. Her daily housekeeping, combined with the more efficient efforts of Shaindele, had worked wonders, transforming the little apartment into a friendly, orderly space that was a pleasure to be in.

The more time she spent in Yaakov Lehman's house, the more she thought about him. Once, helping Shaindele to iron his white shirts (with the new steam iron she'd purchased, pretending it was only on loan), she found herself imagining his broad chest and long arms, the back of his white neck that would feel the smooth caress of the newly pressed collar. The first time she opened his closet door to put away his clothes, she had been dumbstruck by the Styrofoam head form with his wife's wig, feeling as if she'd glimpsed a ghost. She wondered why he kept it there and how he could stand looking at it day after day.

She tried to imagine how they had been together. Were they romantic? Did they bicker? Or did they have that warm, familiar relationship she'd glimpsed in other religious families, where husbands and wives kept a respectful distance from each other in public but in private joked and laughed and bared their hearts like any other couple. How close had they been? And would it ever be possible for Yaakov Lehman to allow another woman to take her place in his heart and in his home?

She knew he had been dating. Shaindele, who on all other matters was as tight-lipped as an MI5 agent, was uncharacteristically expansive on this particular topic. "One is a rich widow with a designer apartment, and the other one a divorcée who lives in Monsey. She comes from a very important family." The girl smiled (in delight or spite, Leah couldn't decide). "Every day, they are calling the shadchan, begging her to arrange the wedding."

"So, your father talks to you about such things?" Leah asked her sweetly, without batting an eyelash. Shaindele's face flushed deep red, and she turned away to sulk.

The little witch, Leah thought, shaking her head. *But why should this concern you?* she scolded herself. *Of course he will marry again. One of those women or their near equivalent. And why not? He would never consider someone like you, someone born impure from a mother who never went to the ritual baths, who had lived like a pagan most of her life, getting drunk in seedy bars and sleeping with strangers. No matter that it was from despair and not promiscuity and that it had only happened two or three times. A man like Yaakov, who was a virgin until he married his virgin bride, would never lower himself. Besides, he is not available,* she comforted herself, *a man with a chained heart, straitjacketed by his yearning for another woman, a woman no other will ever be able to match. A woman whose hair he keeps in his closet, like a shrine.*

And then one day, the wig and its ghostly white head were gone. She was flabbergasted, yearning to read all kinds of significance into its disappearance. But perhaps, after all, it meant nothing. Perhaps Shaindele had simply put it in her own closet for the future, or her mother-in-law had found a needy bride who could make use of it. But she could not help imagining that Yaakov himself had reached up and taken it down, finally banishing it from his life. And if so, what could that mean? The more she tried to force herself not to think about it, the more she was powerless to stop.

Cleaning up the bathroom, she sometimes touched his toothbrush, trying to imagine him standing there looking at himself in the mirror as he used it. What did he see? Had the improved condition of his children and the house eased the misery she had glimpsed in his eyes? Did he ever smile, the way he had smiled in his wedding photo, the way he had smiled at her when she talked to him about the children's nicknames? Did he ever think about her, she wondered, when he saw the newly washed dishes, the neatly stacked piles of folded laundry, the children in their clean pajamas, fresh from their bath? What did he say to Icy and Cheeky when they talked about her?

Gently, she tried to probe. "Icy, what did Tateh say when you showed him the picture you drew?" or "Did Tateh like the vegetable soup I made yesterday?"

Icy would stare at her and smile, then forget all about the question, asking for more chocolate cake or another ice cream cone.

He wasn't the kind of man she was used to. She didn't like beards as a rule. How would it feel against her skin, brushing against the smooth surface of her cheek and around her lips? she thought, shocking herself. More and more, she longed to see him again, to look into his sad, blue eyes and ask him all the questions that went through her head all day long. But they were like ships that passed in the night. He was gone long before she arrived, and she was out the door before he returned.

But lately, he had been leaving her little notes of thanks around the house. She found them addressed to her inside plain white business envelopes.

Dear Leah,
Chasya showed me the picture you drew together of the Bais Hamigdash. It is very wonderful! She seems so happy these days, and so well. The doctors are very pleased with her progress. I tell them she takes a secret medicine. We both know it's the Leah pill.
May God bless you for your chesed *to me and my children.*
Yaakov

Dear Leah,
The casserole was so tasty. It puts my mind at rest to know that my children are enjoying such nourishing, delicious food. Thank you! As for me, it is wonderful to have a warm meal when I return at night. May HaShem bless you for your kindness.
Respectfully,
Yaakov

She read them again and again, holding them close to her heart before refolding them and placing them carefully back into her pocket.

And then, one day, she found a pretty bouquet of red and white roses and pink chrysanthemums on the dining room table. There was another note:

Dear Leah,
Chasya told me about the flowers you took her to see in the park. She said, "Leah knows all the names of all the flowers." I thought you might like these. I have no idea what they are called.
Every blessing,
Yaakov

She cut off the ends of the stems and put them into a vase, then searched for an aspirin to add to the water to prolong their blooms. Oddly, she couldn't find any. Filling the vase with water, she placed it carefully on the dining room table, hoping they'd last through to the weekend anyway, brightening the family's Shabbos table.

But the following week, there was a box of chocolates with another note:

Dear Leah,
I meant for you to take the flowers home. Just a small thank-you for
all the wonderful things you do for my family. So this week, I am
trying again, but with candy. I hope you will take this with you and
not let my children finish it off.
             Every blessing, and may HaShem bless you for your chesed.
                                                            Yaakov

She smiled to herself. Of course the children had eaten most of it, but as instructed, she took the rest home. They were delicious praline fillings covered with glatt kosher Swiss chocolate, which tasted exactly like non-kosher Swiss chocolate. She tried to eat only one a day so she would have a reason to keep the box. It was suddenly important to her, that box, his notes. She wanted to write him back but couldn't think of what to say.

Despite all the time she had spent among Orthodox Jews, she was still not completely conversant with the norms. It was as if there existed a thick book filled with rules that were invisible except to them. She was constantly terrified of saying or doing something that was inadvertently out of bounds that might jeopardize her relationship with the children. It was unthinkable. But doing nothing was rude.

She took out a piece of pretty lilac notepaper and began to write.

Dear Rav Lehman (Yaakov),
Thank you very much for your thoughtful, kind gifts. I am happy to
be of help to you. Your wonderful children give me more than I
could ever give them. There is no need to buy me anything. Your
thanks are also not necessary, but I appreciate them deeply.
                        May God bless you and yours,
                                Your friend,
                                Leah Howard

Yaakov came home from school late, his head filled with principles of accounting, tax laws, and microeconomics. He had almost finished his second semester at Touro College. With the credits the college offered for his yeshiva studies, he had only another two semesters and summer school before being able to take the certification exam for his CPA. Then he would be able to get a well-paying job, enough to support his family and pay off his debts. He dreamed of the day when he would be able to pay his children's tuition without begging for a payment plan or a discount; when he would be able to respond generously when asked for charity.

Most of all, he dreamed of being able to meet the matchmakers' exorbitant demands concerning Shaindele's future husband, demands that included a monthly stipend for seven years so that the young man could continue learning. Such a groom would bring honor to his daughter and the Lehman family. Without such a dowry, he knew, his precious daughter would have to settle for a groom whose rosh yeshiva could give only a grudging recommendation and whose prospects would not include those achievements most admired in their world that took place solely between the four walls of the yeshiva.

The irony of finishing his degree and finding a full-time job, effectively locking him out of his beloved study hall forever, exiling him from the place where he felt most at home and where his true talents lay, in order to support another scholar was not lost on him. His heart ached to think of it. But there was nothing to be done. Like other balabatim, he would sneak in learning during precious moments stolen from the drudgery of his working life, on Shabbos and holidays and Sundays, or late in the evening or early in the morning. Meir would have to find a new *chavrusa*. That idea alone filled him with despair.

He tried not to think of it, to be grateful for all the mercies God had shown him over the past few months. Shaindele was in her room, studying. The kitchen was clean, all the dishes and pots put away. A place mat with a clean plate had been set for him at the table. A note on the refrigerator door told him there was fresh soup and a casserole he could heat up for his dinner. He popped his head in to say hello to his daughter, then checked his sleeping children. Their warm, still bodies and peaceful breathing felt like a blessing. He closed the door gently so as not to disturb them. In his bedroom, he hung up his jacket. It was only when he sat down on the bed to take off his shoes and put on his slippers that he noticed the pale, lilac envelope on his pillow. His heart skipped a beat before he even opened it. It was from her. It had to be.

He pried it open gently, trying not to damage the delicate stationery. His heart beating faster, he slipped the note carefully out of its envelope and began to read. A wave of disappointment came over him, wishing it had said more. But then again, perhaps not. She called herself his "friend." It was a generous term, a kind one. But what kind of friend was he to her? He took and took and took. There was no symmetry in their relationship. Her loving his children was just more of her giving and him taking. Perhaps the flowers and the candy had not been a good idea. They were silly, really, when you thought about it. Something goyishly romantic. How had he not realized that? But what else could he do?

For the first time since they had met at the hospital, Yaakov Lehman admitted to himself that he could not get Leah Howard out of his mind. Often, before he fell asleep at night, the color of her hair passed through his mind, or the shape of her cheek, or even her battered backpack with its sewn-on patches and labels from all over the world. She was young and unencumbered. Like Rachel, she, too, was beyond his reach.

The matchmakers had started calling again. Through his mother-in-law, he was constantly put under pressure to meet this one or that one or think again about those he had already met and rejected. Sooner or later, he supposed, he'd have to give in. He didn't expect to be alone the rest of his life. And in their world, to have the companionship of a woman meant marriage, no more and no less.

How he dreaded getting on that merry-go-round again! The entry into the homes of strangers, the confrontation with the anxious, pleading eyes of desperate women, the vulnerability of putting himself on the line for rejection! Something inside him rebelled against it. Always, always he had done what was expected of him. He had followed the laws, written and unwritten, of his world. He thought of Zissele. If only he had not! If only he had been stronger, more assertive, done for her what she needed instead of what was expected. If only he hadn't given in to social pressure! He had failed her, failed his children. And now he was being pressured again.

He picked up Leah Howard's letter. Could there be something between the lines? He had to find out. He owed her that. He owed himself that.

20

"How would you like it if we invited Leah to come for Shabbos?" Yaakov asked Chasya one morning as he was helping her get ready for kindergarten.

The child looked up at him with her big, soft brown eyes, her small lips quivering. "Oh, Tateh!" she cried. "Can we?"

Shaindele stopped combing Mordechai Shalom's hair, her hands going numb. "Tateh, you can't mean it!"

He turned to his daughter, his nostrils flaring. "And why not? She does so much for us, and we give nothing back. Is that *hakoras tovah*?"

Shaindele bit her lip, devastated at his anger, but even more so at his total incomprehension of what a truly terrible idea this was in all ways. *Hakoras tovah*—gratitude! And what about his gratitude to her, his own daughter? How could he put her in such a position?

Not only was Leah Howard an unmarried girl and he, her father, a widower, but Leah Howard was also a *baalas teshuva* born into a nonreligious home, who had spent her whole life up to now involved in all kinds of *pritzus*; a woman with wild, curly, red-gold hair that although tied back neatly in a ponytail still hung halfway down her back; a woman who every time she opened her mouth made it clear she was not one of them.

While she correctly and piously used expressions like *Baruch HaShem,* she couldn't get the *ch* sound right. It came out like a *k* or an *h* instead of the guttural sound akin to clearing the back of your throat, an instant giveaway someone was a hopeless outsider. She said *humash* instead of *chumash.* She would say, *staying at their house,* instead of *staying by them.* She would say she was *studying,* instead of *learning,* going to *classes* instead of going to *shiurim.* And once, when she wanted to *bentsch,* she said she needed to say *grace after meals.* She might as well be a shiksa! Even English she didn't talk good! More than once, Shaindele had caught her saying in front of the children words like *cool,* or *oh, man,* or *dude,* or *gosh.* Shaindele had no idea what these words could mean but suspected it was *nivul peh.*

Inviting Leah Howard to join the family for Shabbos was like putting up a neon billboard on Eighteenth Avenue announcing that this woman, this outsider, was not just a piously motivated do-gooder who came in on weekdays to do the chores and babysit but was a friend, practically a member of their family!

In her mind's eye, she saw the perfect face of Freidel Halpern, her blue eyes wide with shock and condemnation. She contemplated the speed with which the word would go out from Freidel to Freidel's brothers and then to her distinguished parents, spreading like contagion to all the matchmakers, killing off any chance she might have had in finding the wonderful shidduch of her dreams. Instead of a handsome, distinguished scholar, she'd be offered plain, short, overweight men, middling learners from nondescript families. As for the Halpern brothers, she might as well yearn for a trip to the moon.

Even without Leah Howard, their family had image problems. Only the family's impressive *yichus* from both sides had protected them so far from the natural fallout over her mother's mysterious death. But even now, she could feel the slow leak of air from the puncture holes in that life raft keeping them afloat, destabilizing their position moment by moment. Now, instead of doing all in his power to keep the boat steady and steer them toward a safe shore, her father had inexplicably decided to stand up and jump up and down by inviting Leah Howard for Shabbos, deliberately trying to drown them all!

"Tateh, you don't understand," she pleaded.

"Didn't we have this talk, Shaindele? I'm surprised at you." His eyes were hot with anger and disappointment.

Shaindele quickly looked down, tears of helpless fury overflowing and racing down her cheeks. She wiped them away as fast as she could.

He was overcome by misery. He'd allowed himself to believe she'd had a change of heart, sincerely repenting her slanderous lies and gossip-mongering. But now he saw clearly that was simply wishful thinking. Her obedience had been nothing more than a fear of punishment.

Of all the things that were most important to Yaakov Lehman, raising his children to observe not only the letter but the spirit of the Torah's laws was supreme. The ability to instill good values, honesty, benevolence, and loving-kindness in the souls entrusted to his care by his beloved Creator was a sacred obligation and his supreme duty, even more than Torah learning. After all, one learned in order to do.

As he looked at his furious, ungrateful child, weeping out of snobbery because her father wanted to show appreciation to a good woman who had worked so hard to help their unfortunate family in their hour of need, he felt his heart sink with an acute sense of failure.

"Shaindele, Shaindele." He shook his head slowly, his eyes moist and downcast. "After our last talk, I was so encouraged. You've been so kind, so helpful, I felt sure it meant that you had uprooted the causeless hatred toward Leah from your heart. But I see now that is not yet true. I take the blame entirely upon myself. I have failed you and your mother. It was up to me to bring you up to be the fine person your mother and I both saw in you from such a young age. What has happened to my kind, loving Shaindele?" He looked at her tenderly, sorrow and disappointment etched in his mouth and eyes.

It pierced her heart. A week ago, even a day ago, she would have melted with contrition under such a look, her heart aching, doing whatever he asked of her. But now, she simply didn't care. She longed to open her mouth and spit out the truth in his face: how he, in his recklessness, was endangering her entire future! But for Shaindele Lehman to do such a thing would be like a lamb suddenly roaring like a lion. Raised to respect her parents the way she respected God Himself, the words stuck in her throat. Instead, silent tears of frustration rolled down her cheeks.

Stricken and helpless, Yaakov reached out to smooth back the shiny, dark hair on his daughter's head. She flinched. He drew back his hand, almost feeling his heart shrivel like a grape left out in the sun, his warm sympathy evaporating.

"Do you remember how hard it was right after Mameh died? How you had to stay home from school? How the house was upside down, the children crying day and night?" His voice was hard and demanding.

She nodded unhappily.

"Can't you see what a difference she's made to us all?"

Shaindele said nothing. She finished combing her brother's hair, clipping his skullcap firmly to his head. "Come," she told the child, turning away from her father, "I'll get your bag. I'll take you to cheder."

"Please, Shaindele," Yaakov called after her.

She ignored him, hurrying down the stairs with her brother in her arms, away from his words and his voice, which were swallowed up by the roar of fury in her ears and the noise of her shoes slamming against the pavement. While her heart was full to bursting, her lips, dammed by law, custom, tradition, and respect, could let nothing out. Only her mind and thoughts were free. No one could command them.

How could he be so stupid? she thought. Her intelligent, kind father whom she had always respected for his wisdom and piety, who always knew exactly the right thing to do? What was wrong with him?

Now she knew the truth. She had lost both mother *and father*, she mourned. She was all alone, with no one to look out for her interests. Her mind worked feverishly to find a solution. And then, instinctively, she understood exactly what to do.

It was late June. The heat from the sun pouring into her classroom in the old school building was stifling. Nechamke Solomon was sitting by an open window, the sun baking her head. When she got up to go to the blackboard, she stumbled, then fainted. The class was in an uproar. Without thinking twice, Shaindele also got up, put one foot in front of the other, then gracefully fell to the floor as well.

She felt the school nurse patting her face. Someone else put an arm around her back and lifted her up, placing a glass of ice water in her hand and sticking a straw into her mouth.

"We're going to call your father to come pick you up," Mrs. Erlich, Rabbi Halpern's secretary, told her as she lay in the nurse's office on a cot next to Nechamke.

"*No!* He's . . . he's . . . far away. In Lakewood. Call my grandmother."

Fruma Esther came as fast as her orthopedic shoes would carry her.

"What's this, Shaindele?"

She sat up. Her bubbee wasn't the kind of cuddly grandmother that sided with children against their parents. Sensing just a whiff of rebellion or disrespect, her grandmother could be harsher and more punishing than her father and all her teachers rolled into one. And once her grandmother got it into her head that a child was lacking in character and piety, she never forgot, targeting the offender with countless admonitions and lectures and maybe worse . . . *Besser an erlecher patsh fin a faltshen kuss.* Better an honest slap than a deceitful kiss, she would often say. Still, this was an emergency.

"Bubbee, I need to talk . . . to tell you . . ."

She glanced up at Mrs. Erlich, then catching hold of her grandmother's eye, gave a tiny, meaningful shake of her head before lying back down.

Fruma Esther was no dummy.

"*Mertsishem,* she'll be fine. I'll take care of her, Rebbitzen Erlich."

The woman reluctantly backed off. "*A zai gezunt.*"

Checking that Nechamke was really asleep, Shaindele whispered to her grandmother the entire, sordid tale of the Shabbos invitation to Leah Howard.

Fruma Esther patted the white, soft hand of her granddaughter, who looked so much like her Zissele. "*Chas v'shalom!*" she said firmly. "*Bli neder, mein kindt,* your bubbee will take care of this."

Shaindele felt an enormous weight roll off her heart. She sat up, then stood.

"Where are you going, child?"

"*Baruch HaShem,* I'm feeling better now. I'll go back to class."

"Are you sure, *shefelah*?"

She leaned down and kissed the old woman's worn cheek, etched with a half century of wrinkles, one for every challenge and every trouble she had faced down in battle.

"I feel fine now."

It wasn't easy getting old, Fruma Esther told herself as she sat up in bed the next morning, massaging her knees. Every day, something else that had been working just fine stopped. Now, it was her knees. First it was the back of them, the hamstrings pulling her calves like vicious hoodlums; and then it was the front, the kneecap aching with every step. She rubbed them with Bengay. The odor made her feel faint.

She got up, getting dressed slowly, every movement accompanied by aches and pains. And when she stretched her arms over her shoulders to pull up her zipper, she felt her back give out.

"*Oy, oy, oy!*" she moaned, falling back heavily on the bed. Now she had done it, she couldn't move. She tried to talk herself out of it.

"Who will help your Zissele's family if you don't get involved? You have to get up! You have to talk some sense into your *choson* before he finishes off the family's reputation! Before poor Shaindele's chances for a good shidduch are ruined!"

Her back listened but was not impressed. It stayed put, reacting to any attempt on her part to get up with a punishing swiftness that took her breath away.

Now she was sorry she didn't have one of those little telephones people kept close to them. Yaakov, too, was without one. For some reason she didn't fully understand, the rabbis were against the little phones. Something about pritzus. But now she heard, they had kosher phones. How easy it would have been to simply dial his number and have him pick up! She could tell him everything without moving more than her fingertips!

She lay there helplessly, hoping it would pass, imagining the conversation.

"My dear Yaakov," she would begin warmly. "I know how hard it has been for you and how you are struggling since losing my Zissele; God should watch over us and save us from more pain. *Chas v'chalilah,* I don't want to criticize, but if there was a snake crawling under the kitchen table while you and the children sat around singing Shabbos songs, would you want me to control myself from warning you? There is a snake in your home, a young woman that has wormed her way into your lives. Who is she? What do you know about her, really? Like a stray cat, she comes into our neighborhood. Who were her parents, her grandparents? So now, she is religious. She wears long skirts and shirts that cover her elbows and button under her chin. But when an alley cat wants something, it can be clever. It can come into your home and pretend to be a house cat, but it will never escape its nature. Who knows what dangerous things she is bringing into your home, into the minds of your children when you are not there, things picked up roaming the streets? You should listen to Shaindele, who hears what goes on. She is sick with worry, your Shaindele. She fainted in school . . ."

Well, maybe not that part about the alley cat. Yaakov was such a tzaddik. He would immediately complain it was *loshon hara,* which of course it was, but for a worthy cause! One had to protect the family. There was no higher value than that.

"People are talking," she would tell him, even though, strictly speaking, that wasn't exactly true. But she imagined that it wasn't far from the truth! How could they not talk? A young woman, newly religious, a young widower, and she with those ridiculous long, red curls like Esau! She was practically living in his house. As long as it remained a business relationship, the tongues would wag more slowly. But the moment she started coming over for intimate Shabbos meals like one of the family, any shackles on their tongues and their imaginations would be set free.

The thought so alarmed her that she wrenched her body into a sitting position. The result was agonizing. But strangely, the pain seemed to exhaust itself, lifting and taking some time off.

"*Baruch HaShem.*" She sighed, slowly bending down to tie her shoelaces. Adjusting her wig, she hurried out the door.

Outside, the sun bore down on her, casting its blazing clarity over her plans. Where was she going? she thought. To the kollel? Was that what the family needed, a public confrontation in front of all the students? The very thought horrified her. She could try to talk to Rav Alter again. But honestly, he hadn't been much help the last time she went that route. True, Yaakov had agreed to start the shidduch process, but look what had come of it! Nothing. And then, just as she was turning the corner, another thought struck her. Taking a slight detour, she headed toward her friend Rebbitzen Basha.

She pressed the intercom.

"Yes," a fuzzy voice came through.

"Basha, it's me, Fruma Esther. Can I come up?"

"Such a question!" The buzzer immediately sounded.

She pushed open the door and stood at the foot of the steps wondering how her old friend still navigated them. Sighing, she held on to the bannister, pulling herself up. She was breathless when she reached the door, which was already open, Rebbitzen Basha standing there with a half smile on her face. The two friends embraced.

"Such a shlep!" Fruma Esther wheezed. "How do you manage without an elevator?"

"*B'li ayin hara, Baruch HaShem,* my feet are still good!"

"*Kaynahora.*"

"Come *zits sich,* Fruma Esther."

"Thank you. So hot. I'm shmoiling!"

"I'll bring you a cold drink."

"I'm taking up your time?"

"A pleasure to give you my time," Basha called from the kitchen, soon returning with a pitcher of iced tea and a plate of rugelach.

Fruma took a drink gratefully, then bit off a piece of rugelach. "You made these yourself, or it's from the bakery?"

"What bakery? I'm cooking and baking like a meshuggener."

Fruma Esther suddenly looked around. The house was in an uproar, boxes of food and good china piled up everywhere.

"*B'ezras HaShem,* the *vort* for my grandson is tomorrow."

Heshy's engagement party! "I forgot all about it! Mazel tov! Such a lovely girl. I know it wasn't easy, but you see it all turned out for the best for Heshy."

The two women sighed, nodding. Heshy, born with a clubfoot, still had a slight limp. The girl, too, had a bit of a problem with cross-eyes. But the two families' great-grandparents were both from the same little town in Hungary, and the girl's father was a wine merchant who was taking Heshy into the business as soon as he finished a few years of learning.

Besides, she was a sweet, modest girl who was grateful to Heshy and adored him. The engagement had been joyful for both sides.

"God be blessed. And what's the good news about your *choson*?"

Fruma Esther shrugged. "The women are willing. But he's not."

"Be patient, Fruma. A man doesn't get over a Zissele like yours overnight."

She nodded resignedly.

"So how is the family managing?"

"*Baruch HaShem.* Shaindele helps. I help when I can."

Basha pressed. "But all the laundry, the cooking, the cleaning, and the afternoons when Shaindele is in school and the children are home?"

"That girl, the *baalas teshuva* you sent, that Leah, is there all the time."

Basha smiled uncertainly. From her expression, it didn't look as if Fruma Esther was there to shower her with thanks. "A lovely girl. Such *chesed*!" she tried.

Fruma Esther sat up straighter. "It's a problem."

"What could be a problem? Someone does such a *chesed,* that's a problem?"

"The children are very attached to her. And now Yaakov wants to invite her for Shabbos."

Basha leaned back. She drummed her fingers on the table. "Do you know if they have an understanding?"

Fruma Esther, for whom such a thing was light-years worse than what she had been contemplating and trying to prevent, suddenly felt her heart miss a beat. Of course! The Shabbos invitation was just the beginning! How had she not seen this coming? "*Chas v'chalilah!*"

"Fruma Esther, I'm surprised at you! Aren't you always the one who told me to have *bitachon?* When my Heshy couldn't find a shidduch, weren't you the one to say I should be open and let HaShem work his miracles? You think we wanted a cross-eyed *kallah*? But this was God's will."

Blood rushed to Fruma Esther's face. "Cross-eyed but frum! From a frum family! This Leah, who are her people?"

"She lived with us for a few months. She is a lovely, sincerely frum girl."

"You didn't answer my question."

"You shouldn't hold it against her. It's to her credit she found the right *derech* with no help from her family."

"What do you know about them?"

Basha hesitated. "I am not comfortable talking about Leah. You need to ask her, or Yaakov needs to ask her. All I can tell you is she is a very warmhearted, fine girl filled with love and *yiras shomayim*."

"That is today. But yesterday? She ate *terefah* and slept with men, and ate on Yom Kippur, and dressed like a *prutza,* just like the rest of her family, whoever they are. And who will swear that she won't get tired of all the laws and restrictions and backslide, return to her old ways? Would you let your son marry her?"

Basha was silent, her face troubled. "We are all *baale teshuva,* Fruma Esther. Every one of us backslides. Can anyone swear to you that someone born into an important, frum family with lots of *yichus* won't go off the *derech*? Do I have to mention names? There is not a frum family in Boro Park that has not suffered. And they did everything they thought was right from the moment the child was born. Do you know how many young people in Boro Park died from drug overdoses this year alone?"

"What are you telling me?"

"Sixty-one. I know because Reb Aryeh is involved in setting up a counseling center. Leah Howard ran away from all that. She came here because she decided on her own that this is a better *derech.* The life she wants."

"You are involved in *kiruv,* Bashe. Your house is always filled with girls like Leah. You're used to it. But our family is not. Our children are more sheltered. We don't want to open the door to such things, to let the *gashmius* and the *tumah* into our lives."

"It seems to me that the only thing that Leah Howard has brought into your lives is love and *chesed,*" Bashe said mildly, standing up. "Did you forget how sick your Chasya was? How Leah dropped everything and ran down to the hospital to be with her? Is she better now?"

Fruma Esther fidgeted. "*Baruch HaShem,*" she admitted, squirming.

Basha sat down. She extended her hand to her old friend, cupping her gnarled fingers. "It's not the life you planned."

Fruma Esther shook her head.

"But it's the life HaShem has given you."

"I was going to ask you to talk to Leah."

Basha took back her hand. "About what?"

"Tell her it's not good. Not for her, not for Yaakov, not for the children. Tell her not to come for Shabbos, even if he invites her. And certainly not for anything more than that."

"Why are you so against her, Fruma Esther? You are a kind woman, a fair person, a great rebbitzen. This goes against our Torah. As it is written: *Where a penitent stands, even angels cannot stand.* Our patriarch, Avraham, came from a family of idol worshippers. And Yaakov married the daughters of Laban, an evil man, a schemer and an idol worshipper. Did our forefather Yaakov hold that against our matriarchs Leah and Rachel? You can't help what your family is, but you can overcome it. Leah and Rachel were our matriarchs, the origin of the Jewish people. And all of us are descendants of slaves. How can any of us look down our noses at any Jew, any convert?"

"It's because of Shaindele," Fruma Esther blurted out. "Her shidduch chances."

"Shaindele is old enough for a shidduch? Already?"

"She's sixteen soon."

"Oy, I still think of her as a little girl tagging after Zissele with her doll carriage." Tears sprang to her eyes.

Fruma Esther's eyes also misted. "She fainted in school yesterday. She is terrified the family name will be ruined and her shidduch choices along with it. Her mother isn't here to protect her, and her father is so burdened. I have to do right by her."

Nothing else needed to be said. Despite everything Rebbitzen Basha believed, the laws of the shidduch were inexorable. If Yaakov Lehman dropped out of kollel and married a *baalas teshuva* from an unknown family, there was no question it would seriously impact the kind of shidduch his daughter Shaindele could expect. It would be held against her. This would also be true of her older brothers, who would be looking for shidduchim soon, but less so; men were always more valuable than women. The two grandmothers looked at each other. Who were they to fight the world?

"I don't know how, but I'll talk to her," Rebbitzen Basha said, feeling suddenly tired and very old.

"*Baruch HaShem*," Fruma Esther murmured, clasping her hands.

"*HaShem Yishmor*," Rebbitzen Basha replied, shaking her head, devastated.

Dear Leah,
We wish to invite you to join us for a Shabbos meal on this Friday
night so that we may serve you for a change! Please say yes. Chasya
is already jumping up and down with happiness at the thought.

Every blessing,
Yaakov

Leah held the invitation in her hand and read it again. How could he have known that it was just for this she'd been longing? Religious life was lived as a series of doorways all leading toward the grand salon that was Shabbos.

All during the week, people shopped, cooked, and cleaned with the ultimate goal of Shabbos always in mind; a day when the food would be the finest, the wine the sweetest, the conversation the most interesting. To be involved with a religious family during the week and denied the opportunity to enter with them into the joy of Shabbos was a true deprivation. While various people in the neighborhood had been kind enough to invite her, she was always the guest and a stranger, except when dining with Rebbitizin Basha. As a single person, it wasn't socially acceptable for her to make her own Shabbos dinners and invite guests. It would be lovely to share Shabbos with the family she felt so close to already.

She remembered her very first Shabbos experience.

Two weeks after moving in with Dvorah, her new roommate knocked on her door. "How would you like to come to Friday night dinner with me and some friends? They're lovely folks, and we always have a whale of a time."

It had been very difficult being stuck in a house and a neighborhood where from Friday night until Saturday sundown—more or less twenty-five hours—you couldn't drive, use public transportation, write, use electronics of any kind—including cell phones, computers, televisions, or radios—and even had to avoid opening a refrigerator if the automatic light hadn't been turned off! While she'd managed to sneak out to the subway early Saturday mornings, spending the day far from all these restrictions, she felt unsafe doing that on Friday nights. Stuck in the house with nothing to do but read, it was extremely boring.

So, despite her bitterness about being forced to participate in yet another religious ritual, she answered, "Why not?"

Dvorah smiled. "A few things. You'll feel more comfortable if you wear a dress or a skirt and blouse, something with sleeves that isn't too mini or too body-con."

"There's a dress code?"

She shrugged. "It's a religious experience, and modesty makes it more spiritual for everyone. You want a man to look into your eyes, not at your cleavage, when he's talking about God."

She laughed. "Right. Gotcha."

She sat in the living room watching Dvorah light candles. First Dvorah made a circular motion with her hands over the tiny, flickering flames, then pressing her eyelids closed with her fingertips, she just stood there swaying silently for what seemed like forever. When she finally recited the blessing with her lilting Irish-accented Hebrew, an inexplicable twinge of sadness filled Lola's heart as she remembered the tall, silver candlesticks wrapped up in tissue paper languishing in her mother's bedroom closet.

"Gut Shabbos," Dvorah said, turning to her with a bright smile.

"Why were you standing there swaying like that for such a long time?"

"We believe that on Friday night, a special conduit opens up in heaven for women. During the time a woman lights candles, her prayers go straight up to heaven. So I go down the list: I pray that my father's diabetes shouldn't get any worse, and my mother's sciatica shouldn't act up. I pray that my brothers, Tim and Jimmy, shouldn't get into any accidents when they drink too much, and that my niece doesn't get bullied at school for being chubby. I pray that my boyfriend succeeds at his business, and that this week, I'll succeed in inching a little closer to God. And I pray for you."

She was startled. "Me?"

Dvorah nodded. "That you find some peace and happiness."

She turned away, both touched and annoyed, wiping her suddenly damp eyes with the back of her hand.

It was a twenty-minute walk through streets crowded with Chassidim, old men and little boys and every age in between, their glossy black satin coats shimmering, their shirts a dazzling white, their beards large and bushy or short and clipped. "Gut Shabbos, gut Shabbos," they greeted each other, nodding, smiling.

"Does everyone in this neighborhood know each other?" she asked Dvorah.

"No, silly. That's just what you say when you see another Jew on Friday night."

"But they don't say it to us."

"That's because they aren't supposed to be looking at women."

"It makes me feel invisible."

Dvorah shrugged. "And how do you feel as a woman when you walk down certain streets in Manhattan by yourself and strange men call out 'greetings' to you?"

Two points for Dvorah.

Their hosts lived in a brownstone on the third floor. "We can wait for the Shabbos elevator, or we can walk up."

"Shabbos elevator?"

"It runs on a timer, automatically stopping on every floor, so you're allowed to use it."

"It's okay. I'll climb up with you."

A tall woman wearing an elaborate headdress and a long, elegant housecoat greeted them. She hugged Dvorah and then extended a smooth, white hand to Lola. It was adorned with gold jewelry and expensive rings.

The woman noticed her staring. "One advantage of being married to a religious man. Every holiday, he is obligated to buy me a piece of jewelry. It adds up."

"What a lovely idea!"

"Believe me, we have it coming to us!" She laughed, ushering them both in.

It was a large apartment with an enormous dining room table set for at least twenty.

"I see you are all set up. I came early especially to help you, Rebbitzen," Dvorah chided.

"The advantage of having ten children, four of them teenage girls, is not having to do anything for Shabbos. Why don't you and your friend sit down in the living room and relax?"

Two young, smiling girls peeked out of the kitchen. They were such pretty girls, with thick, long, shining braids and faces scrubbed pink. They wore mid-calf skirts and wrist-length blouses. A few moments later, a third girl came in carrying a baby.

"This is our youngest addition, Zevulun Aaron," their hostess said.

He was like one of those cherubs floating on the ceilings of Venetian palaces, she thought, amazed. The girl who carried him tickled him and he laughed.

"Should I lay him down, Mameh?"

"Better not. I don't want he should fall asleep before kiddush." She turned to them, apologizing. "It will be a while yet until the men come home from shul. The service is long, and then they schmooze. I would offer you something, but we don't eat before kiddush."

"That's fine! Please, it's so good of you to invite me!" Lola said sincerely.

"How long have you been a convert?" the rebbitzen asked.

Dvorah leaned forward on the couch. "Actually, Lola is Jewish by birth. She's my roommate."

"Ah. I see. So this isn't your first Shabbos?"

She hesitated. "Actually, my boyfriend and I were very interested in Judaism. We went to classes and even a few Shabbos dinners organized by Jewish campus organizations."

"Which college?" she asked.

"Santa Clara."

"We say *S Clara* and *Simcha Monica*." She smiled. Before she could digest the strangeness of that, their hostess quickly continued. "And are you both—you and your boyfriend—still interested in Orthodoxy?"

She shifted uncomfortably. "Not really."

"May I ask why?"

She looked down, feeling a twinge of resentment. This was starting to feel like an inquisition. In revenge, she decided on total honesty. "I'm just not sure I believe in God at all anymore."

There was a hushed silence. "But you did, once?"

"Yeah, maybe. I don't know. When I was a little kid. I hope you're not offended."

"Not at all, personally. I just feel sad. To have no connection with your Creator. How lonely." The rebbitzen shook her head. "I hope you won't mind my asking, but what happened?"

"My boyfriend—my fiancé—died in a completely stupid hiking accident a few months before our wedding. That was last year."

She heard a small, shocked intake of breath from Dvorah, who was hearing this for the first time.

"How very, very terrible for you!" the rebbitzen said. There were actual tears in her eyes. "You know, my parents are both survivors. My mother saw her mother and her baby sister led off to the gas chambers by Mengele. My grandmother was the most religious woman. The wife of an important rabbi. She kept every law, so strictly. And yet, that was her fate."

"So, your mother . . . did she . . . believe?"

"She said everything she went through just brought her closer to God and that everything God does is a *chesed*."

Lola leaned back, her body going limp. "I don't understand how she could still believe that after everything she'd seen."

"My mother always said that God cannot prevent people from exercising their free will, even if that allows them to create gas chambers and concentration camps. . . ."

Or to slip down off mountains, Lola thought.

"She told me that believing in God doesn't mean you will never have anything bad happen to you. It just means He will be there by your side to help you get up and keep going when you live through terrible times. He was there with my mother. She was only eleven, and yet Mengele thought she was older and let her live. God saw to it that a woman from my mother's hometown, a woman who had lost her own daughter, was there in the same barracks. This woman took care of my mother like she was her own. This woman—her name was Magda—told my mother that God would be with them and that my mother would be part of the future and through her, this woman would also have a future."

"Did the woman also survive?"

The rebbitzen shook her head. "But my mother did; she had seven children, forty-three grandchildren, and eleven great-grandchildren. And still counting! Not a day goes by that my mother doesn't bless the woman who took care of her in the camps and bless God for all His kindness and miracles in giving her this family."

It took her breath away. How was that possible? How was it possible to still believe after bearing witness to such tragedies; to feel gratitude instead of hatred, love instead of bitterness? She looked around at this house with its walls full of imposing family photographs of smiling people. She looked at the table set so beautifully for a festive family meal, at all the empty seats that would soon be filled. She listened to the baby giggling in the bedroom and the sounds of running water in the kitchen interspersed with girlish laughter. Death, destruction . . . it was history. It was the past. Out of its cold ashes, new life had sprung, these lovely, smiling faces of people filled with gratitude for what remained—gratitude for life.

Footsteps were heard in the doorway, and soon a group of men and boys trooped in.

"Guten Shabbos, Rebbitzen Magda," a smiling, bearded man said.

She looked at the rebbitzen, startled.

The woman looked back at her, smiling. "There are fifteen Magdas in our family. There will be more. The future."

The boys took their places around the table, and then the girls. A baby seat was rolled in, and an alert and smiling baby placed carefully inside. The rabbi went around the table, laying his hands gently on the heads of his sons and daughters, whispering a Hebrew prayer.

"What is he saying?" she asked Dvorah.

"For the boys, 'May you be like Ephraim and Menashe,' and for the girls, 'Like Sarah, Rebecca, Rachel, and Leah.' May God bless you and guard you. May God show you favor and be gracious to you. May God show you kindness and grant you peace."

She tried to imagine what it must feel like to have your father's hands rest softly on your head, to hear his voice whisper those blessings over you every week. The room, despite the crowd of people, was hushed for a moment. The silver goblets gleamed in the soft candlelight along with the silver-handled bread knife and the gold threads in the embroidered red velvet cover that rested on two enormous homemade loaves of braided egg bread.

"They call the bread *challah,* after the show bread in the ancient temple," Dvorah whispered. "The whole table is supposed to represent the tabernacle, to raise up the animal act of eating to something holy, something spiritual. That is the whole point of the Shabbos. You take an ordinary day and turn it into something special. You ennoble time itself. They say a special spirit enters into a person on Shabbos." Her eyes shone.

The rest of the meal, Dvorah supplied a running commentary. There was the kiddush, the sanctification of the wine—wine, that alcoholic beverage used in Roman orgies and that destroyed people in bars and nightclubs. Here it was measured out carefully in a silver goblet, sanctified, everyone allowed only one sip. And then there was the communal singing: the song blessing the angels who had accompanied the men home from the synagogue; the song of the husband blessing his industrious and faithful wife whose worth was "above rubies." And finally, there was the ritual of pouring clean water from a two-handled cup twice over your hands to sanctify them before they touched the bread, the staff of life. Only then did the meal begin.

The food was endless, platters of sweet fish eaten with scarlet, tongue-burning horseradish; steaming bowls of chicken soup, thick with noodles and vegetables; platters of brisket, roast chicken, potato kugel, carrots and yams sweetened with honey. And as they ate or the plates were being cleared away, the men and boys were called upon to share some insight into that week's portion of the Torah read in the synagogue. "A Shabbos meal without some words of Torah is like eating ham," Dvorah whispered into Lola's amused and startled ear.

"Dovid Hamelech, one of our tzadikim and gedolim, was *nichshal.* We hold that God judges his tzaddikim *k'chut hasahra.* For such a great man, even the smallest sin the *sotan* is *mekatreg.* Chazal tell us, Dovid did *teshuva.* There was a *kapara* and the *shechina* returned. We should all be *zoche* to such a thing."

"What language is that?" she asked Dvorah. She hadn't understood a single word. Yes, there were some English words and the construction of the sentence, its grammar, seemed like English, but nothing else.

"It's Yinglish." Dvorah smiled. "This is the translation: 'King David was one of our greatest saints and kings, and yet we believe that God judges even His saints to a hair's breadth. And Satan, the prosecuting angel, went after him. But David repented, and God forgave him. May we all be worthy of such forgiveness.'"

"How did you figure that out?"

"Remember when we first met? You couldn't understand what I was saying either! It's like immigrating to any new country. Eventually, you figure out the local idiom."

These little lectures were sometimes followed by lively discussions, in which even the girls joined in. And finally, before the last course was served, the entire room lit up with song. The tunes were simple and repetitive, with choruses sung over and over, so that by the middle of each song, even she could remember the tune and repeat some of the foreign words. Some of the children accompanied the music with special hand gestures that went around the table, like a wave at a football game. Others tapped in rhythm.

It wasn't just a meal, she thought. It was a big family celebration. A celebration of family, the kind that opened its doors and its heart to let in strangers, embracing them. And they did this *every single week!* She tried to imagine what kind of life that would mean, what the rest of the week would look like if you knew every Friday night there would be this wonderful coming together, this abundance, this nourishing spiritual experience.

How different Friday night and Saturday were in the real world: the mad search for connection in bars and discotheques among strangers, everyone running around showing off their bodies, fueled by too much alcohol as the deafening *boom, boom, boom* of music and the blinding strobe lights made it impossible to hear or talk to anyone. How many times had she been driven to desperate hookups just to escape? And how many times the morning after had she looked in the mirror feeling degraded and dehumanized? And all that was considered "normal." It was what people did. And this family, this dinner, would be considered "fanatic," "ritualistic," and therefore, "dangerous" and "abnormal." How ironic was that?

By the time dinner was over, it was almost midnight. She felt exhausted as well as uplifted. The rebbitzen embraced Dvorah and then turned to her. "You had what to eat?"

"Too much!"

"Don't be a stranger, Lola. You are welcome back anytime. And may the God you don't believe in heal your wounds."

Her hug and kiss were warm and genuine.

Everything God does is a chesed. And what about what had happened to Josh, to the love of her life? How could that possibly have been a *chesed*? But if there actually was a God, a person could never see what He saw, because He could look into the future until the very end of time. What if Josh had never taken that hike but had ALS and was destined to spend the rest of his life in a wheelchair, dying slowly as he endured terrible suffering? Or what if he had survived the fall and had brain damage or been a paraplegic, never able to hike or run again? *Perhaps that would have been better for me,* she thought, but it would not have been his choice.

But that was a cop-out! Deal with the fact that a young life had been uselessly cut short by a silly accident and that human life was filled with dangers and chaos. But if that was the case, wasn't it better to feel that when that chaos engulfed you, there was a benevolent God ready to help you through, rather than the emptiness of an indifferent universe?

All the way home through the dark, quiet streets, she felt the flicker of something she had not known for many months. A tiny twinge, a small tap, almost unnoticed, began to beat inside her. She recognized it. It was the tiny tattoo of hope jump-starting her flatlining spirit; hope that it was perhaps possible to forgive, to live again in this imperfect and dangerous world.

She had never seen those people again. Soon afterward, her life with Dvorah had also come to an abrupt end, taking a complete and total turn. But the experience that Friday night had changed something inside her, lighting a tiny pilot light.

Now, holding this invitation, looking forward to joining Yaakov and his children at their Shabbos table, she felt herself fill with a thrilling anticipation that that tiny light was finally going to burst into flame.

21

The letter from her mother was sitting in front of her door. Pinned to it was a note of apology from a stranger who said that it had been mistakenly delivered to someone who lived in his building, and that he had found it lying in the hallway. He apologized for taking so long to find her. The postmark was months old.

She put it down on the kitchen table unopened. Of all the luck! On a day when she was feeling so happy, this was all she needed. She stared at it for a while, and it stared back.

There was nothing to be done. Her mother probably thought the worst already because she'd gotten no answer. She made herself a hot cup of coffee with cinnamon, sat down in her favorite chair, and tore open the envelope.

"*Dearest Lola,*" it began, the name scratched out and *LEAH* written over it. She sighed.

> *I got your letter. You say you're sorry for getting rid of every way for me to contact you—your phone, your computer. You say you think maybe I was worried because for A MONTH I HAD NO IDEA*

WHAT WAS GOING ON WITH YOU. Ya think? Good guess! Try hysterical. But honestly, I don't know if your letter makes me feel better or worse than not hearing anything at all.

What can I say? This is all very strange stuff, and you know how I feel about it, so there is no use pretending I'm okay with it. On top of that, two weeks ago, Ravi picked himself up and took off for India. I'm not sure when or if he'll be back. He read your letter and said he agreed with you about Americans polluting their souls and about the sleaziness and stupidity turning the world into Pottersville. *He said that your letter made him think about his own heritage. And so, he is back in India (okay, I'm not blaming you, but gee whiz!).*

I spent quite some time steaming mad at both of you. And then I started to think that some part of me is just missing. Maybe it got loose and fell off when I hightailed it out of my bedroom and sped off to California. Or maybe I was just born without it, like some people were born with four toes. I just don't believe in God. In any God. I think that kind of faith is either a curse or a gift. And if it's a gift, my name was left off the Christmas list.

I just don't get it, and I never will. I see the world and everything that goes on in it, and it all seems so really human to me—the way people live and love and cheat and fight and kill each other. It seems so random. If there were a good and compassionate God, it would be more orderly, make more sense, no?

But you were never like me. To you, the sun setting every evening wasn't something you took for granted. You'd drag me over to the window or outside to the backyard, astonished, pointing to the sky, proof that God had a set of brushes and the sky was His canvas.

I've come to accept that we are different. How that happened, go figure. I thought you'd be my clone, and I tried to raise you like I wished I'd been raised. You say I raised you to believe in freedom and that this is your choice and I should be happy for you. That first part is true enough. But when you have a child and they choose to reject everything you believe in, let's see how happy you'll be. Let's see how happy you'll be when they just give up on all their dreams and ambitions. You weren't just dreaming your dreams, you know; you were dreaming mine, too. And now I'm left with nothing, nothing at all.

This family you are volunteering for, that's sweet. But don't fall in love with those kids. They are some other woman's family, and they will never love you the way they loved her. You're young. You have plenty of time to have your own kids.

I understand that you are learning new things, seeing a different way of life and because you are you, you're full of enthusiasm. But let the mother you think knows nothing and is pretty much useless tell you this: people are just people. Nobody is a bigger saint than the next one; they just hide their true selves better. Sooner or later, you'll figure out for yourself that this community you're madly in love with and want so much to be a part of is just like the rest of the world.

Even if that isn't the case, why do you have to be such a fanatic? Don't you have any right to your own past, your own dreams? Why do you have to hate everything you once loved and be willing to leave it behind because you think you've found something better? I don't understand why you can't just be yourself and take on more things. Why can't you curl up with Vogue *or* Marie Claire *or* People *on your Shabbos? What would be so terrible? Especially since on Saturdays you're now stuck doing nothing, for Pete's sake! (I don't know how you aren't going stir-crazy.) Why does everything have to be either-or, with slammed doors and vicious piñata-bashing until everything you once were falls out? And let me remind you, if you've forgotten, that who you once were was pretty damn awesome! You practically ran that marketing department, and the company would have gone public if their CEO hadn't been a sleazy shyster. It's not your fault the product was shit, so stop beating yourself up over it! (See, I didn't even mention Andrew, may he rot in jail, the rutting, cheating loser!)*

So Ravi writes me he's seen his daughter, and she's changed so much. She won't call him baba je *(Daddy) anymore; that's what she calls her stepfather. But still, she means a lot to him. I think his heart aches. He's so much like you, so confused about where he belongs. But if he starts growing his hair again, I'm not taking him back. Why is it that the people I love most love this invisible God more?? I don't know how someone seemingly normal can be involved in such bizarre stuff.*

Okay, so I'm rambling. I'm not a writer like you, and lately, I'm not thinking straight. All these ideas go around and around in my head, especially at two in the morning. What can I do? I smoke a joint. Take a sedative. Drink a beer. The hell with meditation. All that does is make me concentrate on how fat my stomach is getting. I just try to get through one day (or night) at a time.

So, where was I? Okay, your letter. You say you want me to give you absolution (sorry, wrong word). Okay, I forgive you for anything you've done to me. But what I can't and won't forgive is what you are doing to yourself. You had some hard breaks, kid, it's true. And I wasn't Mother Knows Best. And your father was a brilliant heel. And your beautiful, kind fiancé fell off a cliff. And your rebound boyfriend turned out to be a fraud and a pig. Trust me, I get all that. I may be a high school dropout hairdresser, but I'm not a complete moron.

But you know what? You've also been so incredibly lucky: you are beautiful and smart and have a great degree. You experienced real love with a truly good man who adored you and was faithful to you and wanted to marry you. How many people can say that? So lightning didn't strike twice and your latest guy was a bust. But don't give up. You'll find another Josh. Don't change everything about you he loved. Go back to your old life. Don't do this for me. Why should you care what I think? I never cared what my parents thought. Do it for yourself.

You'll never be happy with these strangers. They'll never appreciate you and never accept you unless you hide your true self from them. That's their problem. What are you going to do—hide forever, deny yourself forever? And what if you slip up? What then? Get thrown out (my dream scenario, I admit) and start all over somewhere else? Do you really have time for that?

I have this regular customer, Bella, a really nice Jewish lady from New York who retired to Boca Raton, and we got to talking about our kids, and she told me her daughter got involved in one of these baale teshuva *programs in college and she turned into a mean, selfish, manipulative crook who's living on Medicaid, food stamps, and WIC—Women, Infants, and Children nutrition program— even though she's got a second degree and an able-bodied husband who decided to be a "scholar" and does nothing but sit around all day "learning" except when he takes time off to get her pregnant. Bella says her daughter's destroyed their family and gotten rid of every friend she ever had because she is so hateful and abusive. Bella says she herself was always very traditional but now she HATES religious Jews. She said before this, her daughter was the sweetest, nicest, most warmhearted, giving, spiritual person. "Becoming a BT destroyed her and just about killed us," she told me.*

Is that what is going to happen to you? To us?

If I don't hear from you, I guess I will have my answer, but it will break my heart. Please, please don't cut me off. Even if we don't agree. You are still my daughter, and I love you more than anything.

Love and kisses,
Mom

Leah dove for the phone. Her hand trembling, she dialed.

"Mom?"

"Who is this?" She sounded tired and suspicious.

"Mom, it's me, Leah."

"Lola? Is it really you?"

"Mom, I'm sooo sorry. That letter you sent, somebody just now brought it over. Mom, I would have called you right away, I promise."

"I've been through hell, Lola. When you didn't answer—"

"I know, Mom, I can just . . . Listen, that's not going to happen to us, to you and me, what you said happened to your customer Bella. I'm not going to be hateful and abusive and cut off my family and friends. I'm not going to go on welfare. I have a business, Mom, my own business, and it's actually doing very well."

"It's so good to hear your voice. You do sound happy. Are you really happy, Lola?"

"Sometimes. Most of the time."

"I miss you so much."

"I miss you, too." It was really true. For all her faults, her mother was irreplaceable.

"Can you take off some time, come down to Florida? I'll send you a ticket."

"It's not the money or even the time. There is this little girl, and she's been sick. I don't want to leave her at the moment. Can you come out here?" There was a brief silence. "Mom?"

"How can I stay in your apartment in Boro Park with all those fanatics all over the place? I'll wear the wrong shoes, or pants, or my lipstick will be the wrong shade, and they'll stone me."

Leah opened her mouth to deny it but then thought better of it. There was more than a little truth in her mother's fears. She tried to imagine Cheryl Howard with her bleached-platinum hair, tight jeans, and crop top on these pious streets and shuddered. And as much as she tried not to let her thoughts wander in that direction, she could not stop herself imagining how it would affect her, ruining her own reputation. As far as BTs were concerned, the less their nonreligious parents showed up, the better off they were. Even without that, getting accepted was no walk in the park.

"Mom, I want you to come! You don't have to stay with me. You can stay in the city, and I'll come to you. We'll spend time together."

"You're ashamed of me, right? In front of your new friends?"

"I'm new here, I want to be accepted," she said honestly.

"Yeah, and if I show up, they'll know the truth about you, right?"

"It's no different from someone's parents showing up with a Trump hat at their kid's college. Parents are always embarrassing their children. It's normal."

"Not for you. Not for us. I used to come to see you at Santa Clara all the time. Josh didn't head for the hills when he saw me."

"Please don't talk about Josh," she said quietly.

"You know I'm right."

"Okay, you're right. But this is my problem, not the community's. I have to work on myself."

"And in the meantime?"

"Come to New York! I'll rent a hotel room for you. I'll meet you at the airport. We'll go shopping."

"And see a play?"

She wasn't sure about that. She hadn't been to a theater in two years. "I don't know. Just come!"

"I'll think about it."

"And Ravi?" Leah said delicately.

"Still in India. I don't want to talk about it."

"I understand. But maybe it's for the best, Mom."

"It's horrible."

"Okay, I hear you. Have you thought about going there?"

"Where?"

"To India, to see him."

"I think his family would love me as much as your friends in Boro Park. No, he either comes back and takes off the turban, or we're done."

"And if he comes back and leaves on the turban?"

"I don't want to think about it, Lola."

"So, are you coming?"

"Maybe. But in the meantime, can we talk on the phone like normal human beings? Like Americans?"

"Would that make you feel better?"

"You're kiddin' me, right?"

"Then okay. Here is my cell number." She repeated it.

"Thank you Lo . . . I mean Leah. It's a relief."

"Think about coming, please?"

"I will. I love you."

"I love you, too."

She heard her mother sigh. "I'll call you tomorrow."

"Okay, Mom. Good night. Love you."

"Love you, too."

22

"Leah," Rebbitzen Basha said over the phone, "how are you?"

"*Baruch HaShem,* Rebbitzen! So good to hear your voice!"

Rebbitzen Basha swallowed. She hadn't been in touch for weeks. But she said, "You disappeared on us. Such a stranger you've become." She tried being jovial. "It's for a good cause, right?"

"Yes," said Leah happily to the woman who had introduced her to the Lehman family. "Without your help, who knows what would have become of me?"

"Become of you? What could become? Nothing bad could happen to such a wonderful young woman like Leah Howard."

Leah smiled but said nothing, waiting to hear the reason for the call.

"Leah, are you still there?"

"Yes, I'm listening, Rebbitzen."

"I'd like you to come over."

"I'm always happy to see you. It's just I'm so busy right now."

"Busy, shmizzy. I need to see you."

"Something happened?"

"Something has to happen? All is gut, *Yisborach HaShem.* Just . . ."

"Isn't your grandson getting engaged this week?"

"You remembered!"

"You invited me. It's on my calendar. I wouldn't miss it for the world."

Rebbitzen Basha groaned inwardly. She had forgotten completely that she'd called Leah and invited her to the *vort*. Now there would be no way to separate this ugly business from the beautiful simcha she was preparing. That was the situation. Shabbos was only a few days away. If she was going to do what she promised, it would have to be now.

"Maybe you could come by today?"

"Well, I have to be at the Lehmans' when the kids come home at one. And I have a client I need to speak to at ten."

"Come over for lunch?"

"You don't have to feed me, Rebbitzen," she laughed, relaxing.

"If you would only see how much food I'm preparing, you wouldn't say that. My kitchen will explode! Help me out?"

"Okay, sure."

Leah hung up the phone, amused and pleased, looking forward to going to the home where she had been treated so warmly. That, and the glow of the Shabbos invitation from Yaakov Lehman, infused her spirit with optimism. Things really were looking up!

"Come in, come in." Rebbitzen Basha greeted her at the door, hugging her and kissing her cheek. "Let me look at you, Leah. You look so skinny! There's no food by you?"

Leah laughed. With running after the kids, skating, and general happiness, she had lost a ton of weight, getting rid of all the seminary calories that had come along with her Torah studies. The amount of junk food consumed in between lectures on modesty and chastity had been prodigious, some arguing that it was the result of newly pious women sublimating their sexual urges in chocolate consumption. "I'm exercising more."

It wasn't just the weight. Rebbitzen Basha studied the new shine in the young woman's lovely eyes. Her lips, too, had a refreshingly upward curve. And the white forehead was makeup-free and as smooth and freckled as a peasant girl's. She looked so young, so happy. With all her heart, Rebbitzen Basha wished she could simply feed her, love her, and send her on her way to Yaakov Lehman and his children. But she had made a promise, and more than that, she had felt the pain—justified or not—of one of her closest friends, a woman who had lost her husband and then her daughter. She could not turn her back on her.

"Leah-le, come sit by me a minute." She patted a space on the worn sofa.

Leah sat down.

"Rebbitzen Lehman came to see me yesterday. She told me that you have been invited by her son Yaakov to spend Shabbos with them."

"Yes." Leah nodded, beginning to smile and then, seeing the expression on Rebbitzen Basha's face, thinking better of it.

"She is worried."

"About what?"

"Leah, Yaakov Lehman is a widower. You are an unmarried woman who spends a great deal of time in his home. I know most of the time, you are not there together, but if you come for Shabbos, he will be there. You understand?"

"Okay," she said, shrugging. What was there to understand?

"I can see on your sweet face you don't understand anything. Leah-le, people will talk."

"About what?"

"That there is something between the two of you."

Leah blushed. "And would that be so terrible? After all, we are both single."

"Yes, but in our world, a single man and a single woman do not meet up without formality. This protects both their reputations, not to mention the reputation of their families. Yaakov Lehman is a good man, a kind man, perhaps even a bit of a tzaddik. When he invited you, he didn't think about these things, because he is above such things. Unfortunately, this community is not. They have much to learn and a long way to go to reach his spiritual level. If you go to his house on Shabbos, though, people's tongues will wag."

"Ugly gossip is their problem, not mine." She shrugged again.

"Ugly gossip can destroy Shaindele's chances for a decent shidduch."

Leah stared at her. "Is that true?"

Rebbitzen Basha nodded unhappily. "Shaindele is so worried about it, she fainted in class yesterday. Fruma Esther had to go and get her."

"And this is the reason Shaindele gave her for why she fainted," Leah murmured. It wasn't a question. She felt sick. "She's never liked me! From the beginning, she's tried to get rid of me. But it's not just me. She doesn't want anyone in the house because she doesn't want anyone to see how she's abusing the children. She's hitting them, you know. Chasya told me this in the hospital."

"No? Really. Oy vey." Rebbitzen Basha squeezed her hands together. "She is a troubled girl. You should have met her before her poor mother died. Such a sweet, kind, lovable child! She has been through Gehenna."

Leah's heart was cold.

Rebbitzen Basha put her hand over Leah's. "You could ruin Shaindele. It is in your hands. But you also have the power to do a *chesed* to this girl and to this family. If you care for this family, don't complicate Yaakov's life by hurting his daughter. However she's behaved, it is Yaakov who will suffer if his daughter is denied a decent shidduch. He will never forgive himself."

"But it was Yaakov who invited me!"

"Yes, because he isn't thinking straight. You have to protect him by doing the right thing for both of you. You have to be the one to tell him something came up and you can't make it. You have to keep your distance."

Leah didn't say anything. How could she? The woman who had been so kind to her and had provided the safe ground from which she had launched her new life was asking her—begging her—for a favor. It could not possibly be from bad motives. Her heart was heavy, but what could she do?

"All right, Rebbitzen. If you think it would be for the best."

Do I think that? Rebbitzen Basha asked herself, ashamed. "Who knows what is for the best, Leah-le? All we know is what seems to be the right thing at the time. God should help us all to do His will and find favor in His eyes."

Leah rose, her feet leaden. Over the course of the fifteen minutes that she had been there, she felt she'd aged.

"You're not going? I have lunch all ready for you!"

"Please forgive me, Rebbitzen, but I think I've lost my appetite. If you don't mind, I'll go now."

"Forgive me, Leah. You know I want only the best for you."

"Of course, Rebbitzen."

"You're still coming to Heshy's party, right? Don't forget!"

"Of course, Rebbitzen."

Leah felt flushed and tired. Her heart ached as she wound her way home. She had an hour to get to the children. *What should I do? How will I face them?* All week, Icy had been starting every sentence with, "When you come to us for Shabbos . . ." The little girl had made so many plans. In which chair Leah would sit. How they would listen to kiddush together and sing all the Shabbos songs. How Icy would wear her "*kallah*" dress, her favorite, a white dress with lace on the sleeves. "You never saw me in my *kallah* dress, because it's a Shabbos dress, and I never see you on Shabbos," she told Leah. "But this Shabbos, when you come, you'll see me. I'm so beautiful!"

Leah had laughed and picked her up and swung her around the room, and they had sung Shabbos songs together: *Who loves Shabbos? Tateh and Mameh. Who loves the Shabbos? Bubby and Zaidie. Who loves the Shabbos? Everybody!* What was she going to tell Icy now? And what would she tell Yaakov?

Would she tell him the truth or make up some story? She hated the idea of it. Like a character in some sleazy telenovela where everybody keeps secrets from one another, causing endless misunderstandings and anger, when all they had to do was just tell the truth to clear everything up. "Be honest, you morons!" she'd always shouted at the screen.

But could she be honest? What was there to say? "Icy, Shaindele hates me and is trying to get rid of me?" "Yaakov, your eldest daughter is up to her old tricks, manipulating everyone to hide her crimes?" "Yaakov, your saintly mother-in-law is involved, gossiping all over town?"

But even if she had the guts to do it, how was that going to solve anything? If, as Rebbitzen Basha said, her going over to the house on the weekend when Yaakov was there would set tongues wagging and place him and his family in social disgrace, what did it matter who caused this harmful thing to be prevented? It was all for the best, anyway, even if people's motives were base.

She had no desire to cause Yaakov Lehman any harm. Both outing Shaindele or accepting his invitation would do exactly that.

Still, confusion gnawed at her. Was her friend Rebbitzen Basha to be trusted? Or was she exaggerating? Leah hadn't been a member of this community, this society, long enough to know. Before making any decision, she had to be sure.

She said nothing to the children when she saw them, and that night she called Shoshana.

"Dr. Glazer. Who is this?"

"It's me, Leah."

"You sound terrible! What's wrong?"

"Everything."

"Calm down."

"Shoshana, can we meet for coffee tonight?"

She had just finished a ten-hour shift and was falling asleep, but Leah never called her, always waiting until Monday night when they met at the rink to share her news. She'd seemed fine on Monday! Happy, even. What could have happened in two days? "Give me fifteen minutes to get out of my pajamas, and I'll pick you up in front of your house."

"I'm bothering you. You're tired; forget about it."

"I'll just sit here and suffer in the dark," Shoshana teased her. They both laughed.

"Okay. I'll wait for you downstairs."

It took her more like a half hour, but there she was. She swung open the door on the passenger side. "Hop in. Where to?"

"Oh, I don't care, just someplace with no yentas staring at us."

"*Oooh,* you finally figured out where you live." Shoshana giggled.

It was a cozy place with a redbrick wall and antique jewelry display cases that held a delicious display of doughnuts, croissants, and danishes.

"It's not kosher, so there's no temptation." Shoshana laughed. "Although, I have to admit that I sometimes will get a butter croissant. They have to make it with real butter so I know it's not lard."

Leah, who had never heard of the possibility of eating something that had no rabbinical stamp of approval, was surprised. "There is so much I still don't know," she groaned.

"Did you ever hear this one? How many BTs does it take to screw in a lightbulb?"

Leah smiled. "No. Tell me."

"What, you're allowed to do that?" Shoshana laughed. Then she turned serious, laying a sympathetic hand over Leah's. "Talk."

Leah told her everything.

Shoshana leaned back and sighed. "I knew you were going to run into this sooner or later. I'm actually surprised it's taken this long."

Leah stared at her.

"Honey, let me tell you how this BT thing works. Our community does everything it can to encourage nonobservant Jews to come back to a Torah-true way of life. We show you how wonderful our lives are, how pure. We invite you into our homes for Shabbos. We take you around to all the synagogues to show you how merry we are, how we dance and sing on Simchas Torah. We convince you to get rid of your tattoos, to stop polluting your pure soul with McDonald's cheeseburgers and bacon, to reject the prurience of discos and nose rings, not to mention late-night hookups in bars . . ."

"But it's not a joke; this really *is* a better way of life."

"You know what? I agree. Yes, it is. So, you un-ink yourself, sew up the slits in the backs of your skirts, slip out the belly button ring, and become super careful about what you eat and do for entertainment. You move in with us, on our holy streets. In fact, you start looking just like us! But not exactly. We can always tell who you are a mile away. Your sleeves are longer, your hems are lower, your stockings thicker but not the right shade. You go a little overboard in everything to compensate for your 'sinful' past, which we've taught you to loathe and feel ashamed of. You try so hard, but it's no use; the minute you open your mouth, you get the lingo wrong. Your grammar is too good. You throw in unnecessary prepositions: What are you doing *on* Sukkos? Where are you going *on* Shabbos? You would never say, 'I want that you should take her number.' Those things could be forgiven. But some things are unforgivable."

"Like what?" Leah asked miserably.

"That you really are sincere. That you really love God. That you pray like an angel with your whole heart. That you are shocked at gossip. That you do everything by the book, while we, who were born into this world and have never known anything else, have long ago forgotten the reason for anything we do! We go through the motions because that's how we were brought up."

Leah hung her head wordlessly, listening. "But Yaakov's not like that."

"Okay. Not Yaakov. And maybe some others. But I'm trying to make a point. Now here comes the best part. So you've given up your old life and you are living next door to us. So naturally, you start thinking maybe you'll go out with our sons or our daughters, our widows or widowers. Wrong! That's when all the alarm bells start going off. *Oh, no.* Back off, sister. What makes you think you will be good enough, now or ever, to actually become *part* of our pure and holy families? We will *never* forgive the nonreligious parents who gave you birth, the marijuana that's entered your lungs, the clams that have slid down your throat. You are forever tainted." She paused. "Didn't you ever wonder about those men they fixed you up with?"

"You also complained about your shidduch dates."

"But I didn't get fixed up with cripples, autistic men, frisky, married Africans, misfits. With you, they were scraping the bottom of the barrel."

Leah said nothing.

"The truth is, we loved saving your soul, but when your body hangs around in our neighborhood, it's a nuisance. You will never be good enough for us. It doesn't matter that you are ten times purer, more spiritual, more sincere. It doesn't matter that the Torah exhorts, pleads, threatens, *begs* Jews to accept the stranger, the outsider, the penitent and convert *hundreds of times* in the *text,* not in some obscure commentary on a commentary in a footnote. *It doesn't matter.* You will *never, ever* be accepted as one of us. It's just that simple. And I'll tell you something else—if you try to get around this by marrying another BT, don't expect your kids to be accepted into our schools. This goes on forever."

Leah looked at her, devastated, tears filling her eyes. In a flash, all her shidduch dates came back to her, those disgraceful men who had been sent to her door. No one was so low Tovah Klein had not considered them to be her equal or higher. Now it all made sense. Shaindele closing the door in her face when she came over for the first time; being told her *chesed* was no longer necessary, even though it was, desperately. And even Rebbitzen Basha, kind Rebbitzen Basha, had talked her out of coming for Shabbos because her very presence would pollute the entire Lehman family.

It was so painful, as painful almost as a death. She wondered how she was going to go on. What had her mother said? *You'll never be happy with these strangers. They'll never appreciate you and never accept you . . . Sooner or later, you'll figure out this community you love so much and want to be part of is pretty much like the rest of the world.*

What if she was right? What if these things were true? And if they were, then could anything else be true? The society that she had looked up to, all the wonderful things she'd been taught about living a Torah life, a life she was making so many painful sacrifices to join in order to be part of a better world, a world where people were kinder and more honest, more authentic, where they honestly believed in and served a gracious God, was that also a fake? Was everything she had been taught simply PR? And if that was the case, what was she going to do now?

"Aren't there any exceptions?" she asked weakly.

"Of course."

"Who?"

"Ruth Blau. She was a convert and wound up marrying the most extreme fanatic leader of the most extreme fanatic sect, Neturei Karta, people who hate everyone except themselves. Still, their leader married her, and when his flock complained bitterly, he told them to shut up. But he was old, and she was hot stuff. Also a crazy fanatic like himself. It was a match made in hell. But it happens."

"So you think I should back off?"

"You are asking *me* for relationship advice?" She rolled her eyes.

"I'm asking you."

She cleared her throat. *"I have a love, and it's all that I have, right or wrong . . ."* she sang in a high falsetto, mocking herself.

"West Side Story, right?"

"Exactly. Ask me about love, and I sing songs from *West Side Story* like Maria, who wound up with a dead boyfriend. So don't ask me."

"Just tell me this: Can my accepting this one Shabbos invitation hurt Yaakov and ruin Shaindele's shidduch chances?"

"That's nuts, but also quite accurate. But it's not the one invitation. It's the implication."

"Implication?"

"That you and Yaakov Lehman are involved."

"Would that be so terrible?" she whispered, her voice weak. She was close to tears.

Shoshana sat up. "So it's true?"

Leah leaned back, looking at the floor. "I think about him all the time."

"And what does he think?"

"He leaves me notes. Flowers. Candy."

"You've got to be kidding."

"I never said anything because I was afraid I was just . . . misunderstanding."

"What did the notes say?"

"He thanked me for my *chesed*." Leah made the supreme effort to make the sound correctly, like she was choking and clearing her throat.

"Go on."

"That's it. But, Shoshana . . . I can't explain it . . . I just know. He cares."

"You are setting yourself up for heartbreak, my friend. Even if he cares, his family will turn over heaven and earth to make sure he never acts on it. Look what they are doing about a single, innocent Friday night dinner invitation with the whole family! Imagine if you started going out alone on shidduch dates!"

"So it's hopeless?"

"You are both entering a world of pain. In our world, the chassidim and the misnagdim—both of whom are strictly observant and share the same God, the same values, the same Torah—have been at each other's throats for hundreds of years. This will be worse."

"So I just tell him no, I can't do it, ever? I can't come for Shabbos, meet with him, in any way?"

Shoshana shrugged helplessly. "Tell him you don't think it's a good idea. You'll be shocked at how fast he gets it and moves on."

Leah felt suddenly cold. She hugged herself. Icy would be so disappointed. But if this was just going to lead to a long, drawn-out war of endless misery for all involved, including the children, it was better to end it now before more casualties were added to that of her own heart. Everybody in that family had suffered enough. She had also suffered enough.

"Okay."

When Shoshana dropped her off, she reached over and squeezed her hand sympathetically. "You'll live through this, Leah. Believe me."

At that moment, she wouldn't have sworn to it. Leah leaned over and kissed Shoshana's pale cheek. "Thanks for the *shiur*."

"Believe me, I am so sorry I had to be the one to tell you all this. I'm sorrier than I can say."

"It's not your fault, Shoshana."

"It's the system. The ugly system and the great and powerful wizards hiding behind the curtains manipulating everything—they are responsible for destroying our beautiful world."

Leah didn't take the elevator, walking slowly up the steps to her apartment. She needed time to think. She went in, locked the door, then sat down at her desk. She took out a piece of her flowered, lavender stationery.

Dear Yaakov,
I'm sorry. I can't make it this Shabbos. Maybe another time?
Every blessing,
Leah

She looked over the letter. With a sudden burst of anger, she squeezed it to a pulp in her fist, then threw it away, shaking her hands and flexing her fingers to get back some feeling.

Dear Yaakov, she began again.
On second thought, I can't accept your kind invitation to join you for Shabbos. I know you'll understand why. It is better this way.
Every blessing,
Leah

She folded it carefully and slipped it inside an envelope, sealing it so that she would have to tear it apart to change even one word. She slipped it into her purse to take to the Lehmans' the next day.

Her steps were heavy as she walked over there the following afternoon, her mind burdened.

"Leah!" Icy reached out and hugged her. Leah picked her up in her arms, cuddling the warm little body.

Cheeky squealed with a dopey grin, holding out his arms to her. She picked him up, too.

"Can we go to the park today? Please, Leah, please! I want to take my dolly with me in her carriage."

"Sure, why not?" She smiled.

Chasya skipped joyfully ahead as Leah followed slowly behind, grasping Mordechai Shalom's little hand. He was thrilled to be walking, relishing his newfound freedom from the carriage. And then, for no reason at all, the toddler suddenly leaned over, pressing his soft, little lips to her hand, kissing her.

Quick tears sprang to her eyes, and a flow of love as powerful as a riptide pulled her forward. Her mind might have backtracked, understood that certain things didn't make sense anymore, but her heart—her heart was in this all the way. The lyrics in that love song from *West Side Story* were true. When love comes so strong, there really *isn't* a thing you can do. She couldn't backtrack, she couldn't escape. Life flowed in one direction only: forward. She had no choice but to continue.

She leaned down and lifted the little boy into her arms, kissing him, feeling his warm, responsive, loving little arms around her neck in response. That, at least, she knew was real.

23

It was late when Yaakov got home. His exams had been brutal. He was disgusted with himself that he'd been unsure of some of the answers. He had never in his life failed at learning anything, no matter how difficult. Maybe it was just his age, he thought. His wits were not as sharp as they used to be. He found that idea somehow comforting. For if he were doomed to leave the study hall, it was better to feel that his chance to shine there was limited anyway.

He felt exhausted and ready for dinner and bed as he walked into the living room. But the moment his eyes spied the little lavender envelope on the dining room table, his heart pounded joyfully. Another letter. From *her*.

He opened it respectfully, as if it were something delicate that would change or be ruined by carelessness or haste. But as his eyes moved swiftly over the words, his fingers tightened involuntarily, crushing the paper. His arm fell as he took a step backward, sinking heavily into a chair. He took off his glasses, lifting the letter close to his eyes, rereading every word to make sure he hadn't misunderstood. Then he jumped up angrily, refolding it and sliding it back inside its envelope before shoving it into his pocket. Hardly knowing what he was doing, he walked around in circles, finally stopping by the window. He stood there, staring out into the narrow sidewalks of old concrete, the pale, dusty trees, the dark parade of black suits and hats—like soldiers in some medieval army.

This was where he lived. In this place. And for most of his life, he had wholeheartedly believed it the best possible place on earth, and the people who lived there—his friends and neighbors, people who stood next to him as he poured out his heart in the synagogue, people whose intelligent comments enlightened him in the study hall—the best possible people.

He thought about her letter. He did not pretend that he didn't know what she was talking about, just as she in her letter did not pretend this was a simple matter of postponing the invitation to a more convenient time. He admired her for that and would not demean himself or her by reacting with wide-eyed innocence and denial. He could just imagine what people had been saying behind their backs: a Torah scholar, a widower, inviting an attractive young woman, a *baalas teshuva,* to join him at his Shabbos table with only his children as chaperones.

He did not blame them for their opinions, but what right, what *right,* did anyone have to speak to her, to shame her? *He* had invited her. If they had a problem with that, they should have had the decency to come to *him* and say it to *his* face instead of ganging up on a pure, innocent person whose feelings—like those of any newly religious person who has left behind their old life and embarked on a difficult new path among judgmental strangers—were easily hurt. *Baale teshuva* were so *vulnerable.* They lived in a fog of criticism: for their past behavior, for not getting all the words, all the little details, of their new lives correct immediately. Most of all, for their sincere piety, which, he thought with growing fury, irked the complacency of those who had been going through the motions since childhood and had long forgotten what it was all about.

Hypocrites! Of course they had approached her instead of him! She was such an easy target: exposed, accessible, lacking the knowledge to turn their ugly arguments against them. Whereas he would have had no trouble sending them to Gehenna.

What had they said? What arguments had they trotted out to shame and pressure her into doing their will? It must have been very bad, because he knew how much she was looking forward to Shabbos with the children—he didn't dare hope that might it have been for his sake—as much as he had been looking forward to hosting her. Leah would never have willingly disappointed Chasya and Mordechai Shalom unless she had been squashed pretty hard under someone's ugly boot. And that was simply unforgivable.

He looked in on Chasya and Mordechai Shalom, who were both curled up and fast asleep. Shaindele's door was shut, even though she no doubt had heard him come in. He put his hand up to knock on her door. Then, his jaw tensing with anger, thought better of it, moving silently away.

He got into bed and tried to sleep. Despite his exhaustion, he could not. His whole body was clenched into a fist of helpless fury, his heart thumping malevolently as if it wanted to tunnel its way out of his chest. What to do, what to do? He tossed and turned, uncomfortable in his own skin. He thought of Rachel, the pleasure and excitement of their short time together, the devastation of her rejection. Didn't people know what he had been through? What is it they wanted from him? Wasn't it enough, he thought with heart-stopping fury, that he had let his wife die to please them and their sense of propriety?

He inhaled sharply, shocked. Was that true? Had he let Zissele die? Could he have saved her? Maybe. *No!* Of course not! He couldn't have saved her. Nothing could have saved her. *And now, perhaps, nothing will save me.* To fulfill everyone's expectations, to please them, he would have to lower his head and move dumbly toward the first Monsey widow that came his way. He would have to live with her in misery and heartache for the rest of his life. Then *they* would be happy. Then *they* would shut their mouths and stop their gossiping. Or not. If they didn't gossip about him, then they'd gossip about his new wife, even if she was the most staid, boring, overweight, middle-aged matron ever to pull a dull brown wig over her mown, dry, short hair. They'd talk about how she didn't give enough charity, or how her wig was too long or not long enough. They'd whisper that her dresses were too expensive and not appropriate for the wife of a poor widower. Or that she dressed in shamefully cheap clothes, embarrassing the important family she'd married into. There was a problem to find something to talk about? And yet they expected—and he expected it himself—to live an entire lifetime restrained by what people *might* say behind your back. To present yourself always in a way that would find favor with scandal-mongers and gossipers. Did that make any sense at all?

Most of the time, he had it easy. A member in good standing of the community who had known these people all his life, a *man,* he could stand up to them. But Leah . . . It wasn't right that he had made her position more difficult than it already was. As much as he wanted to plead with her to reconsider, to convince her to ignore whatever it was the yentas had said to her, he wasn't sure it was the fair and decent thing to do. And so he lay there in the dark, falling into a black abyss of hopelessness where he stayed until the light of morning lifted him, reminding him of his sacred religious obligations, which no bitterness or fury could delay.

24

"There is someone I think you should meet, Leah," Shoshana told her breathlessly as they were Rollerblading around the rink.

"Really?"

"Yes. He is the cousin of a friend of mine. He owns a small florist shop in Manhattan. He is thirty-nine. Never been married. Newly religious."

"What does he look like?" she asked wearily.

"Well, not tall, but dark and—I don't know—maybe handsome. More short and sweet." She laughed.

"Too short for you?"

"Well, the thing is . . ."

Leah was shocked to see her friend's face suddenly redden. Shoshana skated over to the edge of the rink, making her way to the locker room. Leah, surprised, followed her.

"What's wrong?"

"Sit down, Leah," Shoshana ordered her.

She obeyed.

"When you told me about Yaakov, I wanted to share the truth with you. But somehow, I just couldn't bring myself." She took a deep breath. "Leah, I am not single. I'm in a relationship."

Leah sank down on a bench, stunned. "When?"

"Four years."

Four years! Leah took a deep breath. "Who is it? Why are you keeping it a secret?"

"He's a pediatrician, divorced. He's not . . . Jewish."

She didn't know which part of this revelation was the worst. Cumulatively, it was breathtakingly horrible. Leah reached out for her friend's shoulder in sympathy. She suddenly understood: Maria. *West Side Story: Right or wrong, what else can I do?* How had Shoshana kept such a secret for so long? The Jewish part could be fixed. But the married part? "Was he married . . . when you . . . when it . . . ?" Leah asked.

Shoshana nodded. "Unhappily. I didn't break that up. It was dead long before I entered the picture."

"And are you . . . in the picture?"

"I love him!" She put her head between her hands, her whole body trembling like the leaves of an aspen in the breeze.

"So all these shidduch dates . . ."

"I do it for my parents. If they knew the truth, it would kill them."

"So what now?"

Shoshana shrugged helplessly.

"He could convert, no?"

"He offered."

Leah exhaled. "So?"

"My parents want a Talmud scholar from an important Hungarian Chassidic family."

"You can't always get what you want."

Shoshana looked up. "That's from a rock song." They both smiled.

"You have to tell them."

"I know, I know, I just keep putting it off. My father has a heart condition. My mother has hypertension and diabetes."

"I'm sure they'd both like to be at your wedding."

"No one will convert him if they know he's doing it to marry a Jewish girl."

"Why is that?"

"Because an Orthodox conversion is not done for convenience. It has to be sincere, to be the genuine desire of the participant, not an expedient to another goal."

"The rabbis don't have to know he has a girlfriend."

"Well, I've thought of that. But he doesn't seem to be in any rush, to tell you the truth."

So, that was it. They sat together wordlessly.

"Anyhow, about the florist . . ."

"You went out with him?"

Shoshana nodded. "He was very nice, really. Funny, considerate, intelligent. Really wants to get married and start a family."

Leah hesitated. "Sounds good."

"Shall I give him your number?"

Leah hesitated, thinking of Yaakov Lehman. Shabbos had come and gone. He had not reacted at all to her letter. There had been no more candy. No more notes. He was simply gone. This annoyed and upset her. She'd expected—hoped?—he'd at least try to talk her out of it, encourage her to come, proclaim the innocence of his intentions and of the invitation. Obviously, she wasn't worth the effort. *He will never look at you in any other way than as his household help,* she told herself cruelly. And if he did, then what? It would just make matters worse, increasing the misery all around for everyone. There was simply no future there.

"Sure, why not?" she said impulsively.

Shoshana smiled. "Great! I'll give him your number."

They arranged for him to pick her up. But that afternoon, Cheeky started howling that his ear hurt. She didn't want to leave him. But when she called her date to cancel, he persisted.

"I'll wait for you to get finished, no problem."

"It might take a while. I don't want to leave him with his older sister, so I'll need to wait until his father gets home from night school, and that might be a little after nine."

"I can come get you directly after work, no problem."

She didn't know whether to be flattered or put off by his persistence. She gave him the address.

"I'll wait outside for you. I drive a black BMW."

She sat in the living room, Cheeky curled up in her arms. The child's face was flushed, but he had finally fallen asleep. His little body was hot against her chest. She heard the key turn in the lock.

Yaakov Lehman lifted his head when he saw her, his face flushing with heat.

"You're here!"

She put her finger to her lips, pointing to the sleeping baby. "He's got an earache and he's running a fever," she whispered. "I gave him a teaspoon of Tylenol. But tomorrow, he should see a doctor."

He nodded, concerned. He looked at his sleeping boy whose cheek rested on Leah's soft bosom, his golden curls touching her neck, which was smooth and pink beneath her modest blouse. Her hair was held back by a colorful headband and braided into a loose chignon. But the curls, rebelling at every turn, created a halo around her face. She wore no makeup except for a tiny green line on her upper lid that made her eyes shine. Her young arms were full and gentle around his son.

They looked at each other silently, the room around them swelling almost to bursting in its attempt to contain all that lay unspoken between them.

Finally, she got up. "I'm sorry, but I have to go. Should I lay him down? Or do you want to take him?"

She was leaving! He was wounded. She had to go! Just when he had come home, and she was already running away.

She studied him, shocked at what she saw in his face. He was crestfallen.

"Oh, of course. Yes. It's . . . I'm . . . so sorry . . . to keep . . . you need to . . . of course," he mumbled.

They stood looking at each other wordlessly, their eyes shyly shifting to the sleeping child that lay between them.

"Of course. I'll take him." Yaakov held out his arms, moving closer, his cheek almost touching hers, his arms inches from her body. Gently, awkwardly, Leah lifted the small child off her shoulder, moving closer to Yaakov, breathing in the genuine odor of a clean man's body in clean clothes cooled by the night air. As she moved closer, delicately shifting the child from her arms into his father's, Yaakov's shoulder accidentally brushed hers. It felt electric. She could tell he felt it, too. Both of them stepped back. She lowered her gaze to his gentle, large hands, studying them as they curled protectively around the little boy, clasping him to his heart. The child barely stirred.

"Is it . . . a class?" he asked her, appalled at his forwardness.

She looked at him uncomprehendingly.

"Where you have to go now," he added, blushing. Was it his business? But he could not help it. He had to know why she was leaving him, leaving the child.

Her eyes met his steadily. "No. It's a shidduch date."

He immediately looked down. "I see." He nodded, devastated. Of course. *What did you expect?* He wanted to cry like a small child, to bray and howl with pain.

Leah watched all this pass over him, including his failed effort to hide it. She was spellbound, almost transfixed by a feeling that was equal parts confusion, wonder, and hope. She felt afraid for him, for his vulnerability, his transparent honesty that left him as defenseless as the baby in his arms. He was totally open. There wasn't a duplicitous bone in his body. Whatever dwelled in his heart, he broadcast to the world in his eyes. It was a dangerous way to live. Something inside her wanted to protect him, the same way she wanted to protect his son.

"It's the first time. We've never met," she said, feeling irrationally apologetic.

"Those are hard." He smiled painfully. "I hope you enjoy yourself!"

"Do you?" she asked him softly, searching his eyes. Was it possible? Or was she imagining what she saw there? Yearning, hope, barely concealed despair? And yes, fathomless passion? Was it real? Were they really telling her everything she longed to know?

She took her things and left, closing the door gently behind her.

He listened as her footsteps grew fainter and more distant, leaning back on the couch as he softly rocked the child. His body was aching, bereft. The room seemed to have emptied out, leaving him alone. But then, suddenly, he felt flooded with the warmth of the child's body, the softness of his hair. Slowly, he caressed the little boy's sweet shoulders and firm little back, his mind awash with a million rebellious ideas, wanting to shout with pain and incredulity and happiness, wanting to break the bonds that held him, like Samson stretching the ropes of the Philistines until he pulled down the pillars that held up the roof, raining down rubble and destruction on everything, himself included. Yes, he was ready for it. Let the pillars smash! Let the stones crush him, too! What did any of it matter if he could not have her? They had taken one woman from him. He would not let them take another.

His name was Aaron Gluck. And he was nice, really nice, she thought. White teeth, a ready smile, comfortable in his own skin. Considerate.

"I understand you love to Rollerblade. I thought maybe we could go ice-skating?"

How thoughtful, she thought, looking at his nicely shaved, kind, smiling face.

"Well, normally it would be fun, but I've had a long day. Would you mind if we just—"

"Sure, no problem."

He took her to a nice, kosher coffee shop about ten minutes away. It was empty and quiet, and he was pleasant and funny and didn't ask any intrusive questions. Shoshana was right. Leah *did* like him. And they had a lot in common. He was also newly observant from a secular family.

"I think I enjoy being Orthodox because it makes me feel special. Otherwise, my life would be so dull, so ordinary. I like the idea of being connected to something larger than myself. The idea of following a path that is always winding its way upward to purity, goodness, holiness."

"Yes, so do I." His words touched her. It was so hard for Jews born into Orthodoxy to understand the incredible joy of discovering a place within yourself that truly connected to God. They either took such a feeling for granted or had never had it and didn't want it, content to pretend, their outward obedience to stringencies covering for their lack of any real faith, she thought with a new bitterness.

"It's hard for people like us to find a shidduch among the Orthodox." He shrugged. "Believe me, I've tried."

"It's terrible, isn't it? After all the things that are written in the Torah about not mistreating the stranger?"

"Awful. But what can you do? Not everybody lives up to their ideals."

"It hasn't made you bitter?"

He smiled. "I'm not a bitter person. I'm a florist. I love color and beautiful scents and nature. There's no room in me for anything ugly and dark. In the end, you have no choice over how others behave, only about your own reaction."

She nodded, impressed.

"So, what do think?" He looked at her hopefully.

"I like you," she told him honestly. "But the truth is, I think I'm in love."

He blinked, leaning back in his seat. One forefinger nervously tapped the table.

"Then why did you agree to go out with me?"

"It happened about ten minutes before I met you."

His smile returned. He leaned in. "Does the person know?"

She shook her head.

"And what would happen if he found out?"

"He'd be surprised, then appalled, and then, ever so politely and gently, I'd get kicked out of his life."

"I'm confused."

"Join the club."

They smiled at each other across the table, but a bit sadly.

"Any hope you might change your mind?"

"Probably. I'll probably change my mind the minute you drop me off and I walk into my empty, lonely house tonight."

"So, why don't we just try seeing each other again?"

She shook her head. "It wouldn't be right. To you, I mean. You are a great guy—"

He put his hand over his heart and grimaced. "Ouch!"

"No, please, I mean it. You are probably the nicest guy I've met in the entire time I've been going out on these shidduch dates."

"I like you, too," he said warmly, without pretense.

"Why?"

"Really?"

"Yes, I'd like to know."

"For one thing, you are beautiful."

She blushed in confusion. She couldn't remember the last time a man had told her that! For such a long time, she had felt old and fat and hated her reddish, frizzy hair. But as he said it, she remembered how surprised she'd been the last time she bought clothes, realizing that she was back to the size she'd worn in college.

"And you're honest. You say how you feel. I feel I can trust you."

"Thank you, Aaron."

"Don't mention it, Leah."

For a few minutes, no one said anything. He motioned for the check. "This is what I propose. Hold on to my number. No pressure. If you change your mind, get kicked out, fall out of love, call me. Let's take this thing where it needs to go." He wrote down his phone number on a napkin and slid it over to her. "A back-up. Put it somewhere safe," he pleaded.

She nodded, smiling, as she folded it carefully, putting it into her purse.

He dropped her off outside her apartment building.

"Can I walk you up?"

"Please, no," she said wearily.

He sighed, walking around and opening the door for her.

"You won't lose my number, right?"

"I have it, Aaron."

"Well, good night, I guess."

"Good night, Aaron. And thank you for being so nice."

She walked up the stairs, not wanting to wait an extra second for the elevator, yearning for sleep and oblivion. She stopped, gripping the bannister. Before her door, on the very last step, sat Yaakov Lehman.

He got up silently, searching her eyes.

"You know where I live?"

"It wasn't hard to find out."

"Cheeky?"

"Sleeping. The Tylenol. Shaindele's watching him."

She nodded. "Yaakov, what are you doing here?"

"I . . . needed to tell you. To talk to you, about Shabbos. I was very disappointed."

She looked anxiously around at the deserted staircase, concerned. That's all she needed, for some nosy neighbor to witness this encounter. It would spread out like feathers in the wind through the entire community. "Please, Yaakov, come inside."

He followed her over the threshold.

"I won't close the door all the way so there's no *yichud*," she said.

He hadn't even thought of that! "Thank you."

"About Shabbos," she continued. "I was also looking forward to it, but you know, it would be misunderstood. The community would say it was improper. It might taint your family's reputation, hurt Shaindele's chances when the time came for shidduchim. After all, I'm unmarried, a *baalas teshuva*," she said, repeating dutifully every argument that had been used to convince her.

He made a small, impatient gesture. "I've heard all this before."

She was shocked. "About me?"

"Nothing to do with you. But the very same things exactly, told to me by all the great tzaddikim in our community. People who are on such a high level. Did you know that everyone in our community is a tzaddik? On such a high level? At least that's what they tell themselves, and it's up to the rest of us to keep pretending it's true. And to do that, it's all right to lie, to cheat, to reject newcomers as not 'worthy' enough to live among us. Even to ruin lives. I listened to them when they told me not to do what was right because it would taint the family's reputation, ruin my children's shidduchim. I killed my wife, Leah. She died because of me. And now my poor children are motherless orphans. All because I listened to them."

She was shocked. "Yaakov, please—"

"No, Leah, this is the truth. We reject people like you because we don't want outsiders to see what's really going on here. Otherwise, people might begin to realize that we are not all great tzaddikim, and *that* no one is ever allowed to know. Rejection of people like you is the best way to pretend that only the most holy are allowed inside."

"Yaakov, you are the most holy."

He shook his head violently. "I ruined my family," he said starkly.

"Don't."

But he couldn't stop. "Because I let them convince me that saving face was more important than saving a life. Don't listen to them, Leah. Please, don't listen to them!"

The bitterness poured out of him like pus from a wound. His eyes seemed dead, his shoulders defeated.

"Yaakov, you are best man I've ever known."

He shook his head adamantly. "No, the kindest thing you could say about me is that I'm a fool." He suddenly stopped, looking deeply into her eyes. "Leah, if I asked you to go out with me, would you go out with me?"

"Go out? I don't understand." She tried to turn her face away.

But he was relentless. He moved closer, as close as he could without actually touching her.

"Leah, if you got a call from a respectable shadchan who asked you if you would go out with Yaakov Lehman, a widower with five children, a man who is only a part-time learner, who has as yet no income but has good prospects, would you agree to go out with him?"

She wiped her eyes. "Yes, Yaakov. I would go out with you."

His eyes came back to life. He exhaled, a smile lighting up his face as his broad shoulders, held back tensely, eased into their natural posture. He looked once again like the man she knew.

"But, Yaakov, we have to be very, very careful. It all has to be done in the proper way, not to bring any shame on your family, any gossip, so that your children—so that Shaindele—won't suffer. Please, Yaakov!"

"We will be the most respectable couple, with a saintly matchmaker breathing down our necks so that even the throats and tongues of the most sinful gossipers will have nothing to say. I promise you!"

His joy was infectious. For the first time, the little apartment seemed bathed in a warm glow that banished the chill of loneliness. It seemed homey and full, she realized as she smiled into his happy face, her heart full to bursting.

25

Fruma Esther Sonnenbaum sat uneasily in the waiting room of the eye clinic of Mount Sinai Hospital. It was crowded like a buffet table after Yom Kippur, she thought irritably, staring at the women in their immodest tight pants and the men with tattoos, wishing now she had asked someone to accompany her. She sighed. No, it was better this way. There were enough *tsuris* for her family right now. They needed another? As for all the yentas who would have lined up to take her and then told the entire neighborhood what good people they were to help the poor, unfortunate widow of the great Rav Sonnenbaum whose own family was no longer in a position to help her given the unfortunate and heartbreaking events with which God had visited upon them of late . . . no, thank you.

She had been seeing Dr. Margolis going on seven years now. She remembered the shocking moment she realized that there was something terribly wrong with her eyesight—not that it had ever been good, mind you. From the age of six, she had been prescribed prescription lenses. "She will probably need glasses her entire life," the young doctor in the white coat had told her mother, who pursed her lips as if swallowing a bitter but necessary pill. The words had echoed in her own shocked, childish heart. "All her life!" She was only six.

She had grown used to the yearly visits to the optometrist, the endless "does it look better this way or that way" of the vision tests to determine if a still thicker lens was necessary to make sense of a blurry world. Almost always, the answer was yes. But then seven years ago, she had been helping one of the grandchildren with homework and the graph paper had suddenly seemed all misshapen and wobbly instead of a neat little grid.

She thought she was going blind or losing her mind.

But it turned out to be neither.

"An epiretinal membrane," Dr. Margolis told her.

"*Vus is dus?*"

"It means you have a thin piece of tissue over your retina. If it doesn't bother you, you don't have to do anything."

"It bothers me."

"Well, we can operate."

"On my eye? You want to use a knife on my eye?" she'd gasped.

"It's a very successful operation. Takes half an hour, but then you'll probably need surgery a few months down the line for a cataract."

"I have a cataract?"

"No, not now, but if you do the surgery to remove the membrane . . ."

So, they would solve one problem and cause another. Suddenly, it didn't bother her. Not enough for that.

But every year, she could feel the tissue encroaching on her vision, pulling on her eyeball like an impatient and undisciplined child. It was just a matter of time before she would see almost nothing clearly from that eye.

She pondered long and hard how such a thing had happened to her. "We don't know," Dr. Margolis told her. But then he added, "Sometimes it starts out as an infection and there is scar tissue."

An infection! She remembered when it had started. She had visited the cemetery where she had recited psalms, weeping copiously over her late husband Yitzchak Chaim's grave. The very next day, her eye had grown red and filled with pus.

Perhaps she had wiped away her tears before ritually washing her hands as was the law, allowing the evil spirits that lurked among the dead to damage her eye? The doctor had given her a little tube of antibiotic gel to put on her inner eyelid, but it had taken weeks to go away.

The idea of losing her eyesight terrified her more than anything. As Rashi wrote concerning Isaac, of whom it is written "his eyes were dim": *Blind and housebound either caused the evil inclination to be removed, or those two qualities along with the removal of the evil inclination created the status of a dead person.*

If she could not read the holy books and the sweet words of *chazal*; if she could no longer make out the words in the prayer books—not the everyday prayers that she knew by heart but the special *piyyutim* in the holiday liturgy with their complicated poetry and anagrams, verses *no one* could learn by heart; if she could no longer help her children and grandchildren, give alms to the poor, cheer up her friends in the old-age home; if she were instead to become a burden, dependent on others for care, she would absolutely prefer to be dead and buried with dirt thrown over her.

She had not come to that. She still had one good eye that allowed her to read her holy books—the Torah portion and the haftorah, *Duties of the Heart,* and *Mesilat Yesharim,* except that now it took longer. But several months ago, to her shock and horror, her good eye had been diagnosed with a similar condition. She knew if her good eye ceased to function, she would be left stumbling and bookless in a blurry world that no eyeglass prescription could fix.

She tried to think why HaShem, blessed be His Name, had brought this terrible trouble down upon her. For she had no doubt, God was just and His punishments were meted out measure for measure. What sins had she committed with her eyes?

Never in her life had she gone to a movie theater. Nor had she ever owned a television set. And she was not in the habit of reading anything that was not published by Feldheim, Artscroll, or Targum, all 100 percent glatt kosher publishing houses that would never have dreamed of putting into print anything that did not have strict rabbinical approval, usually from more than one rabbi, if not a dozen, who wrote laudatory letters of recommendation that filled up page after page before the first chapter even began! But there must be something she was missing, some act involving a sin that involved her eyes. Otherwise, she could find no explanation for why she was now discussing the dreaded operation that required her to have her eyeball sliced open and shaved, and her natural lens replaced with plastic.

When her turn came, she sat behind the machines as they looked into her retina, watching the bleeping and flashing bright lights as they photographed the inside of her poor eyes. *Please God,* she prayed. *Please!*

Her cell phone—one of several Yaakov had determinedly acquired and distributed among the family soon after Chasya got out of the hospital, insisting it was vital they be able to contact one another at all times—rang and rang, but she did not answer.

Yaakov hung up the phone, frustrated. He was like a man with a parched throat desperate for a drink of water. It must be arranged, quickly, before Leah changed her mind! Or, he reluctantly admitted to himself, he changed his. For this was, he knew, a hazardous undertaking fraught with risks. His entire world would be up in arms against the idea.

He was disappointed that Fruma Esther had not answered his call, even though, of all people, she was sure to be the strongest opponent of his relationship with Leah. Had she not already made that clear? Yet in the past, she had also been his firmest ally and most outspoken advocate of remarrying. In his heart, he hoped her love for her grandchildren and her sincere desire to be of help to her daughter's family would outweigh any ugly prejudice.

He considered calling the shadchan who had arranged his prior shidduch dates directly, but put down the phone. All he needed was a lecture on why not accepting the divorcée from Monsey or the windfall insurance heiress from Brooklyn with her designer couches was a sin bordering on the criminal! Still, was not matchmaking a business after all? Wasn't the woman trying to earn a living? What could be easier than selling a product that was presold to its only customer?

Encouraged, he dialed.

"Shalom aleichem, who is this?"

"Rebbitzen Kimmeldorfer, this is Yaakov Lehman."

He heard a deep intake of breath, then silence.

"Shalom?" he repeated.

"And shalom to you, Rav Lehman."

There was no mistaking the tone. It was hostile. He cleared his throat.

"How are you?"

"How should I be?"

"I'm calling to ask you a question."

"I'm listening."

"I'm interested in a shidduch."

"This is news to me, Rav Lehman."

"Well, yes, I know it must have been difficult for you, and I ask *mechilah*."

"Difficult for me? For *me*! Am I looking for a husband for myself? Am I waiting by the phone to hear? Am I a poor, husbandless divorcée or widow with an excellent reputation and with financial means to have anyone I want and still—"

"I apologize. But surely I told them right away that I wasn't interested. At least that is what I told my mother-in-law. She must have called you."

"Must have? I don't think so. What I heard from your dear mother-in-law was that you liked them both, but you were having a hard time making up your mind after that youngster rejected you. What was her name again?"

"Rachel," he whispered, swallowing hard. What was he going to say, that he had told his mother-in-law months ago that he had absolutely no interest at all in either one of those women, and there was zero chance of his changing his mind? Obviously, this information had not filtered down to Suri Kimmeldorfer.

"Then I ask *mechilah* again," he offered mildly. "You are completely justified—as are the saintly women you set me up with—to feel pained and insulted. I take full responsibility."

There was a beat while the woman recalibrated. "So, you have a better answer for me now?"

"I'm afraid not. But I have another proposition."

"I'm listening."

"I have met a woman through my family and have broached the subject of a shidduch, but she wants to do it through a respectable shadchan. And so, of course, I thought only of you."

"I see." There was a pause. He could just envision the little wheels turning in her head. "What's her name?"

"Leah Howard."

"Howard? What kind of name is Howard?"

"A Jewish name."

"Is her family from Brooklyn?"

He realized that he had no idea where Leah Howard's family was from. He had never asked her, and he didn't care. "From Manhattan," he guessed. He might as well have said Goa, India, for all the familiarity Suri Kimmeldorfer had with Jews from that far-off borough, which was forty-five minutes removed by car ride and an hour and a quarter by subway *if you got lucky* with the F train. Women from Manhattan were like women from Far Rockaway: geographically undesirable.

"You say you know this woman?"

"Yes," he admitted, and closed his lips.

"I'll have to look into it."

This he hadn't expected. "What do you mean 'look into it'? I have told you, this is what I want."

"I have a reputation to maintain, Rav Lehman." She sniffed.

Yaakov felt the beads of sweat in his armpits and across his forehead sprout like dandelions under the relentless rays of a harsh sun. He was totally confused. Why would she consider it praiseworthy to keep pressuring him to accept incompatible women with whom he had nothing in common yet consider helping to facilitate his marriage to the woman he loved a frontal attack on her respectability and thus livelihood? But he had never been involved in the delicate machinations of the male-female relationship before marriage that were best left to experts. Even his first wife had come to him after his mother had made all the arrangements. It was all a great mystery. Still, the urgency he felt would not allow him to back down.

"I ask your *mechilah* once again, Rebbitzen. I am sure you are doing God's holy work. But I tell you this: I feel sure this is God's will. Can you not help to fulfill this mitzvah? If not, I will take no more of your time."

The alarming finality in the tone of his voice did not go unnoticed. She had been in this business a long time and knew unerringly when she was about to lose a customer, perhaps forever. And what a customer! The

Lehmans were aristocracy. One word from Fruma Esther, and her business would lose at least half its clientele.

"Well, if this is what Rebbitzen Fruma Esther believes would be best," she conciliated.

"There is no need to involve my mother-in-law."

Now the woman's ears pricked up like a hunting dog who hears the tread of paws in the deep hedgerows of the countryside, invisible but clearly present. "In fact, now that we're talking, Reb Lehman, I'll tell you very frankly, I'm surprised to hear your voice on the other end of the phone instead of hers. Why didn't *she* call me about Leah Howard?"

What could he say?

"My dear mother-in-law is a *tzadakis* and has done so much to help me. But as you know, she has many children and grandchildren. It is hard for her to be involved in everyone's life all at once. I am trying to ease her burden."

"Very praiseworthy, Reb Lehman," said Rebbitzen Kimmeldorfer, who wasn't thrown off the scent for a millisecond. "But since she and I have been in touch about your shidduch for such a long time, believe me, I think she would want to be involved. *Chas ve'shalom,* I wouldn't want her to feel insulted or left out."

"*Chas ve'shalom,*" he repeated helplessly.

"So why don't I try to call her and talk to her?"

He gave up. "That would be very kind of you, Rebbitzen."

"*HaShem Yisborach* should bless you and your family, Reb Lehman. You should know no more sorrow."

"Yes, well, thank you and shalom."

"Shalom."

Even if the slight, nearly nonexistent, possibility existed that Suri Kimmeldorfer would call Leah to arrange a shidduch after she spoke to Fruma Esther, still he couldn't wait. Besides, it was much more likely that such a conversation would result in an outraged Fruma Esther on the doorstep of his yeshiva, where she would drag him in to see Reb Alter, who might—or might not—join in the battle against his heart's desire.

Even in the best case, where everyone behaved like angels from heaven on their day off from guarding the Holy Throne of Glory, when all was said and done, he didn't want Leah to spend another twenty-four hours in doubt, worst-case scenarios leaping through her mind with a hundred demeaning suggestions. He didn't want her to think for a moment he was having second thoughts.

He needed someone to help him, someone he trusted implicitly, to whom he could open his heart and bare his incredible need and his terrible dilemma; someone who was sincerely righteous and who would not judge, but unhesitatingly and selflessly do immediately what he needed done. He needed a true friend who was also a tzaddik.

He picked up the phone and dialed.

26

He had known Yaakov Lehman as a young bridegroom, filled with excitement and longing. He had known him as a young widower, almost broken by sorrow. But never had Meir Halpern heard the desperation bordering on despair in the voice of his *chavrusa* that he heard now.

"Of course I will help you, Yaakov! It is wonderful that you have finally found your *beshert.* But I don't understand what you want *me* to do."

Slowly, patiently, in the almost singsong tone he used to expound and extrapolate the intricacies of difficult Talmudical passages, Yaakov explained to his *chavrusa* what he wanted him to do.

"You want me to be your shadchan?" Meir said, summing up the strange request with shocking simplicity.

"Yes," Yaakov answered. "I want you to be my shadchan. I want you to call Leah Howard and tell her what a wonderful man I am and plead with her to go out with me. And then I want you to tell everyone the shidduch was your idea."

Meir didn't know what to say. A serious, dedicated Talmud scholar from a large and distinguished family, as long as he could remember, his path in life had always been marked out for him, a path he walked easily and comfortably.

"But, Yaakov, what do I know about matchmaking?"

"My friend, the match is already made. As it is written: *Forty days before conception a heavenly voice rings out: this man for this woman.*"

There was a mutual silence as both men thought of the woman whose tragic loss had made it necessary for a second heavenly voice to ring out.

"I am happy for you, Yaakov, and of course I will help you. I just don't understand why you need me. You are both adults. You know each other. Why can't you simply—"

"Thank you, Meir. She, Leah, has asked me to do this in the most respectable way, through a shadchan, so that no tongues will wag. She is worried about *loshon hara.*"

"But why should anyone speak *loshon hara*? You are both God-fearing Jews, both pious and observant, both unmarried and unrelated. She doesn't have your mother's name. You are not from the priestly class, and she is not a divorcée. I cannot see any biblical or halachic impediment . . ." His voice trailed off in utter confusion.

"It's not a question of halacha, Meir. You know how people are. The gossip. She wants to be certain that from the beginning no one will have what to say because we did everything in the most pious and acceptable way according to our traditions and customs."

"Most admirable," his friend said approvingly. "Have you tried a regular shadchan? They would be happy of the income."

"I have tried, but the woman wants to 'investigate' first."

"What? Why?"

"Because Leah is a *baalas teshuva.*"

"But this is against the Torah! Against the halacha!" Meir exclaimed. "As it is written: *You shall not oppress the stranger.*"

"As it is written, Meir, but not as it is practiced," he said patiently. "If I wait to find a shadchan who won't 'investigate,' who won't be talked out of it by my mother-in-law—"

"Rebbitzen Sonnenbaum? She's against this?" he asked, the first doubts creeping into his voice.

"I don't know; I haven't asked her," Yaakov said hurriedly, his patience waning. "But I know this: she wants to marry me off to a rich widow from a prominent family or a well-to-do divorcée with *yichus* because that's what she sincerely believes would be best for the family. But it wouldn't. Not for me."

"But if you spoke to her . . . explained . . . surely—"

"Meir—" He cut him short. "There is no time! I can't keep Leah waiting. She'll think she is somehow not good enough and that perhaps I have changed my mind. She has had so many ugly experiences with prejudice in our community. I just don't want her to feel oppressed again. And so, Meir, I am asking you to call her now."

"It's forbidden to hurt or oppress newcomers! It's an *issur d'oreitah*, a direct command from God Himself in His own words!" Meir said as if still in the study house discussing a theoretical, philosophical problem, his voice gaining certainty.

"Meir, please!" Yaakov cut him short.

"Look, Yaakov, I would do it gladly, but what do I know from matchmaking?"

Yaakov felt sad for Meir, sympathizing with his friend's sincere distress. Were the situation reversed, he would have felt exactly the same. "Meir, do you remember the conversations with the shadchan you had before you married Bruriah?"

Meir tried. It was so long ago. "I think so. A little. Maybe."

"So, this is all you have to do. Please, Meir. Help me."

Meir Halpern came home early from the study house. Removing three toy trucks and a teddy bear from the weathered living room couch, he sat down heavily. Wiping his sweaty, nervous hands across his dark pants, he lifted the heavy black hat off his head and placed it beside him.

"Tateh!" his four-year-old son cried out, running to him, then laying his curly head down on his father's knees. Meir caressed the child's curls, then lifted him up and kissed him. "Bruriah!" he called over his shoulder.

His young wife hurried in from the kitchen holding a baby in her arms. Their two-year-old daughter tugged at her skirt.

"You're home." She looked at him curiously. "What's wrong?"

"Nothing. Just . . . I have an important phone call to make. Could you please take the children into the other room for five minutes?"

"Important?" she asked, arching her brows in surprise as she gently took the four-year-old's hand and gathered him to her side.

"It's a double—no, a *triple* mitzvah," he said, nodding. He saw her smile, and his heart expanded, imagining for a terrible second what it must have been like for Yaakov to lose his Zissele. He waited, watching her shepherd his children into the kitchen. Putting his misgivings behind him, he picked up the phone.

"Shalom aleichem. Is this Leah Howard? My name is Meir Halpern. Who am I? I'm . . ."

Could he call himself a shadchan? Or would that be a lie? But since in this instance, he was acting in the capacity of one, perhaps it wasn't a lie? But if he didn't call himself a shadchan, perhaps it would not satisfy her need for respectability and community approval? So, an untruth in the service of a mitzvah was acceptable, especially if it avoided embarrassment for someone. To embarrass a person was like murdering them, as it is written. . . .

"Hello? Are you still there?" she said, confused by the long silence.

He cleared his throat. "I am a shadchan," Meir Halpern finally declared. "I have heard many wonderful things about you, Leah. About your piety and your *chesed*. About your devotion to study and keeping mitzvoth. I want to propose a match to you. A fine, pious Talmud scholar who tragically lost his wife. He has five children, two still small. He has just turned forty-one. Would you be willing to meet him?"

He smiled, listening to her response. "Very good. So I will tell him to call you to make arrangements?" He listened, nodding, then gently set the receiver back into its cradle. He exhaled slowly. "Bruriah, you can let the children back in now. I'm done."

The room erupted with life as the children, hopping and crawling, crowded in along with his wife, who was talking softly to the baby. She sat down next to him, whispering into his ear.

"Well, mitzvah accomplished?" She smiled.

"I think so," he said, smiling back.

"What was it all about?"

"I'm now a shadchan."

Her look was incredulous and amused.

"Yes, I have made a match for my *chavrusa,* Yaakov the widower."

"Who is the girl?"

"Her name is Leah. She is a *baalas teshuva* who was one of the community volunteers helping him with his children."

"What do you know about her? Her family? What she did before she came here?"

Meir shifted uncomfortably. "I don't know."

"But a shadchan is supposed to investigate before he makes a match! How much will the dowry be?"

"I don't know. We didn't talk about it."

She shook her head. "A fine shadchan you make!"

"I don't think I will do it again, Bruriah."

"That's a good idea, Meir. So what *do* you know about this girl?"

"Only that—if it be God's will—she will make my friend Yaakov happy."

"For a time. Like any marriage," Bruriah said wisely.

"*Even if a man lives many years, let him enjoy himself in all of them, remembering how many the days of darkness are going to be,*" he quoted, wiping the sweat from his forehead and kissing his wife on hers as he took the baby from her arms.

27

Leah put down the phone, her heart racing, her eyes moist. Yaakov had kept his word! And with a swiftness and honesty that took her breath away. Everything would be out in the open now, arranged according to the strictest tradition. Anyone who would be offended now by their relationship was clearly in violation of all the Godly laws written in the Torah. It was their problem, not hers.

But as usual when a thing most hoped for and dreamed of suddenly goes from the far-off realm of vague imaginings into the fleshy, solid presence of reality, she found it hard to make the transition. While in the past, she slept as if drugged, her worries and hopes too distant to prey on her fears, now she found that however she tried, sleep would not come. Like bees swarming from an overturned hive, her thoughts darted in and out, stinging and menacing, as well as dropping tantalizing bits of sweet nectar.

What if, she thought, turning over once again to find the unfindable comfortable spot that would let her sleep, *what if, in spending time together, in growing more familiar, we suddenly realize how incompatible we are?* After all, they had nothing in common—not lineage nor upbringing nor even language, hers a product of her California upbringing, his the rare distillation of thousands of years of Jewish wanderings and holy books, glued together with the recent Eastern European immigrant past washed up on the shores of New York City.

What if, at closer inspection, he saw how newly minted was her acceptance and practice of a lifestyle and customs that had been his and his family's bread and butter for decades, if not centuries? What if she made mistakes, said the wrong blessing, put on the wrong clothes, forgot to do something she should, mistakenly did something she shouldn't? Would he look at her differently? *Would he change his mind?*

What if she changed hers?

Boro Park was such a different world—another planet, really—where native-born Americans spoke English like foreigners. As much as she tried to talk herself out of it, that bothered her, that uneducated speech. It made her feel as if people were in some way primitive. When they said things like "I'll go by you" instead of "I'll go to you." Or "How's by you?" instead of "How are you?" It grated. But if she was a snob, they were worse.

Although she did her best to keep all the laws, still, she was singled out as a "penitent." She found the very term *baalas teshuva* repellant. As if those who used it against her had nothing to do penance for! Or the idea that a person born of a mother who didn't go to the ritual baths was somehow inferior, tainted. How she sometimes longed to stand on a soapbox in the center of Boro Park and shout at them, "We were all born from a human womb and began with a putrid seed! Do you think father Abraham's mother, who was married to an idol worshipper, went to the mikvah? Do you think Moses's mother, who was an Egyptian slave, went to the mikvah? You and I both came naked into this world, bawling our heads off. What we make of our lives doesn't depend on whether our mothers dunked naked into a little pool of much-used water filled with hairs. We were born pure, all of us. Or all born tainted. So give it up, you wretched snobs!"

Could she commit to living the rest of her life in that world? And if not, could she go back to her old life? Did she want to?

Her life had changed so radically, she thought. There was a new rhythm, something ordered and meaningful.

It started with the Days of Awe in September, beginning with Rosh Hashana followed by days of deep introspection that culminated in fasting and prayer and the long, urgent call of the ram's horn, that went off like a bomb siren, increasing in urgency and intensity. *Hurry!* it seemed to shout. *There is no time! Search your life! Become a better person! There is no time!* How different from the secular New Year's celebrations she had been part of—the loneliness and attempts at false hilarity washed down with alcohol to numb herself to the relentless passage of time.

She thought of Sukkos, moving out of your house for a week to eat and even sleep in a flimsy little booth, reminding you that homelessness was man's natural state, and everything solid in your life was temporary, a gift from God. The first time she'd grasped the lemony, ripe citron in her hands together with the tall green fronds of the date palm, the myrtle and willow leaves, waving them up and down, back and forth, toward heaven and toward earth, it had felt almost pagan, connecting her to ancestors from a distant past who had lived close to the earth, in harmony with the changing seasons, the planting and harvesting.

And then came December and Chanukah, candles shining from every window on the street, the light growing more robust with every night's addition of a new candle until the windows blazed, banishing the darkest nights of the year, reminding you that miracles did happen, and black nights, danger, and sadness could be collectively banished, transformed into light and joy. She thought of Purim, which saw the staid streets burst into color, becoming a carnival with endless little brides and queens, little soldiers and tiny high priests in their white robes and glued-on beards, carrying loaded baskets of cakes and sweets to friends and neighbors, the only holiday one was encouraged to get drunk out of frivolity and joy. And soon after, the open windows, the pails of water flowing down gutters as people scrubbed their homes for Passover, readying themselves for the sacred retelling of the tribe's beginnings: Abraham, Isaac, Jacob, Moses, Aaron, the ten plagues of Egypt, and the miraculous journey through the desert to the promised land.

Here in Boro Park, time didn't pass; it was embraced, celebrated, every month with its rituals and reminders of who you were and where you came from and the God Who watched over you. The very thought of leaving all that behind, going back to the thin fabric of her old life, was chilling.

Yet at the very base of all those rituals was the belief—the hope—that leading a religious life made you a better person; that living among religious Jews meant living among good people, raising your children to be like them. With a heavy heart, she realized this was not so.

Although it was true of some—she thought of Yaakov and some of the rabbis who were her teachers—many others, perhaps even most, were at best simply ordinary human beings and at worst narrow-minded, cliquish, prejudiced gossipers with the same moral failings as most people. Indeed, there was something hard and unforgiving and almost brutal among those who considered themselves the most piously stringent in their observance, something ugly and positively vicious in their unrelenting persecution of those who deviated from their standards. They were nothing like the compassionate, kind, forgiving God they desired—or pretended to desire—to serve. With their bullying, they had succeeded in creating a little closed and unwelcoming kingdom, an unforgiving and brutal place where the truly pious, indeed, goodness itself, deprived of life's blood, couldn't survive.

Was that too harsh? She didn't know.

But her deepest worry was not if she could live in Boro Park. After all, people picked up and moved all the time. No, her deepest worry of all was something else entirely.

How, she thought, *can I be sure I am in love with the man and not just with the father of my beloved children?* After all, their courtship had been shockingly brief, a few notes, some words exchanged. You haven't yet agreed to marry, she comforted herself. Just to go out. And she knew way more about Yaakov Lehman than any other man she had agreed to meet on a shidduch date.

She thought about his eyes, so warm and true and expressive, the way they lit up when he looked at his children, when he looked at her. She loved how honestly they reflected every nuance of his heart: his pain, his regret, his disappointment, his sadness, as well as his joy. His eyes never lied, never obfuscated or hid. They mirrored whatever was happening in his soul.

And then there were his hands, those large, gentle, dependable hands with their graceful, clean fingers. You would never hesitate to put a tiny baby inside them, or the hand of a child needing guidance. You would never worry that they would be harsh or unkind or abrupt. They were soft. They were patient. They were strong. She would never be afraid to have them hold hers, or touch her.

She loved his body, tall and lean and broad shouldered. He was handsome. Handsomer than either Joshua or Andrew had been. And while she couldn't imagine him climbing a mountain, she could see him running another kind of marathon: standing in place and praying for hours without eating or drinking. There was something of the ascetic in him, but not in an aggressive way. He looked like a man who lived a great deal in his mind. And yet because of the laws of the Torah—which exhorted men to live also in the body, to be connected to the ordinary cares of normal people—he was also deeply connected to life. He was a man who laughed, who loved, who had children and raised them.

She loved his reticence and modesty, his gentlemanly deference and protectiveness around her and his daughters and even his mother-in-law. In the secular world, it was impossible to find a man who had not been infected by the worst accomplishments of feminism: the idea that women should be treated as men not only in their paychecks but also in their physical strength. Yes, she could open her own door, carry her own packages, lift heavy objects. But what woman wanted to be treated like that, unless you were a brainwashed Soviet comrade? She loved how Yaakov treated her.

But most of all, her soul was seared by the love he had for her, of which she had no doubt. She had experienced it and knew how it felt. She could hear it in the tone of his voice, in its breathlessness when he approached her. She could see it in the way his eyes roamed over her, as if she were a precious, almost sacred object to be studied and admired. She could see it in the corners of his mouth as they turned upward with joy each time she walked into a room.

And then, there was this: the time she had grabbed a handful of his white shirts to place them into the washing machine and instead had impulsively buried her face in them, breathing them in.

She turned over, her body shot through with sudden passion. His neck, she thought. His shoulders. His chest. His lips. Yes, that could not be denied. It was alive in her, and it was alive in him, the longing, the need.

Leave it alone! What does it matter? she begged herself. Maybe, God willing, if she decided it was right, she would be his, and he would be hers. For better, or for worse. And she would get used to Boro Park, and they would get used to her. Or not. And with that, she finally slept.

Yaakov called her early, giving her just enough time to ritually wash her hands and recite her prayers.

"Shalom aleichem, Leah. It's Yaakov Lehman."

"Yes," she whispered hoarsely. "I know."

"What is wrong?"

"Nothing. Just . . . I didn't sleep very well. Excited."

"So, the shadchan called you about me?"

She smiled to herself. So this was how it was going to be played. "Yes, Reb Lehman. I was expecting your call. He said very nice things about you. Told me that you were a fine catch."

"He didn't!"

"No, he didn't," she teased. "But he did say you were sincere in wishing to remarry."

"'That I am, Leah-le.'" His voice caressed her as it sank into intimacy, dropping the forced formality of role-playing. "You want that I should come tonight? I *mamash* can't wait. I will find someone to watch the *kinderlach*."

She sucked in her breath at the language. *It will be all right,* she thought. *I'll get used to it. Maybe I'll learn to speak the same way.* "Who will you get? Shaindele?"

"Why not?"

"Are you going to tell her what's going on?"

"I am. I feel we shouldn't hide and pretend."

"You know she isn't going to be happy, to say the least."

"She is young and sometimes *farmisht*. But she has a good heart, Leah. She will want me to be happy, for you to be happy. *B'ezrat HaShem* she should be *zoche* to be as happy as we are in her own shidduch."

"She's never wanted me to be part of your family. Even that first time, I could hardly get her to open the door and let me squeeze inside."

"She still suffers from losing her mother. Please, Leah, don't hold her *narishkeit* against her."

"No, of course not, Yaakov. I'm just warning you what to expect. But whatever happens, please, Yaakov, don't get angry at her! Let her say what she feels, let her be honest. Make it clear to her that you understand how hard it is for her to accept that you have a new woman in your life, but that it doesn't mean you've forgotten her mother. Please, most of all, tell her that our relationship has nothing to do with her! She will never be displaced. She'll always be your beloved daughter and that you will always love her more than anyone or anything."

"You are a *tzadakis,* Leah."

"No, just a woman. I understand womanly rivalry." She smiled. It was so easy to be generous to Shaindele now that the girl had been so thoroughly vanquished on all fronts. She did feel genuine sympathy for the girl, who was obviously bitterly confused and unhappy—just not enough to fulfill the little schemer's fantasies and magically disappear. Life is tough, and then you die. The child would just have to learn to put up with her.

"So, when can I come to you?" he asked breathlessly, making an extra effort to speak correct English.

She felt touched. "Go home and see your children first. They wait for you all day. I'll be ready whenever you can come."

"Where should we go?"

"Take me wherever you took your other shidduch dates," she told him, laughing.

He was waiting at her door at eight thirty in his best black suit and the blue tie he had worn to meet Rachel.

"I rented a car," he told her excitedly when she opened the door.

He didn't know what he was doing, what he was saying. He was so happy, so overjoyed that she was there, smiling up at him with her big green eyes and long, curly hair. So sweet! So young in a way that had nothing to do with age! He felt the joy spread down his body like a slow anointing with holy oil, warm and soothing, from head to toe.

"Shalom, Rav Lehman," she said softly, her voice teasing. "So nice to finally meet you."

He sobered up only slightly, trying to get back into character. "Hello, Leah. I've heard so much about you. The shadchan sang your praises."

"Given that he's never met me, he must be very creative." She laughed, watching a slow blush creep up Yaakov's cheek. Or was that simply the golden reflection of her own happiness? "Would you like to come in? But of course, I will have to leave the door open so there will be no fear of *yichud*."

He smiled, the car keys almost electric against his palm, the idea of being alone with her—open door or not—dizzying. "Why don't we just go?"

They walked out into the late spring night, Leah pulling the pretty lavender pashmina around her shoulders against the gentle chill.

"You look very nice, Leah. I like . . . the color of your shawl," Yaakov said awkwardly, trying to behave the way he imagined normal American men behaved on dates with normal American women. He was terrified she would suddenly realize who he was and think better of the whole thing.

Leah found his attempts charming but a bit dissonant. "Relax, Yaakov. It's just me."

"I'm not relaxed?" He frowned.

"No, you are as tightly wound as a little boy's sidecurls."

He exhaled. "I just want it should be perfect. To be everything you would want, Leah."

She looked at him, his eyes, his hands, his beautiful warm smile.

"It is," she told him.

He took her to the same revolving lounge on Broadway where he had sat with Rachel in what seemed like a lifetime ago. But for some strange reason, it all seemed so new, as if it were the first time. He couldn't remember anything about it, most of all the girl who had sat opposite him. He wondered vaguely what had happened to her, hoping she had also found happiness. He felt generous, giving. Everyone deserved to be happy! He wished God's blessings on every living creature, on every blade of grass, on every stone.

He could not even remember what Rachel looked like. Leah was an eraser, he thought. Whatever had come before her was neatly wiped away from his memory and thoughts. He could see only her, hear only her, want only her. There was no divorcée, no rich widow, no Rachel, even no Zissele. He was not himself, not the Yaakov who had known all those women.

He was a young man with no past. This beautiful young woman was the first woman he had ever met and fallen in love with. The room turned around and around, the city spinning out of control as his body and mind filled with such fierce and unfamiliar longing he felt almost sick with desire.

"I would want . . ."

She turned to him, studying his face, his flaming cheeks and bright eyes. She frowned. He looked feverish.

"Yaakov, is something wrong?"

"I would want . . ." he repeated, even more softly, placing an elbow on the table and leaning in toward her as far as he could without touching her. "I would want to hold you in my arms."

The words were electric, making the air between them almost crackle with sparks.

"Oh, Yaakov . . ." She shook her head, a feeling of excitement exploding in the pit of her stomach. "Oh, Yaakov, if only you could!"

He took his elbow away, leaning back in his chair. "I never in my life said that to any woman on any shidduch date."

"Of course not." She laughed. "They would call the shadchan immediately, and you would be blacklisted."

"Yes," he agreed with a self-mocking smile. "Off their lists they would throw me. They would never find me another shidduch." He looked up, his heart in his eyes, so tender and vulnerable. "Leah, I don't want another one. All I want is you. Forever."

She knew that in the haredi world couples decided to marry after only one or two dates. Still, it was startling to her. Everything was moving at such supersonic speed, she thought, dizzy, but strangely not apprehensive. She knew this man through the children he had fathered, the home he had created, the community he was part of. She knew him as well as she had known Josh and much better than she had ever known Andrew; knew him and had fallen in love with him long ago, she realized, before they ever exchanged a single word. That was the shocking truth.

"Yaakov, are you sure? Very sure? You don't know anything about me, not really."

"I know everything I need to know, Leah, Leah, Leah," he sang, drunk on joy.

"What am I going to do with you?" she said, laughing softly, tenderly. "Marry me?"

"Are you sure, Yaakov? Really sure?"

"By me, it's for sure. But what about by you? Is it for sure by you, Leah? That is the question."

She leaned back and sighed. "I was never surer of anything in my life."

"So, if this is the situation, should we call the shadchan and tell our families?"

"No," she said firmly. "Not yet. First, I want you to know everything about me. And when you've heard it all, and you know it all, then you can decide."

"It doesn't matter to me," he protested.

"But, Yaakov, it matters to me. I can't marry someone unless I'm very sure he knows the truth. I can't worry that down the road you might find out something about me that would make you change your mind."

"I would never be so *nichshal*."

"That wouldn't be a failure. It would just mean you were human. And even if what you say is true, I can't live with that uncertainty."

He leaned back. "So tell me everything, Leah. Whatever you want. If that is what you need to do, do it."

She looked around self-consciously, suddenly aware of the relaxed, casual New York couples sipping lattes or cocktails. It was not a place for drama, to make themselves more conspicuous than they already were. "Not here, Yaakov. Let's walk down to the park."

The New York street was buzzing with sounds and activities. He walked beside her silently, content. This was all he wanted, he thought. To be with her. He didn't need to talk, didn't need to hear. But soon they turned into a small, quiet park with a single bench.

"Let's sit for a while."

He sat down next to her. Even pierced and half-hidden by skyscrapers, the moon was large and bright, transforming her into molten silver, bleaching the color from her hair, her cheeks. She seemed strange to him, otherworldly almost. A strange, unknown creature, utterly desirable in her strangeness. He didn't want her to speak. He didn't want anything to interfere with the soft, silver gleam that entranced him. But he saw that she would, that nothing could stop her. He dreaded it. Not for the revelations that would emerge—nothing would make him change his mind—but for how he would have to follow suit, revelation for revelation. He thought of it with horror as he watched her take a deep breath as if about to dive underwater. He felt suddenly breathless.

She started from the beginning, going out of her way to use the most shocking language as if intent on pushing the narrative toward extremity. "My mother was a teenager when she got pregnant with me after a one-night stand." "I only met my father twice. He had lots of illegitimate children all over the place." She described her traditional grandparents and how her mother had scrubbed away any vestige of her Judaism, bringing her up with Christmas trees and trips to see Santa. "For her, there was nothing religious about Christmas. It was simply an American holiday, and we were Americans. But one year, she took out a Christmas movie from the video store about a little girl who prays to God to give her a pony. It was Hollywood, so of course she got it. And I thought, *I can also do that, pray!* So I began praying for all kinds of things, making up prayers in my own childish words. When my mom caught on, she was furious. She told me that anyone who is so weak that they can't depend on themselves and have to make up a mythical, imaginary being to get what they want was a pitiful excuse for a human being. She said that God was 'just a bigger version of the tooth fairy.'"

"Tooth fairy?"

"When American kids lose a tooth, they put it under their pillows—"

"Why?"

"Because in the morning they will find the tooth gone and a present instead. Their parents tell them it was the tooth fairy, but at a certain point, every kid figures out it's his parents."

"So that is what God was to your mother—the tooth fairy?"

"Pretty much."

"Oy vey."

She paused, studying him. Were his cheeks redder? Or was she imagining it?

He took her pause as an opportunity to cut the story short. Her parents, her life before she came to Boro Park, what did any of that matter? He loved who she was now, who she had become. The rest was an old story, unimportant and a bit unreal to him. "And still, despite it all, you found your way to God."

"I think I always believed. My mother told me that when I was very small and she took me to the beach for the first time, I sat there just staring at the ocean and the sand and didn't say a word until finally I asked her, 'Who made it?' She always laughs at that story, but I think that was my first encounter with God."

She told him about the Hebrew school classes, and the year her mother had given in and made a seder. "She invited our Hispanic neighbors to join us. Instead of reading the Hagadah and talking about the Jewish exodus from Egypt, we talked about Caesar Chavez and his oppressed workers and how we shouldn't eat grapes. And next to a box of matzo, she put a loaf of sesame bread, so the neighbors wouldn't think we were weird."

A small, involuntary gasp escaped his throat. She nodded, perversely pleased.

"Leah, you don't have to do this. It isn't important!"

"Please!" she begged. "It's important to me. You need to know who I am, where I came from."

He sighed, nodding in silent acquiescence.

"But despite my upbringing, deep in my heart, I think I always knew I was a Jew and that there was a God and He was real." She hesitated. "Then I got proof."

It had been years since she had spoken about it, but it had to be done. How else would he understand?

"We lived around the corner from a rough neighborhood full of immigrants. They were poor, and there was alcoholism and drugs. I was walking home from Hebrew school through the park one afternoon. It was already getting dark. I saw a man in front of me. He had a book in his back pocket that kept inching up until it finally fell out. I ran to pick it up and return it to him. He was in his twenties, Hispanic, with a pockmarked face and shifty eyes. He asked me if I knew how to read, then handed me his book. When I looked at it, I felt sick. It was a pornographic comic book. I could see he'd added his own obscene words and drawings to the filthy cartoons, pressing a pencil brutally into the page, darkening certain body parts—you can imagine which. I handed it back to him, confused, then scared. I had enough sense to know I had to get away, so I told him it was late and I had to go home, but he followed me. He said he'd walk me home so we could "ask mommy permission" about all the things he wanted to do to me. He named a few. I guess he thought that was funny and that I'd be too young and too stupid to get it. But I understood exactly what he was talking about and that I was never going to get home."

Yaakov leaned forward, steepling his hands as if in prayer.

"The park was empty. I saw his eyes flitting to the bushes, and a terrible fear settled over me as I realized something really horrible was about to happen to me and that there was nothing at all I could do to stop it."

He gripped the sides of his chair, his knuckles white.

"So I whispered, 'Please, God, help me.' Just at that very moment, a streetlamp went on, and this big black man came jogging by with his little boy. I looked at him, and he began to slow down, taking both of us in. The pervert saw it and stepped back, then took off. I ran to the man and his son and jogged alongside them all the way home."

He gripped his hands, resting his elbows on his knees and bowing forward, his eyes boring into the dark pavement as he imagined what could have been. He wanted so much to hold her, to comfort her. "*Baruch HaShem,*" he whispered. "*Such hashgacha pratis.*"

She nodded. She, too, had always believed that, and that belief had led her to enroll at a college with religion classes. She described Santa Clara, Father Joe, and the big, blond Baptist farm girl who had been her roommate. "When she found out I was Jewish, she started throwing all these quotes from the Bible at me. She was so shocked I'd never heard them before. 'Don't you know how lucky you are to be an Israelite?' she said. I still remember one of her quotes, because it touched me so deeply that I looked it up and memorized it. *'Inquire about bygone ages that came before you, ever since God created man on earth, from one end of the heaven to the other: has anything as grand as this ever happened, or has its like ever been known? Has any people heard the voice of a god speaking out of a fire as you have, and survived? Or has any god ventured to go and take for himself one nation from the midst of another by prodigious acts, by signs and portents, by war, by a mighty and outstretched arm and awesome power, as the Lord, your God, did for you in Egypt before your very eyes?'*"

He nodded in recognition, repeating the passage in Hebrew.

"'What I wouldn't do to have been born into such a holy and chosen people as you!' my roommate said, and she meant it. She made me feel as if I had won the lottery simply because my mother was a Jew and being Jewish was in my blood, in my genes. 'Your people made a covenant with God. You can't get out of it. It's forever,' she used to scold me. She, and my classes with Father Joe, and later my fiancé, Joshua, made me want to know more."

"You loved him very much?"

She nodded, a lump forming in her throat. "He was a very spiritual person, very connected to God, much more than I. But for him, God was in the mountains, in the sound the wind made through the trees, in sunrises and sunsets." Slowly, tearfully, she described how she had lost him.

A low sound, a cross between a moan and a cry, escaped him.

She turned to look at him. His eyes were clouded with tears. It was more than sympathy, she understood. It was a cry of recognition from a heart that had also known shattering, life-changing tragedy.

"Oh, Leah-le!"

"I blamed HaShem. It took me some time to figure out that my anger was connected to my faith. You can't be angry at something you don't think exists."

"This is true," he said quietly, deep in thought. "Sometimes, it is easier to be angry at God than to put the blame where it belongs, on ourselves."

His wide blue eyes were soft with love for her and filled with pain for both their tragedies.

She told him about PureBirth, about struggling with her guilt, about wishing she had done more. And finally, she told him about coming to Boro Park. "I'd tried everything the secular world had to offer and still felt empty. I wanted something else, something that would give meaning to my life. In your world, I found so many of the things I'd longed for all my life: safety, order, rules, limitations, real community, deep values. But I have to be absolutely honest with you, Yaakov. I've also discovered some things I wasn't prepared for."

He looked at her, surprised. "What things?"

She was afraid to speak, afraid what she had to say would ruin everything. Perhaps he could forgive her past, but this was about the present.

Still, she couldn't start a life with him without being truthful. She owed him that. She owed herself that.

"I used to think religious people were kinder, nicer, had better characters, but I found out they're just like everybody else, just people. Some are better, some are worse. There are the sincere ones, like you, but also the opposite: the butcher who won't pay his bills until I threaten him with lawyers; the little girls who look me up and down in the street and tell me I dress like a shiksa; the matchmakers who treat *baale teshuva* like something they have stepped in and have to wipe off the bottom of their shoes.

"There is so much—what's that word?—*gaiva*, misplaced pride; so many people who call themselves frum who most of the time don't think about God at all. It's all about themselves: how many important rabbis they know, how strict they are about what they eat and what they wear. There is no end to the rules they make up to show off. Sometimes, it feels almost like a cult. They don't do it to serve God; they do it so they can lord it over everybody else. It's what in my other life we used to call *social climbing.* They are so strict about laws that were never written in the Torah and so lax about the laws that are actually there! I can't ever be one of them, Yaakov. I won't."

"How was it for you before, in the goyish world?" he asked her. It wasn't a challenge, just a simple question.

She thought about it. "I guess the same. So many hypocrites, people busy preaching acceptance and tolerance but hating and rejecting everyone who isn't exactly like them. It breaks my heart when I think about how few genuinely good people there are in the world. You're one of them. I want to be one of them, too, to raise children who love God and keep the Torah." She hesitated, taking a deep breath. "I just don't know if I can do it in Boro Park."

She looked down at her hands, tired and a bit hopeless. "I guess you understand now why everyone is so against us getting together. I can understand why people always worry about *baale teshuva* backsliding to their old ways, but I'll tell you this honestly: I will never go back to my old, secular life because there is nothing there for me. I love you, Yaakov. So much! But I'm not the same as your family, your friends and neighbors, and I never will be. This is the truth. I won't blame you if you decide to end things now." She shrugged, her shoulders already accepting defeat.

He said nothing, his face shrouded in darkness, the moon's silver light pooling beneath the golden halo of streetlamps. And as the minutes passed and the silence grew, her heart began to ache with a growing premonition of disaster and defeat. He would reject her now. She knew it. He was just searching for the right words, the kind words, to use. Knowing Yaakov, he would make every effort to do it gently.

"I don't understand you," he finally said, breaking the silence with shocking suddenness, shaking his head.

Her head flew up. She searched his face as her heart sank. "What do you mean?"

"Here you are, opening your heart to me, telling me every shame and disgrace you can think of about yourself like an accusing angel. You're worried I'm going to change my mind? That you're not good enough for me? But, Leah, why don't you ask me anything about myself, about *my* sins? Because if you did, you'd hold that I am not good enough for you."

She smiled. "Impossible. I know everything there is to know about you, Yaakov. You're an open book."

"Leah, you never asked me once about my wife, about Zissele. Not once. I told you I killed her. How could you marry such a man?"

"I know you didn't kill your wife, Yaakov. Your mother-in-law told me everything about Zissel as soon as I started working at your house. I know she got sick and died tragically and that you did everything you could to save her. I know what it's like to feel guilt over losing someone you loved. For years, I felt that I had killed my fiancé. Again and again, I went over that moment he slipped. And each time, I imagined my arm shooting out faster, my hand gripping his more firmly, pulling him to safety. But that's a fantasy, Yaakov. There was nothing I could have done to save Josh. He would have pulled me down with him. It was an accident, but I wasn't responsible, just like you aren't responsible for the death of your wife."

"How do you know that? Why are you so sure?"

She stared at him, chilled. "Now you are scaring me."

"You should be scared! I was a worthless husband. I did everything wrong. I didn't even try."

"What could you have done?"

He looked at her, his face contorted in grief. *"Keep my statutes, and my judgments, which if a man do he shall live by them . . ."*

"I don't understand." She shook her head in helpless confusion.

"Live by them! The Rambam says, *For the sick man we may violate a hundred Sabbaths!* And we're not permitted to do it through a non-Jew or a child, but the scholars and saints of Israel must do it! *And he shall live by them, and not die through them.* Zissele was sick. It was my sacred obligation to help her. But I did nothing because of the shame. And now she's dead."

He held his face in his hands, rocking gently in grief.

She stared at him, stunned. "Yaakov, what are you saying?"

"My Zissele didn't die because of an illness. She killed herself."

Leah's mouth fell open in horror. "Oh, Yaakov."

Tears streamed down his face, unheeded. "It started right after our first child was born. Everyone said she was tired. But it was more than that. She wouldn't eat, wouldn't get dressed. And her mother and her friends would spend hours by her, helping her to take care of the baby, helping her to get dressed, spoon-feeding her, taking her out for walks. It took months. And then the depression passed. She became my Zissele again. But with every baby, it came back, and every time, it was worse, until finally, with Mordechai Shalom, there was no Zissele left. I didn't know her anymore. She didn't know herself. Like always, we tried at home. But this time, nothing helped. She needed a doctor, a hospital. My mother-in-law, I begged her . . ."

"What did your mother-in-law say?"

"She, too, finally agreed. Together, we took Zissele to the doctor, the psychiatrist. Right away, he told us it was serious. She needed to be in a hospital. 'Committed,' he told us. Even if she didn't want, even by force. He warned us she could hurt herself. But Zissele swore to her mother she was getting better, that she just needed time. We should give her more time, she begged. My mother-in-law sided with her. She said it would ruin the family's *yichus* to have a mother in a mental hospital. Our children would never get decent shidduchim and that by itself would destroy her Zissele. She'd be even more depressed. How could I argue? All of it was true, every word! No one wants to marry into a family with mental illness. Even having Moshe Rabeinu in your *yichus* would be worthless in such a case.

"My mother-in-law said she would move in by us. She would take care of Zissele, like before. She said we should ask the rabbis, get permission to stop having babies, at least for a while. We should let her rest and then, for sure, Zissele would come back to herself, just like before. I wanted so much to believe that! And so I did nothing. Are you listening to me, Leah? I didn't do anything. And then . . . and then . . . my Zissele . . ." He covered his face with both his hands and sobbed, his big shoulders shaking with uncontrolled grief.

Now it will be over, he thought. All over between him and this young woman, this woman he loved for bringing joy back to his heart and happiness back to his children. The young woman who had just admitted she loved him. But all by herself, she had figured out the dark truth about the community of which he was a part. Now she would realize he wasn't any better than the people she had spoken about. He was the same, one of them. That terrible secret kept imprisoned so long in the locked chambers of his heart had escaped. Like the fumes of a poisonous gas, there was no way to contain it now. It would be out there, enveloping and polluting their relationship, isolating him forever.

In the darkness of despair, he felt something touch him. Her fingers, he realized, shocked, as he felt his hands gently peeled from his face. He looked at her as she reached out, taking his trembling hands in hers, holding them gently. According to all the laws of modesty, it was forbidden. He must not touch her. She must not touch him. He was stupefied, too shocked to move or protest. He watched, fascinated, as she lifted his hands to her lips, kissing his knuckles one by one.

"You should find somebody better. I am a broken man."

This is the truth, she thought. *His heart is broken.* He was a man with a broken heart. And she, who was she? A woman whose heart had long ago rolled off a mountain in one of the most beautiful places on earth, shattering into a million shards.

So many mistakes. So many bad choices. So many tragedies and hurts brought to innocent people with the best of intentions or with no intention at all. It was so hard to be human. It was so hard to be alive.

"How could you love such a man, Leah?"

She did not let go of his hands. "I could. I do."

28

Yaakov gathered his family around him: Shaindele, Chasya, Mordechai Shalom, and his tall, shy, teenage yeshiva boys, Elchanon Yehoshua and Dovid Yitzchak. In the big easy chair sat his mother-in-law, Fruma Esther.

He told those standing to sit down around the dining room table. There, with Mordechai Shalom in his lap, and his arm draped gently around Chasya, he began to speak.

"My dear family," he said, smiling, "ever since the terrible *nesoyon* of losing our saintly Zissele, our family has been in mourning. But HaShem, may His name be blessed, has decreed an end to our suffering! He, in His enormous *chesed,* has granted me a new *ezer k'negdo,* an *eshes chayil,* to help me and our family make a new beginning."

He saw Shaindele stiffen with shock as if struck; his mother-in-law's eyes go wide with questioning. He hurried so that he wouldn't lose courage. "I am, *imyertza* HaShem, getting married. The *vort* will be next Thursday night."

His mother-in-law rose, her face frozen except for a tiny, nervous tic just outside the corner of her eye. "Mazel tov, my *choson.* And now, maybe, you should be so kind and tell us—as we are all waiting to hear—who is the *kallah?*"

He smiled even more broadly, patting an excited Chasya's little head. "You all know her. Like Rivka, about whom it is written, *'And Isaac was comforted after his mother's death,'* she's brought the *shechinah* back into our home. We could not have managed without her. Her name is Leah Howard."

Chasya gasped, then laughed, climbing up on her chair and reaching up around her father's neck to hug him. Then she climbed down, taking Mordechai Shalom's small hands in hers and pulling him to the floor. "Leah is going to be our mommy!" she told him. "Our Leah!" The two little ones danced around the living room floor as the older children sat in motionless, wordless silence, watching.

Yaakov, happily watching the little ones, his vision blurred with tears of joy, did not immediately notice the older ones. Only when Shaindele rose unsteadily to her feet did he turn his attention to her and to the boys. "Never, never, never!" she screamed in hysteria, sobbing, as her grandmother jumped up and took her into her arms. The two little ones froze, their smiles turning to frightened sobs, while the older boys glanced at each other in embarrassment, high color rising in their cheeks as they lowered their gazes to the floor.

Yaakov froze in wonderment and dismay, unable to comprehend what he was seeing and hearing. He got up and walked over to Shaindele.

"My dear child," he said gently. "I know this is a surprise by you. Also by me. But I believe that this is HaShem's plan for us. In His kindness and *hashgacha pratis,* He has answered my prayers—all our prayers—and brought Leah to us. I hope that you will welcome her as she deserves to be welcomed and that you will bring no shame to our good name by not treating her as the precious gift from HaShem she is."

It was as if he'd poured oil on a fire. Shaindele wrenched herself out of her grandmother's embrace, eyes blazing as she confronted her father. "*We* should bring no shame to our good name? *Us?* What about *you?* How can you do this? To Elchanon Yehoshua, to Dovid Yitzchak, to me? No shadchan will work with us! It's bad enough that you are leaving the kollel to become a *baal bayis,* but how could you bring a woman like her into our family to replace our saintly mother? A woman who was born from an unclean *niddah*? A person who has tainted her soul by filling her stomach with terefah food, pig and shellfish, a person who was a *mechalal* Shabbos, *who had a tattoo* and who knows how many men—"

"Enough!" Yaakov finally exploded. "And who are you, Shaindele? Are you not a Jew? Was not the forefather of all Jews the son of pagan idol worshippers who ate every forbidden thing? Have I not brought you all up to be God-fearing Jews? And yet you desecrate the Torah! Is it not written: *Do not oppress or ill-treat the stranger*? Our sages tell us that to *oppress* means to cheat him in business. But *ill-treat* means to use wounding words against him. Rabbi Yohonan said in the name of Rabbi Shimon bar Yochai that to wound with words is much worse than to cheat in business, because you can give back the money you steal but you can *never* restore the pride of the person you hurt. And what about me, your father. Am I not owed respect? Is this *kibood av*? You should be ashamed of yourself!"

Shaindele sobbed, running to her room and slamming the door with a loud crash.

Fruma Esther got to her feet, her whole body shaking with rage. "Can I speak to you privately, Yaakov?"

He hung his head, his hands gripping the table. "Whatever you want to say to me, you can say right here, in front of your grandchildren." Then he raised his head, looking directly into her eyes with steely determination. "But then, I may also have some things to tell your grandchildren, things I have never spoken of before, Rebbitzen."

She stared at him, dumbfounded at the threat. She straightened her back with dignity. "So, I wish you and the children mazel tov again. It's time for me to go home."

Devastated, she gathered her purse and the shopping bag filled with empty plastic containers from the last batch of food she had brought over, making her way unsteadily to the door. The older boys accompanied her.

She touched their faces. Such fine boys. She was so proud of them. But it was as if she were on the far shore watching them struggle against monster waves, their heads slowly going under. She was helpless. "*HaShem yishmor.*" She sighed, kissing the mezuzah and walking down the steps. Like Hagar deserting her son Ishmael in the desert, she thought, because she could not bear to witness what would happen to him without food and drink in the desert sun.

"Boys, sit down," Yaakov said gently, putting his arms around his sons. "I know this must be a great surprise. You haven't had the chance to meet Leah the way the younger children have."

The boys did not look at their father, their gazes lowered. Obviously, Shaindele had met the bride-to-be. Her reaction frightened them. They, too, would soon be in the shidduch market. Their entire futures depended on a good match to a fine family with the means to support them so they could continue their Torah learning until one day they themselves could become the heads of Talmudic academies. This was their dream. And now, if what Shaindele said was true, that dream was in jeopardy. There was a short silence.

Finally, Elchanon Yehoshua spoke up. "Tateh, is it true what Shaindele said?"

"By us, we don't discuss *loshon hara,*" Yaakov answered with uncharacteristic sharpness.

"But, Tateh, why would Shaindele—" Elchanon Yehoshua began.

"Your sister has suffered more than anyone since Mameh left us," Yaakov cut him off. "Her life is filled with *nesyonos.* She is sometimes *nichshal.* We must pray for her."

"And Bubbee? What about Bubbee? What did she want to talk to you about?"

"This was a surprise for her also. She had different shidduchim in mind. But God, blessed be He, had other plans. I am sure that once Bubbee has a chance to think about it, she will also see that we have been blessed."

"But what things were you going to tell us that we never heard before?" Elchanon Yehoshua pressed.

Yaakov laid a gentle hand on his son's. "This is not the time, Elchanon Yehoshua. But one day we will talk about it," he said gently. "About your mameh."

"Leah is going to be our mommy!" Chasya sang again, released now from the shadow of her older sister. The term *mommy* she had learned from Leah. Her mameh was gone, but Leah would be her mommy. She danced with the baby. Yaakov lifted them both into his arms, waltzing through the living room. "Yes, little Icy, little Cheeky, you will have a mameh again. We will all have a wonderful mameh again to light our Shabbos candles, to bake our challah, to read to us." *And to lie beside us in the cold, dark night.*

"So, how did it go?" Leah asked him later that night.

"*Baruch HaShem,*" he hedged.

"Okay, so now tell me what *really* happened."

He hesitated. You weren't allowed to lie, except to prevent hurting someone's feelings. "Chasya and Mordechai Shalom jumped up and down. Chasya kept saying, 'Leah is going to be our mommy!' like it was a song."

Leah wiped away the quick flash of tears that welled up in her eyes. "I love them so much. And what about the others?"

"The boys were *mamash* surprised, but I know they are happy for me. They are good boys."

"And Shaindele?"

He hesitated. "I don't know what's wrong with that girl."

"But you let her talk, right? Like we discussed?"

"Such a mistake." He looked down, ashamed, shaking his head.

"That bad?" She felt her pulse quicken. She wasn't surprised, but still, it dampened her joy. "She's worried about her shidduch; you know that. She's not wrong."

"I don't care how much *yichus* and how much learning a boy has, if he cannot show respect to a wonderful person like you, he is not a good shidduch for any child of mine."

"It's not the boys; it's the shadchanim. They're the ones you'll have to deal with."

"Any shadchan who doesn't respect a woman like you is not a God-fearing Jew and not fit to find a shidduch for my daughter or my sons."

"Yaakov, Yaakov . . ." She shook her head sorrowfully. She hated that she was going to be the cause of any difficulty for him or his children, but she loved him for his uncompromising stance. "Maybe I could talk to Shaindele?"

"Absolutely not!"

She was taken aback. It wasn't a tone Yaakov Lehman used.

"But why, Yaakov? Maybe, if I talked to her, woman to woman . . ."

He took a deep breath. "I can forgive many things, but not deliberate lying. Especially since I already warned her about it."

"What did she lie about?"

"The tattoo. She keeps talking about your tattoo."

Leah froze. "Yaakov, I had a tattoo."

He was amazed. "But I never—"

"It was on my wrist, and it was very important to me. I got it with my late fiancé, just before he died."

"But I never noticed."

"Because before we met I had an accident, and burned my hand. The skin just peeled off. No more tattoo. Would it have a made a difference?"

He hesitated. The truth was, he couldn't be sure. "I might not have allowed myself to get to know you. I also have my blindspots and prejudices."

You can never know if something that happens to you is a good thing or a bad thing, she thought in wonder, remembering the prayer in which she had beseeched God for help. And as painful and horrible as it had been, her accident had been His answer. It had brought this wonderful man into her life.

"Your daughter isn't a liar, Yaakov."

"God be blessed, at least that!" he murmured in relief. "Still, her behavior, her language, is unacceptable for a religious girl."

"Don't be too hard on her. I'm sure if I could just—"

He raised his hand. "For everything, there is a time. Once you are her stepmother, you will have all the time in the world to talk to her. But until then, you need to leave her alone. Let her get used to the idea. Pushing her now will only make things worse."

She thought about it. Sadly, it was true. "All right, but it goes against my nature. I so much want to be her mother, too."

"In time, all in good time." He tried to smile reassuringly, even though he felt no such confidence in time as a healing agent for this particular wound. Shaindele could hold a grudge forever. He changed the subject.

"Have you told *your* family yet?"

"I'm going to call my mother tonight. I wanted to wait, to see how it went with you first."

"Oh, so you were afraid I'm changing my mind?" He grinned, wagging a finger at her. "When will you learn that what HaShem decides, no person can change? He has brought us together. It's a blessing."

It was. *It is,* she thought, dreading the phone call she had to make.

She decided instead of a phone call, she would use Skype so she could see her mother's face and her mother could see hers.

The app rang, and suddenly there she was, Cheryl Howard in the flesh. She had a new haircut, short and spiky, the color a light platinum over dark roots. Her mouth was painted a bright red. She was wearing one of those off-the-shoulder blouses that made her look almost naked.

"Oh my God!" Cheryl shouted. "Ravi, come here quick! Look who's on Skype!"

So Ravi was back. He poked his head into view. His dark hair had grown. It was shoulder length now, Leah noted, wondering if that had significance.

"Hello, Lola. How are you? Your mother has been very worried about you."

"Hi, Ravi. She was worried about you, too. How was your trip?"

He hesitated, then shrugged.

She swallowed. "Well, I'm glad you are both here together. I have some news." She took a deep breath. "I'm getting married."

"Oh my God!" Cheryl shouted, moving off frame. The screen filled with Ravi, who turned, gesticulating wildly. Then he, too, moved off camera. In the background, she heard him shouting at her mother to come back.

"Hello? Are you still there?" Leah said into the screen.

Cheryl's head bobbed back into view, her blue eyes wide and shell-shocked, her red lips tightly stretched. "So tell me about him."

"His name is Jacob—Yaakov, actually."

"Oh my God! He is one of *those,* isn't he?" She said it with a combination of horror and mockery.

"He is a religious Jew, as am I, Mom."

"He's one of *those*! He's one of *those*!" she shouted.

"I'm going to hang up right this second if you don't stop."

"Okay, okay. I'm stopping." She took a deep breath. "Tell me about him."

"He's forty. A widower. He has five kids—"

"Oh my God! Oh my God! I can't believe it! You know what's going to happen to you, don't you? You're going to be his slave. He already killed one wife, and now you're going to be number two! After you've popped out another five kids for him! You're going to be his slave, work yourself to the bone taking care of his kids while he sits on his ass in some room reading, not earning a penny! You're going to support him, right? That's also part of this deal, isn't it?"

Leah didn't even know where to begin to answer, the accusations were so broad, so breathtakingly wrong.

"I'm getting the family I always wanted, Mom. I love him. I love the kids. I'm going to work as hard as I can to be a good wife, a good mother."

"You're marrying into a cult! I would have been happier if you'd told me you were joining an ashram in India!"

"You would have been happier if I'd told you I was miserable and contemplating suicide but living on the Upper West Side," she said bitterly.

She saw her mother's red lips open in surprise. "That's not fair."

"Isn't it? Look at me, look at my face. I haven't had an antidepressant in two years. I haven't had an inhale of marijuana in three. I am in love with a wonderful man and his wonderful children. And most important, he's in love with me! He's *committed* to me. To having me as his wife, to raising a family with me! I am working, building my own successful little business and supporting myself. I am part of a community. After everything I've been through, everything I've suffered, why can't you be happy for me? I have everything I've always wanted."

"You do look good," Cheryl conceded. "But I can't help being worried about you."

"*Now* you are worried about me? When I was spending my time cruising sleazy Manhattan bars and nightclubs on Saturday nights, risking my health and my safety with one-night stands, that didn't worry you. But *now* you are worried? When I'm in a committed, monogamous relationship with a strictly monogamous and committed man who wants to marry me?"

Cheryl looked thoughtful. "You know I only want the best for you."

"No, I don't know that. But if it's true, show me now by smiling, by being happy for me."

Cheryl forced herself to smile. "So, what, like, you are . . . like, engaged?"

"The formal engagement is called a *vort.* It's a party. It's on Thursday night."

"Which Thursday night?"

"In a week and a half."

Oh my God! Cheryl mouthed wordlessly. "Does he have a beard?"

"Yes, Mom."

"*Oh my God!* But he doesn't wear those *things,* those curls by his ears, does he?" She was almost breathless.

"No, he doesn't. They are tucked behind his ears. He isn't a chassid."

"Okay, thank God for that. And what does he do?"

"He's getting a CPA soon. Look, Mom, I'm calling to invite you and—" Leah swallowed hard, trying not to conjure up the image of her mother in her present outfit and Ravi in his long hair and jeans surrounded by religious Jews at the little apartment in Boro Park, feeling almost sick at the thought. "And . . . Ravi to join me."

"Just a minute."

Her mother left the screen. Leah heard whispering, and then her mother shouted something unintelligible. Finally, Cheryl returned. "Well, that's not a lot of notice. We both work."

"I totally understand," she breathed, relieved beyond words. "So maybe you can make the wedding?" There would be a larger crowd then. Her mother and Ravi wouldn't exactly blend in, but at least they wouldn't be two exclamation points. "It's two months from now."

"*Two months?* Why so fast? I'm not sure we can make arrangements so fast," Cheryl said, stalling for time, truly in shock. "I was going to suggest you come home for a while. To think it over, talk to some of your old friends."

"I haven't been in touch with anyone for a while, Mom. Maybe after the wedding sometime, Yaakov and I and the children can take a little vacation. Mom, stop making that face, or I'm going to hang up."

"It's not on purpose! I can't help how I feel. You're being suckered into something. I've done my research. I know all these people. They treat women like dirt, like beasts of burden."

Leah's heart sank, but she controlled her temper. It would be disrespectful to turn off the camera and disconnect. And you had to respect your parents; it was one of the Ten Commandments. You didn't have to obey them if they demanded you sin, but you had to show them respect. It took everything she had to say gently, "That hasn't been my experience, Mom, and I'm not going to change my mind. So are you coming to the *vort* and the wedding or not?"

"Honestly, I don't know. I can't tell you; not right now. Give me some time to think about it."

"Okay, Mom." Leah felt the sudden urge to cry. "I'm going to go now, Mom."

"Okay, take care," Cheryl said formally, turning off the faucet of her despair. "I love you."

"I love you, too."

29

The next day, Rebbitzen Fruma Esther walked slowly through the streets of Boro Park, her body weak with sorrow and confusion. What was going to happen now? Uncharacteristically, she couldn't think of a plan, of what to do next. The obvious things: pressuring Leah, talking to her son-in-law's rav, had all backfired in the past. And what had Yaakov meant when he had said to her that he also had some things to tell the children? And why did it sound like an ugly threat, like he had something to say? What had gotten into him? This wasn't the son-in-law she knew, her kind, scholarly, saintly Yaakov. Something had happened to him. He had coarsened. Tragedy will do that. Everybody is a big tzaddik when life is running smoothly.

But perhaps, perhaps, she thought, the idea unfolding slowly, tentatively in her mind like the blurry letters of the words in front of her bad eye, he rightfully held something against her, something to do with Zissele. But that would have to wait. First and foremost, she needed to find out who was responsible for going behind her back to make such a terrible shidduch.

Suri Kimmeldorfer vehemently denied any knowledge or responsibility for a shidduch between her son-in-law and some redheaded *baalas te-*

shuva. "For sure, he asked me to set it up. But I told him I'd have to investigate first, to talk to you, Rebbitzen. He never called me back. Are you telling me he is engaged now? And to this *baalas teshuva,* the redhead?" After all those months, and she had lost out on an easy fee. She kicked herself.

"Yes, that one. But you did the right thing," Fruma Esther told her, nevertheless holding her completely responsible that her Zissele's fine husband had fallen into the wrong hands. What did it matter if she was blameless in this particular case? The fact was that if the silly, incompetent woman had just done her job, come up with another pretty Rachel or some other over-the-hill virgin, some poor rabbi's daughter so desperate for any kind of husband she could easily be pressured, this would never have happened! If only she had just leaned heavily enough on such a girl instead of pushing her bitter, wrinkled divorcées and fat widows on Yaakov, who knows? But that was water under the bridge. She would have to let it go for now because she had troubles of her own.

Her long-delayed eye operation was scheduled for the next day. Such terrible timing! But she couldn't cancel. The surgeon was a specialist, and it had taken months to get this appointment through the clinic. If she canceled, she'd have to go to him privately, and that would cost thousands of dollars she didn't have. She'd told no one. Who was there to tell? The family was in such an uproar. She didn't call a friend either, who might ask nosy questions. Nothing must reveal the turmoil that had engulfed her family.

She lay down on the operating table as the surgeon took a huge needle and hovered over her. The pain as he injected the local anesthetic into her eyeball was excruciating, but she was ashamed to show weakness, biting her lips and swallowing her anguished cry. They gave her an oxygen mask and covered her with blue plastic sheeting, exhorting her to keep absolutely still. They didn't have to say it twice. She had a choice? Bad enough they were going to slice open her eyeball and use a tweezer to rip off the membrane covering her retina—akin to pulling Scotch tape off tissue paper—all she needed was to make it harder for the surgeon by jiggling around like a child.

She lay there, hands folded over her chest, trying to put her mind somewhere else. She thought about the trip she had taken as a child to the

Catskills with her parents, the old country hotel with the groaning break-fast table weighted with slabs of fresh butter, chilled pitchers of milk, colorful bowls of pot cheese, sour cream, scrambled and hard-boiled eggs, and baskets of country breads. Her mind drifted off to the flowering plants, the wide shade trees, and the soft green grass that surrounded the modest bungalows. Sometimes, real images intervened: blurry shapes in vivid blue, intense violet, and deep green. She could even see the little tweezer as it poked around, catching the little fibers in its grasp. Finally, after what seemed like hours, she could feel them remove the plastic sheeting and cover her eye with a bandage. They helped her to sit up and then helped her into a wheelchair.

"Who has come to take you home?" the nurse asked her.

"I need someone to take me home? I'll get home by myself," she answered, dizzy and hoarse.

She heard the nurse move away to have an urgent, whispered conversation with people she could not see. "No one told her this before?" she heard someone shout.

She tried to remember, and then vaguely it came back to her. Yes, they had told her to bring someone. But she wasn't like these spoiled American women. She assumed she could manage. Who knew she was going to feel like this?

The nurse returned. "We have some volunteers at our hospital. Perhaps one of them would agree to go with you. We can't release you without accompaniment."

"But, what, do I need to bother somebody?" she protested weakly. She felt so tired. She wasn't in any pain, but one eye was covered completely, which made her feel unbalanced. She couldn't even wear her glasses over the bandage! How would she even get to the taxi? What if she fell and injured the eye! Now she began to regret her decision not to involve the family. But it was too late. She couldn't call anyone now. They would come running down in a panic, disrupting their lives. They would hover over her, exactly what she didn't want! Besides, it would take hours. "Maybe if you know somebody who wants to do a mitzvah," she finally gave in.

The woman's name was Marsha Feigenbaum—a Jewish name, for sure. But she didn't cover her hair, and she wore pants. Even with one eye and no glasses, Fruma Esther could see that. Still, she was very kind, and no youngster. Maybe they were even the same age! Here she was, healthy, active, helping others. God had blessed her.

The volunteer sat down quietly nearby, and when Fruma Esther's name was called by the doctor, Marsha helped push the wheelchair into his office and afterward repeated what the doctor had said about filling the prescriptions and putting in the eye drops, one from each bottle three times a day, as soon as the eye bandage was removed the next day. She was to return in the morning. Very generously, she offered to drive Fruma home and to pick her up the next day and bring her back.

"You drive alone, from Manhattan to Brooklyn?" Fruma Esther asked in awe.

"Yes. Don't you drive anymore?"

"Me? Drive? I never learned how, and we never had a car." She shrugged. It was something she had always longed to do. "Is it hard? To drive?"

The woman laughed. "Not after fifty years."

Fifty years! "And your eyesight? It's good enough to drive?" she asked anxiously. That's all she needed, a car accident on the way home from the hospital. She'd be blind!

"I have never had an accident. I'm an excellent driver," Marsha assured her.

There was a choice? She slumped down in the wheelchair. She was in God's hands and this strange woman's.

Together with a hospital orderly, she was guided out of the wheelchair and into Marsha's car. All the way to Boro Park, the woman inquired gently about how she was feeling, only leaving her alone in the car for the time it took to get the prescriptions filled at the pharmacy. And when they arrived home, the woman helped her out and went up with her in the elevator.

"I will ring your bell tomorrow," the woman said, guiding her to a comfortable chair. "Don't try to come downstairs by yourself."

"Such a mitzvah. God should bless you," Fruma Esther told the woman sincerely.

Somehow, it was easier for her to accept this kindness from a stranger than to involve her family or people she knew from the neighborhood. With this secular woman who didn't know her at all, who was from a different neighborhood, a different world, she could somehow be herself— old, frightened, sick—things she felt she could never allow her family, who depended upon her, or her friends, who looked up to her, to see.

Surprisingly, she felt no pain at all. "Even an aspirin I didn't take," she told Marsha the next day when she came to pick her up.

"Are these your children?" Marsha asked.

Fruma Esther squinted to see where she was pointing.

"And grandchildren and great-grandchildren," she answered proudly, without thinking.

"Such a big family! But still, you came alone to your operation."

And needed a stranger, a volunteer, to chauffeur you around. This the woman didn't say, but it was what Fruma Esther heard. She felt suddenly ashamed. "They would have come. They would have fought over who would come if I had told somebody. But I didn't tell nobody. What, did I need them to worry? They're busy, believe me. They have enough to worry about." She sighed, thinking of Yaakov and Shaindele, Elchanon Yehoshua and Dovid Yitzchak.

"You should let them help you. Such a big, lovely family," Marsha said wistfully.

"You have children? They're married?"

"A son and a daughter. My daughter is married but no children."

"God should give you a *kallah* for your son, and many grandchildren," Fruma Esther blessed her.

"He died, my son. Five years ago," the woman said softly. "He was gay, and he had AIDS."

Fruma Esther thought of how her friends, relatives, neighbors, members of her synagogue, and shadchanim would view this woman with her uncovered hair, her immodest clothing, and the *shanda* of homosexuality that tainted her family. They would dismiss her completely—this lovely, kind, generous woman, so full of *chesed,* so innocent she would admit such a thing about her son to a stranger—pronouncing herself unworthy, sinful, and far removed from God. Inexplicably, she felt ashamed, even angry. It was *so* wrong! People judged from outside, but God saw into the heart.

Perhaps he had made some bad choices, Marsha's son. But illness happened to the guilty and to the innocent. Children had free will. What could you do about it? Nothing. You did everything for your children. Everything. You wrung out your kishkes and hung them out to dry. But what could you do if they made mistakes, hurt themselves? "I also lost a daughter. Two years ago. She killed herself," she blurted out to her own astonishment. She had never said those words before to any human being, living or dead, doing her best to not even think them.

"I'm so very sorry," the woman said, taking her hand tenderly.

"They . . . the doctor, he wanted to commit her. A mental hospital. *Postnatal depression,* they called it. Severe. But I wouldn't let them. I thought I knew better what was good for her, for my own daughter. She went through this after every one of her babies. Many women do. I did. But she was a good girl. Before, she always got over it. But this time . . . she . . . I . . . I . . . maybe . . . I made a mistake."

"It is so easy to make mistakes when you are a parent. The easiest thing in the world," Marsha said. "But you can only do what you think is best at the moment. Maybe you will be smarter the next day, or the next month, or in five years. But it doesn't help you at the moment. You need to forgive yourself."

Could she? Ever? Can you do *teshuva* over something as terrible as causing, or at the very least not preventing, a death? Deep in her heart, she knew Yaakov blamed her. And if the truth came out, her grandchildren would, too. And she deserved it.

"I'll bring you back today. But are you going to be able to manage on your own?"

"God willing, I will be fine," she answered, bringing her mind back to the present. "And if, God forbid, I need help, I have many friends."

Later that morning, after they'd removed the bandage and Marsha dropped her off at her apartment, she offered to put in the eye drops.

"Please," Fruma Esther said gratefully. "I don't know how."

Patiently, Marsha showed her how to tilt back her head and pull down her lower lid to make a pocket. She showed her exactly how to hold the little bottles upside down right at the corner of her eye and to squeeze just enough to get out one drop. "Don't blink and keep your eyes closed. That way, more of the medicine will remain in."

When it was time for her to leave, Fruma Esther pressed a box of pralines into Marsha's hand, the best, most delicious, most expensive chocolates available at Moishe's Candy Shoppe in Boro Park. "From Belgium."

"This is not necessary," Marsha protested, trying to return it.

But Fruma placed an insistent hand over hers. "Let me treat you, Marsha. Sometimes to take a gift is also a good deed."

She gave in, clutching the box. "Well, it's very kind of you. Look, I'm leaving my card on the table. You can call me anytime, if you need a lift to the hospital, or"—she hesitated—"if you just want to talk."

Her next appointment was in two weeks. She felt sad that she would not be seeing Marsha for so long. Sad and lonely. Lonelier than she had ever felt in her life.

The eyepatch was gone, but she had a clear plastic cover to wear over her eye at night. When she tried to look out of that eye, it was like looking through a fishbowl, a big, black bubble bobbing around in front of her. The doctor said it would get smaller and smaller, then disappear. But in the meantime, it was driving her crazy. She spent the day sitting in her armchair, thinking.

Her own pregnancies and memories of giving birth came back to her, the shuffling through days and nights with no sleep, her nipples two spots of agony, bleeding and raw, competing with the ache and burning pain of the stitches lower down. And even when the baby slept, you lay there worrying. Would it stop breathing? Was it eating enough? You prayed for sleep, that your body and mind would slow down, stop torturing you, let you rest. You dreaded the sound of the baby's cries. And finally, you dreaded the baby. You sat there in the dark as everyone slept, wondering why no one had ever told you it would be this hard. A *bracha*, a blessing, is what they called every birth. No one ever contradicted that.

But Zissele—her sweet, lovely daughter—had told her the truth. With the first birth, the depression had lasted a week. The second, two weeks, and with each birth the time had lengthened, the symptoms growing more and more severe, until with the fifth, it had been impossible to cope. She did not recognize her Zissele, her sweet child.

"It's a mistake. A terrible mistake," Zissele sobbed, rocking up and back in the chair that had been in their family for a hundred years, the nursing chair. "I can't do this. I'm so tired, I can't sleep."

"Of course you're tired, maideleh. You have a new baby. A blessing from God. It will get better, like always."

But it didn't. She started to shake and tremble. She complained she was freezing, even though it was an unusually warm September. Her clothes were soaked with sweat and milk, but she refused to change them, refused to shower. "How am I going to do this? I can't, I can't." She wept, inconsolable over something no one could see or understand. "How am I going to go back to work? We will go bankrupt!"

All the reassurances, all the hugs and kisses from her, the children, Yaakov, this time, nothing helped.

"I am a *rosha*. I am weak, spoiled, lazy, ungrateful," Zissele wept. "I don't deserve my family, my husband. God will punish me for being a bad mother. For not being an *eishes chayil*. He will punish my family. Something terrible will happen to my children because of me. They will be better off without me."

What could you say to such meshuganah behavior? She brought Zissele to the rabbis and the rebbitzens, who reassured her that God loved her and that being a tired new mother was not a sin. They exhorted her to have faith, to say tehillim. But she could see Zissele wasn't listening.

Zissele became convinced her baby was going to die. She became a fanatic about boiling everything that came into contact with him: pacifiers, toys, towels. If anything fell on the floor or the counter, it had to be boiled again. She started to refuse to hold the baby because she didn't want to give him her own germs, sure it would kill him. "He can't get sick." She wept. "If he gets sick, he will cry all through the night, and then I won't get any sleep. I have to sleep!" She started to boil her own clothes and insisted on paper plates and plastic utensils that could be thrown away after she touched them. She opened doors with her elbows.

Zissele stopped taking care of herself so completely that Fruma and Yaakov took turns dressing and feeding her, although most of the time Zissele had been too tired to eat. Together, Fruma, Yaakov, and Shaindele took care of the baby, the laundry, the dishes, the cooking, the shopping, the other children. She made Yaakov return to yeshiva, and Shaindele to school, taking the whole burden on herself, day and night. At night, as Zissele dozed on the living room couch, she would sleep beside her in an armchair. "My heart is beating so fast. It is going to explode!"

Zissele would cry out several times a night. And then Fruma would hold her Zissele in her arms and rock her like a baby. "*Sha,* Zissele. *Sha, shtil,* my Zissele. Try to sleep, my dear little *shefele.*"

By the end of the month, when it was clear Zissele was only getting worse, Fruma and Yaakov agreed they could do no more and that Zissele needed a doctor. He gave her medicine that helped her sleep, but then she began acting strangely. If they took her shopping, she would talk to herself so loudly people would turn around to look. She seemed confused and couldn't talk straight, answer a simple question. She started to do crazy things: grab Chasya by the hair, chew up pieces of newspaper, stand by the window and bang her head against the glass.

For months, they consulted more rabbis, they spoke to healing women from the community who recommended herbal teas, meditation, massages, hot baths, long walks, acupuncture, Reiki, breathing exercises, and reciting certain psalms. Some of these things seemed to help Zissele for the moment, but they didn't last.

Then one day, while they walked to the park with the baby in the carriage, Zissele suddenly got down on her knees and screamed. Then she rolled around on the sidewalk, sobbing, "No! How did this happen? What am I going to do?" On the way to the doctor, she tried to jump out of the taxi. And all the time, she wept—without reason, without control, without hope.

"I want to die. I have to die," she would say. "I have to die before I kill the baby. Don't ever leave me alone with him!"

That was the last straw. They took her back to the doctor, who said, "This is very serious. You must take her to a psychiatrist who specializes in this." They made an appointment. The psychiatrist said she needed to be committed to a hospital for mental patients, that she was a danger to herself and to the baby. He reserved a room for her for that very night.

She remembered that night, sitting at Zissele's bedside as her daughter stared at the walls and wept. "Zissele, they want you should go to the hospital."

"No hospital!" Zissele begged. "Think of the shame. Think of the shidduchim for the children! Who will want to marry into a family with a crazy mother who is in a mental hospital! Please, Mameh. I will try harder. Give me another chance!"

She sounded so reasonable. So like her old, sweet self. "Yaakov, let's try a little longer. I think she's getting better," she told her son-in-law that night. He hesitated, but she had insisted. "We must try, give her another chance, because once she is committed, there is no turning back. Everyone will know. It will taint the family name forever," she pleaded.

Reluctantly, he agreed. "But if she isn't better by the end of the week, she goes into the hospital," he warned. And she agreed.

But they didn't have another week. The very next day, the phone call she would never forget came from Shaindele first thing in the morning, during the one hour when she went home to change her clothes and Yaakov had already left for yeshiva. Shaindele said she couldn't unlock the bathroom door and that her mother had been in there for almost an hour. She had knocked and knocked, she told her grandmother, weeping, but there had been no answer. Shaindele had been hysterical, calling the local ambulance service, *hatzalah,* who broke down the door. But it was too late. They found Zissele curled up on the floor, an empty bottle of aspirin beside her. Only a small flicker of life remained in her as they transported her to the emergency room, a spark that was soon extinguished.

Her dear, innocent, sweet child. And her poor, sweet granddaughter who had seen it all but understood nothing. They told Shaindele her mother had gotten sick, something to do with childbirth. But who knew what Shaindele really thought?

She rocked slowly now in that same rocking chair, the nursing chair, which she had brought home with her after the funeral. Her heart was so heavy. She, too, had seen everything but understood nothing. She had been blind.

For a moment, she sat there motionless, a great revelation breaking over her like a wave. That was it, her punishment for having failed her Zissele, for having failed Yaakov and Shaindele, Elchanon Yehoshua, Dovid Yitzchak, Chasya, and Mordechai Shalom. She had willed herself not to see what she didn't want to see, and as a result, her daughter had died. And now, God in His great justice, was taking away her eyesight. It was measure for measure. God judged people, even His saints, to a hair's breadth. But God was also merciful, and there was no sin for which a person could not repent. And what was true repentance? Being in the same situation and acting differently.

She thought about Leah Howard. What was really her objection to this kind woman who had brought order and happiness back to her son-in-law and to her grandchildren? Her secular background? Was it not even more praiseworthy that coming from such a family she had found a sincere path back to God? The way she dressed? She was stylish, but not immodest. Her hair? It was the hair God had given her, without artifice, and it was beautiful.

No, it was none of those things but simply the fact that her friends and neighbors didn't think any *baal teshuva* was good enough to marry into their families. It was the fact that their unfair and harsh judgment, dishonest as it was, would diminish her own family's stature, ruin its reputation. But she had already made the most supreme and ultimate sacrifice for the sake of her family's precious reputation. Now she realized, it had all been for nothing.

Pay no attention to outward things, God had chastised the prophet Samuel when he went to anoint the next king of Israel and was impressed by David's tall, handsome older brothers. But it was the short, young, red-headed David that the Lord had chosen. *For not as man sees does the Lord see,* God told his prophet. *A man sees only what is visible, but the Lord sees into the heart.*

It was time to repent her sins. She did not want to be blind anymore.

30

"Can I come in?"

Rebbitzen Basha quickly buzzed in her old friend. She was surprised. Fruma Esther usually called before coming over. It was just a coincidence that she was at home, as Wednesday morning was her usual time to shop for her meat order for Shabbos.

She stood by the door, her brows knitting in anxiety. "Is everything all right, Fruma Esther? Your eye, it's so red!"

"It's not my eye that is red," Fruma Esther wheezed, "it is my face. I am so ashamed."

Rebbitzen Basha's kind face was full of concern. "Come, sit. I'll make tea."

Fruma Esther sat down on the couch heavily, her feet almost giving way as an "Oy" escaped her. It was so good to get off her feet, such a relief not to have to worry about bumping into walls or tripping over cracks in the old sidewalks of Boro Park. She reached gratefully for the teacup and saucer offered her, looking greedily at the plate of rugelach drenched in chocolate and honey. She would take just one. But her stomach jiggled as she reached for it, reminding her of vague resolutions to eat less. *Just one bite, a little bite,* she negotiated with herself. What could it hurt? She needed something to sweeten her bitter soul.

"Yaakov is getting married."

Rebbitzen Basha was happily surprised, her hearty "Mazel tov" resounding and pure. But studying her friend's crestfallen face, she stopped. "Isn't this what you prayed for? So why the long face?"

"It's Leah. Leah Howard."

Rebbitzen Basha leaned back, exhaling. Then a huge smile lit up her face. "God is good!"

Fruma Esther was taken aback. "You're not surprised?"

"Very. And overjoyed. *Baruch HaShem!* Ever since I had that talk with her and convinced her not to go to the house for Shabbos, I've been eating my heart out. You shouldn't know, she was so hurt, so upset. Better I should cut out my tongue than do such a thing ever again! But I did it for you, to help you. And she hasn't come back to see me since. She didn't even come to my Heshy's *vort.* I can't blame her. Such a lovely girl. Believe me, Fruma Esther, your family is getting a jewel. So, you're here because you want me to make trouble again, to stop it? I'll tell you right now, from me you won't get such help again. Never."

"I don't want to make any trouble," Fruma Esther said so softly her friend thought she'd misheard.

"You what? My hearing, you know, not so good."

"I want to help. I want to do *teshuva,*" Fruma Esther said loudly. "But I don't know how. Yaakov is mad at me. Shaindele is crying. There's trouble between the child and her father. And I'm to blame."

"You can fix it."

"How?"

"First, you shmooze with Shaindele. Tell her the truth about what happened to her mother. It's time for her to know, Fruma. Otherwise, she blames her father, she blames the world. She can't move on with her own life."

"How . . . do you . . . who told you?"

"You thought I didn't know? You live here how long and you still dream you can keep secrets in Boro Park, Fruma Esther? You of all people should know what's what. The rabbis had to decide the halacha after

Zissele . . . when she . . . passed away, whether she could be buried in the Jewish cemetery. My husband was one of the rabbis they consulted."

"They decided it was an accident. They let her be buried properly," Fruma Esther said, trembling as she remembered the fear that, as a suicide, Zissele would be buried outside the community's cemetery. It had been a tremendous *chesed.* "Who else knows?"

"Only my husband and the two other rabbis who were asked to decide. My husband never said a word, but they sat in my living room. I couldn't help overhearing. I didn't tell anyone, and I never will. But the child—Shaindele—she was there when it happened, no? When the ambulance came? She saw the whole thing with her own eyes. She must have questions. She should know the truth."

"I wanted to spare her from the shame."

"There is no shame in being sick, Fruma Esther," Rebbitzen Basha told her. "I tried to tell you that years ago."

"But a mental sickness, it's not like cancer. People talk. It's a *shonda.*"

"It's a *shonda* that they should talk!"

"Yes, Basha, I know that now." She sighed. "All right. I will talk to Shaindele. Then what?"

"And then you can do something nice for Yaakov and Leah. You can hold the *vort* at your house."

She hadn't thought of that. "My house? You want I should invite my friends, all the rabbis?"

Rebbitzen Basha nodded. "Maybe not at your house; there won't be room. Hire out the big hall in shul. I'll help you with the food and setting up. But yes, you should organize it. The widow of the great Admor Yitzchak Chaim Sonnenbaum, the sister of the late Rabbi Eliezer Ungvar, must invite everyone, all the most important rabbis. They can't refuse you, you know that. They wouldn't dare not come. Show them that you are 100 percent behind it. And at the *vort,* you need a big smile on your face, all the time. Talk to everyone. Tell them what a special person Leah is, how full of *chesed,* how much she has helped Yaakov and the children. Just the truth, Fruma Esther. Just the truth." Rebbitzen Basha hesitated. "And if you can, you could say the shidduch was your idea. That would stop the *rechilus* for good."

Fruma Esther's eyebrows raised in surprise at the last idea, but then settled back into place. The two pious old women, grown wiser and sadder for the years they had lived and struggled to keep God's word, looked at each other.

It was not a secret that for all the efforts of the community—its rabbis and institutions—to reach out to secular Jews and bring them into the fold, once they succeeded, there was no place to put them. The sad and ugly truth was that the frum community didn't want these people. They didn't want their *frei* parents and siblings showing up, giving bad ideas to the community's own children about how to dress and behave. And deep down, there was the persistent idea that somehow, belief in God and Yiddishkeit was worn like a skin by those born into the life and was only a coat for the newly observant, easily taken off and discarded at any moment. And so despite their sincerity and years of learning Jewish law, the general consensus was that *baale teshuva* were not to be trusted as far as kashruth and observance were concerned. Somewhere in Boro Park, the child of two *baale teshuva* was sitting alone because her friends were forbidden by their frum parents to come over and play with her lest they be given a cookie with a less-than-stellar hechsher or hear music or see forbidden books left over from her parents' previous lives. All these things lay in the background as Rebbitzen Basha and Fruma Esther looked at each other.

"We can't change the world, Basha."

"Yes, but we don't need to, Fruma Esther. We just need to make a little room in our world, in our community, our streets, our own homes, our own hearts for Leah Howard. She will be your grandchildren's stepmother. You have to fight for her, Fruma Esther. You have to fight for your grandchildren and any children she and Yaakov will, God willing, have together."

She blinked, her bad eye making the room go blurry. The future was unclear, frightening. So many places to stumble! All the things she feared most in the world would crash down on her and on her family if she followed her friend's advice. She would be criticized. She would be talked about behind her back. But there was no choice. She couldn't finish her life in blindness and sin. When she went to meet her Creator, her life would be an open book to Him. He would turn the pages and read not what people said about her but what she had actually done and what was in her heart. So many pages she wished she could erase. The Creator, in His kindness, gave man that great gift: to erase the bad by doing good. If you were in the same situation and behaved differently, then your sins faded on the page, like old ink gone dry, first becoming illegible and then disappearing altogether, leaving the page blank.

"Can you make those almond cookies, the ones you made for Heshy's *vort*?"

Rebbitzen Basha smiled in relief. "As many as you like, my dear friend."

"Help me get up. I have so many things to do. But first, I have to talk to Shaindele."

Fruma Esther Sonnenbaum walked slowly, her footsteps still uncertain, yet somehow lighter, as if some cripplingly heavy bundle she had been forced to carry on her back had finally been delivered. She would go directly to Bais Yaakov, she thought, get permission from the principal to take Shaindele out of class. Oh, the child would be surprised. She would worry something happened, *chas ve'shalom*. But she would smile as she took her granddaughter's soft little hands in hers, patting them reassuringly. They would have a talk, and then the heavy bundle would fall from her lovely granddaughter's small shoulders as well.

She smiled to herself, nodding pleasantly to acknowledge the many greetings that followed her down the street as she made her slow but steady progress. As she expected, the principal, Rabbi Halpern, couldn't have been nicer or more accommodating. He even insisted on walking her down to Shaindele's classroom and going inside to fetch the child. To her surprise, when he exited the classroom, he was alone.

"She didn't come in today," he told her. "Is she ill?"

She shrugged, smiling as she apologized. But the real smile, the natural outgrowth of unburdened relief, was now a forced artifice, plastered on her face for show as she walked quickly to her son-in-law's house. She rang the bell. When there was no answer, she stood there knocking and knocking until a neighbor opened the door to see what was going on. Fruma Esther smiled at her, too.

"A woman is waiting outside," someone told Yaakov, interrupting a lively discussion between himself and Meir about tithes. He got up quickly, hurrying out with a growing sense of discomfort. No one who knew him would interrupt his precious learning time unless it was an emergency. The idea ballooned in his head like cotton wool pressed against a cut, growing larger and more blood-filled with every step.

It was Fruma Esther. "I'm very sorry to disturb you, but I need to speak with Shaindele."

Now his dread lapsed into confusion touched with annoyance. "Shaindele? Where should she be at this hour? She's in school."

Slowly, she shook her head, watching her son-in-law's face collapse with the panic that was slowly filling her heart.

Fruma Esther and Yaakov hurried home, but it was empty. Yaakov picked up the phone and called Leah, not because he thought his daughter would have confided in her but because he needed to hear her voice.

"I'm coming right over," she told him.

All three of them sat in the living room silently.

"Maybe she discussed her plans with one of her friends," Leah suggested.

"All her friends are in school. I don't want to take them out of class," said Fruma Esther, shaking her head. "The school doesn't need to know about every *narishkeit*."

Leah thought about it. It had only been a few hours. There was no point in getting Shaindele into trouble with her school unless there was absolutely no choice. "Yes, all right. We can wait and call them at home."

"I'll call my family, my brother in Baltimore, although if he knew something, he surely would have called me."

Soon he returned, crestfallen. "He hasn't heard anything. He'll call the second he does. I also spoke to the boys." He shook his head, disconsolate.

The hours passed. Leah went to pick up the little ones from school and day care. Their happy childish voices and bright smiles were like putting on the lights in a dark room. Yaakov kissed them and held them close.

It had been more hours than they could bear to think of since anyone had seen or heard from her. An innocent young girl, and she was out there in the world, alone. They prayed to God to have mercy. And then they waited.

31

It was the most logical thing to do, Shaindele had told herself that morning as she wandered around Penn Station lugging a small suitcase. But the place was so big, so confusing! She had never been in Manhattan all by herself. At the most, she'd only ever traveled fifteen or twenty minutes from home on local Boro Park buses.

The shoes, she thought, were a mistake. She thought she'd get dressed up, like for Shabbos, but the most she had ever walked in them was to and from shul. Now, they were pinching her toes viciously, the too-slim heel tipping her forward, making her feel as if she were about to pitch over at any moment. She reached down to massage her raw, aching heel, glancing around at the noisy crowds.

There were so many strangers wearing such immodest clothing! She straightened, lowering her eyes, trying to calm her panic. Taking a deep breath, she bunched her tender young lips together in determination. *It will be all right,* she told herself as she scanned the signs. *You're not stupid. You can read.* If all these people had figured out where to go, she could also figure it out.

Eventually, after many twists and turns, she found herself at a row of counters with a sign that said Tickets. She joined the line. It was long, but standing in one place was easier than walking around in circles. It was already ten o'clock. She thought about her classmates, her teachers. She wasn't worried anyone would wonder where she was; she had been late and absent so many times over the past year and a half. *They think I'm home washing dishes again,* she thought as a secret smile crept slowly across her face. *If only they knew!* Eventually, her turn came. "I want to buy a ticket to Baltimore," she told the man behind the counter.

That was the beginning of her trouble. What time, which station, what kind of ticket? he asked. But she had no answers.

"Do you want the stop at the airport, or at Penn Station in Baltimore?" he asked again, impatiently. Then a man behind her—mean-looking, with tattoos all over his arms—said, "Move it, girlie; I have a train to catch." The combination so frightened her that she lost her voice for a moment and even considered running away. Gathering all her courage, she turned back to the ticker seller.

"Not the airport."

"And what time did you say you want to leave?"

That at least was easy. "Right away."

He tapped on a computer. "There is an Acela Express leaving at 11:00 a.m. That's an hour from now."

"Okay. How much?"

"It's $124, one way."

Her heart sank. She had counted her birthday and Chanukah money. There was barely one hundred dollars. "Maybe something is cheaper?"

He tapped on his screen. "I can get you on the Northeast Regional. It's about twenty minutes longer than the Acela Express, but it's only $84 one way. There is one seat left in coach, and it's about to leave. Do you want it?"

"I'll take it," she answered quickly, zipping open her little pink wallet and counting out her money, which included quarters and dimes. She pushed it toward him. Maybe it was the coins, or how little her hand looked on the counter, but he suddenly looked over the counter more carefully. "Are you traveling alone?"

She nodded, quickly pocketing the ticket he handed her as small winged creatures took flight in her stomach.

"How old are you?"

"I'm sixteen."

"Okay. But just know that if you're younger, they won't let you travel without filling out some forms. Do you have any ID?"

"ID?"

"Move it already!" the man behind her practically shouted.

She turned, hurrying away with her suitcase, occasionally looking over her shoulder, frightened the ticket seller might send someone after her who would demand she relinquish her ticket. She *was* sixteen, but she knew she was small for her age and had nothing to prove she was telling the truth; Bais Yaakov didn't give out student IDs. All at once, she felt her confidence shaken. She had not even left the city and already was faced with so many things she hadn't planned for or thought about, making her feel childish and incompetent. And now she needed to find the right track before her train left the station, taking her precious, expensive seat with it!

Hopelessly lost, she looked around for someone to ask. She was afraid to ask a man, having never spoken to a strange man in her life. In fact, she had practically never spoken to anyone who wasn't an Orthodox Jew. She looked for a woman, preferably with children. So many were black. She had no experience at all with black people. There weren't any in Boro Park, except for the very, very rare convert, or various strangers briefly passing through.

Finally, she saw a booth with the word *Information* banded across the top. But the line was so long! She'd miss her train! Pushed beyond her fears by the real possibility of winding up penniless and forced to return home in shame, she finally approached an older woman with a cane who was sitting on a bench. The woman listened to her kindly, but then shook her head, answering her in a language that wasn't English. More time wasted! Now her terror became real.

"Excuse me, miss. I overheard you asking that lady where to get the train to Baltimore?"

Horrified at being approached by someone she didn't know, she nevertheless looked up hopefully. It was a black woman wearing a sleeveless blouse tucked into skin-tight pants. Around her neck was a huge cross. Shaindele trembled, forcing herself to be calm.

"Yes."

"I'm going in that direction, so you can follow me if you want. I'll get you there."

Shaindele nodded wordlessly, walking behind the woman, taking care to keep a safe distance. The woman glanced behind her once or twice, then shrugged, rolling her eyes. Eventually, they emerged onto an outdoor platform filled with trains. But the woman didn't turn around, disappearing into the crowd without a word.

Shaindele watched her go, panicking as she looked over the huge area with so many trains. *How will I know which one?* What if she made a mistake, got on the wrong one, and wound up far away among strangers with no money to get back? The thought was terrifying. But soon she realized that there were official-looking people checking tickets. She presented hers and was directed to her train. "But you'd better hurry, honey; it's about to leave."

She ran, dragging her suitcase, the word *honey* echoing offensively in her ears with its rude familiarity. The suitcase felt much heavier now than it had in the morning when she'd secretly returned to what she knew would be an empty house to fetch it. Quickly, she climbed aboard just in time to hear the whistle of imminent departure. Once safely inside, she felt stirrings of regret about her behavior toward the kind stranger who had helped her to find the correct platform. Why had she been so afraid to walk beside her? Why, she'd never even said thank you, which was probably why the woman had gone off without a word. She looked down the platform hoping to see her again, wishing she'd be on the same train so she could make amends. But she was gone. *I must stop being so afraid of trusting people. I must start acting like a grown-up instead of a little girl,* she berated herself.

She walked through the cars, checking the seat numbers against those on her ticket, glancing once again at the price. Almost all her money! *It doesn't matter,* she comforted herself. Uncle Chaim would pick her up from the station. They would take care of her. She didn't need money.

With relief, she found her seat, leaning back and settling her small valise beside her in the aisle.

"Would you like some help putting that up?"

He was a man, a stranger. Despite her good intentions, Shaindele froze, looking down stiffly, ignoring the question, until he shrugged and moved away. But soon another stranger came by, another man.

"You might want to put that suitcase someplace where it doesn't block the aisle," he told her brusquely as he stepped over her and the bag, brushing against her as he made his way to the window seat.

She was stunned. He was yelling at her! And he had touched her! And now he was sitting next to her, a stranger, a man! She felt sharp tears come to her eyes as she jumped up, grabbing her bag and hurrying down the aisle. She went through several cars until she found a place to stand. Shaking, she held on tightly to a pole as the train began to lurch forward rapidly, her breath coming in quick, sharp bursts. She felt almost faint. *It doesn't matter, it doesn't matter,* she tried to tell herself, helpless against the rising tide of panic that once again flooded wildly through her body like waves lifted by hurricane winds.

She saw a conductor walking toward her. She looked down, wondering if the ticket seller had told someone to take her off the train because she couldn't prove her age.

"You should really find your seat," he told her.

"I found my seat," she answered, still looking down.

"So why aren't you sitting in it?"

She shrugged.

"Hey, how old are you? Are you here alone?"

His voice was suddenly suspicious, she thought. *Oh no!*

"I'm sixteen," she said shrilly. "And I have a ticket."

"Sixteen? Are you sure? If you are under sixteen, you needed to check in with customer relations at the station and fill out a form. Did you do that?"

"I'm sixteen," she insisted, hot, angry tears filling her eyes as she lifted her head and looked at him defiantly.

"Got some proof? An ID? Something from your high school?" The silence lengthened.

"I go to Bais Yaakov in Boro Park. I'm in tenth grade. They don't give out IDs."

"Can you tell me your date of birth? Quick now."

She told him.

He did a fast calculation in his head, looking her over carefully, his eyes focusing on the long sleeves, the mid-calf skirt, the old-fashioned thick braid. "Bais Yaakov, huh? What kind of place is that?"

"A strictly religious Jewish school just for girls."

He exhaled, his eyes becoming kinder. "First time alone on a train?" he asked her.

She nodded gratefully.

"Okay. You shouldn't be standing here between cars. Let's take you back to your seat."

She followed him. He helped her put up her suitcase and punched her ticket. "You know when to get off, right?"

"Baltimore. Penn Station. How many stops?"

He told her. "But don't worry. I'll come back to make sure you get off at the right place. You wait for me."

"Thank you very much. You are very kind," she told him, trying to make amends for her previous behavior.

The man in the window seat leaned over, ignoring her and addressing the conductor. "Thanks for putting up the bag. She had it blocking the aisle. Got all huffy and left when I pointed it out to her."

"Did she?" The conductor crinkled his eyes at her. "And what tone of voice did you use to speak to this young lady?" he asked.

The man leaned back, clearing his throat, obviously disgruntled.

The conductor winked at her. "You have any problem," he said pointedly, "you come find me, all right?"

"Thank you," she whispered, close to tears.

She leaned back, trying to calm herself. *I can do this,* she told herself. *I can run away. Escape. I just have to stop being so afraid all the time to talk to goyim. Look how nice that woman had been! And the conductor! I'm out in the world now,* she told herself. *I have to learn to get along, to stop being so suspicious of everyone.* It was a big world, even though she had only ever seen a tiny part of it. All that was going to change. It was already changing, she thought happily, looking out the big picture window at the strange, unknown fields and houses that flew past. She sighed in happiness, finally relaxing.

For months, she had been secretly plotting. It was the most logical thing to do, she told herself again. To join her brothers in exile. Of course, her uncle and aunt would be surprised to see her. But surely they would never turn her away or send her back home once she explained what was going on back there. Surely, she told herself, they would share her outrage and stand side by side with her, ready to help.

They were, after all, not only her family but also strictly God-fearing and righteous members of the haredi community like her family, her father, *used* to be. Surely they would understand the urgency of her plight and the fact that she was doing the only thing she could to ensure her future: embarking on an urgent search for a shidduch which *must* be found for her before the disastrous union between her father and Leah could take place and blacken her family's reputation, bankrupting the store of goodwill in the community for their good name and *yichus*. She was like three-day-old meat in the refrigerator, she thought, which urgently needed to be cooked and eaten before it went bad and became worthless.

Once she married, she'd be safe, she thought. A respectable matron in a different community where people knew her uncle but not her father. There, no one would care who her father had married. Of course, her aunt and uncle, her brothers, her grandmother would be shocked at first. But once they reflected on the situation, she was certain they'd all form one unit, siding with her and her husband against her father and his reckless choice. And once she got settled, she and her husband would insist on taking in Chasya and Mordechai Shalom to protect them. But not right away, she reflected guiltily. She needed to wait. Hopefully, with time, certain unfortunate memories would fade from their minds. Children forgot quickly, didn't they?

She thought about her life as a married woman. It had to be easier than her life now. First of all, there would be no children to take care of—that is, until she had her own. And that, God willing, would take time. The longer the better as far as she was concerned. Secretly, she wondered if it might never happen, like with some couples. She didn't care. Look how miserable every birth had made her mother! But no, being childless was impossible. After ten years, the rabbis would insist your husband divorce you and take a new wife to fulfill the mitzvah. But all you needed to do was have one, she comforted herself. Then your husband and your mother-in-law wouldn't be able to complain or feel cheated. Just one, she thought, to keep people's tongues from wagging that your husband had made a bad shidduch or that God was punishing you for your sins. And even that could take years. She wrinkled her nose in distaste at the prospect of having to care for a demanding, dirty infant.

Don't think about that now, she told herself. *Think about the nice little apartment in Baltimore you'll move into with your husband and how you'll only have two dishes to wash after every meal, along with a small pot or two. Think about how on Shabbos your in-laws will invite you over, your mother-in-law doing all the work and treating you like a queen.* For just the two of them, there wouldn't be much laundry. Once a week, she'd put up a load. As for the dreaded ironing, she could manage every two weeks, or when her husband ran out of white shirts. She'd make sure he had dozens of them. Or maybe she'd never have to iron. She smiled to herself. Maybe she'd be one of those lucky young wives who sent out their laundry. Such things were not unheard of, even though the women who did it were gossiped about and looked down upon for their extravagance.

Who cares? Let them talk! There was no crime in being rich. Of course, he'd still have to be a scholar. But where was it written that all scholars had to be poor? Were there no righteous Jews in Belgium in the diamond business who had handsome, scholarly sons interested in frum New York girls with impeccable *yichus*?

Only . . . she was a bit young. Even for the shadchanim. Sixteen was unusual, but not unheard of, she assured herself. She'd heard of more than one girl in Brooklyn, and many in Jerusalem's Meah Shearim, who had married at that age or even younger with their parents' consent, which wasn't hard to come by when an unusually advantageous match came along they didn't want to risk losing.

Besides, in only six months she'd be seventeen, and then there would be absolutely no problem. The opposite: a seventeen-year-old, especially one from a good family, was considered a real catch, her youthful inexperience a guarantee of special purity, like the first drops of oil produced in the olive press, extra virgin.

She blushed at the comparison, feeling the first tiny pricks of misgiving. While she was ready to have her own home and, most importantly, to be freed of the drudgery of taking her mother's place, she was less certain about certain other duties that came along with being someone's wife.

Did she really want to get into bed with a man? The very idea was outlandishly repulsive and unimaginable given the strict boundaries between men and women with which she had grown up. You couldn't even sit at the same table at a wedding feast with your father and brothers, let alone a young man who was a stranger. Why, you were chastised if you even rolled up the linen curtain at the top of the mechitza in the women's section to watch the men dancing on Simchas Torah! How, then, could they expect a girl to make such a sharp transition just because she'd walked down the aisle and had a ring stuck on her finger and blessings rained down on her head?

But everybody did it. And afterward, they sat pale and blushing through seven days of family dinners in their expensive new wigs, shiny rings that had never been exposed to dirty dishwater sparkling on their fingers. If they'd been through something horrible, you'd never know about it. Still . . . She chewed nervously on her lower lip. There was no way to guarantee you wouldn't be the exception.

She had heard whispers of girls who got divorced after only two or three months of marriage. What could be so bad in only two, three months that you'd risk the disgrace of divorce, not to mention having to give back all your wedding presents, including your new rings? It had to be *that*. Or something to do with *that*.

Would he expect, demand, that she go to bed with him every night when she wasn't a *niddah*? Or just once a week on Friday night and the night she returned from the mikvah? What, she thought, if she hated it? What if it was painful, humiliating?

She shifted uncomfortably in her seat, trying to dismiss her fears, to conjure the pleasant dreams that had filled her head while making her escape plans: the lovely new furniture her in-laws would buy for their scholarly son's pretty, young bride. The magnificent white dress she would have made for her. The stunning blond wig she would wear after cutting short her own thick, brown hair—which she hated. The piles and piles of wedding presents . . .

What would she do all day? Would he expect her to work to support him? Well, everyone would expect that. It was what the wives of brilliant scholars did, supporting Torah learning and thereby earning merit for themselves in this world and in the World to Come. It was what her mother had done, what she wanted to do. But what could she do to earn a salary?

She hadn't even graduated high school yet! She supposed she could always be a secretary to religious people, or a cashier in a religiously owned store, or even a waitress in a glatt kosher restaurant. She felt a stab of misery at the thought of such drudgery.

She had always dreamed of being a teacher like her mother. She liked school and had been an excellent student. She'd even considered going on from high school to a place like Touro College. But it was very possible her husband wouldn't agree, not if they needed money, or, worse, she got pregnant right away. She imagined herself sitting in class behind one of those little desks, her belly swollen, everyone secretly looking at her with equal parts envy and pity, the way she'd looked at the pregnant, married seniors.

She clenched the sides of her seat, trying her best to forget that ever since Leah had come to help, she had been able to really concentrate on her studies again and that after the wedding, Leah would be there full-time, taking even more of the burden from her shoulders, maybe even allowing her to go back to being a child again.

But it was impossible. When her father married Leah, she herself would become an object of pity, the recipient of sly glances and barbed, hurtful remarks. A familiar childish pique and jealousy filled her heart. It would be horrible, unthinkable! A disgrace that would ruin her life and the lives of her siblings, no matter how obvious the benefits.

Besides, once Leah married her father, what was to stop her from slacking off, forcing Shaindele to take over all her old chores again and then some? Her father would not stick up for her. He probably wouldn't even notice. As always, he'd disappear—into his new marriage, his studies, and eventually his job. Pure and simple, she told herself stubbornly, she was stuck. *This* was her only option. It was logical.

She closed her eyes, trying to imagine the young man who would come into her life. She had a certain template for him: the black suit and Borsalino hat. Of course, he would only wear white shirts, but maybe also colorful silk ties. At least, she hoped so. He would be taller than she was, which wasn't hard, but not so tall she'd have to arch her neck when she looked at him. He would speak in a soft tone and only once in a while look into her eyes, because to look directly was too *chutzpadik,* unworthy of a scholar. And he would know things, holy things. And he would teach her to be a better person. Holier. Someone who didn't lose her temper, which the rabbis taught was akin to idol worship. She so much wanted to be a better person, she thought, yawning. Then she closed her eyes and slept.

When she woke up, she saw people hurrying to get off. She had no idea where she was. Then she thought she heard somebody say Baltimore. Her stop! She looked around for the conductor, but he was nowhere to be seen. Afraid the doors would close, dragging her off into the unknown, she pulled down her suitcase and hurried off. When she finally realized what she had done, it was too late.

32

It was getting dark outside.

"We should call the police," Fruma Esther whispered, trying not to alarm the little ones who were playing in the living room after their baths.

"They'll only tell you to wait twenty-four hours," Leah said, shaking her head. "Besides, you don't need the police to show up here at the house. The neighbors—"

"Let them think what they want!" Fruma Esther exploded. "The yentas!"

Leah and Yaakov stared at her wonderingly.

And then the phone rang.

Yaakov jumped up, gripping it as if it were a live creature attempting to escape. His brows knitted, then smoothed.

"*Baruch HaShem!*"

Leah and Fruma Esther turned to him and then to each other, exhaling with relief.

"She what?" he said, sitting down, his eyes growing wide and startled as he listened. "I don't know what to say. Leah, my *kallah*, and Bubbee

Fruma are here. Let me talk it over with them, and I'll call you back. Thank you!"

He put down the phone, then clutched his skullcap as if the top of his head was about to blow off. "She's in Baltimore with my brother. She took the train."

"God be blessed!" Fruma Esther said, clutching her heart. But after her initial relief, she was suddenly furious. "All by herself! By train! Went to Manhattan, bought a ticket, without a single word? What was she thinking? Who knows what could have happened to her! And letting her family suffer like this. HaShem watch over us, I can't even think—"

"Is she all right?" Leah interjected. "What took so long? It's only a few hours to Baltimore by train."

"She got off at the wrong stop, in Philadelphia. She was rushing and left her purse behind. She had no money. She didn't know what to do. Finally, a conductor saw her crying and took pity on her, put her on another train. Someone helped her look up my brother's number and lent her their phone to call. It took hours."

"Ach, she must have been so frightened." Fruma Esther sighed.

"What is she doing there, Yaakov?" Leah asked, dreading the answer.

He looked at her strangely. "She told my brother that she wants him and her aunt to find her a shidduch."

Fruma Esther clasped her hands together, twirling her wedding band around with her thumb and forefinger, her heart beating faster than was appropriate for such an old piece of equipment. "*Oy gevalt,*" she whispered.

Leah laughed. "Married? She's a baby! He's sending her home, right?"

Yaakov said nothing.

"Yaakov? You're going to call him back and tell him to send your sixteen-year-old daughter back home, right? Am I correct?"

"Let her get married, then!" Yaakov exploded. "I've had enough!"

"What are you talking about? You can't be serious." Leah raised her voice.

"She has done nothing but try to destroy this family with her anger and chutzpa. She put Chasya into the hospital. And now, she does this, to us, to *me,* after everything we've been through, after everything we've suffered! It was heartless, selfish. Enough! I have done all I can to raise her, to educate her in the right middos. But I've failed. I can't do any more. There is something deeply wrong with that child. Let my brother try, then. Maybe he'll have better luck. And if it comes to it, let her husband try!"

"Yaakov," Fruma Esther placated. "Please."

"You can't mean it. She's a silly teenager. You don't try to find husbands for silly teenage girls. You try to talk them out of it." Leah was furious and shocked. Could this even be happening? Could this man she loved, this man she thought the world of, be advocating such a third-world solution to his unhappy daughter's first serious rebellion? She was devastated and confused.

He saw the disappointment in her eyes, and his heart sank. Now Shaindele would get what she wanted, he thought, his fury growing. "Don't fall into her trap, Leah. She is trying to break us up. Don't you see that?"

Leah shook her head. "You give her too much credit. She isn't some diabolical monster. She's a scared, confused kid who thinks marriage is the only way out for her."

"Out of what?" he suddenly shouted. "Out of a loving home? A fine family who would do anything for her?"

"She was there, Yaakov, when Zissele . . . when it happened," Fruma Esther said softly. "And we never told her the truth. Who knows what she thinks? And then we made her take over the house, the children. It was too hard for her. She's still a child herself."

Yaakov sat down heavily, his legs collapsing beneath him, all his anger suddenly gone.

Leah knelt beside him. "She tried so hard to take her mother's place, but she didn't know how. She must have felt like such a failure."

He looked up, tears in his eyes. "I can understand her bubbee defending her. But you, Leah? Why would *you* defend her? She's been terrible to you."

She held his gaze steadily, thoughts rushing through her head. Why indeed? In a certain way, this would be the absolute, perfect solution to the Shaindele problem, a deus ex machina where two celestial fingers plucked the little troublemaker up and made her disappear into some preferably far-off shidduch where she would never again be able to exercise her toxic influence over her life or Yaakov's or the children's.

"This isn't about me," she said softly, her eyes caressing him. "This is about your daughter. About you. About this family being whole again. There have been too many upheavals in everyone's life, Yaakov. Shaindele will only find misery if she tries to become a wife and a mother when she isn't ready. After everything that happened to her mother, are you willing to risk that?"

He wanted to put his arms around her, to rest his weary head on her soft shoulders. She was God's blessing to him. He said a silent prayer for the innate, healing goodness inside her that had come pouring into his life, saving him from heartbreak, anger, and sin. He rested his head in his hands, squeezing his temples. "I don't know what to do."

"But I do," Fruma Esther said, getting unsteadily to her feet. "Call your brother. Tell him first thing in the morning to put her on a bus back to New York."

"He'll want to drive her," Yaakov said doubtfully. Despite his fury, she was still his little girl.

"Tell him no. She wants to pretend she's all grown up? Then she can take a bus back by herself. It will be good for her. She'll have a long time to think about what she's done. And I'll be waiting for her when she gets off."

33

Expecting her furious father, Shaindele was surprised and tremendously relieved to see her bubbee instead. Climbing down the steps from the bus gingerly, her feet a bit wobbly after the four-hour drive—twice as long as the train ride down—that is, if she'd gotten off at the right stop! Coming back, there had been only one brief stop so she couldn't get lost. It was also in Philadelphia. She'd stayed on the bus, eating the challah-and-cheese sandwich her aunt had given her, along with a generous package of sweets.

On the one hand, she was embarrassed that she had been treated like a misbehaving child, her wishes ignored. But on the other, she felt a great burden had rolled off her back. The more she'd sat in the train next to a strange man, then wandered for hours around a terminal full of strange men, the more odious the idea of marriage had become to her. She didn't want a man, any man, to touch her, she realized. She couldn't bear the thought. She wasn't ready, she wasn't ready! Not for that. Secretly, she'd been half-afraid that Leah would talk her father into letting her stay and get married. But that hadn't happened.

Fruma Esther held out her arms, and Shaindele fell into them, weeping.

"Sha, sha. It's all right, *shefelah*. Don't. It's going to be all right."

She wiped her eyes and picked up her valise.

"Come."

Shaindele followed dutifully, taking her place silently beside her bubbee on the long taxi line. What could she say? She was ashamed, grateful not to be scolded, to be left alone. When it was finally their turn, she climbed into the taxi.

"One twenty-one eighty-three Springfield Boulevard, Jamaica, Queens," the old woman told the driver.

"What? We're not going home?" Shaindele felt a rush of panic, almost paralyzed with fear. Where was she being taken? To some home for wayward religious girls? Some institution or halfway house where they sent you for years, trying to straighten you out? She had heard whispered rumors of such places. So, her family didn't want her back after all! She should have known. That Leah! Of course she would try to get rid of her!

"Please, Bubbee. Let's go home. I promise to behave myself."

But the old woman was silent, staring straight ahead.

"Please, Bubbee, where are you taking me?"

Fruma Esther gently touched her granddaughter's miserable face. "We're going to visit your mameh. I want to talk to her, and I want you should listen to what I have to say."

Shaindele shrank back into her seat, feeling small and confused. What could this mean?

It was a long ride out to Montefiore Cemetery in Queens. They sat side by side, their bodies shaking with the jerks and stops of the car, even occasionally touching, but they hardly spoke, each sunk in their own private fears and expectations. When they finally arrived, they wove silently through the granite and marble gravestones until they found it.

Zissele Sarah . . . beloved wife and mother . . . daughter of . . . Her price was far above rubies.

"Come, *shefelah*. Let's sit a minute."

She led her granddaughter to a nearby bench, and both of them sat down. "Do you know, Shaindele, when you were born, your mother was so happy. She wanted a girl so much. She was always afraid it might happen to her like what happened to our neighbor, Surele. She had seven sons, Surele, one right after the other. Everyone said it was a blessing, and that Surele must be a saint, like the wife of the high priest who God also granted seven sons because even the walls of her house never saw her hair. But your mother didn't think to have seven sons and no daughter was a blessing! She kvelled when she held you in her arms. You looked just like she did when she was born. Exactly the same."

"Really?" A small smile found its way to the young girl's unhappy face.

"I should make up a story? And you were like her in other ways, so sweet, so kind. Just like your dear mameh, who was such a good girl. She only ever gave us *nachas.* She was so proud of you and your brothers and sister."

"But, Bubbee, she was always so sad! Especially when Mordechai Shalom was born. She cried all the time. I thought . . . I was afraid we made her unhappy, that we made her sick, because it's so hard to take care of such a big family. I tried to help her, Bubbee, really I did! But I'm not a very good *balabusta.*"

Fruma Esther leaned back to stare at her, shocked. "So, that's what you think? That your mother got sick because you didn't help her enough?"

Shaindele nodded, and that small movement caused the moisture in her eyes to spill over, dropping down her cheeks like tiny diamonds that sparkled in the sun. Fruma Esther reached over, wiping them away.

"Listen to me, Shaindele. Your mother had an illness, a mental illness. It happens sometimes to some women after giving birth. No one knows why, even the smart doctors. Hormones, they said. Too many, not enough. They're just guessing. Every time your mameh gave birth, she got that illness, went through that sadness. It's nobody's fault. It had nothing to do with how much work she had to do. Do you remember how the women would come to the house and bring food and take bags of laundry to do? Do you remember how I moved in after every birth? Your mother was taken care of."

"Why didn't Tateh help her more? Why was he never home?"

"We insisted—your mameh most of all—that your tateh go back to the yeshiva, so that in the *zchus* of his learning, God would heal your mameh."

"Then why didn't you take her to a doctor?"

"Oy, did we take her to doctors! This one gave her the green pill, another one gave her the pink pill, but *gornisht helfn.* The sickness, it only got worse, until she couldn't stand it. It made her do meshuga things, to think meshuga thoughts. We took her to a psychiatrist, a top man. But he wanted we should put her into a mental hospital. Your mother, she begged me not to do it. She was so afraid for the shame, afraid for the family's good name. For your shidduchim, Shaindele. And I gave in to her. You understand what happened here? I was also afraid, *more afraid of shame than of death.* Your tateh, he fought with me. He said we should do like the doctor said. But I wouldn't allow it. Your mameh begged me. 'Let me try one more time. I can do it.' And I believed her, because she was my daughter, and because I wanted to believe her. It was easier. But in the end, your poor mameh just couldn't stand the suffering anymore. She gave up."

"I don't understand."

"Shaindele, that morning when you were home with her, your mameh swallowed a whole bottle of aspirin. By the time she got to the hospital, it was too late. They tried to save her, but there was nothing anybody could do."

The girl's face froze in horror. "I knew she was in the bathroom too long! I should have broken down the door when she didn't come out! But I . . . I was busy with Chasya. She was crying and wouldn't stop. She is always so difficult. If it hadn't been for her—"

Fruma Esther grabbed the girl firmly by the shoulders, shaking her. "Listen to me, Shaindele! It wasn't your fault! It wasn't your little sister's. Even if you broke down the door, what would it matter? If not that time, it would have been another time. She wanted the pain to end. If anyone is to blame, it's me."

"But how could she do that to me, to us? How could she leave us? How could she leave *me* to take her place! It wasn't fair! I wasn't ready. How should I know how to take care of children and a house! I needed her . . . I need her, and she isn't here, and she will never be here." She sobbed.

Fruma Esther pressed her to her bosom. She was such a child, a little girl still. Why hadn't anybody understood that? Because in their world, a sixteen-year-old girl was almost a *kallah moide,* a girl ready to be a wife, a mother. But Shaindele wasn't. She was still a child. To that, too, she had been blind, to her granddaughter's pain, her youth, her guilt, her neediness. All the while, she had been focused on what the neighbors would say, on her own responsibilities, on Yaakov, never giving a thought to what Shaindele, her granddaughter, had been going through.

"I know it's been hard on you, Shaindele, but it's your tateh who has suffered most of all. You have no idea, your poor tateh! Without your mameh's salary, he had to take out loans from the *gmachim* to pay for rent and for food. Now the government helps him. But still, he owes so much money. He even thought about becoming a schnorrer! Did you know that? He took a bus to Lakewood. Got a certificate—"

Shaindele shook her head, shocked.

"But he couldn't do it. Instead, he went back to school at night so he can get a good job and pay back all the money and give you a decent dowry when the time comes. It was the hardest thing in the world for him to leave the yeshiva. But he's doing it out of love for his family—for you, Shaindele."

The girl's cheeks reddened with shame, understanding for the first time the full dimensions of what her father had been going through.

"They said things about Tateh, about him leaving the kollel."

"Who said? What things?"

"The girls in school. They made me feel ashamed of him for wanting to be a *baal bayis* instead of a talmid chochom. I *was* ashamed."

"Such gossipers and defamers! And they call themselves God-fearing! They will become the kind of people that condemn a poor woman for being sick, the kind of people I was so afraid of I let your mother die." She wept. "So lonely he's been, you don't know, my poor Yaakov. I tried to find him a shidduch, believe me. But the ones the shadchonim came up with, they were nothing like your mameh. Divorced women like bitter herbs; widows thinking only about *gelt*. They didn't make him happy. He didn't think they would love his children. The one shidduch he was interested in, an older single girl, rejected him because he was too old, too poor, with too many children."

"That girl that came over, Rachel? She didn't want him? Not the other way?"

She shook her head. "He was heartbroken, your poor tateh. Not every woman is willing to take on a widower with a big family and no money, Shaindele. But now, *Baruch HaShem,* he has found someone. For the first time since your mother got sick, I see some happiness in his eyes. No one can know what fills another person's heart or why. But Leah fills your father's heart. And he and you children fill hers. She loves Chasya and Mordechai Shalom, and would love you, too, if you just gave her a chance to know you, the real you. Just try. You know, you share many things. She, too, had a hard childhood and lost someone she loved. And I'll tell you something else." She hesitated. "Your father was willing for you to stay in Baltimore. To get married. He was angry. But Leah . . . Leah told him to forgive you. That you were just an unhappy child."

"Really?" Something hard shifted in the young girl's heart, softening. "Bubbee, what are you saying? That you think it's all right now, this marriage? With such a person?"

"More than just all right. I think it's a blessing. I think it's God's will. Ruth, the great-grandmother of King David, was a Moabite, an idol worshipper. But her heart was pure and she loved God and she wanted with all her heart to leave her own family and their ways and be part of Naomi's. And look how HaShem blessed her and Naomi's family! Leah will also bring us blessings."

"But what about *my* shidduchim? What will people say?"

Fruma Esther sat up straight. "They will say they'd have great mazal to marry into the family of the Admor Yitzchak Chaim Sonnenbaum and Rav Eliezer Ungvar! The shadchanim are picky, but I am pickier. You will only marry the very finest boy. I give you my word." She trembled with emotion as she said this. Who knew if it was true? But God is good. She depended on Him not to make her family suffer anymore.

The two women, old and young, sat side by side weeping softly, thinking of what could have been.

"Forgive me, Shaindele, for all my sins. For not saving your mameh."

Shaindele grasped her grandmother's wrinkled hand warmly in her own. "I remember how you sat with Mameh, day and night. You never went home. You worked so hard."

"But the one thing I should have done, the only thing that would have saved your mameh, I didn't do."

They wiped their eyes.

Fruma Esther held her granddaughter's hand. "Come, let's talk to your mameh."

Side by side they stood by the cold, gray headstone that even the spring sunshine could not warm, both thinking of the pretty, vital young woman who had once laughed and loved and given birth.

"Zissele, I came here with your daughter. See how beautiful she is! Such a good girl! Such *nachas* for you. I came to ask your *mechilah*. You should forgive me, my dear daughter, for not giving you the help you needed. I was confused and weak. I should have convinced you it was no shame to go into a hospital if you were sick. But I didn't. I promise to do *teshuva*, to take care of the *mishpocha*, to fight until my last breath if anybody tries to harm them. Your family is well. Yaakov has finally found a kind woman who cherishes your children and cares for them as if they were her own. They will be a happy family, Zissele, the kind you always wanted them to be. And when the time comes, we will find, with God's help, the finest shidduch for your beautiful daughter, someone worthy of her, and of you."

Shaindele listened wordlessly, and when her grandmother had finished, offered up her own silent prayer.

Dearest Mameh, I forgive you for leaving me. Rest in peace. I'm so sorry for everything you suffered and for not being able to help you, for not calling the ambulance faster. I didn't know. I'm sorry for being so angry all the time— at you and Tateh, at the children. I felt lost. I wanted an easier life, like my friend's. Forgive me for losing my temper, for being unkind to Chasya and Mordechai Shalom because I could see in their eyes they knew what a bad job I was doing taking care of them. Forgive me for hating Tateh's bashert, *Leah, and trying to get rid of her. She's better at everything than I am, and the children love her. I was jealous. I'm so ashamed. I promise,* bli neder, *from now on, to help Tateh, to be happy for him and Leah. She is a stranger but a good person. And on the* zchus *of my* teshuva, *may God grant me a good shidduch. But not until I'm ready! Pray for me, Mameh! Watch over us. We will always love you.*

As was customary, they placed small stones on the grave as a sign of respect. Then they poured water from a cup over their hands twice, ritually purifying themselves from the dust of the dead. Arm in arm, they turned toward the exit and the long ride home.

EPILOGUE

The *vort* of Yaakov Lehman, the widowed son-in-law of the late Admor Yitzchak Chaim Sonnenbaum, had all of Boro Park talking. People who had not been invited traded information about the number and prestige of the guests who had filled the catering hall to bursting. They spoke about the words of the Torah that the great rabbis who attended had spoken in honor of the Sonnenbaum family, and the praise they had heaped upon Yaakov himself as a distinguished scholar who had undergone great trials.

People who had actually been there, however, remembered different things, things they found difficult to put into words but kept close to their hearts: The way the eyes of the bride-to-be shone like little gleaming jewels out of her pale face. The way Rebbitzen Fruma Esther linked arms with her on one side, while her granddaughter Shaindele linked arms with her on the other. The shine on Yaakov's face when he looked at Leah, like that of the high priest exiting the Holy of Holies on Yom Kippur, having successfully performed his duties and made atonement for the entire people of Israel. They remembered how Yaakov and Leah had held his youngest children in their arms, and how the children had hugged them and laughed.

There were other things, too, things many found remarkable and impossible to understand: the presence of a woman in a sleeveless red dress with uncovered, bleached-blond, spiky hair. The man in the Sikh turban who stood next to her. The tall, beautiful black girl with marvelous hair. The large, fierce-looking Israeli in a knitted skullcap who talked all night to a young, wig-wearing religious woman with an Irish accent who held a gorgeous blue-eyed baby in her arms. There was also a beautiful young woman some whispered was a rabbi's daughter, a doctor, who had herself recently become engaged to a convert and a divorcé, also a doctor.

Most of all, those present would remember the moment that someone loaned the woman in the red dress a shawl to cover her hair and shoulders so that she could be honored with an invitation to share the ceremonial plate with Fruma Esther as it was smashed, like the cup under the wedding huppah, to symbolize that even during the most joyous celebrations, we must not forget our tragedies.

Whether or not the invited guests gossiped about these strange things later to others, ruining reputations and causing misery and unhappiness, is hard to know. It is just as easy to imagine that those who came to this special occasion, which included many great rabbis and scholars of the Talmud, were scrupulous in keeping the laws of the Torah and therefore said not a single word that might be construed as negative, preferring instead to simply express their gratitude that the unhappiness of a widower and his orphans, well-respected members of their community, had been transformed by the Holy One Blessed Be He into joy. And that they—as a community—had had the great privilege of embracing a pious young woman who had, like Ruth, at long last found her way to them, and to the God who had clearly directed the uneven steps of her long journey home.

ACKNOWLEDGMENTS

I suppose the genesis of this book would have to be Far Rockaway, New York, where, as a seven-year-old, I entered the Hebrew Institute of Long Island as a scholarship student and where for the next ten years I received a Jewish education that transformed my life. I thank Simon Cohen, the philanthropist whose funding made it possible to educate poor Jewish children who would otherwise have grown up in ignorance both of their heritage and the unique relationship between themselves and their God and people.

During the course of writing this book, I reached out to others who had experienced this same transformation. Some were kind enough to answer my questions about their own journey toward faith, with its spectacular scenery as well as its detours and obstacles. Thank you so much, Karen Furman, Judi Kirk, Kate Kramer, Eva Goldstein-Meola, Devorah Taitz, Lissa Goldman, Leone Hersh, Vickie Lecy, Lisa Bellin, Tara Carey, Shoshana Kent, Karen Cohen, Jessica Vaiselberg, and Aura Wolfe. Your words were inspiring.

I also found the following books extremely informative, and I thank their authors: *Becoming Frum: How Newcomers Learn the Language and*

Culture of Orthodox Judaism by Sarah Bunin Benor; *Tradition in a Rootless World: Women Turn to Orthodox Judaism* by Lynn Davidman; *Rachel's Daughters: Newly Orthodox Jewish Women* by Debra Renee Kaufman; *A Tale of Two Souls: My Hand of God Story* by Ilana Danneman; *Frumspeak: The First Dictionary of Yeshivish* by Chaim M. Weiser; and *Behind the Smile: My Journey Out of Postpartum Depression* by Marie Osmond. I thank the many other women whose riveting accounts of postpartum depression I read on the internet for helping me to understand and describe some of the consequences and symptoms of this disease.

A special thanks to author Mark Oppenheimer, whose excellent article "The Beggars of Lakewood," published in *The New York Times Magazine* in October 2014, gave me a fascinating virtual visit to that community and its beggars and helped me to depict it more realistically in chapter 4.

Although I was not a stranger to Boro Park, having spent a year there as a student in the Sara Schenirer Hebrew Teachers Seminary in 1968, I must give a very warm and heartfelt thanks to family friend Charna Klein and her husband, Tom, who not only hosted me in their lovely Boro Park home during the writing of this book but gave me a tour and an insightful update into the community's fascinating culture and customs. In addition, my deep appreciation to my son Akiva Ragen for his helpful description of yeshiva life and the relationship between *chavrusa* study partners, which I could not have figured out without him. A thank-you also to my son-in-law Oren Bratt for allowing me to include his personal story of finding an apartment in Manhattan (my daughter warned you that this would happen if you talked to me!). A special thanks also to my talented copy editor, Sara Ensey, for her careful eye and insightful comments.

Last but not least, my deepest thanks to my talented editor, Jennifer Weis, and my intrepid and encouraging agent, Mel Berger at WME, who have nurtured whatever gifts I have and continue to make it possible for me to share my ever-evolving understanding of the special world I entered fifty years ago and continue to inhabit.

GLOSSARY

baal bayis. (singular) **baale batim** or **balabatim.** (plural) pronounced *baleh bawsim.* Literally, "house owner," but used in an often derogatory way to indicate status: bourgeois, prosperous merchant, or working class as opposed to scholar.

baal teshuva. Literally, "possessor of repentance." Refers to one who leaves a secular lifestyle to become religiously observant. **baalas teshuva.** (feminine) **baalos teshuva.** (feminine plural) **baale teshuva.** (plural) Refers to penitents of both sexes. **Teshuva.** Penitence. To repent is to "**do teshuva.**"

Bais Hamigdash. Temple in Jerusalem.

balabusta. Laudatory term for an efficient, hardworking housewife.

baruch she'bara brios naos b-olamo. Blessed be He who created wonderful creatures in His world, a blessing made upon seeing any unique natural wonder.

bashert. One's perfect match as ordained by God.

bitachon. Faith.

bli neder. A formula that accompanies a vow used to prevent a person from swearing in vain.

bracha. A blessing.

bracha levatala. A useless blessing that takes God's name in vain, such as wishing for a certain gender of child when a woman is already pregnant.

bri'ah. God's creation. The universe.

BT. Short for **Baale Teshuva.**

chas v'chalilah. God forbid. Also **Chas v'shalom.**

chavrusa. Talmudic study partner.

chazal. Acronym for the Hebrew "our sages, may their memory be blessed."

cheder. Religious nursery school.

choson. Groom and/or son-in-law.

davening. Praying.

dafka. Specifically and emphatically.

dreykops. A scatterbrain who talks endlessly but says nothing.

eshes chayil. Woman of valor, a virtuous wife and mother, also name of Friday night hymn of praise traditionally sung by husbands to their wives.

ezer k'negdo. Man's helpmate. Biblical description of Eve.

farmisht. Confused, befuddled, and dysfunctional.

fleishig. A person's state during the six hours after eating meat, when no dairy may be consumed.

frei. Literally, "free." A derogatory term of those not adhering to God's laws.

frum. Devout or pious. Committed to the observance of Jewish religious law that often exceeds the bare requirements of **halacha**, the collective body of Jewish religious laws.

gashmius. A derogatory term meaning indulgence in earthly pleasures.

gmach. Free loan fund that distributes a wide variety of goods and services as a good deed. **Gmachim.** (plural).

gornisht helfn. Nothing at all helped.

goyishe narishkeit. Gentile childish foolishness.

haredi. Ultra-Orthodox Jews.

HaShem. Literally, "the name." A periphrastic way of referring to God in contexts other than prayer or scriptural reading, because the name itself is considered too holy for such use. **HaShem Yaazor.** God should help.

HaShem Yisborach. God be blessed. Interchangeable with **Baruch Hashem** and **Yisborach HaShem.**

HaShem Yishmor. God watch over us.

hashgacha pratis. Divine providence.

hechsher. Rabbinical stamp of approval, mostly referring to kosher status of food.

heimish. Homey, informal, cozy.

imyertza HaShem. God willing. Also abbreviated as: **Mertsishem.**

kallah moide. A young girl ready for marriage.

kapara. Expiation for one's sins.

kaynahora. May the evil eye not see. Said in times of joy.

kibood av. The biblical obligation to honor one's father.

kinderlach. Little children. Often used as an endearment.

kiruv. Outreach to non-Orthodox Jews to encourage belief in God and adherence to Orthodox Jewish law.

kollel. Talmudic academies of higher learning for men after high school, usually married men.

levayah. Funeral.

Litvish. Of or pertaining to Jews from Lithuania.

machashefa. Witch.

maggid shiur. Rabbi that lectures in a yeshiva or kollel.

mamash. Really, truly, actually.

mechalal Shabbos. A desecrator of the Sabbath.

mechilah. Formal forgiveness for sin.

mein kindt. Literally, "my child." Term of endearment.

middos. Character traits.

midrash. Ancient Rabbinic commentary attached to the biblical text.

mishagas. Craziness. **meshuganah, meshuga.** A crazy person.

misphocha. The family.

Moshe Rabeinu. Moses our teacher.

nebbech. Sad, unfortunate.

niddah. A woman who is in a state of spiritual impurity during and after menstruation, preceding immersion in the ritual bath.

nigun. Tune, usually sung with sacred texts.

nesoyon. Spiritual test, usually something difficult or tragic. **Nesyonos.** (plural)

nivul peh. Desecration of the mouth by using foul language.

off the derech. Literally, "off the path," referring to someone who has ceased to observe Orthodox Judaism.

oneg Shabbos. A pleasurable gathering on Friday night or Saturday to honor the Sabbath day, which might include food, drinks, songs, and games.

parnosa. Income.

parsha. Torah portion.

prutza. An immoral woman, a whore.

rachmones. Piteous.

Rambam. Acronym for one of the greatest Jewish philosophers Moses ben Maimon (1135–1204), commonly known as Maimonides.

rechilus. False slander.

Rosh Yeshiva. Head of Talmudic academy.

rosha. Hebrew word for villain.

Shabbos. Affectionate term for Sabbath day.

shadchan. Matchmaker. **shadchonim, shidduch.** (plural). Match arranged by shadchan.

shayich. Relevant. Its opposite, "not shayich," which denotes something that is irrelevant or a waste of time.

shechina. Divine presence.

shefelah. Literally, "little lamb." Term of endearment.

Simchas Torah. Holiday in which Torah scrolls are taken from the ark and honored with dancing and singing.

Talmid chochom. A Torah scholar.

tisha b'Av. The ninth of Av, a day of fasting and mourning to commemorate the destruction of the Second Temple by the Romans.

tumah. Spiritual impurity.

tzitzis. Four-cornered, fringed ritual garment worn by males under their clothes.

vort. Yiddish, literally, "word," an engagement party where couple give their word to marry.

yeshivish. A version of ultra-Orthodoxy rooted in the Lithuanian followers of the Vilna Gaon who emphasized logic and scholarship as opposed to the Chassidic emphasis on feeling and emotion.

yichus. Good pedigree, important lineage. Observance.

yiras shomayim. Literally, "fear of heaven," a pious, praiseworthy fear of sin.

zchus. Merit, reward.